Tales of the South Pacific
The Fires of Spring
Return to Paradise
The Voice of Asia
The Bridges of Toko-Ri
Sayonara
The Floating World
The Bridge at Andau
Hawaii
Report of the County Chairman
Caravans
The Source
Iberia
Presidential Lottery
The Quality of Life
Kent State: What Happened and Why
The Drifters
A Michener Miscellany: 1950–1970
Centennial
Sports in America
Chesapeake
The Covenant
Space
Poland
Texas
Legacy
Alaska
Journey
Caribbean
The Eagle and the Raven
Pilgrimage
The Novel
The World Is My Home: A Memoir
James A. Michener's Writer's Handbook
Mexico
Creatures of the Kingdom

with A. Grove Day
Rascals in Paradise

with John Kings
Six Days in Havana

CREATURES OF THE KINGDOM

ILLUSTRATIONS BY KAREN JACOBSEN

RANDOM HOUSE
NEW YORK

JAMES A. MICHENER

CREATURES OF THE KINGDOM

STORIES OF
ANIMALS AND NATURE

Library of Congress Cataloging-in-Publication Data

Michener, James A. (James Albert)
Creatures of the kingdom / James A. Michener. — 1st ed.
p.   cm.
1. Animals—Fiction. I. Title.
PS3525.I19C74   1993
813'.54—dc20   92-46075

Manufactured in the United States of America

24689753

FIRST EDITION

Book design by Carole Lowenstein

This anthology is dedicated
to Theresa Potter,
my longtime secretary,
who conceived the idea
and made the selections

CONTENTS

FOREWORD

When I try to locate myself in the scheme of things I discover that I am a rather puny member of the animal kingdom—weight 166 pounds, while an elephant weighs two tons, a gorilla 880 pounds—living in a small town (Doylestown 8,717 population—Shanghai 11 million, Calcutta 9 million), in a small state (Pennsylvania 45,333 square miles—Alaska 569,600, Texas 267,338) in a relatively small nation (United States 3,618,770 square miles—Russia, 8,649,490, Canada 4,014,263) in one of the smaller continents (North America 9.3 million square miles—Asia 17, Africa 11.7) on quite a small planet (if Earth is given the index 1, Jupiter is 1403, Saturn 832), attached to a sun that is only an average star (millions of other stars are bigger and brighter), off to the edge of one of the smaller galaxies (it has only 400 billion stars, while most of the other 100 billion galaxies appear to be larger, sometimes massively so).

I cannot, therefore, ever think of myself as exceptional in any respect. I know that man could never have survived the violent volcanic upheavals in the Pacific Ocean that created the glorious chain of Hawaiian islands. The first tenants of the newly born Rocky Mountains surely did not walk upright. My kind has lived here on Earth only a few million years; the dinosaurs thrived for a hundred million. And I am not homocentric enough to think that man embodies all that is best in the animal kingdom, in which he plays a dominant part. He cannot slither along on his belly like a snake or use his nose to feed himself the way an elephant can. He has not the incredible hearing system of a bat, the sense of smell of a bloodhound, or the capacity to survive underwater like a slug. He cannot cast off his aging skin like a crab or stand motionless for hours on one foot like a blue heron. Man is a wonderful creature, majestic in his mental capabilities, but in many other respects he is either limited or downright deficient.

If man assesses himself honestly when he compares himself with the other animals, he can avoid getting a swelled head. The great reward of making such a comparison is the discovery of a vital truth: since man shares this earth with other creatures, he is morally obligated to treat them as members of his own family.

It is hideous to terminate a natural species, especially when one contemplates the millions of years it may have taken for that creature to evolve from a prehistoric prototype. The fact is that once a species, whether flora or fauna, has been killed off, it is lost forever. The primordial conditions that either allowed or encouraged it to evolve are now gone. There is no longer any seminal ooze in which various life forms can thrive and develop; there are no vast, permanent swamps on whose shores they can climb or take root to make their way to transforming themselves. The temperatures of oceans have cooled, the chemical components altered. It may be technologically impossible for a reptile to evolve into a bird the way the pterodactyl presumably did. The conditions of place and time are not right.

There is, of course, a radical possibility. Astronomers seem to agree that the earth has about four billion more years of existence and during that time it is possible that some cataclysm of the kind that may have altered history in the past could recur to wipe out man and allow a new creation to repeat instantly. (I do not believe or accept that speculation; I believe that genesis will come about in an orderly, continuous way in obedience to the definable laws of nature.) Within the span of man's custodianship, which has been brief, of natural treasures like water, forests and clean air, we must do our best to protect and preserve all that exists.

I feel pain in my heart when I study the latest reports on species that are in danger of total extinction. Picture these magnificent animals tramping through the bush or plodding their way over desert sands: the tiger, the gorilla, the giant panda, the elephant, the Bactrian camel, to name only a few. That is a catalog of majesty, a treasury of great images, an evocation of how diverse and powerful and noble nature can be when creatures are allowed to undergo eight or ten million years of evolution. Ten million years from now, our elephant could possibly become something even more wonderful, if we do not terminate the process now.

I am reminded of something in a lighthearted vein—a cartoon that appeared some years ago, in what magazine I do not remember. It showed two imaginary creatures climbing ashore out of the primordial ooze, one male, one female, obviously intent on a common purpose. But they are both distressed and frustrated, for planted on the sand dune they had hoped to use is a handsomely lettered sign, such as one sees on military bases, that says NO EVOLVING.

I am not an impartial witness to developments in the animal kingdom. I love animals, have always lived with them, have tried to understand them, and have written about them with affection in an effort to remind others of what a significant enrichment to human life they can be. This anthology of some of the many passages I have written about various animals testifies to that abiding love.

I've had warm relationships with many kinds of animals. I have a photograph that shows Java, one of the gentlest, most caring dogs my wife and I ever had, hovering nearby to protect me, if need be, from the strange woman who was photographing us—Java is in the foreground, where she always tried to be if anything seemed to threaten me. In Maryland two stately blue herons took residence in a swamp behind our house, standing silent hour after hour as they waited for fish to swim by. Victor and Victoria, my wife named them, and they became members of our family, communicating with us, waiting for fish scraps, guarding our house.

A family of bluebirds nested six inches from my study window and grew to ignore my typing. I lost a running battle with a squirrel who believed that the sunflower seeds I put out for the cardinals and evening grosbeaks were intended for him. Once, for several days in the Brazilian wilderness along the banks of the Amazon, I became familiar with a monstrous boa constrictor, tamed by others, who climbed about my arms and shoulders.

But the wild animals I remember best among the buffalo, the Kodiak bears, the bald eagles and the salmon I have studied were two hyenas, one in southern Spain and one on the Serengeti Plain in central Africa. The latter frequented a tourist camp—a kind of motel in the savannah—where he made himself a beloved pet. Lurching about, grinning in his hideous way at his friends, growling when necessary, he became passionately addicted to bottled beer, and we used to watch as he wandered from one bar table to the next, neatly reaching for half-filled bottles and chug-a-lugging their contents. Toward sundown he would stagger off to find someplace to sleep it off, and when the tourists who'd been out on the veldt watching the hordes of animals returned to their cottages, we always knew where our hyena was, for we would hear screams, indicating that some traveler from London or Berlin or San Francisco had found the hyena asleep on his or her pillow.

My relations with the hyena in Spain were of a more personal character. A famed Spanish naturalist had brought home to the Cádiz area a female hyena that he had more or less tamed. Tied to a tree with a chain so long that she could roam about, she was always delighted to see me because she knew that I would roughhouse with her. As we wrestled, I punched her rather forcefully while she nipped at my ankles and wrists. But always the time came when she would take my forearm in her powerful jaws, tighten her teeth with increasing power, as if to say: If I wanted to, Buster, I could bite your arm in half. Then she would release me, throw her powerful arms around me and hug me for the sheer joy of companionship. I had the same relationship with a semi-tamed boa constrictor in the Amazon. He, too, could have crushed me had he wanted to, but he, too, enjoyed rough play.

It was on the Serengeti that I had my most extraordinary experience with animals. John Allen, the English protector of the great herds that passed through and a man who cherished his relationship with animals, took me first on a low-flying plane trip over a large portion of the Serengeti to show me the elephants, giraffes and water buffaloes, but it was when he landed near a hillock so that we could have a picnic that I saw African wildlife at its most awesome: coming straight at us was a mixed herd of at least five hundred thousand wildebeestes and zebras on their way to new feeding grounds.

John, one of his assistants armed with a powerful rifle, my wife and I walked out among the animals and in time found ourselves deep in the midst of this enormous migration. It was eerie. Slowly, the animals came directly at us, but when they reached a spot about ten yards from us they mysteriously parted, half to the left, half to the right, leaving us in a lozenge-shaped free zone; as soon as they passed, they closed ranks again, heading purposefully for their feeding grounds. I tried several times to touch the passing animals, but, without ever seeming to look at me, they maintained that ten-yard distance and rushed past. It was an experience few have had, being in the dead center of a vast herd on the move.

But the part I recall most often is what happened as we returned to our car. Our path took us past the wooded hillock we had used as a guide point, and as we approached it, John Allen moved my wife and me to the inside nearest the copse, while he and his armed assistant unlimbered their guns and walked well to our right, away from the scrub. When we were safely past I asked: 'What was that all about?' and Allen explained: 'Lions infest those woods, and sometimes they leap out to grab unwary travelers. Tom and I had to stand back so that if the lion leaped at you we had free range to shoot him dead before he got you.'

I asked: 'Do you ever miss? Or does the gun ever fail to shoot?' and he said reassuringly: 'It's our business to see it doesn't.' Not many novelists in their seventies have been used as lion bait.

These excerpts from my various books depict the way I think and feel about animals. Each segment was an integral part of the novel in which it appeared, just as animals have been an integral part of my life. The animals entered my pages as naturally as they occupied the veldt or the ice cap or any other habitat.

Those of us who love animals and try to write about them accurately are often, and sometimes with reason, charged with the literary sin of the 'pathetic fallacy,' which the dictionary defines as 'the attribution of human emotions or characteristics to things or animals; e.g., angry hurricane, vengeful cobra.' Purists who object to such usage can be vehement in their objections, and, probably, rightly so. The hurricane that is born off the West African coast, gathering power as it whips westward across the Atlantic, is not angry at the island of St. Croix. But if you are on St. Croix when the hurricane hits, you can be forgiven for thinking that the storm is venting its anger.

I have tried, not always successfully, to avoid the pathetic fallacy when dealing with animals, but if some purist denies that the drunken hyena in the Serengeti lodge had a self-satisfied smirk on his face as he lurched off to bed, or that my dog Java evidenced a protective love for me, I cannot accept his or her censure.

I have often been asked whether I have allowed my personal life or characteristics to appear in my novels. The answer is 'Yes, the old buffalo Rufous in *Centennial* comes close to a self-portrait.' While researching that work I paid prolonged visits to a ranch that supported a small herd of bison, and as I studied them, imagining a time when millions roamed the western plains, I began to identify with a grizzled fellow who remained more or less off to one side as if he were contemplating the fate of his herd. (Talk about the pathetic fallacy!) At the conclusion of my visits, when I had to turn to other subjects, I felt as if I understood the old geezer and, reluctant to leave him, I put him in my book. I am pleased and touched when readers tell me that they too grew to like him.

—JAMES A. MICHENER
Eckerd College
28 January 1991

CREATURES OF THE KINGDOM

FROM THE BOUNDLESS DEEP

ILLIONS UPON MILLIONS of years ago, when the continents were already formed and the principal features of the earth had been fixed, there was, then as now, one aspect of the world that dwarfed all others. It was a mighty ocean, lying to the east of the largest continent, a restless, ever-changing, gigantic body of water that would later be described as pacific.

Over its brooding surface immense winds swept back and forth, whipping the waters into towering waves that crashed down upon the world's seacoasts, tearing away rocks and eroding the land. In its dark bosom, strange life was beginning to form, minute at first, then gradually of a structure now lost even to memory. Upon its farthest reaches birds with enormous wings came to rest, and then flew on.

Agitated by a moon stronger then than now, immense tides ripped across this tremendous ocean, keeping it in a state of torment. Since no great amounts of sand had yet been created, the waters where they reached shore were universally dark, black as night.

Scores of millions of years before man rose from the shores of the ocean to perceive its grandeur and to venture forth upon its turbulent waves, this eternal sea existed, larger than any other of the earth's features, more enormous than the sister oceans combined, wild, terrifying in its immensity and imperative in its universal role.

How utterly vast it was! How its surges modified the very balance of the earth! How completely lonely it was, hidden in the darkness of the night or burning in the dazzling power of a sun younger than ours.

At recurring intervals the ocean grew cold. Ice piled up along its extremities and pulled vast amounts of water from the sea, so that the wandering shoreline of the continents sometimes jutted miles farther out than before. Then, for a hundred thousand years, the ceaselessly turbulent ocean would tear at the exposed shelf of the continents, grinding rocks into sand and incubating new life.

Later the fantastic accumulations of ice would melt, setting cold waters free to join the heaving ocean, and the coasts of the continents would lie submerged. Now the restless energy of the sea deposited upon the ocean bed layers of silt and skeletons and salt. For a million years the ocean would build soil, and then the ice would return; the waters would draw away; and the land would lie exposed. Winds from the north and the south would howl across the empty seas and lash stupendous waves upon the shattering shore. Thus the ocean continued its alternate building and tearing down.

Master of life, guardian of the shorelines, regulator of temperatures and sculptor of mountains—the great ocean was all these.

Millions upon millions of years before man appeared on Earth, the central areas of this tremendous ocean were empty, and where famous islands now exist nothing rose above the rolling waves. Of course, crude forms of life sometimes moved through the deep, but for the most part the central ocean was marked only by enormous waves that moved at the command of moon and wind. Dark, dark, they swept the surface of the empty sea, falling only upon themselves, terrible and lonely and puissant.

Then one day millions of years ago, a rupture developed in the rocky bed of the ocean. It occurred near the middle of the sea, a bit closer to what would later become the western United States than to the shores of eastern Asia. Some great fracture of the earth's basic structure had occurred, and from it began to ooze a white-hot liquid rock. As it escaped from its internal prison and came into contact with the ocean's wet and heavy body, the rock instantly exploded, sending aloft through the nineteen thousand feet of ocean that had pressed down upon it columns of released steam.

Upward, upward, for nearly four miles they climbed, those agitated bubbles, until at last upon the surface of the sea they broke loose and formed a cloud. In that instant the ocean signaled that a new island was building. In time it might grow to become an infinitesimal speck of land that would mark the great central void. No human beings then existed to celebrate the event. Perhaps some weird and now-extinct flying thing spied the escaping steam and swooped down to inspect it; more likely the roots of this future island were born in darkness and brooding nothingness.

For nearly forty million years, an extent of time so vast that it is almost meaningless, only the ocean knew that an island was building below its surface. For nearly forty million years, from that extensive rupture in the ocean floor, liquid rock seeped out in small amounts, forcing its way up through what had escaped before and contributing to the accumulation that was building on the floor of the sea. Sometimes a thousand or ten thousand years would pass before any new eruption of material would take place. At other times gigantic pressures would accumulate beneath the permanent rupture and with unimaginable violence rush through the existing apertures, throwing clouds of steam miles above the surface of the ocean. Waves would be generated that would circle the globe and crash upon themselves as they collided twelve thousand miles away. Such an explosion, indescribable in its fury, might in the end raise the height of the suboceanic island a foot.

For the most part, the slow constant seepage of molten rock was not violently dramatic. Layer upon layer of the earth's vital core would exude, hiss when it met the cold seawater, and then slide down the sides of the mountains, for this bound together what had gone before, and established a base for what was to come.

And then one day, at the northwest end of the suboceanic rupture, an eruption of liquid rock occurred that was different from any others that had preceded it. It threw forth the same kind of rock with the same violence and through the same vents in the earth's core, but this time what was erupted reached the surface of the sea. There was a tremendous explosion as the liquid rock struck water and air together. Clouds of steam rose miles into the air. Ash fell hissing upon the heaving waves. Detonations shattered the air for a moment and then echoed away in the immensity of the empty wastes.

But rock had at last been deposited above the surface of the sea. An island had risen from the deep.

In the long history of the ocean many such piles had momentarily broken the surface and then become submerged again. What was significant about the initial appearance of this first island along the slanting crack was the fact that it held on and grew. Stubbornly, inch by inch, it grew. In fact, it was the uncertainty and agony of its growth that were significant, and only by relentless effort did it establish its right to exist. For the first ten thousand years after its tentative emergence, the little pile of rock in the center of the sea fluctuated between life and death. Sometimes molten lava would rise through the internal channels and erupt from a vent only a few inches above the waves. Tons upon tons of material would gush forth and hiss madly before falling back into the ocean. Some, fortunately, would cling to the newborn island, adding many feet to its formation.

Then from the south, where storms breed in the deep, a mighty wave would form and rush across the world. Its coming would be visible from afar, and in gigantic, tumbling, whistling, screaming power it would fall upon the little accumulations of rocks before surging past.

For the next ten thousand years there would be no visible island, yet under the waves, always ready to spring back to life, there would rest this huge mountain, rising nineteen thousand feet from the floor of the ocean, and when a new series of volcanic thrusts tore through the vents, the mountain would patiently build itself for another try at breaking through the surface. Exploding, hissing and spewing forth ash, the great mountain would writhe in convulsions as it tried to pierce the waves. Its island would be born again.

This was the restless surge of the universe, the violence of birth, the cold tearing away of death; and yet how promising was this interplay of forces as an island struggled to be born, vanishing in agony and then soaring aloft in triumph.

For a million years the island hung in a precarious balance, a child of violence; but finally it was firmly established. Now each new lava flow had a solid base upon which to build, and inch by inch the debris agglutinated until the island could be seen by birds from long distances. It was indeed land, habitable for men had there been any then existing, with shelters for boats, had there been boats, and with rocks that could have been used for building homes. It was now an island, in the real sense of the word, taking its rightful place in the center of the great ocean.

But before life could prosper on this island, soil was needed, and as yet none existed. When molten lava burst upon the air it generally exploded into ash, but sometimes it ran as a viscous fluid down the sides of mountains, constructing extensive sheets of flat rock. The action of wind and rain and cooling nights began to pulverize the newly born lava, decomposing it into soil. When enough had accumulated, the island was ready to support life.

The first living forms to arrive were inconspicuous, indeed almost invisible—lichens and low types of moss. They were borne by the sea and by winds that howled back and forth across the oceans. With a tenacity equal to that of the island itself these fragments of life established themselves, and as they grew they broke down more rocks and built more soil.

At this time on the distant continents separated by the ocean there was a well-established plant and animal society composed of trees and animals and insects. Some of these forms would have adapted easily to life on the new island but were prevented from taking residence by two thousand miles of open ocean.

The first sentient animals to reach the island were fish, for they were everywhere in the ocean, coming and going as they wished. But they could not be said to be a part of the island. The first nonoceanic animal to visit was a bird. It probably came from the north on an exploratory mission in search of food. It landed on the still-warm rocks, found nothing edible, and flew on, perhaps to perish in the southern seas.

A thousand years passed, and no other birds arrived. One day a coconut was swept ashore by a violent storm. It had been kept afloat on the bosom of the sea by its buoyant husk, traveling more than three thousand miles from the southwest, a marvel of persistence. But when it landed, it found no soil along the shore and only salt water, so it perished, but its husk and shell helped form soil for those that would come later.

The years passed. The sun swept through its majestic cycles. The moon waxed and waned, and tides rushed back and forth across the surface of the world. Ice crept down from the north, and for ten thousand years covered the islands, its weight and power breaking down rocks and forming earth.

The years passed, the empty, endless, significant years. And then one day another bird arrived on the island, also seeking food. This time it found a few dead fish along the shore. When it emptied its bowels on the waiting earth it evacuated a tiny seed that it had eaten on some remote island. The seed germinated and grew. Thus, after the passage of eons of time, growing life established itself on the rocky island.

Now the passage of time becomes incomprehensible. Between the arrival of the first, unproductive bird, and the second bearing the vital seed, more than twenty thousand years had elapsed. In another twenty thousand years another form of life arrived—a female insect, fertilized on some distant island on the night before a tremendous storm. Caught up in the vast winds that howled from the south, she was borne aloft to a height of ten thousand feet and driven northward for more than two thousand miles to be dropped at last upon this new and remote island, where she gave birth to the first insect native to the island.

The years passed. Other birds arrived, but they bore no seeds. Other insects were blown ashore, but they were not females or, if they were, they were not pregnant. But once every twenty or thirty thousand years—a period longer than that of historic man—some bit of life would reach the island by accident, and by accident it would establish itself. In this hit-or-miss way, over a period of time that the mind can barely grasp, life populated the island.

It was one of the most significant days in the history of the island when a bird staggered in from some land far to the southwest, bearing in its tangled feathers the seed of a tree. Perched upon a rock, the bird pecked at the seed until it fell on the soil, and in the course of time a tree grew. Thirty thousand years passed, and by yet another accident, the seed of another tree arrived, and after a million years of sheer chance, after five million years of storms and birds and drifting sea-soaked logs bearing snails and borers, the island finally had a forest with flowers and birds and insects.

Nothing, nothing that ever existed on this island reached it easily. The rocks were forced up fiery chimneys through miles of ocean to burst onto the surface of the earth. The lichens that arrived came borne by storms. The birds limped in on deadened wings. Insects came only with hurricanes, and the seeds of trees arrived in the belly of some exhausted wandering bird.

Timelessly, relentlessly, in wind and rain the island was given life, and this life was sustained by constant volcanic eruptions that spewed forth lava that broke down into life-sustaining soil. In violence the island evolved, and in violence great beauty emerged.

The shores of the island, weathered by the sea, were stupendous cliffs that caught the evening sun and glowed like serrated pillars of gold. The mountains were tall and jagged, their lower levels clothed in dark green trees, their upper pinnacles glittering with ice, while the calm bays in which the grandeur of the mountains was reflected were deeply cut into the shore. Valleys and plains, waterfalls and rivers, glades where lovers would have walked, and splendid sites where towns could have been built, the lovely island had all these assets, these alluring invitations to civilization. But no man ever saw them, and the tempting glades entertained no lovers, for the island had risen to its beauty long, long before the age of man; and at the moment of its greatest perfection it began to die. In violence it had been born; in violence it would die.

There was a sudden shudder of the earth, a slipping and a sliding, and after a period of thousands of years, the island had sunk hundreds of feet lower into the ocean, and ice nevermore formed upon its crests. The volcanoes stopped erupting, and no lava poured forth to create new soil to replace what had sunk into the sea. For a million years winds howled at the hills, the ocean gnawed away at the ramparts. The island began to shred away, to shatter and to fall back into the ocean from which it had sprung.

A million years passed, and then a million more, and the island that had grown so patiently at the northwest tip of the great crack in the ocean floor began to slowly, slowly vanish. The birds that had fed upon its hills went elsewhere, bearing in their bowels new seeds. From its shore fertilized insects were storm-blown to other islands, and life went on. Once every twenty or thirty thousand years some fragment of nature escaped from this island, and life went on.

But as the island subsided, a different form of life sprang into increased activity. In the warm, clear, nutritious waters that surrounded the shores, coral polyps began to flourish, and slowly they left behind them as they died their tiny calciferous skeletons a few feet below the surface of the sea. In a thousand years they built a submerged ring around the island. In a thousand more years they added to its form, and as the eons passed, these tiny coral animals built a reef.

Ice melted in the north, and the coral animals were drowned, overcome by the unprecedented weight of the water. The seas' temperature dropped precipitously and the animals died. Torrents of rain poured down from island hills and silted up the shoreline, strangling the tiny coral. Or new ice caps formed far to the north and south, pulling water away from the dying island. The coral reef was exposed and it died.

Like everything to do with this island, throughout its entire history, the coral lived precariously, poised between catastrophes and always building. And so it was that these tiny animals built a new island to replace the old as it gradually wore itself away and sank into the sea.

How terrible this passage of life and death! How meaningless that an island that had been born of such force and violence, that had been so fair, so willing to accommodate man should he ever arrive . . . how sad it was that this island had grown in agony and died in agony before ever a human eye had seen its majesty.

For more than ten million years, the island existed silently in the unknown sea and then died, leaving only a fringe of coral where seabirds rested and gigantic seals played. Ceaseless life and death, endless expenditure of beauty and capacity, tireless ebb and flow and rising and subsidence of the ocean. Night comes and the burning day, and the island waits, and no man arrives. The days perish and the nights, and the aching beauty of lush valleys and waterfalls vanishes, and no man will ever see them. All that will remain is a coral reef, a calcium wreath on the surface of the great sea that had given the island life, a memorial erected by the skeletons of a billion billion billion little animals.

Such coral reefs, when they form a circle in the sea—and there are hundreds of them in the Pacific—are a distinctive and beautiful feature of this ocean. A typical one might protect a circular lagoon two miles in diameter with no land in the middle. Others, of equal size, will have rising from their center remnants of the original volcano that built the island along whose flanks the coral built their reefs. Such a combination—a rugged volcano remnant two thousand feet high rising from the middle of a lagoon and surrounded by a perfect circular reef with only one opening to the outside ocean—can be a magical place, none more so than Bora Bora, the most enchanting island in the world.

While the first island was rising to prominence and dying back to nothingness, other would-be islands, stretching away to the southeast, were also struggling to attain brief existence followed by certain death. Some started their cycle within the same million years as did the first. Others lagged. The latest would not pierce the surface of the sea until the first was well into its death throes, so that at any moment from the time the first island began to die, man, had he then existed, could have witnessed in this two-thousand-mile chain of islands every sequential step in the process of creation and disintegration.

Like an undulating wave of the sea itself, the rocky islands rose and fell; but whereas the cycle of an ocean wave lasts a few minutes at the most, the cycle of the rise and fall of these islands took about sixty million years. Each island, at any given moment of time, existed certainly and securely within that cycle: it was either rising toward birth and significance or it was perishing. If man had been able to witness the cycle, he could not have identified which part of the cycle a given island was in. But the impersonal, molten center of the earth knew, for it was sending that island no new supplies of lava. The waiting sea knew, for it could feel the cliffs falling into its arms a little more easily. And the coral polyps seemed to know, because they sensed that it was now time to start erecting a memorial to this island, which would soon be dead—that is, within twenty or thirty million years.

Endless cycle, endless birth and death, endless becoming and disappearing. Once the terrifying volcanic explosions ceased on any island, that island was already doomed: a new ice age was beginning, which would freeze out all life. Limitless cycle, endless change.

After the first rupture had produced an island that kept its head above water permanently, a miracle occurred that was one of the wonders of our planet. As the rupture remained fixed in the crust of the earth, far below the surface of the sea, a constant supply of new magma available for the formation of new islands continued to pour out for millions of uninterrupted years. But now the great subterranean plate of rock on which the Pacific Ocean rests continued its inexorable creeping movement that began with the creation of our planet and will presumably continue as long as the earth exists. It edges a fragment of a millimeter each decade, forever in a northwest direction, 290 degrees on a compass, but always this deeply hidden Hot Spot, as it came to be called, remains exactly where it originally broke through.

This explains what happened in the construction of these beautiful islands in the middle of the Pacific. The first one, whose birth I have just described, is located at the extreme northwest of the chain; it was relatively small and would bear the name Niihau. It required millions of years to build, but when it was safely above the surface of the sea, it was carried off by the drifting of the plate, always to the northwest to vacate the Hot Spot so the future Kauai could be built by the same process. When this new island wandered off, its place was taken by Oahu, and four others in turn. But always the Hot Spot remained in place, so that when mankind finally reached the islands, it was busy creating the biggest of all, the island of Hawaii itself, with its two massive active volcanoes proving that it still stood directly above the Hot Spot. However, since new islands appear to be aborning beneath the surface of the ocean, perhaps even huge Hawaii is already moving off the Hot Spot and joining the other islands in this beautiful fleet as they continue their predestined journey away from the United States and toward Japan.

Toward the end of the master cycle, when the western islands were dying and the eastern ones were abuilding, a new volcano pushed its cone above the surface of the ocean, and in a series of titanic explosions erupted enough molten rock to establish securely a new island, which after eons would be designated by men as Oahu, capital island of the group. Its subsequent volcanic history was memorable in that its habitable land resulted from the wedding of two separate chains of volcanoes.

After the parent volcano had succeeded in establishing an island, its mighty flanks produced many subsidiary vents through which lava poured. Then a greater volcano, separated from the first by miles of ocean, sprang into being and erected its own majestic construction.

For eons the two massive volcano systems stood in the sea in fiery competition, and then, inevitably, the first began to die back, its fires extinguished, while the second continued to pour millions of tons of lava down its own steep flanks. Hissing, exploding, crackling, the rocks fell into the sea in boundless accumulations, building the later volcano ever more solidly, ever more thickly at its base on the remote floor of the ocean.

In time, sinking lava from the second master builder began to creep across the feet of the first, and then to climb its sides and finally to throw itself across the exposed lava flows that had constituted the earlier island. Now the void in the sea that had separated the two was filled, and they became one. Locked in fiery arms, joined by intertwining ejaculations of molten rock, the two volcanoes stood in matrimony, their union a single fruitful and growing island.

Its soil was later made from dozens of smaller volcanoes that erupted for a few hundred thousand years, then passed into death and silence. One exploded in dazzling glory and left a crater looking like a punch bowl. Another, at the very edge of the island, overlooking the sea, was transformed into a gaunt headland shaped like a diamond.

When the island was fully formed—and what an enchanting island it was—some force of nature, almost as if by subtle plan, hid in its bowels a wealth of incalculable richness. It was not diamonds, because the island was 250 million years too young to have acquired the carboniferous plant growth that produced diamonds. It was not either oil or coal, for the same reason. It wasn't gold, for neither the age nor the conditions required for the creation of that metal were present on this island. It was none of these commonly accepted treasures, but it was a greater one.

The volcanic basalt from which the island was built was porous, and when the tremendous storms that swept the ocean struck the island, the waters they disgorged ran partly out to sea in surface rivers but seeped partly into the heart of the island. Billions of tons of water thus crept down into secret reservoirs of the island.

They did not stay there, of course, for since the rock was porous, there were avenues that led back out to sea, and in time the water was lost. But any animal, a man perhaps, could intercept the water and use it, for the entire island was a catchment; the entire core of the island was permeated with life-giving water.

But that was not the special treasure of this particular island, for a man could bore into almost any porous rock on any island and catch some water. Here, on this island, there was to be an extra treasure, and the way it was deposited was something of a miracle.

When the ice came and went, causing the great ocean to rise, and when the island itself sank slowly and then was rebuilt with new lava—when these titanic convolutions were in progress, the south shore of the island was alternately exposed to sunlight or buried fathoms deep in ocean. When the first condition prevailed, the exposed shore was cut by mountain streams that threw their debris across the plain, depositing there claylike soils and minute fragments of lava. Sometimes the sea would bring bits of animal calcium or a thundering storm would rip away a cliff face and throw its remnants over the shore. Bit by bit, over a hundred thousand years at a time, the shore accumulated its debris.

Then, when the ocean next rose, it would press down heavily upon this shelving land, which would lie for ages, submerged under tons of dark green water. But while the great brutal ocean thus pressed down hydraulically, it at the same time acted as a life-giving agent, for through its shimmering waves filtered silt and dead bodies, and water-logged fragments of trees and sand. All these things, the gifts of both land and sea, the immense weight of ocean would bind together until they united to form rock.

Cataclysmically the island would rise from the sea to collect new fragments washed down from the hills, then sink beneath the waves to accumulate new deposits of life-building slime. But whenever the monstrous ocean beat down heavily upon the shore for ten thousand years at a time, new rock would be formed, an impermeable shield that sloped down from the lower foothills and extended well out to sea. It was a caprock, imprisoning in a gigantic underground reservoir all that lay beneath it.

What lay trapped below, of course, was water. Secretly, far beneath the visible surface of the island, imprisoned by this watertight cap of rock, lay the purest, sweetest, most copious water in all the lands that bordered upon or existed in the great ocean. It lay there under vast pressure, so that not only was it available, but it was ready to leap forth twenty or thirty or forty feet into the air, and engulf with life-giving sweetness anyone who could penetrate the imprisoning rock and set it free. It waited—an almost inexhaustible supply of water to sustain life. It waited—a universe of water hidden beneath the caprock. It waited.

The adventurous plants and insects that had reached the earliest northwest island had plenty of time in which to make their way to the newer lands as the latter rose to life. It might take a million years for a given grass to complete its journey down the chain. But there was no hurry. Slowly, trees and vines and crawling things crept down the islands, while in other parts of the world a new and more powerful animal was rising and preparing himself for his invasion of the islands.

Before the two-volcano island with its trapped treasure of water had finished growing, humankind had developed in distant areas. Before the last island had assumed its dominant shape, Egyptians had erected both mighty monuments and a stable form of government. They could already write and record their memories.

While volcanoes still played along the chain, China developed a sophisticated system of thought and Japan codified art principles that would later enrich the world. While the islands were taking their final form, Jesus spoke in Jerusalem and Muhammad came from the blazing desert with a new vision of heaven, but no one knew the heaven that awaited them on these islands.

For these lands were the youngest part of the earth's visible surface. They were new. They were raw. They were empty. Ancient books that we still read today were written before these islands were known to anyone except the birds of passage. Songs that we still sing were composed and

recorded while these islands remained vacant. The Bible had been com-
piled, and the Koran.

Raw, empty, youthful islands, sleeping in the sun and whipped by rain,
they waited. It is proper to review them carefully in their last, unoccupied
moments, those sad, sweet, overpowering days before the first canoes
reached them.

They were beautiful, verdant with wooded mountains. Their cool waterfalls, existing in the thousands, were spectacular. Their cliffs, where the
restless ocean had eroded away the edges of great mountains, dropped
thousands of feet clear into the sea, and birds nested on the vertical stones.
Rivers were fruitful. The shores of the islands were white and waves that
washed them were crystal-blue. At night the stars were close, brilliant dots
of fire fixing forever the location of the islands and forming majestic
pathways for the moon and sun.

If paradise consists solely of beauty, then these islands were the fairest
paradise that man ever invaded. But if the concept of paradise includes the
ability to sustain life, then these islands in the time of Jesus and Muhammad were far from heavenly. They contained almost no food. Of all the
things that grew on their magnificent hillsides, nothing could be relied
upon to sustain life adequately. There were a few pandanus trees whose
spare and bitter fruits could be chewed for minimal subsistence. There
were a few tree ferns whose cores were just barely edible, a few roots.
There were fish if they could be caught and birds if they could be trapped.
But there was nothing else.

Few more inhospitable major islands have ever existed than this group.
Here there were no chickens, pigs, cattle or edible dogs; no bananas, taro,
sweet potatoes, breadfruit, pineapple, guava, gourds, melons or mangoes,
no fruit of any kind; no palms for making sugar. The islands did not have
even that one essential, that miraculous sustainer of tropical life, the
coconut. Some of the fruit had drifted to the shores, but in salty soil along
the beaches they could not grow.

Any man who came to the islands would have to bring with him all his
food. If he was wise, he would also bring most of the materials required
for physical comfort. There were no candlenuts for lamps, no mulberry
bark for making tapa cloth. Nor were there any flamboyant flowers: no
frangipani, or hibiscus, or bright croton, or colorful orchids. Instead of
joy-giving, life-sustaining plants there was a tree whose only virtue was

that its wood when dried yielded a persistent perfume. This was the tree of death, the sandalwood tree. It was not poisonous, but the uses to which it would be put on these islands would make it a permanent blight.

The soil of the islands was not particularly good. It was not rich and black like the soil that peasants were already farming, not loamy and productive like that known to the Dakota and Iowa tribes of Indians. It was red and of a sandlike consistency, apparently rich in iron because it had been formed of decomposed basalt, but lacking in other essentials. If a farmer could add to this soil the missing minerals and supply it with adequate water, it had the capacity to produce enormously. But of itself it was inadequate.

Tremendous quantities of rain did fall on the islands, but it fell in an unproductive manner. From the northeast, trade winds blew constantly, pushing ahead of them low clouds pregnant with pure water. But along the northeast shores of each island high cliffs and mountains rose, and these reached up and knocked the water out of the clouds, so that it fell in cascades where it could not be used and never reached the southwest plains where the red soil was. Of the flatlands that could be tilled, fully three fourths were, in effect, deserts. If one could capture the wasted water that ran useless down the steep mountainsides and back out to sea, bringing it through the mountains and onto the flatlands, then crops could be grown. Or if one could find the secret reservoirs deep in the bowels of the islands, one would have ample water and more than ample food. But barring such a discovery, men who lived on these islands would never have enough water or enough food. The best that could be said of the islands was that they harbored no poisonous snakes, no mosquitoes and no organisms that cause disfiguring diseases.

Of all the growing things that existed on these islands at the time of Jesus, ninety-five of every hundred grew nowhere else in the world. These islands were unique, alone, apart, off the mainstream of life, a secluded backwater of nature, an authentic natural paradise where each growing thing followed its own distinctive pattern of development.

The first seed, which was brought by that adventurous bird, was a grass seed perhaps, one whose brothers and sisters—if the term may be used of grasses—stayed behind on their original islands, where they developed as the family had always done for millions of generations. On these original islands the grass maintained its standard characteristics and threw forth no venturesome modifications; or, if such mutations occurred, the stronger normal stock quickly submerged them, and the primary strain was preserved.

But on the new islands the grass, left alone in sun and rain, became a different grass, unique and adapted to these islands. When men looked at such grass, millions of years later, they would be able to discern that it was a grass, and that it had come from original stock still existing elsewhere; but they would also see that it was nevertheless a new grass, with new qualities, new vitality and new promise.

Birds, flowers, worms, trees and insects all developed unique forms and qualities on these islands. There was then, as there is now, no place known on earth that could even begin to compete with these islands in their capacity to encourage forms of life to develop freely and radically their own best potential.

Why this should have been so remains a mystery. Perhaps a fortunate combination of rainfall, climate, sunlight and soil accounted for this miracle. Perhaps eons in which diverse growing things were left alone to work out their own best destinies was the explanation, as, for example, when a grass reached here it had to rely on its own capacities because it could not be refertilized by grasses of the same kind from the parent stock. But whatever the reason, the fact remains: in these islands new breeds developed, and they prospered, and they grew strong, and they multiplied. These islands were a crucible of exploration and development.

And so, rich with potential, the islands waited. England was settled by mixed and powerful races, and the islands waited for their own settlers. Mighty kings ruled in India, and in China and in Japan, while the islands waited.

Volcanoes, still building the ramparts with fresh flows of lava, hung lanterns in the sky so that if a man in his canoe was lost on the great dark sea, wandering this way and that, he might spot the incandescent glow of the underside of a distant cloud, and thus find a fiery star to steer by.

Large gannets and smaller terns skimmed across the waters leading to land, while frigate birds drew sharp and sure navigation lines from the turbulent ocean wastes right to the heart of the islands, where they nested. If a man in a canoe could spot a frigate bird, its cleft tail cutting the wind, he could be sure that land lay in the direction toward which the bird had flown at dusk.

But, men of Polynesia and Boston and China and Mount Fuji and the barrios of the Philippines, do not come to these islands empty-handed, or craven in spirit, or afraid to starve. There is no food here. In these islands there is no certainty. Bring your own food, your own gods, your own flowers and fruit and concepts. For if you come without resources to these islands you will perish.

But if you come with growing things, and good foods and better ideas, if you come with gods that will sustain you, and if you are willing to work until the swimming head and the aching arms can stand no more, then you can gain entrance to this miraculous crucible where the units of nature are free to develop according to their own capacities and desires.

On these harsh terms the islands waited.

THE BIRTH OF THE ROCKIES

W HEN THE EARTH was already ancient, of an age incomprehensible to man, an event of basic importance occurred in the area of the North American continent that would later be known as Colorado. To appreciate its significance, one must understand the structure of the earth, and to do this, one must start at the vital center.

Since the earth is not a perfect sphere, the radius from center to surface varies. At the poles it is 3,950 miles and at the equator 3,963. At the time we are talking about, Colorado lay about the same distance from the equator as it does now, and its radius was 3,956 miles.

At the center then, as today, was a ball of solid material, very heavy and incredibly hot, made up mostly of iron; this extended for about 770 miles. Around it was a cover about 1,375 miles thick, which was not solid but which could not be called liquid either, for at that pressure and that temperature, nothing could be liquid. It permitted movement, but it did not easily flow. It transmitted heat, but it did not bubble. It is best described as having characteristics with which we are not familiar, perhaps like a warm plastic.

Around this core was fitted a mantle of dense rock 1,784 miles thick, whose properties are difficult to describe, though much is known of them. Strictly speaking, this rock was in liquid form, but the pressures exerted upon it were such as to keep it more rigid than a bar of iron. The mantle was a belt that absorbed both pressure and heat from any direction and was consequently under considerable stress. From time to time the pressure became so great that some of the mantle material forced its way toward the surface of the earth, undergoing marked change in the process. The resultant body of molten liquid, called magma, would solidify to produce the igneous rock, granite, but if it was still in liquid form as it approached the surface, it would become lava. It was in the mantle that many of the movements originated that would determine what was to happen next to the visible structure of the earth;

deep beneath the surface, it accumulated stress and generated enormous heat as it prepared for its next dramatic excursion toward the surface, producing the magma that would appear as either granite or lava.

At the top of the mantle, only twenty-seven miles from the surface, rested the earth's crust, where life would develop. What was it like? It can be described as the hard scum that forms at the top of a pot of boiling porridge. From the fire at the center of the pot, heat radiates not only upward, but in all directions. The porridge bubbles freely at first when it is thin, and its motion seems to be always upward, but as it thickens, one can see that for every slow bubble that rises at the center of the pan, part of the porridge is drawn downward at the edges; it is this slow reciprocal rise and fall that constitutes cooking. In time, when enough of this convection has taken place, the porridge exposed to air begins to thicken perceptibly, and the moment the internal heat stops or diminishes, it hardens into a crust.

This analogy has two weaknesses. The flame that keeps the geologic pot bubbling does not come primarily from the hot center of the earth, but rather from the radioactive structure of the rocks themselves. And as the liquid magma cools, different types of rocks solidify: heavy dark ones rich in iron settle toward the bottom; lighter ones like quartz move to the top.

The crust was divided into two distinct layers. The lower and heavier, twelve miles thick, was composed of a dark, dense rock known by its made-up name of 'sima,' indicating the predominance of silicon and magnesium. The upper and lighter layer, fifteen miles thick, was composed of lighter rock known by the invented word 'sial,' indicating silicon and aluminum. The subsequent two miles of Colorado's rock and sediment would eventually come to rest on this sialic layer.

Three billion six hundred million years ago the crust had formed, and the cooling earth lay exposed to the developing atmosphere. The surface as it then existed was not hospitable. Temperatures were too high to sustain life, and oxygen was only beginning to accumulate. What land had tentatively coagulated was insecure, and over it winds of unceasing fury were starting to blow. Vast floods began to sweep emerging areas and kept them swamplike, rising and falling in the agonies of a birth that had not yet materialized. There were no fish, no birds, no animals, and had there been, there would have been nothing for them to eat, for grass and trees and worms did not exist.

Even under these inhospitable conditions, there were elements like algae from which recognizable life would later develop, but the course of their future development had not yet been determined.

The earth, therefore, stood at a moment of decision: would it continue as a mass with a fragile covering incapable of sustaining either structures or life, or would some tremendous transformation take place that would alter its basic surface appearance and enlarge its capacity?

Sometime around three billion six hundred million years ago, the answer came. Deep within the crust, or perhaps in the upper part of the mantle, a body of magma began to accumulate. Its concentration of heat was so great that previously solid rock partially melted. The lighter materials were melted first and moved upward through the heavier material that was left behind, coming to rest at higher elevations and in enormous quantities.

Slowly but with irresistible power it broke through the earth's crust and burst into daylight. In some cases, the sticky, almost congealed magma may have exploded upward as a volcano whose ash would cover thousands of square miles or, if the magma was of a slightly different composition, it would pour through fissures as lava, spreading evenly over all existent features to a depth of a thousand feet.

As the magma spread, the central purer parts solidified into pure granite. Most of it, however, was trapped within the crust, and slowly cooled and solidified into rock deep below the surface.

What amount of time was required for this gigantic event to complete itself? It almost certainly did not occur as a vast one-time cataclysm although it might have, engulfing all previous surface features in one stupendous wrenching that shook the world. More likely, convective movements in the mantle continued over millions of years. The rising internal heat accumulated eon after eon, and the resultant upward thrust still continues imperceptibly.

The earth was at work, as it is always at work, and it moved slowly. A thousand times in the future this irresistible combination of heat and movement would change the aspect of the earth's surface.

This great event of three billion six hundred million years ago was different from many similar events for one salient reason: it intruded massive granite bodies which, when the mountains covering it were eroded away, would stand as the permanent basement rock. In later times it would be penetrated, wrenched, compressed, eroded and savagely distorted by cataclysmic forces of various kinds. But through three billion six hundred million years, down to this very day, it would endure. Upon it would be built the subsequent mountains; across it would wander the rivers; high above its rugged surface animals would later roam; and upon its solid foundations homesteads and cities would rest.

A relatively short distance below the surface of the earth lies this infinitely aged platform, this permanent base for action. How do we know of its existence? From time to time, in subsequent events, blocks of this basement rock were pushed upward, where they could be inspected, and tested and analyzed, and even dated. At other memorable spots throughout Colorado this ancient rock was broken by faults in the earth's crust, and large blocks of it uplifted to form the cores of present-day mountain ranges.

This rock is beautiful to see—a hard, granitic pink or gray-blue substance as clean and shining as if it had been created yesterday. You find it unexpectedly along canyon walls, or at the peaks of mountains or occasionally at the edge of some upland meadow, standing inconspicuously beside alpine flowers. It is a part of life, an almost living thing, with its own stubborn character formed deep in the earth, once compressed by enormous forces and heated to hundreds of degrees. It is a poem of existence, this rock, not a lyric but a slow-moving epic whose beat has been set by eons of the world's experience.

Often the basement rock appears not as granite but as unmelted gneiss, and then it is even more dramatic, for in its contorted structure you can see proof of the crushing forces it has undergone. It has been fractured, twisted, folded over to the breaking point and reassembled into new arrangements. It tells the story of the internal tumult that has always accompanied the genesis of new land forms, and it reminds us of the wrenching and tearing that will be required when new forms rise into being, as they will.

It must be understood that basement rock is not a specific kind of rock, for its components change from place to place. It has been well defined as 'the layer of rock below which lies ignorance.' In some places it hides far below sea level; at others it marks the tops of mountains fourteen thousand feet high. Throughout most of the United States it lies hidden, but in Canada it is exposed over large areas, forming a shield. Nor was it all laid down at the same time, for variations in its dating are immense. In Minnesota it was deposited more than three and a half billion years ago;

in Wyoming, only two and a half billion years ago; and in Colorado, only a few miles to the south, at the relatively recent date of one billion seven hundred million years ago.

After the basement rock had been accumulated at Centennial, Colorado, later than almost anywhere else in the United States, an extraordinary event occurred. About two billion years of history vanished, leaving no recoverable record. By studying other parts of the West, and by making shrewd extrapolations, we can construct guesses as to what must have happened, but we have no proof. The rocks that should have been at hand to tell the story have either been destroyed beyond recognition or were never deposited in the first place. We are left in ignorance.

This situation is not confined to the region around Centennial, a small area in northwest Colorado, although there the gap is spectacular. At no spot in North America have we been able to find an unbroken sequence of rocks from earliest basement to recent sediment. Always there is some tantalizing gap. Over short distances it can have amazing variations in time and extent; for example, during the missing years at Centennial, massive accumulations of granite that would later form Pikes Peak were being assembled only a few miles to the south.

For hundreds of millions of years at a time the Centennial area must have lain at the bottom of the sea that at intervals covered much of America. The grains of sediment, eroded from earth masses remaining above sea level, would drift in silently and fall upon the basement, building with infinite slowness a sedimentary rock that might ultimately stand five thousand feet thick.

At other intervals the new-forming land would rise from the sea, to be weathered by storm and wind and creeping rivers long vanished. This cycle of beneath-sea, above-sea occurred at least a dozen times; repeatedly magma sent upward by the mantle broke through the crust and crept over the land; repeatedly erosion cut it away and left new forms quite different from their predecessors.

The time required! The slow passage of years! The constant alterations! Now part of an uplifted mountain, now sunk at the bottom of some sea, Centennial experienced wild fluctuations. Because of the erratic wanderings of the earth, the site stood sometimes fairly close to the equator, with a baking sun overhead; at subsequent times it might be closer to the North Pole, with ice in winter. It was a swamp during one eon, a desert the next.

Whenever it came to temporary rest, it should have been exhausted, a worn-out land, but always new energies surged up from below, creating new experiences.

Those lost two billion years lie upon the consciousness of man the way vague memories or ghosts survive in the recollections of childhood. When man did finally arrive on the scene, he would be the inheritor of those vanished years, and everything he did would be limited to some degree by what had happened to his earth in those forgotten years, for it was then that its quality was determined, its mineral content, the value of its soil and the salinity of its waters.

About three hundred and five million years ago occurred what can be called the first event that left an identifiable record at Centennial. Within the mantle, forces developed that produced a penetration of the earth's crust. The basement broke into discrete blocks, some of which were pushed upward higher than their surroundings, to relieve the pressure from below.

The resulting mountains covered much of central Colorado, following fairly closely the outlines that the historical Rocky Mountains would later occupy, and at the conclusion of five or ten million years they constituted a major range.

It was not born in cataclysm. There was no dramatic opening of earth from which fully formed mountains emerged. Nor was there any excess of volcanism. Instead, there was the slow, unceasing uplift of rock until the new mountains stood forth with majesty. They were the ancestral Rockies, and since they left behind them rocks that can be analyzed, we can construct for them a logical history.

From the moment of their birth they participated in a startling series of events. No sooner had they pushed their crests above the flat surface of the land than small streams began to nibble at their flanks, eating away fragments of rock and sand. High winds tore at their low summits, and freezing winters broke away protuberances. At intervals earthquakes toppled insecure rocks; at other times inland seas lashed at their feet, eroding them further.

As the mountains increased in age, the small streams grew into rivers, and as they increased in volume they also increased in carrying power, and soon they were conveying broken bits of mountain downward, cutting as they went and forming great alluvial fans along the margins of the range.

In a beautiful interrelationship, the mountains continued to push upward at about the rate at which the eroding forces were tearing them down. Had the mountains been permitted to grow unimpeded, they might have reached heights of twenty thousand feet; as it was, the system of balances kept them at some undetermined elevation, perhaps no more than three or four thousand feet.

And then, for some reason, the upward pressures ceased, and over a period of forty million years this once formidable range was razed absolutely flat by erosion, with not a single peak remaining as a memento of what had been one of the earth's outstanding features. The fabled ancestral Rockies, a masterpiece of landscape, vanished, its component rocks reduced to rubble and scattered across the growing plains of eastern Colorado, Kansas and Nebraska. Mountains that had commanded the landscape had become pebbles.

Later, as if to seal off the record of their existence, the land upon which they had stood was submerged spasmodically over a period of eighty to ninety million years in the Jurassic and Cretaceous periods, the era of the dinosaurs. Clay, silt and sand were moved in by rivers emptying into the inland sea, filtering down slowly, silently in the darkness, accumulating in soft layers. But with the passage of time and the weight of the water and sediment pressing down, the silt and sand gradually solidified into layers of rock thousands of feet thick. Thus the roots of the once great mountains were sealed off, as if the forces that erected them in the first place had decided to erase them and bury the evidence.

When a mountain ten thousand feet high vanishes over a period of forty million years, what has happened? Each million years it loses two hundred and fifty feet, which means each thousand years it loses three inches. The loss per year would be minuscule.

This extremely slow average rate does not preclude occasional catastrophes like earthquakes or floods that might compress into one convulsion the losses for an average millennium. Nor does it mean that the debris could be easily removed. These mountains covered an extensive land area, and even a trivial average loss, if applied over that total area, would require much riverine action to carry the eroded materials away.

The fact remains that an enormous mountain range had vanished. Since this seems a prodigal action, extremely wasteful of motion and material, a caution must be voiced. The rocks that were lifted from the depths of the earth to form the ancestral Rockies had been used earlier in the construction of other mountain ranges whose records have now vanished. When those predecessor ranges were eroded away, the material that composed them was deposited in great basins, mainly to the west.

The Earth is much like a prudent person who has an allotted span of life and a given amount of energy. Using both wisely, conserving where possible, he can enjoy a long and useful life; but no matter how prudent he is, he will not escape ultimate death. The Earth loses its materials with uncanny thrift: it wastes nothing; it patches and remodels. But always it expends a little of its heat, and in the end—at some unpredictable day billions of years from now—that fire will diminish, and Earth, like man, will die. In the meantime, its resources are conserved.

While the ancestral Rockies were disappearing, an event that was to leave still-visible consequences was reaching its climax along the eastern shore of what would later be known as the United States. The time was about two hundred and fifty million years ago; during preceding periods, reaching very far into the past, a building process of beautiful complexity had been operating. Into the deep ocean depressions east of the wandering shoreline, erosion of prehistoric and very ancient mountains had brought about deposits of sediment that had accumulated to a remarkable depth; at some places the layers were forty thousand feet thick. With the passage of time and in the presence of great pressure, they had formed into rock. Thrust and compression, uplift and subsidence had crumpled these rocks into contorted shapes.

The stage was now set for an event that would elevate the rocks into a mountain range. It occurred when the subterranean plate on which rested the crust that was later to become part of the continent of Africa began to move slowly westward. In time the migration of this plate became so determined—and perhaps it was matched by a comparable movement of the American plate eastward—that collision became inevitable. The predecessor of the Atlantic Ocean was squeezed so severely that it was entirely eliminated. The continents came into actual contact, so that such living things as then existed could move from America to Africa and back again overland.

As the inexorable collision continued, there had to be some kind of dislocation along the edges that were bearing the brunt of the action. It seems probable that the edge of the African plate turned under, its rocky components returning to the crust and perhaps even back into the mantle. We know that the edge of the American plate was thrust upward to produce the Appalachian Mountains, not some ancestral Appalachians, but the roots of the very mountains we see today.

After some twenty million years of steady growth the Appalachians stood forth as a more considerable range than the ancestral Rockies had been. Certainly, they were some of the world's most impressive mountains, soaring thousands of feet into the air.

Inevitably, as soon as they began to emerge, the tearing-down process commenced. First the continental plates drifted apart, with Africa and the Americas winding up in roughly the positions they occupy today. The Atlantic Ocean as it now exists started to develop, its deep inclines providing a basin for the catchment of rock and silt eroded from the heights. Volcanoes operated and at intervals enormous fractures occurred, allowing vast segments of the range to rise while others fell.

As early as a hundred million years ago the Appalachians—only a truncated memory of their original grandeur—began to assume their present shape; they are thus one of the oldest landscape features of the United States. At this time the Appalachians had no competition from the Rocky Mountains, for that range had not yet emerged; indeed, most of America from the Appalachians to Utah was nothing but a vast sea from which substantial land would rise only much later.

In their present condition the Appalachians seem a poor comparison to the Rockies. They are no longer high; they contain no memorable landscape; they do not command great plains; and they are impoverished where minerals like gold and silver are concerned. But they are the majestic harbingers of our land; they served their major purpose long before man existed, then lingered on as noble relics to provide man with an agreeable home when he did arrive. They are mountains of ancient destiny, and to move among them is to establish contact with a notable period of our history.

They have been mentioned here to provide a counterbalance to the great things that were about to happen in the West. About seventy million years ago much of the western part of America lay beneath a considerable sea, and if this configuration had persisted, the eastern United States would have been an island much like Great Britain, but dominated by the low-lying Appalachians.

But beneath the surface of the inland sea there was the portent of great events. The combined weight of sediment and water, pressing down upon a relatively weak basin area, coincided with an upsurge of magma from the mantle. As before, these magmatic pressures from below pushed upward huge blocks of the basement, and bent the more flexible, layered rocks above the basement until a massive mountain range had been erected. The range, running from northern Canada almost to Mexico, was both longer and wider than the ancestral Rockies had ever been and placed somewhat farther east. Its major elevations stood very high, and as these areas were uplifted, the inland sea was drained off.

The mountain range was composed in part of a rock that had formerly appeared in the ancestral Rockies—which is why we know so much about these ancient mountains we have never seen—and formed one of the world's major structural forms, which it still does.

The Rockies are therefore very young and should never be thought of as ancient. They are still in the process of building and eroding, and no one today can calculate what they will look like ten million years from now. They have the extravagant beauty of youth, the allure of adolescence, and they are mountains to be loved.

Their history is reasonably clear. Not all were born as a result of basement block uplift, for certain mountains were squeezed upward by vast forces acting laterally. Others may have arisen as a result of some movement of the American plate. And we have visible proof that some of the southern mountains were built by spectacular action.

About sixty-seven million years ago volcanic activity of considerable range and intensity erupted throughout Colorado. As the mountains rose, the crust cracked and allowed lava to rise to the surface in great quantity. Lava flows were extensive, but so were the explosions of gaseous ash, which sometimes accumulated to a depth of several hundred feet, compressing itself finally into a rock that still exists.

Especially awesome were the vast clouds of gaseous matter that drifted eastward, with internal temperatures rising to thousands of degrees. Whatever they passed over they killed instantly through the exhaustion of oxygen, and when their temperatures fell, the clouds fell too. Their contents then solidified to form crystalline rock, one cloud producing enough to blanket large areas to a depth of seven or eight feet. In other areas, lakes were formed, dammed by lava flow from volcanic fields.

.   .   .

Now for the first time we come to the river that will command attention
for the remainder of this story. It was born coincident with the rise of the
new Rockies, called into being to carry rainfall and melting snow down
from its heights. For millions of years it was not the dominant river of the
region; in fact, five competing rivers led eastward from the Rockies, the
long-abandoned courses still discernible in the drylands. They lost their
identity because of a peculiarity: an arm of our river began to cut southward along the edge of the mountain range, and in doing so, it captured
one after another of the competing rivers, until they no longer ran eastward as independent rivers but coalesced to form the Platte.

When the Rockies were younger, and therefore higher than now, the
river had to be of a goodly size. We can deduce this from the amount of
material it was required to transport. The area covered by its deposits was
about three hundred and twenty miles long and one hundred and forty
miles wide. Depending upon how thick the overlay was, the river had to
transport more than seven thousand cubic miles of rubble. In those early
days it was wide and turbulent. It was capable of carrying huge rocks,
which it disintegrated into fragments of great cutting power, but its main
cargo was sand and silt. Its flow was irregular; at times it would wander
fifty miles wide across plains, and for long periods it would hold to one
channel. During these years it labored continuously at its job of building
the plains of middle America.

About forty million years ago the river's building process was aided by
a cataclymic event. To the southwest a group of volcanoes burst into
action, and so violent were their eruptions, volcanic ash drifted across the
sky for half a thousand miles, held aloft by great windstorms. The ash,
blackening the sky as it passed, blanketed the area when it fell. Perhaps at
some point an entire volcano may have exploded in one superburst, covering the heavens with its burden of fire and lava; eruptions continued over
a period of fifteen million years, and the wealth of the ash that fell upon
Colorado accumulated to a depth of thousands of feet. Combining with
clay, it formed one of the principal rocks of the region.

It is difficult to comprehend the violence of this period. Twenty-three
known volcanoes operated in Colorado, some of them much larger than
Vesuvius in Italy or Popocatepetl in Mexico. Obviously, they could not

have been in constant eruption; there had to be long periods of quiescence, but it does seem likely that some acted in concert, energized by a common agitation within the mantle. They deposited an incredible amount of new rock, more than fourteen thousand cubic miles of it in all.

They glowed through the nights, illuminating in ghostly flashes the mountains and plains they were creating. At times they sponsored earthquakes, and then for some mysterious reason, possibly because the molten magma was exhausted, they died, one after another, until there were no active volcanoes in the region. Only the clearly defined calderas still stand to mark this age of violence.

About fifteen million years ago the area underwent a massive dislocation in a process that extended for ten million years. The entire central portion of America experienced a massive uplifting. Perhaps the continental plate was undergoing some major adjustment, or there may have been a sizable disruption within the mantle. At any rate, the surfaces—both mountains and valleys to the west, and the low-lying flat plains to the east—rose. Colorado was uplifted to its present altitude. Rivers like the Missouri, which then ran north to the Arctic Ocean, began to take form and run south, and the outlines of our continent assumed more or less their present shape. Many subsequent adjustments of a minor nature would still occur—for example, at this time North and South America were not yet joined—but the shapes we know were discernible.

About one million years ago the Ice Age began to send its rapacious fingers down from the north polar ice cap. Because of intricate changes in the climate, triggered perhaps by variations in the carbon dioxide content of the Earth's atmosphere or by accumulations of volcanic dust which intercepted the sun's heat that otherwise would have reached the Earth, large sheets of ice began to accumulate where none had been before.

The glaciers invading North America reached so far south and were so thick, they imprisoned water that normally belonged to the oceans, which meant that shorelines which had lain submerged for the preceding millions of years now lay exposed. The great western glacier did not quite reach the Centennial area; it halted some distance to the north. But at high elevations in the Rockies, small glaciers did form and filled the valleys, and as they moved slowly to lower levels they gouged out the valley bottoms and carved the standing rocks, so that much of the beauty of the new Rockies stems from the work of the glaciers.

They arrived in the mountains at spaced intervals, the first major one appearing about three million years ago; the last, only fifteen thousand years ago. But of course, at high, cold altitudes like the topmost new Rockies small glaciers persisted and still exist.

As the mountain glaciers melted they produced unprecedented amounts of water, which created floods of gigantic proportions. They cascaded down with fierce velocity and submerged traditional rivers, causing them to expand many times their customary width. Much detritus was borne down from the mountains, most of it with sharp cutting edges, and it was this mixture of copious water and cutting rock that planed down the lands to the east.

Sometimes, high in the Rockies, the glacier would impound a temporary rock-and-ice barrier, and behind it an enormous lake would be formed. It would exist for decades or centuries. Then one day there would be a violent cracking sound, and with one vast rush the contents of the lake would surge forth, miles wide until it roared into some confining canyon, where it would compress into a devastating liquid missile, shooting along with terrifying force, uprooting every living thing and ripping away huge boulders from the walls of the canyon before rushing at last onto the plains.

There it would reach the river. A wall of water would fan out across the plains, engulfing both the river and its tributaries. Churning, roaring, twisting, it would scour everything before it as it scratched and clawed its way eastward. In the space of an afternoon, such a flood might carve away deposits that had required ten million years to accumulate.

It was the river that laid down the new land; it was the river that took it away. The endless cycle of building up, tearing down and rebuilding, using the same material over and over, was contributed to by the river. It was the brawling, undisciplined, violent artery of life and such it would always be.

Some sixty-five million years ago—shortly after the emergence of the new Rockies—the river began hauling down an extraordinary amount of rock, gravel and sand, which it deposited in a thick overlay on the flat plains to the east; the deposit was eventually more than two hundred feet thick.

When this process was completed, thirty-eight million years ago, the plains to the east were so built up that they blended harmoniously into the lower reaches of the new Rockies, creating a lovely sweep that extended in unbroken beauty several hundred miles into Nebraska and Kansas. This symmetry did not endure, for the new Rockies experienced a massive uplifting, which raised them above the gentle sweep. As a result, the river now dropped more steeply from the mountains, carrying with it many cutting rocks. It surged eastward and for twelve million years dominated the foothills, cutting them away, scraping down hillocks, and depositing on the plains new layers of rocky, infertile soil.

The great inland sea that had once dominated this area had long vanished, so that the building of this new rock had to be accomplished in open air. The river would bring down deposits, which would spread out in fans. Sun and wind would act upon them, and new deposits would form over them. Gradually, disparate components would begin to solidify, and as heavier forms accumulated on top, those at the bottom would coalesce to form conglomerates.

Each year the plains grew a little higher, a little more stable in their footing. Finishing touches were applied about eleven million years ago when a sandstone rock was laid down, sealing the entire region. This final rock had a peculiar characteristic; at the spot we are talking about, north of Centennial, some variation occurred in the cement that bound the granular elements together. Different from the cement operating in nearby regions, it had been formed perhaps from volcanic ash that had drifted in; at any rate, it created an impermeable caprock that would protect the softer sandstone that rested beneath. At last the vast job of building was ended. From the period when the new Rockies underwent their secondary uplift, some three hundred and twenty feet of solid rock and soil had been laid down, all protected by the caprock, and had there been an observer at the time, he could have been excused had he concluded that what he saw then, eight million years ago, would be the final structure of the plains.

But it was still the river that determined what the surface of the land would be, and starting eight million years ago, it once more began to tumble out of mountains with greatly increased velocity, cutting and swirling and spreading far across the plains. It was engaged upon a gargantuan task, to scour away every vestige of the enormous quantity of land that had been contributed by the new Rockies. In some places it had to remove up to a thousand feet of burden; from extensive areas it had to cut away at least three hundred feet. But it succeeded—except where that extra-hard caprock protected its monolith.

No matter how wild the torrents that raged down from the mountains, nor how powerful the flash floods that cascaded across the plains after some torrential downpour, the monolith persisted. It covered an area no more than a quarter of a mile long, two hundred yards wide, but it resisted all assaults of the river. For millions of years this strange and solitary monolith maintained its integrity.

Neighboring sandstone covers were breached, and when they were gone, the softer areas they had protected were easily cut down by the river. Winds helped; meltwater from ice did its damage; and as the eons passed, the river completed its task—all remnants of the land deposited by the new Rockies were swept away, except the solitary monolith.

And then, about two million years ago, the central portion of the caprock weakened, cracked during a heavy winter and broke away. The softer rock that it had been protecting quickly deteriorated—say, over a period of hundred thousand years—until it was gone.

Two pillars remained, about a quarter of a mile apart, each somewhat elongated in shape; the western was over five hundred feet long and two hundred feet wide, the eastern only three hundred and eighty feet long and a hundred and ninety feet wide. The western pillar was taller, too, standing three hundred and twenty feet above its pediment; the eastern only two hundred and eighty.

They were extraordinary, these two sentinels of the plains. Visible for miles in each direction, they guarded a bleak and silent empire. They were the only remaining relics of that vast plain that the new Rockies had deposited; each bit of land the sentinels surveyed dated back to ancient times, before the mountains were born.

And so the stage is set. One billion seven hundred million years of activity, including the building of at least two high mountain ranges and the calling into being of vast seas, have produced a land that is ready at last to receive and nurture living things.

DIPLODOCUS, THE DINOSAUR

TOWARD DUSK on a spring evening one hundred and thirty-six million years ago a small furry animal less than four inches long peered cautiously from low reeds growing along the edge of a tropical lagoon that covered much of what was to be the present state of Colorado. It was looking across the surface of the water as if waiting for some creature to emerge from the depths, but nothing stirred. From among the fern trees to the left there was movement, and for one brief instant the little animal looked in that direction.

Shoving its way beneath the drooping branches and making considerable noise as it awkwardly approached the lagoon for a drink of water, came a medium-sized dinosaur, lumbering on two legs and twisting its short neck from side to side as it watched for larger animals that might attack.

It was about three feet tall at the shoulders and not more than six feet in length. Obviously a land animal, it edged up to the water carefully, constantly jerking its short neck in probing motions. In paying so much attention to the possible dangers on land, it overlooked the real danger that waited in the water, for as it reached the lagoon and began bending down in order to drink, what looked like a fallen log lying partly submerged in the water lunged toward him.

It was a crocodile, armored in heavy skin and possessing powerful jaws lined with deadly teeth. But it had moved too soon. Its well-calculated grab at the reptile's right foreleg missed by a fraction, for the dinosaur managed to withdraw so speedily that the great snapping jaw closed not on the bony leg, as intended, but only on the soft flesh covering it.

There was a ripping sound as the crocodile tore off a strip of flesh, and a sharp guttural click as the wounded dinosaur responded to the pain. Then peace returned. The dinosaur could be heard for some moments retreating. The disappointed crocodile swallowed the meager meal it had caught, then resumed its log camouflage.

As the furry little animal returned to its earlier preoccupation of staring at the surface of the lagoon, it became aware, with a sense of panic, of wings in the darkening sky. At the very last moment it threw itself behind the trunk of a gingko tree, flattened itself out and held its breath as a large flying reptile swooped down, its sharp-toothed mouth open, and just missed its target. Still flat against the moist earth, the little animal watched in terror as the huge reptile banked low over the lagoon and then came straight at the crouching animal, but, abruptly, it had to swerve away because of the gingko roots. Dipping one wing, the reptile turned gracefully in the air, then swooped down on another small creature hiding near the crocodile, unprotected by any tree. Deftly it opened its beak and caught its prey, which shrieked as it was carried aloft. For some moments the little animal hiding behind the gingko tree watched the flight of its enemy as the reptile dipped and swerved through the sky like a falling feather, finally vanishing with its catch.

The little watcher could breathe again. Unlike the great reptiles, which were cold-blooded and raised their babies from hatching eggs, it was warm-blooded and came from the mother's womb. It was a pantothere, one of the earliest mammals and progenitor of later types like the opossum, and it had scant protection in the swamp. Watching cautiously lest the flying hunter return, it ventured forth to renew its inspection of the lagoon, and after a pause, spotted what it had been looking for.

About ninety feet out into the water a small knob had appeared on the surface. It was only slightly larger than the watching animal itself, about six inches in diameter. It seemed to be floating on the surface, unattached to anything, but actually it was the unusual nose of an animal that had its nostrils on top of its head. The beast was resting on the bottom of the lagoon and breathing in this unique manner.

Now, as the watching animal expected, the floating knob began slowly to emerge from the waters. It was attached to a head, not extraordinarily large but belonging obviously to an animal markedly bigger than either the first dinosaur or the crocodile. It was not a handsome head, nor graceful either, but what happened next displayed each of those attributes.

The head continued to rise from the lagoon, higher and higher in one long beautiful arch, until it stood twenty-five feet above the water, suspended at the end of a long and graceful neck. It was like a ball extended endlessly upward on a frail length of wire, and when it was fully aloft, with no body visible to support it, the head turned this way and that in a delicate motion, surveying the world that lay below.

The head and neck remained in this position for some minutes, sweeping in lovely arcs of exploration. Apparently what the small eyes on either side of the projecting nose had seen reassured the beast, for now a new kind of motion ensued.

From the surface of the lake an enormous mound of dark flesh began slowly to appear, muddy waters falling from it as it rose. The body of the great reptile looked as if it were about twelve feet tall, but how far into the water it extended could not be discerned; it surely went very deep. Now, as the furry animal on shore watched, the massive beast began to move, slowly and rhythmically. Where the neck joined the great dark bulk of the body, little waves broke and slid along the flanks of the beast. Water dripped from the upper part of the animal as it moved ponderously through the swamp.

The reptile appeared to be swimming, its neck probing in sweeping arcs, but actually it was walking on the bottom, its huge legs hidden by water. And then, as it drew closer to shore and entered shallower water, an enormous tail emerged. Longer than the neck and disposed in more delicate lines, it extended forty-four feet, swaying slightly on the surface of the lagoon. From head to tip of tail, the reptile measured eighty-seven feet.

Up to now it had looked like a snake, floundering through the lagoon, but the truth was revealed when the massive legs became visible. They were enormous, four pillars of great solidity but attached to the torso by such crude joints that although the creature was amphibious, it could not easily support herself on dry land, where water did not buoy it up.

With slow, lumbering strides the reptile moved toward a clear river that emptied into the swamp, and now its total form was visible. Its head reared thirty-five feet; its shoulders were thirteen feet high; its tail dragged aft some fifty feet; it weighed nearly thirty tons.

It was a diplodocus, not the largest of the dinosaurs and certainly not the most fearsome. This particular specimen was a female, seventy years old and in the prime of life. She lived exclusively on vegetation, which she now sought among the swamp waters. Moving her head purposefully from one plant to the next, she cropped off such food as she could find. This was not an easy task, for she had an extremely small mouth studded with minute peglike front teeth and no back ones for chewing. It seems incomprehensible that with such ineffectual teeth she could crop enough food to nourish her enormous body, but she obviously did.

After finishing with such plants as were at hand, she moved into the channel. The mammal, still crouching among the roots of the gingko tree, watched with satisfaction as she moved past. It had been afraid that she might plant one of her massive feet on its nest as another dinosaur had done, obliterating both the nest and its young. Indeed, diplodocus had left underwater footprints so wide and so deep that fish used them as nests. One massive footprint might be many times as wide as the fish was long.

And so diplodocus moved away from the lagoon and the apprehensive watcher. As she went she was a veritable poem in motion. Placing each foot carefully and without haste, and assuring herself that at least two were planted solidly on the bottom at all times, she moved like some animated mountain, keeping the main bulk of her body always at the same level, while her graceful neck swayed gently and her extremely long tail remained floating on the surface.

The various motions of her great body were always harmonious; even the plodding of the four gigantic feet had a pleasant rhythm. With the graceful neck and the tapering tail, this large reptile epitomized the beauty of the animal kingdom as it then existed.

She was looking for a stone. For some time she had instinctively known that she lacked a major stone, and this distressed her. Keeping her head low, she scanned the bottom of the stream but found no suitable stones.

This forced her to move upstream, the delicate motion of her body conforming to the shifting bottom as it rose slightly before her. Now she came upon a wide selection of stones, but prudence warned her that they were too jagged for her purpose, and she ignored them. Once she stopped and turned a stone over with her blunt nose. She scorned it—too many cutting edges.

Preoccupied with her futile search, she failed to notice the approach of a rather large land-based dinosaur that walked on two legs. He did not come close to approaching her in size, but he was quicker of motion, and had a large head, a gaping mouth and a ferocious complement of jagged teeth. He was a meat-eater, always on the watch for the giant water-based dinosaurs who ventured too close to land. He was not large enough to tackle a huge animal like diplodocus if she was in her own element, but he had found that usually when the large reptiles came into the stream, there was something physically wrong with them, and twice he had been able to hack one down.

He approached diplodocus from the side, stepping gingerly on his two powerful hind feet, keeping his two small front feet ready like hands to grasp her should she prove to be in a weakened condition. He was careful to keep clear of her tail, for this was her only weapon.

She remained unaware of her would-be attacker, and continued to probe the river bottom for an acceptable stone. The carnivorous dinosaur interpreted her lowered head as a sign of weakness. He lunged at the spot where her vulnerable neck joined the torso, only to find that she was in no way incapacitated, for at the moment of attack she twisted adroitly and presented him with the broad and heavy side of her body. This made him stumble back. As he did so, diplodocus stepped forward, and slowly swung her tail in a mighty arc, hitting him with such force that he was thrown off his feet and sent crashing into the brush.

One of his small front feet was broken by the blow and he uttered a series of awk-awks, deep in his throat, as he shuffled off. Diplodocus gave him no more attention and resumed her search for the stone.

Finally she found what she wanted. It weighed about three pounds, was flattish on the ends and both smooth and rounded. She nudged it twice with her snout, satisfied herself that it suited her purposes, then lifted it in her mouth, raised her head to its full majestic height and swallowed the stone. It slid easily down her long throat into her gullet and from there into her grinding gizzard, where it joined six smaller stones that rubbed together gently and incessantly as she moved. This was how she chewed her food, the seven stones serving as substitutes for the molars she lacked.

With awkward yet oddly graceful motions she adjusted herself to the new stone, and could feel it find its place among the others. She felt better all over and hunched her shoulders, then twisted her hips and flexed her long tail.

Night was closing in. The attack by the smaller dinosaur reminded her that she ought to be heading back toward the safety of the lagoon, back where fourteen other reptiles formed a protective herd, but she was kept in the river by a vague longing she had experienced several times before but could not remember clearly. Like all members of the diplodocus family, she had an extremely small brain, barely large enough to send signals to the various remote parts of her body. For example, to activate her tail became a major tactical problem, for any signal originating in her head required some time to reach the effective muscles of the tail. It was the same with the ponderous legs; they could not be called into instant action.

Her brain was too small and too undifferentiated to permit reasoning or memory; ingrained habit warned her of danger, and only the instinctive use of her tail protected her from the kind of assault she had just experienced. As for explaining in specific terms the gnawing agitation she now felt, and which had been the major reason for her leaving the safety of the herd, her small brain could give her no help.

She therefore walked with splashing grace toward a spot some distance upstream. How beautiful she was as she moved through the growing darkness! All parts of her great body—the gently swaying neck, the stalwart trunk, the slow-moving mighty legs and the delicate tail extending almost endlessly behind and balancing the whole—responded splendidly to one central impulse. It would require far more than a hundred million years of experiment before her equal would be seen again.

She was moving toward a white chalk cliff that she had known before. It stood some distance from the lagoon, sixty feet higher than the river at its feet. Here, back eddies had formed a swamp, and as she approached this protected area, diplodocus became aware of a sense of security. She hunched her shoulders again and adjusted her hips. Swishing her long tail, she tested the edge of the swamp with one massive forefoot. Liking what she felt, she moved slowly forward, sinking deeper and deeper into the dark waters until she was totally submerged except for the knobby tip of her head, which she left exposed so that she could breathe.

She wanted to fall asleep, but the gnawing feeling of hunger kept her awake, even though she could feel the new stone working on the foliage she had consumed that day. The buzzing of the day insects had ceased, indicating that night was at hand, and she knew she should sleep but could not. After some hours the tiny brain sent signals along the extended nerve systems and she pulled herself through the swamp with noisy sucking sounds. Soon she was back in the main channel, still hunting vaguely for something she could neither define nor locate. And so she spent the long tropical night.

Diplodocus was able to function as capably as she did for three reasons. When she was in the swamp at the foot of the cliff, an area that would have meant death for most animals, she was able to extricate herself because her

d to handle
e dispensed
joints were
rection, yet
hey would
head.
developed
ted along
came out
e lagoon,

ot of the
ently one
at the far
had been
net they

vo giant
n unbe-
k of his
n seven
oon.
away
odocus
They
oming
their
kept
hung

erent
had
xer-
ittle
heir
ms.
she
alk

y; although they made a footprint many
t in mud, they could, when it came time
ging muck, compress to the width of a
pull her huge leg and foot from the mud
from the muck at the edge of the swamp;
to cling to, and the leg pulled free with a

,' was so named because sixteen of her tail
enty-seven behind the hips—were made with
great artery that ran along the underside of
another channel topside, and it ran from the
ngest segment of the tail. In this channel lay
inew that was anchored securely at shoulder
ated from either position. Thus the long neck
the precursor of the mechanical crane, which
tremely heavy objects by the clever device of
ley and counterbalancing the whole. The pulley
the channel made by the paired flanges of the
he powerful sinew of neck and tail; her counter-
her torso. Had she had powerful teeth, her neck
ced that she could have lifted into the air the
er in the same way that the claw of a well-designed
many times its own weight. Without the advanced
ulley endowed by nature, diplodocus could have
eck nor her tail, and she could not have survived.
histicated machine, as well adapted to her mode of
t might succeed her in generations to come.
e she had was remarkable, and raises questions as to
veloped. The powerful bones of her legs, which were
the time, were of the most heavy construction, thus
ecessary ballast, but the bones that were higher in her
ssively lighter bulk, not only in sheer weight but also
position, and this delicate construction buoyed up her
t almost to float.
l. Many fenestrations, open spaces like windows, perfo-
e of her neck and tail, thus reducing their weight. These
with their channels top and bottom, were so exquisitely
they can be compared only to the arches and windows of

a Gothic cathedral. Bone occurred only where it was require
stress. No shred was left behind to add its weight if it could b
with, yet every arch required for stability was in place. The
articulated so perfectly that the long neck could twist in any di
the flanges within which the sinews rode were so strong that
not be damaged if a great burden was placed on her neck or

It was this marvel of engineering, which had only recently
and would flourish for another seventy million years, that flo
the shore of the lagoon that night, and when the little mammal
of its nest at dawn, it saw her twisting her neck out toward th
then inland toward the chalk cliff.

Finally she turned and swam back toward the swamp at the f
cliff. Once there she sniffed the air in all directions, and appar
smell was familiar, for she turned purposefully toward fern trees
end of the swamp, from which appeared the male diplodocus she
seeking. They approached each other slowly, and when they
rubbed necks together.

She came close to him, and the little mammal watched as the tv
creatures coupled in the water, their massive bodies intertwined i
lievable complexity. When he rutted he simply climbed on the bac
mate, locking his forepaws about her, and concluded his mating i
seconds. The two reptiles were locked together most of the foren

When they finally separated, each by his or her own route swam
to join the herd, which consisted of fifteen members of the diplo
family, three large males, seven females and five young animals.
moved together, keeping to the deep water most of the time and c
into the river for food. In the water they poled themselves along with
feet barely touching bottom, their long tails trailing behind, and al
in balance by that subtle arrangement of bone whereby the heaviest
close to the bottom, allowing the lighter to float on top.

The family did not engage in play such as later animals of a diff
breed would; they were reptiles and as such were sluggish. Since they
cold blood with an extremely slow metabolism, they needed neither
cise nor an abundance of food; a little motion sufficed for a day, a
food for a week. They often lay immobile for hours at a time, and t
tiny brains spurred them to action only when they faced specific probl

After a long time she felt another urge, one that was irresistible, and
moved along the shore to a sandy stretch of beach not far from the ch

cliff. There she swept her tail back and forth, clearing a space, in the middle of which she burrowed with both her snout and her awkward forelegs. When a declivity was formed, she settled herself into it and over a period of nine days deposited thirty-seven eggs, each with a protective leathery shell.

When her mission ashore was completed, she spent considerable time brushing sand over the nest with her tail and placing with her mouth bits of wood and fallen leaves over the spot so as to hide it from animals that might disturb the eggs. Then she lumbered back to the lagoon, soon forgetting even where she had laid the eggs. Her work was done. If the eggs produced young reptiles, fine. If not, she would not even be aware of their absence.

It was this moment that the furry animal had been watching for. As soon as diplodocus submerged herself in the lagoon, he darted forth, inspected the nest and found one egg that had not been properly buried. It was larger than he, and he knew that it contained enough food for a long time. Experience had taught him that his feast would be tastier if he waited some days for the contents to harden, so this time he merely inspected his future banquet, and kicked a little dirt over it so that no one else might spot it.

After the thirty-seven eggs had baked four days in the hot sand, he returned with three mates, and they began attacking the egg, gnawing with incisors at its hard shell. They had no success, but in their work they uncovered the egg even more.

At this point a dinosaur much smaller than any that had appeared previously, but at the same time much larger than the mammals, spotted the egg, knocked off one end and ate the contents. The pantotheres were not sorry to see this, for they knew that much of the egg would still be left, so when the small dinosaur left the area, they scurried in to find that the broken eggshells did yield a feast.

In time the other eggs, incubated solely by the action of the sun, hatched, and thirty-six baby reptiles sniffed the air, knew by instinct where the lagoon lay, and in single file started for the safety of the water.

Their column had progressed only a few yards when the flying reptile that had tried to snatch the mammal spotted them and, swooping down, caught one infant in its beak to take it to its hungry young. The reptile made three more trips, catching a little diplodocus each time.

Now the small dinosaur that had eaten the egg also saw the column, and he hurried in to feed on six of the young. As he did so, the others scattered, but with an instinct that kept them moving always closer to the lagoon. The original thirty-seven were now down to twenty-six, and these were attacked continuously by the rapacious flier and the carnivorous dinosaur. Twelve of the reptiles finally reached the water, but as they escaped into it a large fish with bony head and jagged rows of teeth ate seven of them. On the way, another fish saw them swimming overhead and ate one, so that from the original thirty-seven eggs, there were now only four possible survivors. These, with sure instinct, swam on to join the family of fifteen grown diplodocuses.

As the little ones grew, diplodocus had no way of knowing that they were her children. They were merely reptile members that had joined the family, and she shared with other members of the herd the burden of teaching them the tricks of life.

When the young were partly grown, their thin snakelike bodies increasing immensely, diplodocus decided that it was time to show them the river. Accompanied by one of the adult males, she set out with the four youngsters.

They had been in the river only a short time when the male snorted sharply, made a crackling sound in his throat, and started moving as fast as he could back to the lagoon. Diplodocus looked up in time to see the most terrifying sight the tropical jungle provided. Bearing down upon the group was a monstrous two-legged creature towering eighteen feet high, with a huge head, short neck and rows of gleaming teeth.

It was allosaurus, king of the carnivores, with jaws that could bite the neck of the diplodocus in half. When the great beast entered the water to attack her, she lashed at him with her tail and knocked him slightly off course. Even so, the monstrous six-inch claws on his prehensile front feet raked her right flank, laying it open.

He stumbled, righted himself and prepared a second attack, but again she swung her heavy tail at him, knocking him to one side. For a moment it looked as if he might fall, but then he recovered, left the river and rushed off in a new direction. This put him directly behind the male diplodocus, and even though the latter was retreating as fast as possible toward the lagoon, the speed of allosaurus was such that he was able to reach forward and grab him where the neck joined the torso. With one terrifying snap of the jaws, allosaurus bit through the neck, vertebrae and all, and brought his victim staggering to his knees. The long tail flashed, to no avail. The body twisted in a violent but futile effort to free itself of the daggerlike teeth.

Allosaurus pushed the giant reptile to the ground, and then, without relinquishing its bloody hold, began twisting and tearing at the flesh until a large chunk of meat was torn loose. Only then did allosaurus back away from the body. Thrusting its chin in the air, it adjusted the chunk of meat in its mouth and dislocated its jaw in such a way that the huge morsel could slide down into the gullet, from which it would descend to the stomach, to be digested later. Twice more the beast tore at the body, dislodging great hunks of meat, which it eased down its throat. It then stood beside the fallen body for a long time as if pondering what to do. Crocodiles approached for their share, but allosaurus drove them off. Carrion reptiles flew in, attracted by the pungent smell of blood, but they too were repulsed.

As allosaurus stood there defying the denizens of lagoon and jungle alike, he presented an amazing appearance; he was as intricately devised as diplodocus. His jaws were enormous, their muscles so powerful that when they contracted in opposing directions they exerted a force that could bite through tree trunks. The edges of the teeth were beautifully serrated, so they could not only cut but also saw; elaborate machines a hundred and forty million years later would mimic their principle. The teeth were unique in another respect. In the jaw of allosaurus, embedded in bone beneath the tooth sockets, lay seven sets of replacements for each tooth. If, in biting through the neck bones of an adversary, allosaurus lost a tooth, this was of little concern. Soon a replacement would emerge, and behind it six others would remain in line waiting to be called upon, and if they were used up, others would take place in line, deep within the jawbone.

Now allosaurus lashed his short tail and emitted growls of frustration. He had killed this animal, which meant a vast amount of food, but could not consume it. Other predators appeared, including the two smaller dinosaurs that had visited the beach before. All remained at a safe distance from allosaurus.

He took one more massive bite from the dead body but could not swallow it. He spit it out, glared at the onlookers, then tried again. Covered with sand, the flesh rested in his gaping mouth for several minutes, then slid down inside the extended neck. With a combative awk-awk rumbling from deep within his throat, allosaurus lunged ineffectively at the watchers, then ambled off to higher ground.

As soon as he was gone, the scavengers moved in—reptiles from the sky, crocodiles from the lagoon, two kinds of dinosaurs from land and the mammals hiding by the gingko tree. By nightfall the dead diplodocus, all thirty-three tons of him, had disappeared and only his massive skeleton lay on the beach.

Wounded diplodocus and the four young dinosaurs that had witnessed this massacre now swam back to the lagoon. In the days that followed she began to experience the last inchoate urge she would ever know. Sharp pains radiated slowly from the place where allosaurus had ripped her. She found no pleasure in association with other members of the herd. She was drawn by some inexplicable force back to the swamp at the chalk cliff, not for purposes of re-creating the family of which she was a part but for some pressing reason she had never felt before.

For nine days she delayed heading for the swamp, satisfying herself with half-sleep in the lagoon, idly poling herself half submerged from one warm spot to another, but the pain did not diminish. Vaguely she wanted to float motionless in the sun, but she knew that if she did this, the sun would destroy her. She was a reptile and had no means of controlling body heat; to lie exposed in the sun long enough would boil her to death in her own internal liquids.

Finally, on the tenth day she entered the river for the last time, stepping quietly like some gracious queen. She stopped occasionally to browse on some tree, lifting her head in an arc on which the late sun shone. Her tail extended behind, and when she switched it for some idle purpose it gleamed like a scimitar set with jewels.

How beautiful she was as she took that painful journey, how gracefully coordinated her movements as she swam toward the chalk cliff. She moved as if she owned the earth and conferred grace upon it. She was the great final sum of millions of years of development. Slowly, swaying from side to side with majestic delicacy, she made her way to the swamp that lay at the foot of the cliff.

There she hesitated, twisting her great neck for the last time as if to survey her kingdom. Thirty feet above the earth her small head towered in one last thrust. Then slowly it lowered; slowly the graceful arc capsized. The tail dragged in the mud and the massive knees began to buckle. With a final surge of determination, she moved herself ponderously and clumsily into a deep eddy.

Its murky waters crept up her legs, which would never again be pulled forth like reeds; this was the ultimate capture. The torn side went under; the tail submerged for the last time, and finally even the lovely arc of her neck disappeared. The knobby protuberance holding her nose stayed aloft for a few minutes, as if she desired one last lungful of the heavy tropical air, then it too disappeared. She had gone to rest, her mighty frame imprisoned in the muck that would embrace her tightly for a hundred and thirty-six million years.

It was ironic that the only witness to the death of diplodocus was the little pantothere that watched from the safety of a cycad tree, for of all creatures who had appeared on the beach, he was the only one that was not a reptile. The dinosaurs were destined to disappear from the Earth, while this little animal would survive, its descendants and collaterals populating the entire world, first with prehistoric mammals, themselves destined to become extinct—titanotheres, mastodons, eohippus—and subsequently with animals man would know, such as the mammoth, the lion, the elephant, the bison and the horse.

Of course, certain smaller reptiles such as the crocodile, the turtle and the snake would survive, but why did they and the little mammal live when the great reptiles vanished? This remains one of the world's supreme mysteries. About sixty-five million years ago, as the new Rockies were emerging, the dinosaurs and all their immediate relations died out. The erasure was total, and scholars have not yet agreed upon a satisfactory explanation. All we know for sure is that these towering beasts disappeared. Triceratops with its ruffed collar, tyrannosaur of the fearful teeth, ankylosaur the plated ambulating tank, trachodon the gentle duck-billed monster—all unaccountably vanished.

A MIRACLE OF EVOLUTION

FIFTY-THREE million years ago, while the new Rockies were still developing and long after diplodocus had vanished, in the plains area where the twin pillars formed, an animal began to develop that in later times would give man his greatest assistance, as well as pleasure and mobility. The progenitor of this invaluable beast was a curious little creature, a four-legged mammal, and he stood only seven or eight inches high at the shoulder. He weighed little, had a body covering of part-fur, part-hair and seemed destined to develop into nothing more than an inconsequential beast.

He had, however, three characteristics that would determine his future potential. The bones in his four short legs were complete and separate and capable of elongation. On each foot he had five small toes, that mysteriously perfect number that was the same for most of the ancient animals, including the great dinosaurs. And he had forty-four teeth, arranged in an unprecedented manner: in front, some peglike teeth as weak as those of diplodocus; then a conspicuous open space; then at the back of the jaw, numerous grinding molars.

This little animal made no impression on his age, for he was surrounded by other, much larger mammals destined to become rhinoceroses, camels and sloths. He lived in seclusion in the shady parts of such woods as had developed and fed himself by browsing on leaves and soft marsh plants, for his teeth were not strong and would have quickly worn down had they been required to chew rough food like the grass that was then beginning to develop.

If one had observed all the mammals of this period and tried to evaluate the chances of each to amount to something, one would not have placed this quiet little creature high on the list of significant progenitors; indeed, it would have seemed then that the beast might develop in a number of different ways, none of them memorable, and that the little fellow might survive a few million years and then quietly vanish.

The curious thing about this forerunner of greatness is that although we are sure that he existed and are intellectually convinced that he had to have certain characteristics, no man has ever seen a shred of physical evidence that he really did exist. No fossil bone of this creature has so far been found; we have a large collection of bones of diplodocus and her fellow reptiles, all of whom vanished, but of this small prototype of one of the great animal families, we have no relics whatever. Indeed, he has not yet even been named, although we are quite familiar with his attributes; perhaps when his bones are ultimately found—and they will be—a proper name would be paleohippus, the hippus of the Paleocene epoch. When word of his discovery is flashed around the world, scholars and laymen in all countries will be delighted, for they will have come into contact with the father of a most distinguished race, one that all men have loved and from which most have profited.

Perhaps thirteen million years after paleohippus flourished, and when the land that would contain the twin pillars had begun to form, the second in line and first-known in this animal family appeared and became so numerous in the area that hundreds of skeletons would ultimately be laid down in rock. Because of this, scientists would know this small creature as intimately as they know their own puppies.

He was eohippus, an attractive small animal about twelve inches high at the shoulder. He looked more like a friendly dog than anything else, with small alert ears, a swishing tail to keep insects away, a furry kind of coat and a face that was somewhat long in order to accommodate the forty-four teeth inherited from his ancestor. The teeth were still weak, so that the little creature had to content himself with leaves and other soft foods.

But the thing that marked eohippus and made one suspect that this family of animals might be headed in some important direction was the feet. On the short front feet, not yet adapted for swift movement, the five original toes had been reduced to four; one had only recently disappeared, the bones that had once sustained it vanishing into the leg. And on the rear foot there were now three toes, the two others having withered away during the course of evolution. But the surviving toes had tiny hooves instead of claws.

One could still not predict what this inconspicuous animal was going to become, and the fact that he would stand second in the sixty-million-year process of creating a noble animal seemed unlikely. Eohippus seemed more suited to be merely a family pet.

And then, about thirty million years ago, when the land that was to form the twin pillars was being laid down, mesohippus developed, twenty-four inches high at the shoulders and with all the basic characteristics of his ancestors, except that he had only three toes on each of his feet. He was a sleek animal, about the size of our collie or red fox. The forty-four teeth kept his face long and lean and his legs were beginning to lengthen, but his feet still contained pads and small hooves.

Then, about eighteen million years ago, a dramatic development took place. Merychippus appeared, a handsome three-toed animal forty inches high, with a bristly mane, long face and protective bars behind the eye sockets.

He had one additional development that would enable the horse family to survive in a changing world: his teeth acquired the remarkable capacity to grow out from their socket as they wore down at the crown. This permitted the proto-horse to quit browsing on such leaves as he found and to move instead to grazing on the new grasses that were developing on the prairies. Grass is a dangerous and difficult food; it contains silica and other rough substances that wear down teeth, which must do much grinding in order to prepare the grass for digestion. Had not merychippus developed these self-renewing grinders, the horse as we know it could neither have developed nor survived. But with this almost magical equipment, he was prepared.

These profound evolutions occurred in what is now known as Colorado on the plains that surrounded the site of the twin pillars. There on flatlands that knew varied climates, from tropical to subarctic, depending on where the equator was located at the time, this singular breed of animal went through the manifold changes that were necessary before it stood forth as the horse as we know it.

One of the biggest changes in the antecedents of the horse appeared about six million years ago, when pliohippus, the latest in the breed, evolved with only one toe on each foot and with the pads on which his ancestors had run eliminated. It now had a single hoof. This animal was a medium-sized beautiful horse in almost every sense of the word, and would have been recognized as such, even from a considerable distance.

There would be minor refinements, mostly in the teeth and in the shape of the skull, but the horse of historic times was now foreshadowed.

He arrived as equus about two million years ago, as splendid an animal as the ages were to produce. Starting from the mysterious and unseen paleohippus, this breed had unconsciously and with great persistence adapted itself to all the changes that the Earth presented, adhering always to those mutations that showed the best chance of future development. Paleohippus, of the many capacities; eohippus, of the subtle form; merychippus, with the horselike appearance; pliohippus, with the single hoof— these attributes persisted. There were dozens of other variations equally interesting that died out because they did not contribute to the final form. There were would-be horses of every description, some with the most ingenious innovations, but they did not survive, for they failed to adjust to the he Earth as it was developing; they vanished because they were not needed. But the horse, with its notable collection of virtues and adjustments, did survive.

About one million years ago, when the twin pillars were well formed, a male horse with chestnut coloring and flowing tail lived in the area as part of a herd of about ninety. He was three years old and gifted with especially strong legs that enabled him to run more swiftly than most of his fellows. He was a gamin by nature and had left his mother sooner than any of the other males of his generation. He was the first to explore new arrivals on the prairie and had developed the bad habit of leading any horses that would follow on excursions into canyons or along extended draws.

One bright summer morning this chestnut was leading a group of six adventurous companions on a short foray. He took them across the plains that reached out from the twin pillars and northward into a series of foothills that contained passageways down which they galloped in single file, their tails flowing behind them as they ran. It was an exhilarating chase, and at the end of the main defile they turned eastward toward a plain that opened out invitingly, but as they galloped they saw blocking their way two mammoths of extraordinary size. Fourteen feet tall at the shoulders, with monstrous white tusks that curved downward from the head, the great creatures towered over the horses. The tips of their tusks reached sixteen feet, and if they caught an adversary, they could toss him far into the air. The two mammoths were imposing, and had they been ill-disposed toward the horses, could have created havoc, but they were placid by nature and intended no harm.

The chestnut halted his troop, led them at a sober pace around the mammoths, coming very close to the great tusks, then broke into a gallop that would take him onto the eastern plains, where a small herd of camels grazed, bending awkwardly forward. The horses ignored them, for ahead stood a group of antelope as if waiting for a challenge. The seven horses passed at full speed, whereupon the fleet antelope, each with a crown of four large antlers, sprang into action, darting after them.

For a few moments the two groups of animals were locked in an exciting race, the horses a little in the lead, but with a burst of speed the antelope leaped ahead and before long the horses saw only dust. It had been a joyous race, to no purpose other than the challenge of testing speed.

Beside the grazing area on which the antelope had been feeding there was a family of armadillos, large ratlike creatures encased in collapsible armor. The horses were vaguely aware of them but remained unconcerned, for the armadillo was a slow, peaceful creature that caused no harm. To their surprise the round little animals stopped searching for slugs and suddenly rolled themselves into a defensive position. Some enemy, unseen by the horses, was approaching from the south, and in a moment it appeared, a pack of nine dire wolves, the scourge of the plains, with long fangs and swift legs. They loped easily over the hill that marked the horizon, peering this way and that, sniffing the air. The wolf serving as the scout detected the armadillos and signaled his mates. The predators hurried up, inspected the armor-plated round balls, nudged them with their noses and turned away. No food there.

With some apprehension, the horses watched the nine enemies cross the grassland, hoping that they would pass well to the east, but this was not to be. The lead wolf, a splendid beast with a sleek gray coat, spotted the horses and broke into a powerful run, followed instantly by his eight hunting companions. The chestnut snorted and in the flash of a moment realized that he must not lead his six horses back into the canyons from which they had just emerged, for the two mammoths might block the way, allowing the dire wolves to overtake any straggler and cut him down.

So with an adroit leap sideways he broke onto the plains in the direction the antelope had taken and led his troop well away from their home terrain. They galloped with purpose, for although the dire wolves were not yet close at hand, they had anticipated the direction the horses might take and had vectored to the east to cut them off. The chestnut, seeing this maneuver, led his fellows to the north, which opened a considerable space between them and the wolves.

As they ran to safety, they passed a herd of camels that were slower-moving. The big awkward beasts saw the apprehension of the horses and took flight, although what the cause of the danger was they did not yet know. There was a clatter on the prairie and much dust, and when it had settled, the horses were well on their way to safety, but the camels were left in the direct path of the wolves. The lumbering camels ran as fast as they could, scattering to divert attacks, but this merely served to identify the slowest-moving and upon this unfortunate animal the wolves concentrated.

Cutting at him from all sides with fearful teeth, the wolves began to wear him down. He slowed. His head drooped. He had no defense against the dire wolves and within a few moments one had leaped at his exposed throat. Another fastened onto his right flank and a third slashed at his belly. Uttering a cry of anguish, the camel collapsed, his ungainly feet buckling under the weight of the wolves. In a flash, all nine were upon him, so that before the horses left the area, the camel had been slain.

At a slow walk they headed south for the hills that separated them from the land of the twin pillars. On the way they passed a giant sloth, who stood sniffing at the summer air, dimly aware that wolves were on the prowl. The huge beast, twice the size of the largest horse, knew from the appearance of the horses that they had encountered wolves, and retreated awkwardly to a protected area. An individual sloth, with his powerful foreclaws and hulking weight, was a match for one wolf, but if caught by a pack, he could be torn down, so battle was avoided.

Now the chestnut led led the other horses into the low hills, down a gully and out onto the home plains. The sight of the twin pillars—white at the bottom where they stood on the prairie, reddish toward the top, and white again where the protecting caps rested—was reassuring, a signal of home, and when all seven of the troop were through the pass, they cantered easily back to the main herd. Their absence had been noted and the older horses came up to nuzzle them. The herd had a nice sense of community, as if all were members of the same family, and each was gratified when others who had been absent returned to safety.

Among the six followers accompanying the chestnut on his foray was a young dun-colored mare, and in recent weeks she had been keeping close to him and he to her. They obviously felt an association, a responsibility each to the other, and normally they would by now have bred, but they were inhibited by a peculiar awareness that soon they would be on the move. None of the older animals had signified in any way that the herd was about to depart this congenial land by the twin pillars, but in some strange way the horses knew that they were destined to move—and to the north.

What was about to happen would constitute one of the major mysteries of the animal world. The horse, that splendid creature which had developed here at the twin pillars, would desert his ancestral home and emigrate to Asia, where he would prosper, and the plains at the pillars would be occupied by other animals. By the year 6000 B.C. he would become extinct in the Western Hemisphere.

The horses were about to move north and they knew they could not accommodate a lot of colts, so the chestnut and the mare held back. But one cold morning, when they had been chasing idly over the plains as if daring the dire wolves to attack them, they found themselves alone at the mouth of a canyon where the sun shone brightly; he mounted her and in due course she produced a handsome colt.

It was then that the herd started its slow movement to the northwest. Three times the chestnut tried unsuccessfully to halt them so that the colt could rest and have a fighting chance of keeping up. But some deep instinctive drive within the herd kept luring them away from their homeland, and soon it lay far behind them. The dun-colored mare did her best to keep the colt beside her, and he ran with ungainly legs to stay close. She was pleased to see that he grew stronger each day and that his legs functioned better as they moved onto higher ground.

But in the fifth week, as they approached a cold part of their journey, food became scarce and doubt was cast on the wisdom of this trek. The herd had to scatter to find forage, and one evening as the chestnut and the mare and their colt nosed among the scrub for signs of grass, a group of dire wolves struck at them. The mare instinctively presented herself to the gray wolves in an effort to protect her colt, but the fierce beasts were not distracted by this trick, and cut behind her to make savage lunges at her offspring. This enraged the chestnut, who sprang at the wolves with flashing hooves, but to no avail. Mercilessly, the wolves attacked the colt, whose piteous cries were cut off almost instantly.

The mare was distraught and tried to attack the wolves, but six of them detached themselves and formed a pack to destroy her. She defended herself valiantly for some moments while her mate battled with the other wolves near the body of the colt. Then one bold wolf caught her by a hamstring and brought her down. In a moment the others were upon her, tearing her to pieces.

The whole group of wolves now turned their attention to the chestnut, but he broke loose from them and started at a mad gallop back toward where the main herd of horses had been. The wolves followed him for a few miles, then gave up the chase and returned to their feast.

Unlike reptiles, mammals have some capacity for memory, and as the trek to the northwest continued, the chestnut felt sorrow at the loss of his mate and the colt. But he did not grieve long because he was soon preoccupied with the problems of the journey.

It was a strange hegira on which these horses were engaged. It would take them across thousands of miles and onto land that had been under water only a few centuries earlier. For this was the age of ice. Vast glaciers crept from the North Pole to areas that are now Pennsylvania and Wisconsin and Wyoming, erasing whatever vegetation had developed there and carving the landscape into new designs.

At no point on Earth were the changes more dramatic than at the Bering Sea, that body of ice-cold water which separates Asia from America. The great glaciers used up so much ocean water that the level of this sea dropped three hundred feet. This eliminated the Bering Sea altogether, and in its place appeared a massive land bridge more than a thousand miles wide. It was an isthmus, really, joining two continents, and now any animal that wished, or man, too, when he came along, could walk with security from Asia to America—or the other way.

The bridge, it must be understood, was not constructed along that slim chain of islands which now reaches from America to Asia. Not at all. The drop of ocean was so spectacular that it was the main body of Asia that was joined substantially to America; the bridge was wider than the entire compass of Alaska.

It was toward the direction of this great bridge, barely existent when the true horse emerged, that the chestnut now headed. In time, as older horses died off, he became the acknowledged leader of the herd, the one who trotted at the head on leisurely marches to new meadows, the one who marshaled the herd together when danger threatened. He grew canny in the arts of leadership, homing in on the good pastures, seeking out the protected resting places.

As the horses marched to the new bridge in the northwest, to their right in unending procession lay the snouts of the glaciers, now a mile away but, later on, a hundred miles distant, but always pressing southward and commandeering meadowlands where horses had previously grazed. Perhaps it was this inexorable pressure of ice from the north, eating up all the good land, that had started the horses on their migration; certainly it was a reminder that food was getting scarce throughout their known world.

One year, as the herd moved ever closer to the beginning of the bridge, the horses were competing for food with a large herd of camels that were also deserting the land where they had originated. The chestnut, now a mature horse, led his charges well to the north, right into the face of the glacier. It was the warm period of the year and the nose of the glacier was dripping, so that the horses had much good water and there was, as he had expected, good green grass.

But as they grazed, idling the summer away before they returned to the shoreline, where they would be once more in competition with the camels, he happened to peer into a small canyon that had formed in the ice, and with four companions he penetrated it, finding to his pleasure that it contained much sweet grass. They were grazing with no apprehension when suddenly he looked up to see before him a gigantic mammoth. It was as tall as three horses, and its mighty tusks were like none he had seen at the pillars. These tusks did not stretch forward, but turned parallel to the face in immense sweeping circles that met before the eyes.

The chestnut stood for a moment surveying the huge beast. He was not afraid, for mammoths did not attack horses, and even if for some unfathomable reason this one did, the chestnut could easily escape. And then slowly, as if the idea were incomprehensible, the stallion began to realize that under no circumstances could this particular mammoth charge, for it was dead. Its frozen rear quarters were caught in the icy grip of the glacier; its front half, from which the glacier had melted, seemed alive. It was a beast in suspension. It was there, with all its features locked in ice, but at the same time it was not there.

Perplexed, the chestnut whinnied and his companions ambled up. They looked at the imprisoned beast, expecting it to charge, and only belatedly did each discover for himself that for some reason he could not explain, this mammoth was immobilized. One of the younger horses probed with his muzzle, but the silent mammal gave no response. The young horse became angry and nudged the huge beast, again with no results. The horse started to whinny; then they realized that the great beast was dead. Like all horses, they were appalled by death and silently withdrew.

But the chestnut wanted to investigate this mystery, and in succeeding days he returned timorously to the small canyon, intrigued by a situation that he could not understand. The puzzle completely eluded him, so he returned to the grassy area and led his herd backward toward the main road to Asia.

It must not be imagined that the horses migrated to Asia in any steady progression. The distance from the twin pillars to Siberia was only thirty-five hundred miles, and since a horse could cover twenty-five miles a day, the trip might conceivably have been completed in less than a year, but it did not work that way. The horses never chose their direction; they merely sought easier pasturage, and sometimes a herd would linger in one favorable spot for eight or nine years. They were pulled slowly westward by mysterious forces, and no horse that started from the twin pillars ever got close to Asia.

But drift was implacable, and the chestnut spent his years from three to sixteen on this overpowering journey, always tending toward the northwest, for the time of the horse in America was ended.

They spent four years on the approaches to Alaska, and now the chestnut had to extend himself to keep pace with the younger horses. Often he fell behind, but he knew no fear, confident that an extra burst of effort would enable him to join the herd. He watched as younger horses took the lead, giving the signals for marching and halting. The grass seemed thinner this year, and more difficult to find.

One day, late in the afternoon, he was foraging in sparse lands when he became aware that the main herd—indeed the whole herd—had moved on well beyond him. He raised his head with some difficulty, for his breathing had grown tighter, to see that a pack of dire wolves had interposed itself between him and the herd. He looked about quickly for an alternate route, but those available would lead him farther from the other horses; he knew he could outrun the wolves, but he did not wish to increase the distance between himself and the herd.

He therefore made a daring, zigzag dash right through the wolves and toward the other horses. He kicked his heels and with surprising speed negotiated a good two thirds of the distance through the snarling wolves. Twice he heard jaws snapping at his fetlocks, but he managed to kick free.

Then, with terrible suddenness, his breath came short and a great pain clutched at his chest. He fought against it, kept pumping his legs. He felt his body stopping almost in midflight, stopping while the wolves closed in to grab his legs. He felt a sharp pain radiating from his hindquarters where two wolves had fastened onto him, but this external wolf-pain was of lesser consequence than the interior horse-pain that clutched at him. If only his breathing could be maintained, he could throw off the wolves. He had done so before. But now the greater pain assailed him and he sank slowly to earth as the pack fell upon him.

The last thing he saw was the uncomprehending herd, following younger leaders, as it maintained its glacial course toward Asia.

Why did this stallion that had prospered in Colorado desert his comfortable homeland for Siberia? We do not know. Why did the finest animal America developed become discontented with the land of his origin? There is no answer.

We know that when the horse negotiated the land bridge, which he did with apparent ease and in considerable numbers, he found on the other end an opportunity for varied development that is one of the bright aspects of animal history. He wandered into France and became the mighty Percheron, and into Arabia, where he developed into a lovely poem of a horse, and into Africa, where he became the brilliant zebra, and into Scotland, where he bred selectively to form the massive Clydesdale. He would also journey into Spain, where his very name would become the designation for gentleman, a caballero, a man of the horse. There he would flourish mightily and serve the armies that would conquer much of the known world, and in 1519 he would leave Spain in small, adventurous ships of conquest and land in Mexico, where he would thrive and develop special characteristics fitting him for life on upland plains. In 1543 he would accompany Coronado on his quest for the golden city of Quivira, and from later groups of horses brought by other Spaniards some would be stolen by Indians and a few would escape to become feral, once domesticated but now reverted to wildness. And from these varied sources would breed the animals that would return late in history, in the year 1768, to Colorado, the land from which they had sprung, making it for a few brief years the kingdom of the horse, the memorable epitome of all that was best in the relationship of horse and man.

THE MASTODON

THE WORLD has known many ice ages, two of which lasted for millennia when much of Europe and North America lay crushed beneath monstrous thicknesses of ice. The winds howled across endless wastes and freezing night seemed perpetual. When the sun did appear, it was unproductive, shining down on deadly ice surfaces. All visible living things perished: grasses and trees, worms and insects, fish and animals. Desolation ruled.

But each protracted ice age was followed by intervals of equal length when the ice mysteriously retreated to release from its frozen prison an Earth bursting with energy and the capacity to restore life in all its manifestations. Grasses flourished to feed the animals that returned. Trees grew, some bearing fruits. Fields, nourished with minerals long unused, bore lavish crops, and birds sang. The future Wisconsins and Austrias exploded into life as the sun brought back warmth and well-being. The world had returned to abundant life.

The first two great ice ages began to evolve so very long ago—say, about seven hundred million years—that they need not concern us. But some two million years ago when the historical record was about to begin, a series of much briefer ice ages arrived, and their dates, extents and characteristics were so well defined that they have been given distinctive names: Nebraskan, Kansan, Illinoian, Wisconsin, and—in Europe—Gunz, Mindel, Riss, Wurm, with the last segment in each group subdivided into three parts, making six in all.

Strangely, although a permanent ice cap came in time to cover the South Pole, which was a continent, to a depth of two miles, none developed at the North, which was only a sea. The glaciers that covered North America stemmed from caps in Canada; those that submerged Europe, from the Scandinavian countries; and those that struck Russia, from sites near the Barents Sea. And because the movement of ice in North America was mainly to the south, Alaska would never lie under a massive ice sheet. It would become known as a cold and barren land covered with ice and snow, but it would never know in all its millennia as much ice as a more habitable state like Connecticut had once known.

The later ice ages created in Alaska a result more dramatic than what happened anywhere else in America, and for a reason that becomes obvious once it is pointed out. If an ice sheet more than a mile thick is going to cover much of North America, the water it imprisons will have to come from somewhere, and it cannot come mysteriously from outer space. It cannot *arrive* on the surface of the Earth; it can come only from water already here, which means that it must be stolen from the oceans. And that is what happened: dry winds whipping across the oceans lifted huge quantities of water that fell as cold rain over the high latitudes and as snow toward the poles. As it was compressed into ice it began to expand outward, covering hitherto barren sites, and causing more and more of the incoming moisture to fall as snow. This in turn fed the existing glaciers and created new ones.

In the recent period with which we are concerned, this theft of water continued for thousands of years, until the snowfields were immensely aggrandized and the oceans seriously depleted. In fact, when the deficiency was at its worst, only some twenty thousand years ago, the level of the world's oceans—all of them—was more than three hundred feet lower than it is now. All the American states that faced the Atlantic Ocean had shorelines that extended miles farther eastward than they do now; much of the Gulf of Mexico was dry; Florida was not a peninsula, nor was Cape Cod a cape. Caribbean islands coalesced into a few huge islands, and the shoreline of Canada could not be seen at all, for it was smothered in ice.

This sharp droppage in the level of the oceans meant that land areas which had previously been separated were now joined by necks of land, which the subsiding waters revealed. Australia was attached to Antarctica by such a land bridge, Ceylon to India, Cyprus to western Asia, and England to Europe. But the most spectacular join was that of Alaska to Siberia, for it united two continents, allowing animals and people to pass from one to the other. It was also the only one that acquired its own name, scientists having christened it Beringia, the lost land of the Bering Sea.

About three hundred eighty-five thousand years ago, when the oceans and continents were in place as we know them today, the land bridge from

Alaska to Siberia was open, and a huge, ponderous animal, looking much like an oversized elephant but with enormous protruding tusks, slowly made his way eastward, followed by four females and their young. He was by no means the first of his breed to cross the bridge, but he was among the more interesting, for his life experience symbolized the majestic adventure in which the animals of his period were engaged.

He was a mastodon, and we shall call him by that name, for he was a progenitor of those noble massive beasts who ranged Alaska. Obviously, a million years before, he had stemmed from the same source that produced the elephant, but in Africa, in Europe and later in Central Asia he had developed those characteristics that differentiated him from his cousin the elephant. His tusks were larger, his front shoulders lower, his legs more powerful, and his body was covered with hair that was more visible. But he behaved in much the same way, foraged for the same kinds of food, and lived to about the same age.

When he crossed the bridge—less than seventy miles from Asia to Alaska—Mastodon was forty years old and could expect to survive into his late seventies, supposing that he escaped the ferocious wild cats who relished mastodon meat. His four females were much younger than he, and as was common in the animal kingdom, they could anticipate a somewhat longer life.

As the mastodons entered Alaska they faced radically different types of terrain, varying somewhat from the land they had left behind in Asia. At the farthest north, facing the Arctic Ocean, lay a thin strip of Arctic desert, a bleak and terrifying land of shifting sands on which little that was edible grew. During the dozen winter weeks when no sun appeared, it was covered by thin snow that piled up into high drifts that were whipped by intense winds across the barren landscape and came to rest in low drifts behind some bridges or rocks.

Since none of his breed could survive long in this desert, Mastodon intuitively shied away from the far north, and this left him three other areas to explore that were more rewarding. Just south of the desert and blending into it in various ways stretched another relatively narrow strip, a tundra, perpetually frozen twelve to twenty-four inches below the surface but rich in rooted plant life when the topsoil was dry enough to permit growth. Here succulent lichens abounded and mosses rich in nutrients and even an occasional low shrub with branches stout enough to provide leaves for grazing. No real trees grew here, of course, for summers were too short to permit flowering or adequate branch development, and this meant that whereas Mastodon and his family could eat well on the tundra during the long summers when nearly perpetual daylight spurred plant growth, they had to make sure they escaped it when winter approached.

That left two rich areas between the northern and southern glaciers, and the first of these was a splendid, hospitable region, the great Alaskan steppe, an area of rich grass growing high most years and yielding some food even in poor years. Large trees did not customarily grow on the steppe, but in a few secluded spots that were protected from searing winds, clusters of low shrubs gained a foothold, especially the dwarf willow whose leaves Mastodon loved to crop. When he was especially hungry he liked to rip off the bark of the willow with his strong tusks, and sometimes he would stand for hours amid a group of willows, browsing and eating a sliver of bark and striving to find among the low branches a bit of shade to protect himself from the intense heat of summer.

The fourth area he had at his disposal was larger than any of the previous three, for in these years Alaska had a predominantly benign climate, which both allowed and encouraged the growth of trees in regions that had previously been denuded and would be again when temperatures lowered. Now poplar, birch, pine and larch flourished, with woodland animals like the spotted skunk sharing the forests with Mastodon, who relished the trees because he could stand upright and nibble at their copious leaves. After feeding, he could use the sturdy trunks of the pine or larch as convenient poles against which to scrape his back.

So between the largess of the new woodland and the more controlled and dependable richness of the steppe, Mastodon and his family could eat well, and since it was spring when they entered Alaska, he naturally headed for a region like the one he had known well in Siberia, the tundra, where he was certain that low shrubs and grasses waited. But now he faced an interesting problem, for the sun's heat that had enabled these plants to grow also melted the top eight or ten inches of the permafrost, turning the softening soil into a kind of sticky mush. Obviously, there was nowhere for the moisture to escape; the earth below was frozen solid and would remain so for countless years. As summer approached, thousands of shallow lakes thawed, and the mush thickened until at times Mastodon sank almost to his knees.

Now he slipped and sloshed his way through the watery tundra, fighting off the myriad mosquitoes that hatched at this time to torment any moving thing. Sometimes, when he lifted one of his huge legs out of the swampy mess into which it had slowly sunk, the sound of the leg breaking free from the suction echoed for long distances.

Mastodon and his group grazed on the tundra during most of that first summer, but as the waning heat of the sun signaled the approach of winter, he began drifting gradually south toward the waiting steppe, where there would be reassuring grass poking through the thin snow. During the early days of autumn, when he was in the dividing line between tundra and steppe, it was almost as if the shrub willows that now appeared low on the horizon were calling him to a safer winter home, but the waning sun exerted a stronger influence, so that by the time the first snows appeared in the area between the great glaciers, he and his family had moved into the forested area that assured an ample food supply.

His first half-year in Alaska had been a spectacular success. Of course he was not aware that he had made the transition from Asia to North America; all he had done was follow an improved food supply. Indeed, he had not left Asia, for those solid sheets of ice to the east had made Alaska in those years a part of the larger continent.

As the first winter progressed, Mastodon became aware that he and the other mastodons were by no means alone in their favorable habitat, for a most varied menagerie had preceded them in their exit from the Asian mainland. One cold morning when he stood alone in the soft snow, cropping twig ends from a convenient willow, he heard a rustle that disturbed him. Prudently, he withdrew lest some enemy leap upon him from a hiding place high in the trees, and he was not a moment too soon, for as he turned away from the willow he saw emerging from the protection of a nearby copse his most fearsome enemy.

It was a kind of tiger, with powerful claws and a pair of upper teeth almost three feet long and incredibly sharp. Mastodon knew that though this sabertoothed tiger could not drive those fearsome teeth through the heavy skin of his protected rear or sides, it could, if it obtained a secure foothold on his back, sink them into the softer skin at the base of his neck. He had only a moment to defend himself from this hungry enemy, and with an agility that was surprising for an animal so big, he pivoted on his left front foot, swung his massive body in a half-circle, and faced the charging sabertooth.

Mastodon had his long tusks, of course, but he could not lunge and impale his adversary on them; they were not intended for that purpose.

But his tiny brain did send signals that set the tusks in wide sweeping motions, and as the cat sprang, hoping to evade them, the right tusk, swinging with tremendous force, caught the rear legs of the sabertooth. Although the blow did not send the cat spinning or in any way immobilize him, it did divert the attack by inflicting a minor wound.

The cat stumbled among the trees, then regained control, and circled swiftly so that it could attack from the rear, hoping with a giant leap to land upon Mastodon's back, from where the vulnerable neck could be punctured. The cat was much quicker than the mastodon, and after a series of feints that tired the larger animal as he tried to counter them, the sabertooth did land with a mighty bound, not on the flat of the back, where it wanted to be, but half on the back, half on the side. It struggled for a moment to climb to a secure position, but in that time Mastodon, with a remarkable instinct for self-preservation, moved under a set of low branches, and had the cat not wisely jumped free, it would have been crushed, as Mastodon had intended.

Repelled twice, the great cat, some nine times larger than the tiger we know today, growled furiously, lurked among the trees, and gathered strength for a final attack. This time, with a leap more powerful than before, it came at Mastodon from the side, but the huge animal was prepared, and pivoting again on his left front foot, he swung his tusks in a wide arc that caught the sabertooth in midair and sent it sprawling back among the trees, one of its legs painfully damaged.

That was enough for the sabertooth. Growling, it slunk away, having learned that if it wanted to feast on mastodon, it must hunt in pairs, or even threes or fours, because one wily mastodon was fully capable of protecting itself.

Alaska at this time contained many lions, huge and much hairier than the kind that would come later. These possessed no handsome manes or wavy tails, and the males lacked the regal quality that would someday be such a distinguishing characteristic. They were simply what nature intended them to be: great cats with remarkable hunting abilities. Like the sabertooths, they had learned never to attack a mastodon singly, but a hungry pride of six or seven could badger him to death, so Mastodon never intruded upon areas where a number of lions might be hiding. Rocky tors covered with trees, deep vales from whose sides groups of lions might attack, these he avoided, and sometimes as he plowed noisily along, bending young and scattered trees to his will, he would see a group of lions in the distance feeding upon some animal they had run to earth, and he would change direction lest he attract their attention.

The water animal with which Mastodon occasionally came into contact was the massive beaver, which had followed him out of Asia. Of giant size and with teeth that could fell a large tree, these beavers spent their working hours building dams, which Mastodon often saw from a distance, but when work was done the great beasts, their heavy fur glistening in the cold sunlight, liked to play at rowdy games, and their agility differed so markedly from the ponderous movements of Mastodon that he was amazed at their antics. He never had the occasion to live in close contact with the underwater beavers, but he noticed them with perplexity when they gamboled after work.

Mastodon had his major contacts with the numerous steppe bison, the huge progenitors of the buffalo. These shaggy beasts, heads low and powerful horns parallel to the ground, grazed in many of the areas he liked to roam, and sometimes so many bison collected in one meadow that the land seemed covered with them. They would all be grazing, heads pointed in the same direction, when a sabertoothed tiger would begin stalking a laggard. Then, at some signal Mastodon could not detect, the hundreds of giant bison would start running away from the terrible fangs of the cat, and the steppe would thunder with their passage.

Occasionally he encountered camels. Tall, awkward beasts who cropped the tops of trees, they seemed to fit in nowhere, moving slowly about, kicking ferociously at enemies, and surrendering quickly whenever a sabertooth managed to cling to their backs. At rare times Mastodon and a pair of camels would feed in the same area, but the two animals, so vastly different, ignored each other, and it might be months before Mastodon saw another camel. They were mysterious creatures and he was content to leave them alone.

In this placid, ponderous way, Mastodon lived out his uneventful life. If he successfully defended himself against sabertooths, and avoided falling into bogs from which he could not scramble free, and fled from the great fires set by lightning, he had little to fear. Food was plentiful. He was still young enough to attract and hold females. And the seasons were not too hot and moist in summer or too cold and dry in winter. He had a good life and he stumbled his gigantic way through it with dignity and gentleness. Other animals like wolves and sabertooths sought sometimes to kill him for food, but he hungered only for enough grass and tender leaves, of which he consumed about six hundred pounds a day. He was of all Alaska's inhabitants in these early years the most affable.

One morning as Mastodon browsed among cottonwood trees near the edge of a swamp in central Alaska, he saw approaching from the south a line of animals much smaller than he had ever seen before. Like him, they walked on four feet, but unlike him, they had no tusks, no heavy covering of hair, no massive head or bulky feet. They were sleek creatures, swift of movement, alert of eye, and he watched with interest and attention as they approached. Not a single gesture, not one movement gave him any indication that they might be dangerous, so he allowed them to come near, stop and stare at him before passing on.

They were horses, the new world's wonderful gift to the old, and they were on their wandering way into Asia, from where their descendants, thousands of years later, would fan out miraculously to all parts of Europe. How beautiful they were that morning as they passed Mastodon, pressing their way into the heartland of Alaska, where they would find a halting place on their long pilgrimage.

Nowhere else could the subtle relationships of nature be so intimately observed. Ice high, oceans low. Bridge open, passageway closed. The ponderous mastodon lumbering toward North America, the delicate horse moving toward Asia. Mastodon lurching toward inescapable extinction. The horse galloping to an enlarged life in France and Arabia. Alaska, its extremities girt in ice, served as a way station for all the travelers, regardless of the direction in which they headed. Its broad valleys that were free of ice and its invigorating climate provided a hospitable resting place.

MATRIARCH, THE WOOLLY MAMMOTH

HOW SAD IT IS to realize that most of the imposing animals that lingered in Alaska during the last ice age and its intervals of temperate climate passed into extinction, usually before the appearance of man. The great mastodons vanished, the fierce saber-toothed tigers disappeared in mists that enclosed the bogs at whose edges they hunted. The rhinoceros flourished for a while, but then waddled slowly into oblivion. The lions could find no permanent niche in North America, and even the camel failed to flourish in its land of origin. How much more interesting North America would be if we had retained these great beasts to enliven the landscape, but it was fated not to be. They rested in Alaska for a while, then vanished from the Americas.

Some of the immigrants did adjust, and their continued presence has made our land a livelier place: the beaver, the caribou, the stately moose, the bison and the sheep. But there was another splendid animal that crossed the bridge from Asia, and it survived long enough to coexist with man. It had a fighting chance to escape extinction, and the manner in which it fought that battle is an epic of the animal kingdom.

The woolly mammoth came out of Asia much later than the mastodon. It arrived at a time of sharp transition when a relatively mild interval was ending and a harsher one beginning, but it adjusted so easily to its new environment that it thrived and multiplied, becoming one of the most successful examples of immigration and the archetypal Alaskan animal of this distant period.

Its remote ancestors had lived in tropical Africa, elephants of enormous size with long tusks and huge ears, which they flapped constantly, using them as fans to keep their body temperature down. In Africa they browsed on low trees and pulled grass with their prehensile trunks. Admirably constructed for life in a tropical setting, they were magnificent beasts.

When such elephants moved slowly north they gradually converted themselves into creatures almost ideally suited to life in the high Arctic zones. For example, their ears diminished in size to about one twelfth of what they had been in the tropics, for now the animals did not require fanning to enable them to live in great heat; they needed minimum exposure to the Arctic winds that drained away their heat. They also rid themselves of the smooth skin that had helped them keep cool in Africa, developing instead a thick covering of hair whose individual strands could be as long as forty inches; when they had been in the colder climates for several thousand years, they were so covered with this hair that they looked like unkempt walking blankets.

But not even that was enough to protect them from the icy blasts of winter in Alaska—especially during the time we are now considering, when the incursion of ice was at its maximum—so the mammoth, already covered with thick, protective hair, developed an invisible undergrowth of thick wool that augmented the hair so effectively that the animal could withstand incredibly low temperatures.

Internally, also, the mammoth changed. Its stomach adjusted to the different food supply of Beringia, the low, tough grasses, wonderfully nutritious when compared with the huge loose leafage of the African trees. Its bones grew smaller, so that the average mammoth, markedly smaller than the elephant, would expose less of its body to the cold. Its forequarters became much heavier than its hind parts and more elevated, so that it began to show a profile less like an elephant's and more like a hyena's, high in front, tapering off at the back.

In some ways the most dramatic change, but not the most functional, was what happened to its tusks. In Africa they had grown out of its upper jaw in roughly parallel form, curved downward before straightening out. They were formidable weapons and were used when males contested for the right to keep females in their group. They were also useful in bending branches lower for browsing.

In Arctic lands the tusks of the mammoth underwent spectacular change. For one thing, they became much larger than those of the African elephant, for in some cases they measured more than twelve feet in length. But what made them distinctive was that after starting straight forward and down, like the elephant's, they suddenly swept outward, far from the body, and down in a handsome sweep. Had they continued in this direction, they would have been enormous and powerful weapons for attack or defense, but what happened was that they arbitrarily swung back toward the central axis, until at last their tips met and sometimes actually crossed, far in front of the mammoth's face. This bizarre condition served no constructive purpose. Indeed, the tusks hampered feeding in summer, but in winter they did have a minimal utility, for they could be used to sweep away snowdrifts so that mosses and lichens hiding below could be exposed for eating. Other animals—the bison, for example—achieved the same result by merely pushing their big heads into the snow and swinging them from side to side.

Protected against the bitter cold of winter and enjoying the plentiful forage of summer, the mammoth proliferated and dominated the landscape long after the much larger mastodon had vanished. Like all other animals of the early period, the mastodon had been subject to attack by the ferocious sabertooth, but with the gradual extinction of that killer, the mammoth's only enemies were the lions and wolves that tried to steal young calves. Of course, when a mammoth grew old and feeble, packs of wolves could successfully chivy it to death, but that was of no consequence, for if death had not come in that manner, it would have in some other way.

Mammoths lived to fifty or sixty years, with an occasional tough customer surviving into its seventies, and to a marked degree it was the way the animal died that has accounted for its fame. On numerous occasions in Siberia, Alaska and Canada—so numerous that statistical studies can be made—mammoths of both sexes and all ages stumbled into boggy pits, where they perished, or were overcome by sudden floods bearing gravel, or died on the banks of rivers into which they fell.

If these accidental deaths occurred in spring or summer, predators, especially ravens, quickly disposed of the cadavers, leaving behind only stripped bones and perhaps long strings of hair, which soon vanished. Accumulations of such bones and tusks have been found in various places and have proved helpful in reconstructing what we know about the mammoth.

But if the accidental death took place in autumn or early winter, there was always the possibility that the body of the dead animal would be quickly covered with a layer of sticky mud that would freeze when hard winter came. Thus the corpse would be preserved in what amounted to a deep freeze, with decay impossible. Most often, one has to suppose, spring and summer would bring a thaw; the protective mud would lose its ice crystals; and the dead body would decompose. Disintegration of the corpse would proceed as always, except that the freezing would have postponed it for a season.

However, on rare occasions, which could become quite numerous over a time span of a hundred thousand years, that first immediate freezing would for some reason or other become permanent, and now the dead body would be preserved intact for a thousand years, or thirty thousand, or fifty. And then, on some day far distant when humans ranged the valleys of central Alaska, some inquisitive man would see emerging from a thawing bank an object that was neither bone nor preserved wood, and when he dug into the bank he would find himself facing the total remains of a woolly mammoth that had perished in that bank thousands of years before.

When the accumulation of viscous mud was carefully cleaned away, a remarkable object would be revealed, something unique in the world: a whole mammoth, long hair in place, great tusks twisting forward and meeting at the tips, stomach contents intact from the time it last grazed, massive teeth in such perfect condition that its age at death could be accurately calculated within five or six years. It was not, of course, a standing animal, plump and clean and encased in blue ice; it was lying on its side, plastered with mud, with leg joints beginning to come apart, but it was a complete mammoth, and it revealed to its discoverers a volume of information.

This next point is important. We know about the great dinosaurs who preceded the mammoth by millions of years because over the millennia their bones have been invaded by mineral deposits that have preserved the most intimate structure of the bone. What we have are not real bones but petrified ones, like petrified wood, in which not an atom of the original material remains. Until a recent find in far northern Alaska, no human being had ever seen the bone of a dinosaur, but everyone could see in museums the magically preserved petrifications of those bones, photographs in stone of bones long since vanished.

But with the mammoths preserved by freezing in Siberia and Alaska, we have the actual bones, the hair, the heart, the stomach—a treasury of knowledge that is incomparable. The first of these icy finds seems to have occurred by accident in Siberia sometime in the 1700s, and others have followed at regular intervals thereafter. A remarkably complete mammoth

was uncovered near Fairbanks in Alaska not long ago, and we can anticipate others before the end of the century.

Why has it been the mammoth that has been found in this complete
form? Other animals have occasionally been uncovered, but not many and
rarely in the excellent condition of the best-preserved mammoths. One
reason was the substantial numbers of the breed. Another was that the
mammoth tended to live in those peculiar areas where preservation by
freezing mud was possible. Also, its bones and tusks were of a size to be
durable; many birds must have perished in these areas in these times, but
because they had no heavy bones, their skeletons did not survive to keep
their skin and feathers in position. Most important, this particular group
of mammoths died during a time of glaciation when instant freezing was
not only possible but likely.

At any rate, the woolly mammoth served a unique function, one of
inestimable value to human beings; by freezing quickly when it died, it
remained intact to instruct us about life in Alaska when the ice castle
functioned as a refuge for great animals.

One day in late winter, twenty-nine thousand years ago, Matriarch, a
mammoth grandmother, forty-four years old and beginning to show her
age, led the little herd of six for which she was responsible down a softly
rolling meadow to the banks of a great river later to be known as the
Yukon. Lifting her trunk high to sniff the warming air and signaling the
others to follow, she entered a grove of willow shrubs that lined the river,
and when the others had taken their places beside her, she indicated that
they might begin feeding on the sprouting tips of willow branches. They
did so with delight because they had subsisted on meager rations during
the recent winter, and as they gorged, Matriarch gave grunts of encourage-
ment.

She had in her herd two daughters, each of whom had two offspring, a
heifer and a bull. Discipline was enforced by Matriarch, for it was the
females who had the responsibility for rearing and educating the young.
The males with their tremendous showy tusks appeared only in midsum-
mer for the mating period; the rest of the year they were nowhere to be
seen.

In obedience to the instincts of her race, and to the specific impulses that stemmed from her being female, she devoted her entire life to her herd, especially to the young. She weighed, at this time, about three thousand pounds, and to keep alive she required each day one hundred and sixty pounds of grass, lichen, moss and twigs. When she lacked this ample supply of food she experienced acute pangs of hunger, for what she ate contained only minimum nourishment and passed completely through her body in less than twelve hours; she did not gorge and then ruminate like other animals, chewing her cud until every shred of value was extracted from it. No, she crammed herself with vast amounts of low-quality food and quickly rid herself of its remains. Eating had to be her main preoccupation.

Nevertheless, if in her constant foraging she caught even a hint that her four grandchildren were not getting their share, she would forgo her own feeding and see to it that they ate first. And she would do the same for young mammoths who were not of her own family but under her care for the moment while their own mothers and grandmothers foraged elsewhere.

This selflessness, which separated her from other mammoth grandmothers, had developed because of her monomaniacal affection for her children. Years ago, before her youngest daughter had borne her first offspring, a once-prepotent older bull joined her herd during the mating season, and for some inexplicable reason, when the mating was completed, he remained with the herd, when normally he should have left to join the other bulls, who foraged by themselves until the next mating season came around.

Although Matriarch had made no objection when this old bull first appeared on the scene to court her daughters—three at that time—she grew restless when he stayed beyond his welcome period, and by various ways, such as nudging him away from the better grass, she indicated that he must leave the females and their children. When he refused to comply, she grew actively angry, but she could do nothing more than show her feelings, because he weighed half again as much as she, his tusks were enormous, and he was so much taller that he simply overwhelmed her in both size and aggressiveness. So she had to be content with making noises and venting her displeasure by rapidly thrashing her trunk about.

But one day as she was eyeing this old fellow, she saw him roughly shove aside a young mother who was instructing her yearling daughter. This would have been acceptable, for bulls traditionally commandeered the better feeding grounds, but on this occasion it looked to Matriarch as if the bull had also abused the yearling, and this she could not tolerate. With a high, piercing scream she lunged right at the intruder, disregarding his superior size and fighting ability, and she was so intent on protecting her young that she drove the bull back several paces.

But he, with his greater strength and immense crossed tusks, quickly asserted his authority and, in a punishing counterattack, slashed at her with such great force that he broke her right tusk at about the halfway mark. For the rest of her life she would be a mammoth cow with a tusk and a half. Unbalanced, awkward-looking when compared with her sisters, she moved across the steppe with the short, jagged tusk, and the loss of its balancing weight caused her to compensate by tilting her massive head slightly to the right, as if she were peeking with her squinty little eyes at something that others could not see.

She had never been a graceful creature. She did not have the impressive lines of her elephant forebears, for she was a kind of lumbering triangle, with the apex at the top of her high-domed head and a long, sloping drop from high forequarters to a dwarfed rear end. And then, to make her appearance seem almost formless, her entire body was covered with long and sometimes matted hair.

In these years when the ice age was at its maximum, Matriarch had at her disposal a somewhat more hospitable terrain on which to feed her family than the harsher one mastodons had known. It was still a four-part terrain: Arctic desert at the north, perpetually frozen tundra, steppe rich with grasses, strip with enough trees to be called a woodland or even a forest. However, it was the steppe that had grown in size, until its mixture of edible grasses and nutritious willow shrubs provided ample forage for the mammoths who roamed it.

Indeed, the expanded area proved so hospitable to these huge creatures that later scientists who would try to reconstruct what life in Alaska was like twenty-eight thousand years before would call the terrain the Mammoth Steppe. In these centuries it looked as if the mammoths, along with the caribou and antelope, would always be the major occupiers of the steppe named after them.

Matriarch moved about the steppe as if it had been created for her use alone. But she conceded that for a few weeks each summer she required the presence of the great bulls who otherwise kept to themselves on their own feeding grounds. But after the birth of the young she, whose responsibility it was to choose the feeding grounds, gave the signal when her family must abandon areas about to be depleted in search of more fertile land.

A small herd of mammoths like the one she commanded might wander, in the course of a year, over more than four hundred miles, so she came to know large parts of the steppe. The richer parts of this steppe provided a variety of edible trees whose ancestors the vanished mastodons might have known—larch, low willow, birch, alder—but recently, in a few choice spots protected from gales and where water was available, a new kind of tree had made its tentative appearance, beautiful to see but poisonous to eat. It was especially tempting because it never lost its leaves, which were long and needlelike, but even in winter when the mammoths had little to eat they avoided it, because if they did eat the attractive leaves, they became sick and sometimes died.

It was the largest of the trees, a spruce, and its distinctive aroma both attracted and repelled the mammoths. Matriarch was bewildered by the spruce, for she noticed that the porcupines who shared these forests with her devoured the poisonous leaves with relish, and she often wondered why. What she did not notice was that while it was true the porcupines did eat the needles, they climbed high in the trees before doing so. The spruce, just as clever in protecting itself as the animals that surrounded it, had devised a sagacious defensive strategy. In its copious lower branches, which a voracious mammoth could have destroyed in a morning, the spruce concentrated a volatile oil that rendered its leaves toxic. This meant that the high upper branches, which the mammoths could not reach even with their long trunks, remained palatable.

In the few places where the spruce trees thrived, they sometimes became part of a remarkable phenomenon. From time to time during the long summers when the air was heavy and the grasses and low shrubs tinderdry, a flash would appear in the heavens followed by a tremendous crashing sound, as if a thousand trees had fallen in one instant, and often thereafter fire would start in the grass, mysteriously, for no reason at all. Or some very tall spruce would be riven, as if a giant tusk had ripped it, and from its bark a wisp of smoke would issue, and then a little flame, and before long the entire forest would be ablaze and all the grassy steppe would be on fire.

At such moments—Matriarch had survived several such fires—the mammoths had learned to head for the nearest river and submerge themselves to their eye level, keeping their trunks above the water for air. For this reason lead animals, like Matriarch with her brood, tried always to know the location of the nearest water, and when fire exploded across their steppe they retreated to this refuge.

Late one summer, when the land was especially dry, and darts of light and crashing sounds filled the air, Matriarch saw that fire had already started near a large stand of spruce trees, and she knew that before long the trees would burst forth in tremendous gusts of flame, trapping all living things. So she began herding her charges back toward where she knew there was a river, but the fire spread so swiftly that it engulfed the trees before she could rush clear of them. Overhead she heard the oils in the trees explode, sending sparks down into the dry needles below. Soon both the crowns of the trees and the carpet of needles below were aflame, and the mammoths faced death.

In this extremity, with acrid smoke choking her, Matriarch had to decide instantly whether to lead her herd back out from among the trees or straight ahead toward the river. Whatever her reasoning, she made the right decision. Bellowing so that all could hear, she headed right for a wall of flame, broke through and found a clear path to the river, where her companions plunged into the water while the forest fire raged around them.

Now came the amazing part: Matriarch had learned that terrifying though the fire had been, she must not abandon this ravaged area, for fire was one of the best friends the mammoths had and she must now teach her young how to capitalize on it. As soon as the flames abated—they would consume several hundred square miles before they died completely—she led her charges back to the spot at which they had nearly lost their lives, and there she taught them how to use their tusks in stripping lengths of bark from the burned spruce trees. Now, purified by the fire that had destroyed the noxious oils, the spruce not only was edible but was a positive delicacy, and the hungry mammoths gorged on it. It seemed as if the bark had been toasted specifically for them.

When the fire was totally out in all parts, Matriarch kept her herd close to the burned-over areas, for the mammoths had learned that rather quickly after such a conflagration, the roots of tenacious plants whose visible growth had been burned off sped the production of new shoots, thousands of them, and these were the finest food the mammoths ever found. What was even more important, ashes from the great fires fertilized the ground, making it more nutritious and more friable, so that young trees would grow with a vigor they would not otherwise have known. One of the best things that could happen to the Mammoth Steppe, with its mixture of trees and grass, was to have a periodic fire of great dimension, for grasses, shrubs, trees and animals prospered in its aftermath.

It was puzzling that something as dangerous as fire, which Matriarch had barely escaped many times, should be the agency whereby she and her successors would grow strong. She did not try to solve this riddle; she protected herself from the dangers and luxuriated in the rewards.

In these years some mammoths elected to return to the Asia they had known in their early years, but Matriarch had no inclination to join them. The Alaska that she now knew so well was a congenial place she had made her own. To leave would be unthinkable.

But in her fiftieth year changes began to occur that sent tremors, vague intimations, to her minute brain, and instinct warned her that these changes not only were irreversible but also cautioned that the time was approaching when she would have to wander off, leaving her family behind, as she sought some quiet place to die. She had, of course, no sense of death, no comprehension that life ended, no premonition that she must one day abandon her family and the steppes on which she found such ease. But mammoths did die, and in doing so they followed an ancient ritual that commanded them to move apart, as if they were symbolically turning over to their successors the familiar steppe and its rivers and its willow trees.

What had happened to signal this new awareness? Like other mammoths, Matriarch had been supplied at birth with a complex dental system that would provide her, over the long span of her life, with twelve enormous flat composite teeth in each jaw. These twenty-four teeth did not appear in a mammoth's mouth all at one time, but this posed no difficulty; each tooth was so large that even one pair was adequate for chewing. At times there were as many as three pairs of these huge things, and then chewing capacity was immense. But as the years passed, each tooth moved inexorably forward in the jaw until it actually fell from the mouth. When only the last two matching teeth remained in position, the mammoth sensed its days were numbered, because when the last pair was lost, continued life on the steppe would be impossible.

Matriarch now had four big matching pairs, but since she could feel them moving forward, she was aware that her time was limited.

When the mating season began, bulls from far distances started to arrive, but the old bull who had broken Matriarch's right tusk was still so powerful a fighter that he succeeded, as in past years, in defending his claim on her daughters. He had not, of course, returned to this family year after year, but on various occasions he had come back, more to a familiar area than to a particular group of females.

This year his courtship of Matriarch's daughters was a perfunctory affair, but his effect upon the older child of the younger daughter, a sturdy young bull but not yet mature enough to strike out on his own, was remarkable, for the young fellow, watching the robust performance of the old bull, felt vague stirrings. One morning, when the old bull was attending to a young female not of Matriarch's family, this young bull, unexpectedly and without any premeditation, made a lunge for her, whereupon the old bull fell into a rage and chastised the young upstart unmercifully, butting and slamming him with those horns that crossed at the tips.

Matriarch, seeing this and not entirely aware of what had occasioned the outburst, dashed once again at the old bull, but this time he repelled her easily, knocking her aside so that he could continue his courtship of the heifer. In time he left the herd, his duty done, and disappeared as always into the low hills fronting the glacier. He would be seen no more for ten months, but he left behind him not only six pregnant cows but also a very perplexed young bull, who within the year should be doing his own courting. However, long before this could take place, the young bull wandered into a stand of aspen trees near the great river, where one of the last sabertoothed cats to survive in Alaska waited in the crotch of a large tree, and when the bull came within reach, the cat leaped down upon him, sinking its scimitar teeth deep into his neck.

The bull had no chance to defend himself; this first strike was mortal, but in his death agony he did release one powerful bellow that echoed across the steppe. Matriarch heard it, and although she knew the young bull to be of an age when he should be leaving the family, he was still under her care, and without hesitating, she galloped as fast as her awkward body would permit, speeding directly toward the sabertooth, who was crouching over its dead prey.

When she spotted it she knew instinctively that it was the most dangerous enemy on this steppe, and she knew it had the power to kill her, but her fury was so great that any thought of caution was stifled. So with a trumpeting cry of rage she rushed in her clumsy way at the sabertooth, who easily evaded her. But to its surprise she wheeled about with such frenzied determination that it had to abandon the corpse on which it was about to feed, and as it did so it found itself backed against the trunk of a sturdy larch. Matriarch, seeing the cat in this position, threw her entire weight forward, endeavoring to pin it with her tusks or otherwise disable it.

Now the broken right tusk, big and blunt, proved an asset rather than a liability, for with it she crushed the sabertooth against the tree, and as she felt her heavy tusk dig into its rib cage, she bore ahead, unmindful of what the fierce cat might do to her.

Despite its injury, the sabertooth managed to free itself and rushed away lest she strike again. But before the cat could muster its resources for a counterattack, Matriarch used her undamaged left tusk to bash it into the dust at the foot of the tree, and then she raised her immense foot and stomped on its chest.

Again and again, trumpeting all the while, she battered the mighty cat, crushing its ribs and even breaking off one of the long saber teeth. Seeing blood spurting from one of its wounds, she became wild with fury, her shrieks increasing when she saw the inert body of her grandson, the young bull, lying in the grass. With her mad stomping, she killed the sabertooth, and when her rage finally subsided she remained, whimpering, between the two dead bodies.

As in the case of her own destiny, she was not completely aware of what death was. In fact, the entire elephant clan and its relatives were perplexed by death, especially when it struck down a fellow creature with whom the mourner had been associated. The young bull was dead, of that there could be no doubt, and in some vague way she realized that his wonderful potential was lost. He would not come courting in the summers ahead; he would fight no aging bulls to establish his authority; and he would sire no successors with the aid of Matriarch's daughters and granddaughters. A chain was broken, and for more than a day she stood guard over his body, as if she hoped to bring it back to life. But at the close of the second day she left the bodies, hardly aware that in all that time she had not once looked at the sabertooth. It was her grandson who mattered, and he was dead.

Because his death occurred in late summer, with decomposition setting in immediately and with ravens and predators attacking the corpse, it was not fated that his body be frozen in mud for the edification of scientists scores of thousands of years later, but there was another death that occurred during the last days of autumn that had quite different consequences.

The old bull that had broken Matriarch's tusk, and had been a prime factor in the death of the young bull, strode away from the affair looking as if he had the strength to survive for many mating seasons to come. But the demands of this one had been heavy. He had run with more cows than usual and had been called upon to defend them against four or five lusty younger bulls who felt that their time to assume control had come. For an entire summer he had lusted and fought and eaten little, and now in late autumn his vital resources began to flag.

It began with dizziness as he climbed a bank leading up from the great river. He had made such treks repeatedly, but this time he faltered and almost fell against the muddy bank that impeded his progress. Then he lost the first of his remaining four teeth, and he was aware that two of the others were weakening. Even more serious was his indifference to the approaching winter, for normally he would have begun to eat extravagantly in order to build his reserves of fat against the cold days when snow fell.

On the day of the first snowfall, with a whipping wind blowing in from Asia and icicles of snow falling parallel to the earth, Matriarch and her five family members saw the old bull far in the distance, at what would later be known as the Birch Tree Site. His head was lowered and his massive tusks rested on the ground, but they ignored him. Nor were they concerned about his safety; that was his problem and they knew he had many options from which to choose.

But when they saw him again, some days later, not moving toward a refuge or to a feeding ground but just standing immobile, Matriarch, always the caring mother, started to move toward him to see if he was able to fend for himself. However, when he saw her trying to intrude on his self-imposed solitude, he backed away to protect it, not hurriedly, as he might have done in the old days, but laboriously, making sounds of protest at her approach. She did not force herself upon him, for she knew that old bulls like him preferred to be left alone. When she last saw him he was heading back toward the river.

Two days later, when thick snow was falling and Matriarch started edging her family toward the alder thickets in which they customarily took shelter during the long winters, her youngest granddaughter, an inquisitive animal, was off by herself exploring the banks of the river when she saw that the same bull who had spent much of the summer with them had fallen into a muddy crevice and was thrashing about, unable to extricate himself. Trumpeting a call for help, she alerted the others, and before long Matriarch, her daughters and her grandchildren were hastening toward the site of the accident.

When they arrived, the position of the old bull was so hopeless, mired as he was in sticky mud, that Matriarch and her family were powerless to aid him. And as both the snow and the cold increased, they had to watch helplessly as the tired mammoth struggled vainly, trumpeting for aid and succumbing finally to the irresistible pull of the mud and the freezing cold. Before nightfall he was tightly frozen into his muddy grave, with only the top of his bulbous head showing, and by morning that too was buried under snow. There he would remain, miraculously upright, for the next twenty-eight thousand years, the spiritual guardian of the Birch Tree Site.

Matriarch, obedient to certain impulses that had always animated the mammoth breed, remained by his grave for two days, but then, still puzzled by the fact of death, she forgot him completely, rejoined her family and led them to one of the best spots in central Alaska for passing a long winter. It was an enclave at the western end of the valley that was fed by two streams, a small one that froze quickly and a much larger one that carried free water most of the winter. Here, protected from even the worst winds, she and her daughters and grandchildren remained motionless much of the time, conserving body warmth and slowing digestion of such food as they could find.

Now once more her broken tusk proved useful, for its rough, blunt end was effective in ripping the bark from birch trees whose leaves had long vanished, and it was also helpful in brushing away snow to reveal the grasses and herbs hiding below. She was not aware that she was trapped in a vast ice castle, for she had no desire to move either eastward into what would one day be Canada or southward to California. Her icy prison was enormous in size and she felt in no way penned in, but when the frozen ground began to thaw and the willows sent forth tentative shoots, she did become aware—how she could not have explained—that some great change had overtaken the refuge areas that she had favored for so many years. Perhaps it was her acute sense of smell, or sounds never heard before, but regardless of how the message reached her, she knew that life on the Mammoth Steppe had been altered, and not for the better.

Her awareness intensified when she lost one of her remaining teeth, and then one evening as she wandered westward with her family, she came upon a sight that confused her. On the banks of the river she had been following stood a structure like none she had ever seen before. It was like a bird's nest on the ground, but many times bigger. From it came animals who walked on only two legs; they were like water birds that prowled the shore, but much larger, and now one of them, seeing the mammoths, began to make noises. Others poured from the large nest, and she could see that her presence was causing great excitement, for they made unfamiliar sounds.

Then some of the creatures, much smaller than herself or even the youngest of her grandchildren, began running toward her, and the speed with which they moved alerted her to the fact that she and her herd were about to face some new kind of danger. Instinctively she began to edge away, then to move rapidly, and finally to trumpet wildly as she started running.

But very quickly she found that no matter where she tried to go with her charges, one of the creatures appeared in the shadows to prevent her from escaping. And when day dawned, confusion intensified, for wherever Matriarch sought to take her family, these beings kept pace, persistently, like wolves tracking a wounded caribou. They would not stop, and when that first night fell they added to the terror by causing a fire to spring from the tundra, and this created panic among the mammoths, for they expected the dry grass of the previous summer to burst into uncontrollable flame, but this did not happen. Matriarch, looking at her children in perplexity, was not able to form the idea: They have fire but it is not fire, but she felt the bewilderment that such an idea would have evoked.

On the next day the strange creatures continued to pursue Matriarch and her mammoths and were finally able to isolate Matriarch's youngest granddaughter. Once the young animal was cut off, the pursuers closed in upon her, carrying in their front legs, the ones they did not use for walking, branches of trees with stones attached, and with these they began to beat the encircled mammoth and stab at her and torment her until she bellowed for help.

Matriarch, who had outrun her children, heard the cry and doubled back, but when she tried to aid her granddaughter, some of these creatures detached themselves from the larger group and beat her about the head with their branches until she had to withdraw. But now the cries of her granddaughter became so pitiful that Matriarch trembled with rage, and with a mighty bellow, dashed right through the attackers to where the threatened mammal was striving to defend herself. With a great roar, Matriarch flung herself upon the creatures, lashing at them with her broken tusk and driving them back.

Triumphant, she was about to lead her frightened granddaughter to safety when one of the strange beings shouted 'Varnak!' and another, a little taller than the others and heavier, leaped toward the threatened mammoth and, with an upward stab, drove a sharp weapon deep into her bowels.

Matriarch saw that her granddaughter was not fatally wounded, but as the mammoths thundered off to evade their tormentors, it was obvious that the young one was not going to be able to keep up. So the herd slowed, and with Matriarch assisting her granddaughter, the huge beasts made their escape.

But to their dismay, the little figures on two legs kept pace, coming closer and closer, and on the third day, at an unguarded moment when Matriarch was directing the others to safety, the creatures surrounded the wounded granddaughter. Intending to crush these intruders once and for all, Matriarch started back to defend her grandchild, but as she strove to reach the attackers and punish them with her broken tusk, one of them, armed only with a long piece of wood and a short one with fire at one end, stepped boldly out from among the trees and drove her back. The long piece of wood she could resist even though it had sharp stones on the end, but the fire, thrust right in her face, she could not. Try as she might, she could not avoid that firebrand. Impotently she had to stand back, smoke and fire in her eyes, as her granddaughter was slain.

With loud shouts, much like the triumphant howling of wolves when they finally brought down their wounded prey, the creatures danced and leaped about the fallen mammoth and began to cut her up.

From a distance that night, Matriarch and her remaining children saw once again the fire that mysteriously flamed without engulfing the steppe, and in this confusing, tragic way the mammoths who had for so long been safe within their ice castle encountered man.

PORTRAIT
OF RUFOUS

I T WOULD BE a dramatic coincidence if we could claim that as the horse left America he met on the bridge to Asia a shaggy, lumbering beast that was leaving Asia to take up his new home in America, but that did not happen. The main body of horses deserted America about one million years ago, whereas the ponderous newcomers did not cross the bridge that the horses had used—for it closed shortly after they passed—but a later bridge that opened at the same place and for the same reasons about eight hundred thousand years later.

The beast that came eastward out of Asia had developed late in biologic time, less than two million years ago, but it evolved in startling ways. It was a huge and shaggy creature, standing very high at the shoulder and with enormous horns that curved outward and then forward from a bulky forehead that seemed made of rock. When the animal put its head down and walked resolutely into a tree, the tree usually toppled. This ponderous head, held low because of a specialized thick neck, was covered with long, matted hair, which absorbed much of the shock when the beast used its head as a battering ram. Males also grew a long, stiff beard, so that at times they looked satanic. The weight of the animal was concentrated in the massive forequarters, topped by a sizable hump, while the hindquarters seemed unusually slender for so large a beast. The animal, as it had developed in Asia, was so powerful that it had, as an adult, no enemies. Wolves tried constantly to pick off newborn calves or superannuated stragglers, but they avoided the mature animals in a group.

This was the ancestral bison, and the relatively few who made the hazardous trip from Asia flourished in their new habitat, and one small herd made its way to the land around the twin pillars, where they found themselves a good home, with plenty of grass and security. They multiplied and lived contented lives to the age of thirty, but their size was so gigantic and their heavy horns so burdensome that after only forty thousand years of existence in America, during which time they left their bones and great horns in numerous deposits—so that we know precisely how they looked—the breed exhausted itself.

The original bison was one of the most impressive creatures ever to occupy the land at the twin pillars in northern Colorado. He was equal in majesty to the mammoth, but, like him, was unable to adjust to changing conditions, so, like the mammoth, he perished.

That might have been the end of the bison in America, as it was the end of the mammoth and the mastodon and smilodon, the sabertoothed cat, and the huge ground sloth, except that about the time the original bison vanished, a much smaller and better-adapted version developed in Asia and made its own long trek across a new bridge into America. This seems to have occurred sometime just prior to 6000 B.C., and since in the span of geologic time that was merely yesterday, of this fine new beast we have much historic evidence. Bison, looking much as we know them today, were established in America and one herd of considerable size located in the area of the twin pillars.

It was late winter when a seven-year-old male of this herd shook the ice off his beard, hunched his awkward shoulders forward as if preparing to fight, and tossed his rufous mane belligerently. He then braced himself as if the anticipated battle were at hand, but when no opponents appeared, he relaxed and turned to the job of pawing at the snow to uncover the succulent and sweet grass below.

He stood out among the herd not only because of his splendid bulk but also because of his coloring, which was noticeably lighter than that of his fellows. He did not comport himself with any degree of dignity, because he was not an old bull.

For reasons he could not clearly understand but which were associated somehow with the approach of spring, he started on this wintry day to study carefully the other bulls and, when occasion permitted, to test his strength against theirs. The two- and three-year-olds he dismissed. If they became testy, which they sometimes did, a sharp blow from the flat of his horn disciplined them. The four- and five-year-olds? He had to be watchful with them. Some were putting on substantial weight and were learning to use their horns as well. He had allowed one of them to butt heads with him, and he could feel the younger bull's amazing power, not yet sufficient to issue a serious challenge but strong enough to upset any adversary that was not attentive.

There were also the superannuated bulls, pitiful cases, bulls that had once commanded the herd. They had lost their power either to fight or to command and dragged themselves along as stragglers with the herd. They grazed about the edges, and occasionally, when there was fighting, they might charge in with the valor of their youthful years, but if a six-year-old interposed himself, they would hastily retreat. Earlier they had suffered broken bones and shattered horn tips, and some of them limped and others could see only from one eye. Some of them had even been attacked by wolves, and it was not uncommon to see some old bull with flesh wounds along his flanks that attracted flies.

It was the bulls nine and ten years old that were worrisome, and these Rufous studied meticulously. He was not at all confident that he could handle them. There was one with a slanting left horn; he had dominated the herd three years ago, and even last year had been a bull to contend with, for he had massive shoulders that could topple an opponent and send him sprawling. There was the brown bull with the heavy hair over his eyes; he had been a champion of several springs and had only a few days ago given Rufous a sharp buffeting. Particularly there was the large black bull that had dominated last spring; he seemed quite unassailable and aware that the others held him in awe. Twice in recent weeks Rufous had bumped against him, as if by accident, and the black bull had known what was happening and had casually swung his head around and knocked Rufous backward; this black bull had tremendous power and the skill to use it.

As spring approached and the snows melted, disclosing a short, rich grass refreshed by moisture, the herd began to mill about as if it wished to move to other ground. One morning as Rufous was grazing in the soft land between the twin pillars, with the warm sun on his back, one of the cows started nudging her way among the other cows and butting the older bulls. This was the cow that made important decisions for the herd and stood ready to fight any member at any time. It was as if the lead bull were the general in battle, the lead cow the prime minister in running the nation.

She now decided that it was time for the herd to move northward, and after butting others of her followers, she set out at a determined pace, leaving the twin pillars behind. She headed for a pass through the low chalk hills to the north, then led her charges up a draw to the tableland beyond. There she kept the herd for several days, after which she led them slowly and with no apparent purpose to the river that defined this plateau to the north. Testing the water at several places, she decided which crossing was safest and plunged in.

The water was icy cold from melting snow, but she kicked her legs vigorously, swimming comfortably with the current and climbing out at last to shake her matted hair, sending showers of spray into the sunlight. From the north bank she watched with a leader's care as older cows nudged yearlings into the river, then swam beside them, keeping the younger animals upstream, so that if the current did overcome them, they would bounce against their mothers and thus gain security for the next effort.

When the main body of the herd was safely across, the old bulls grudgingly and sometimes with growls of protest entered the river, swimming with powerful kicks as the water threw their beards into their faces. When they climbed onto the north bank they shook themselves with such fury that they produced small rainstorms.

Rufous was one of the last to cross, and he did so carefully, as if studying this particular crossing against the day when he might have to use it in some emergency. He did not like the footing on the south bank, but once the lead cow was satisfied that the cows and calves were safely across, she ignored whatever bulls were left behind and set out purposefully for the grazing lands to which she was leading her herd.

When she reached this spot, less than a hundred miles from the twin pillars, she stopped, smelled the ground to assure herself that it was good, then turned the leadership of the herd back to the bulls, assuming once more the passive role of a mere cow. But if any decision of moment was required, she would again assert herself, and when she grew too old to assume this task the responsibility would pass to some other strong-minded cow, for the leadership of the group was too important to be left to males.

It was now spring and the calving season was at hand. The sun would rise, as on a normal day, but some cow would experience a profound urge to be by herself, and she would move with determination toward some unknown objective, and if any other cow or a bull tried to interpose, she would knock the offender aside and pursue her course. She would seek some secluded area, even if it was only behind the brow of a low hill, and there she would lie on the ground and prepare for the birth of her calf.

This year a small black cow left the herd as soon as the new grounds were reached, for her time was at hand. As she passed two old bulls they nuzzled her as if to ask what she was about, but she repelled them brusquely and sought a spot not far from the river where trees gave her some protection. There she gave birth to a handsome black bull calf, and as soon as he appeared she began licking him and butting him with her head and goading him to stand alone. She spent two hours at this task, then began mooing softly to attract the attention of the others, but when they ambled over to inspect her new calf, nudging him with their snouts, she made a show of charging at them, as if to assert unequivocally that the calf was hers.

Among the bison that came to inspect the new calf was Rufous, and his nosy intrusion was an error he would regret. The newborn calf liked the smell of Rufous and for a few moments rubbed his small head against his leg. Some intuition told the calf that there would be no milk in that quarter and he returned to his mother.

Now came the days that would be crucial in the life of the little bison. Within a brief period he had to imprint on his mind the image of his mother, her smell, her feel, the taste of her milk, her look, the sound of her call. Because if he failed to make this indelible and vital connection, he might become unattached when the herd moved and be lost in the strangling dust. If this happened, he would survive only a few hours, for the wolves and vultures, seeing his plight, would close in.

Therefore the mother cow encouraged him to nuzzle her, to taste her milk, to smell her urine and to distinguish her cry. She attended the calf constantly, and when he moved among the other calves that were being born at this time she tried to train him to respond to her cry.

But the calf had proved his inquisitiveness by making friends with Rufous shortly after his birth, and he continued this behavior, moving from one adult to another and failing to establish an indelible impression of his own mother. She tried frantically to correct this defect, but her baby bull continued to stray.

Because one of his strongest memories was that of the smell of Rufous, he tried to associate more with the bull and less with his mother, trying even to get milk from Rufous. This irritated the bull, who knocked the confused infant away. The bewildered little fellow rolled over in the dust, and then ran after another adult bull.

At this point, a fairly large herd of strange bison from the north moved onto the feeding ground, and there was a general milling about of animals, so that the baby bull became lost at the edge of the swirling crush. The two herds were excited enough by their chance meeting, but now they detected strange movement to the west, and this triggered panic on the flank, which quickly affected the mass. A stampede began, and those calves that had been strongly imprinted by their mothers performed miraculously: no matter how swiftly their mothers ran or how deftly they dodged, the calves kept up with them stride for stride, their little noses often pressed against their mothers' flanks.

But the handsome black infant had not been adequately trained and had no intuition of where his mother was, nor could he detect her cry in the confusion. It fell behind, far behind, then gave a little cry of joy, for he smelled a reassuring odor. It was not his mother; it was Rufous, lagging behind because he had been grazing on the sweet grass down by the river.

The bull had no intention of caring for a confused baby and rushed past, but the infant, catching a stronger whiff of the familiar smell, joined the gallop and clung to the older bull's flank. This annoyed Rufous, who tried to kick at the pestering calf as they ran, but nothing would divert the baby bull. With a sense of total security as great as if Rufous had been his mother, he clung to the galloping bull.

But now the wolves that always hung about the edges of a herd, hoping for a bit of luck, spotted the little calf. They had a good chance of picking him off, since the older bull was endeavoring to kick him to one side, so they closed in on the running pair, trying to insert themselves between the baby bull and the mature one.

They failed. Once Rufous recognized their strategy, he became a changed animal. It was his responsibility to protect calves, no matter how bothersome, no matter how distant the retreating herd. Accordingly, he scanned the terrain as he ran and spotted a small embankment that might afford protection.

Twisting his head abruptly to the right, he headed for the rocky bank. As if the young calf had been physically attached to him, he turned at the same moment, and the two galloped to the refuge. There Rufous turned to confront his enemies, keeping the calf beside him and well protected by his large flank.

The wolves closed in, eleven of them, but they were powerless against his horns and massive head, nor could they slip behind him to attack his tendons because he kept his rear tight against the rock. If he had not been hampered by this irritating calf, he could have beaten back the wolves and returned to the herd, but with that encumbrance he could do no more than protect himself.

He did manage one other defense. He bellowed several times—the low guttural cry seemed to roll vainly across the vast prairies. But he was heard. The bison having outrun their fright, had stopped and were aimlessly milling around when the master fighter of the herd to which Rufous belonged, the large black bull, heard the cry of distress and doubled back to investigate. With him came the bull with the slanting left horn, and the closer they approached the intermittent bellow, the faster they ran.

They came up to the encircling wolves in a rush, their hind feet digging in like brakes and throwing clouds of dust. Instantly they perceived what was happening, seeing Rufous trapped against the rocky bank with the calf beside him. With lowered heads and flashing hooves they crashed into the wolves and sent them scattering. The black bull caught one on his horn, tossed him in the air, then stamped on him mercilessly when he fell to earth.

The three victorious bulls, with the calf in the center, slowly walked back toward the herd, which had now stabilized. The calf, exhilarated by the adventure and the comforting smell of his savior, Rufous, trotted happily inside the protective triangle.

When the calf regained the herd and the excitement caused by the wolves died down, he realized he was hungry. Smelling Rufous, he ran to the bull and tried to nurse, but Rufous had had enough. Lowering his horn, he caught the little fellow under the belly and tossed him well into the air. He uttered pitiful cries and crashed to earth. He rose bewildered, and tried again to join Rufous, who lowered his head and gave the calf another toss in the air.

This time his cries reached the distraught mother, who recognized them and rushed to reclaim the infant she thought she had lost. She licked his coat and nursed him and did her best to bring him to her, but he still remembered Rufous as the adult closest to him.

Now the rutting season was at hand. Rufous and the other bulls began a strange but long-inherited chain of behavior. One morning, for no apparent reason, Rufous began suddenly charging at cottonwood trees along the riverbank, tearing into them with wild force as if they were living enemies, then stopping and cleaning his horns against their trunks. The next day as he was walking idly toward the herd he felt an uncontrollable compulsion to throw himself on the ground, twisting and turning in the dust a dozen times until he was laden with sand. Then he rose, urinated heavily in the wallow and threw himself into it again, smearing the muddy urine over his head and body as if to announce to the world, 'When you smell that smell, remember. It belongs to Rufous.'

At this period of the rutting season he did not yet care to confront the other bulls; indeed he stayed well away from them, as if he were unsure of his capacity to challenge them on equal terms, but he continued to fight the cottonwoods and to wallow excessively. He also stood by himself and threw out guttural threats, ignoring those that were being voiced by other bulls in the vicinity.

And then one morning, on a day no different from others that had preceded it, a quiet brown cow that had been completely unassuming felt an overpowering surge of vitality, and her entire personality changed in an instant. She became more rhythmic in her motions, gentler in her manner. She left the cows with whom she had been associating and kicked aside her last year's calf when it endeavored to stay close to her, as she had so painfully taught it to do only a year ago.

She sought out the bulls on the edge of the herd and moved from one to another until she came to its leader. He licked her coat and rubbed his head against hers. Often he rested his shaggy head on the hollow of her back as if it were a familiar pillow. Wherever she moved, he followed, waiting for the proper time for mating.

Now the drama of the rutting season began. A four-year-old bull that had not yet mated with any cow left the lesser bulls with whom he had for some time been sparring and marched boldly up to the courting couple. Ignoring the cow, he took a stubborn stance so that his dark beard was close to that of the black bull. The latter, long prepared for such a challenge but unable to anticipate which bull would issue it, stared for a moment at the intruder.

Then, with shuddering force, the two animals leaped at each other, their shaggy foreheads meeting in an explosive crack that could be heard across the plains. To the surprise of the older bull, this first shattering blow seemed to have no effect upon the young challenger, who pawed the earth, lowered his head and drove with incredible force at the older one's forehead. The black bull was tempted to sidestep and allow the young bull to slide harmlessly off his flank, but he sensed that this opening fight would be crucial, and he intended to settle it unequivocally. So he braced himself, lowered his head and took the charge full on his forehead.

For an instant the horns of the two powerful beasts locked, and it looked as if the kinetic force of the younger must drive the older back, but the black bull had reserves of power. His back legs stiffened. His backbone absorbed the shock. And now he began applying pressure of his own. Slowly the younger bull had to retreat. He could not stand fast.

With a sudden twist, the older bull turned his challenger aside, and as the younger bull's belly was exposed the old warrior lunged at it. He could hear the ribs cracking beneath skin and then the cry of pain. The younger bull withdrew, shook himself to assess the damage, felt his ribs grating and, with no further desire to fight, retreated.

The older bull, victor once more, returned to the cow that he had rightfully won. By this cruel process, cows were assured that they would mate only with the strongest bulls and that the vigor of the species would be preserved.

But this time it was not to be so easy, for no sooner had the victorious bull turned his back on the herd and resumed his attentions to the cow than he heard a belligerent snort. When he turned, he saw the bull Rufous headed toward him in a slow, purposeful march. This was a more serious challenge.

When Rufous stood horn to horn with the older bull, the latter could smell the strong urine in which his challenger had wallowed that morning. It was the smell of a mature bull, one ready to assume his place among the leaders of the herd. So the black bull stood very still, made no movement of any kind, and stared into the eyes of his challenger. The two powerful beasts stood that way for more than a minute, then slowly Rufous broke the gaze, lowered his head and, without raising dust, backed away. This was not a good day for extending his challenge. There would be others more propitious.

The black bull did not raise his voice in triumph, nor did he make any move to follow Rufous to demonstrate once and for all his supremacy. He seemed quite content to have resolved this particular challenge in this way. He, too, sensed that a more likely day would come, a day he could not escape, and that then the issue would be resolved.

As the rutting season progressed, only three bulls served the cows: the black leader, the bull with the slanted horn and the brown bull with the heavy hair over his eyes. Each was challenged repeatedly by younger bulls; each retained his prerogatives, and it seemed as if the summer would end with the three in ascendancy.

And then, as the mating season drew to a close, Rufous experienced the antagonisms he had not felt before. No amount of charging cottonwood trees satisfied him, and rolling about in the mud and urine gave him no release. So one bright morning he sought out an old wallow, which he had known favorably before. It was a prairie-dog town, where the little squirrel-like animals had piled up much used sand. Plodding his way to it, he thrust himself into the soft earth, ignoring the protests of the little animals as they watched their homes destroyed. He wallowed for a long time, till his hair was well filled with dust. Then he rose, urinated copiously and threw himself into it with a fierceness he had not shown before. Now when he got up, his body was well muddied and the matted hair about his head exuded a powerful scent.

With strong determination he marched back to the herd, seeking whichever older bull was courting that day. It was the ugly brown bull. He was with a fine cow, well along in heat, and had it not been for the arrival of Rufous, the two might soon have been mating.

This time Rufous did not waste his time staring into the eyes of his enemy. As soon as he arrived at the scene he lowered his head and charged at the brown bull, but his tactic was not successful because the little bull calf that had adopted him as his mother had caught the scent of the urine-covered body as he passed through the herd and now galloped to suckle. This interrupted Rufous's charge and allowed the brown bull to slash at him as his attack was shorted. A serious gash appeared on Rufous's shoulder and blood began to spurt out.

This enraged him, and he vented his wrath on his would-be son. With a violent toss of his head he caught the persistent calf and threw him high into the air and some distance away. Without pausing to see where he fell or how, he rushed at the brown bull in such a way as to catch him unprepared. There was a resounding clash, and the brown bull fell back.

Instantly Rufous leaped at him, boring in with his powerful horns until he struck the right hip of the brown bull. With a ripping sound he swept his horn along the hip, wounding his enemy severely. Encouraged, he swarmed all over the brown bull, jabbing and thrusting and applying constant pressure. It was as if the brown bull were being attacked from all sides, and in time the pressures began to tell. He fell back further, tried to make one last counterattack and failed. Knowing that defeat was inevitable, he backed off and left the area.

Lowing triumphantly, Rufous took over the waiting cow and licked her coat. He was about to lead her into the cottonwoods when the little calf, recovered from his flight, returned to the strong smell of his supposed mother. Sidling up to Rufous, he again tried to nurse, but this time the victorious bull gently nosed him away. He had other matters on his mind.

For the rest of the year Rufous occasionally caught sight of the old brown bull moving along the outer edges of the herd, an embittered elder whose place had been permanently usurped. Never again would the old fellow mount a cow, for if he were to try, the younger bulls would challenge him, remembering that Rufous had humiliated him.

He was free to stay with the herd as long as he wished, and to feed with it and to play with the calves that other bulls sired, but he could have no part in the leadership and certainly no part in the breeding. Some old bulls elected to remain with the herd; many chose to wander off, a part of nothing, afraid of nothing, impregnable to attack, until the closing days when blindness and worn-down teeth and blunted horns made them vulnerable. Then wolves moved in. The slashing attacks were sustained, sometimes for three days, with a dozen wolves trying to cut down one stubborn old bull until he could fight no more and the fangs destroyed him.

It was now autumn, and the leader cow sensed that her charges ought to be congregating with the larger herd, so she led them northward, and as they moved ponderously, they merged with larger herds, and then with larger still. Bison seemed to be moving in from all directions until the prairie was black. They stretched to the horizon and blotted out the land, but still more came. They moved in accordance with no plan, but only in response to the ebb and flow that their ancestors had observed.

That spring, during the calving season, the herd to which Rufous belonged had contained only thirty-nine members. In summer, when it joined with another small herd, it numbered about a hundred. After the rutting season the augmented herd grew to several thousand. And now, on the northern prairie, it contained nearly a million.

In such a congregation the little black bull with the faulty imprinting would have been destroyed had he not clung close to Rufous. He had no chance of locating his mother, for he could not remember her smell, but the strong odor of his adopted father was easy to identify, and the little fellow stayed close to him.

No matter how sorely Rufous abused his unwanted companion, the latter would not leave him. Deprived of his mother's milk, the little bull learned to depend upon grazing seven months before other calves his age, and whereas they clung to their mothers for protection, he developed an independent nature. By the time snow fell he was willing to bang heads with any animal he encountered. Having already survived one attack from wolves, he was not even afraid of them. As his hump matured, so did his pugnacity grow; he was a tough little bull.

With Rufous he moved freely within the vast herd, sometimes under the leadership of their own cow, sometimes far from her on the outer edge. One day when the herd began to break into the usual smaller units for winter grazing, some hundred thousand bison moved south across the river, and it was fortunate that Rufous and the calf were not in the middle that day. The herd was feeding well west of the twin pillars, heading for the chalk cliff, now forty feet high, and if the bison had approached it normally, they would have separated into two segments, one going west to escape the cliff, the other east.

But on this day a pack of wolves set up a commotion on the eastern flank. This stampeded the bison in that area and they dashed forward. Others, seeing them on the move, joined the flight automatically, and before long a general panic set in until eighty or ninety thousand bison were in motion.

They swept forward irresistibly, overriding anything that came within their path. If a bison stumbled and fell, he was crushed to death by hammering hoofs, and any calf separated even momentarily from its mother was either killed or forever lost.

The center of the stampeding herd drove directly for the chalk cliff, and as the lead animals approached and saw the precipitous drop ahead, they tried to stop, but this they were powerless to do, for the animals surging behind kept coming and forced the first rank over the cliff. Most of them perished in the fall, but those that didn't were soon crushed by succeeding waves of bison as they too plunged over the edge.

The bison on the flanks, of course, easily made their way around the cliff and suffered no fatalities except those few that fell beneath the pounding hooves. But at the center more than twelve hundred perished and wolves did not have to bother trailing the herd for stragglers.

Rufous and the bull calf were on the left flank that day, and when panic struck they galloped easily to safety on the plains below the cliff. The little bull enjoyed the wild excitement of the chase so much that thereafter he roamed with Rufous, and when their herd reassembled under the leadership of their determined cow, the two moved eastward to the twin pillars, where the self-orphaned bull grew into a stalwart animal.

He had a raffish disposition, and at the age of nineteen months, when he was well formed, with sturdy horns growing out of his jet-black head, he was already seeking adventure. One day he limped back to the herd, badly cut up: his rear left leg was shredded above the ankle; his face was gashed; and his right flank was scored by sharp teeth. When Rufous and the other bulls gathered about him to smell whatever clues there were of the disaster, they could tell that the blood on his right horn was not his. Sniffing more closely, they detected the smell of wolf, and next morning three of them, wandering east of the twin pillars, came upon a scene of carnage, with three wolves lying dead beside some low bushes that had been trampled.

It had been a notable triumph, but thereafter the young bull would be lame in his left hind leg. He did not limp badly, but when he dug in for a charge against his fellow bulls he favored that leg, and when the charge came, there was a noticeable drag to the left. This did not deter him from fighting with everyone in the herd. Once he even challenged the lead cow when she was leading them north, but she gave him two swift jabs with her horn to show that she would take no nonsense from brash young bulls.

He liked autumn the best, when the massive herd gathered north of the two rivers. In western America two distinct kinds of bison had always existed, wood bison that kept to the hills, and plains bison. The latter were divided into two herds, the northern and the southern, and the land around the twin pillars marked the dividing line. This was because the southern herd usually stayed below the South Platte, while the northern herd stayed above the North Platte. The neutral land between the two rivers was sometimes occupied by a million or two bison from either herd, but they rarely stayed long.

In these years the northern herd, had it ever assembled at one spot, which it did not, would have numbered about thirty-five million animals; the southern herd, twenty-five million. Even such partial concentrations as gathered along the North Platte could number into the two or three millions, and for them to cross the river might require three days. They darkened the prairies; when they moved, the sky was gray with rising dust. They were magnificent, and in the whole region at this time they had no enemy except the wolf. They were a force of such magnitude that it could never be diminished, a stable community whose laws were so sound and whose behavior was so reasonable that it could reproduce itself perpetually.

It was this herd that the tough bull loved, for when he was a part of it, it seemed to grow larger. If the herd broke into a gallop for some unexplained reason, he longed to be at the very heart of it, going where it led, pulled this way or that by the timeless instinct of the herd. Sometimes, at such moments of wild movement, he bellowed for sheer joy.

He found pleasure in milling around the center, fighting whatever young bulls chose to engage him. The fact that he limped deluded other bulls into thinking that here was an easy enemy, and in the first years he was often challenged, always to the dismay of those who did the challenging, for he was not only strong and canny, but could also be downright mean, with sly tricks that the other bulls had not learned. It was usual, when two bulls found contact in their first violent charge, for them to remain locked, their great foreheads touching, their back legs pumping in a contest of brute strength. But with a weak leg this jet-black bull knew that he must always lose the battle when he fought that way, so when a stolid adversary would dig in for a traditional contest, he would feint forward, make enough contact to fix his opponent in position, then slide to the side, raking his foe with his sharp right horn. He startled many bulls in this way, but he himself was also badly scarred in the brawling. Two ribs had already been broken and the tip of his left horn had been knocked off. He bore many scars in addition to the wolf bites, yet he loved the smell of combat when the vast herd assembled.

But when the excitement bred by the giant herd died down, in some mysterious manner the smaller herd of the twin pillars reestablished itself: the lead cow for that year reasserted her dominance and even fractious bulls like the jet-black one fell in line and willingly took up the trek south to their own familiar territory. Then he marched with Rufous, and the two, the younger one now as hefty as the older, formed as handsome a pair as even the great master herd could have provided.

The younger bull no longer looked upon the older as his mainstay in life; indeed, that ridiculous earlier attachment had been forgotten. To him Rufous was merely the commanding bull of the herd, the one who had not yet been defeated during the rutting season. And here was where the trouble started, for when the jet-black bull was six years old he determined to possess cows of his own. And this placed him in direct opposition to Rufous.

That spring the half-lame bull started to train for the extrarigorous battles he knew lay ahead. He tested his horns against cottonwood trees and bellowed for hours at a time down by the river. He wallowed a good deal and sought fights with younger bulls. With great intensity he watched the three or four older bulls that commanded the cows, and especially he kept his eye on Rufous. It seemed to him that the old tyrant was losing his power.

During the calving season the young bull continued shadow-fighting with trees and galloping suddenly along the edge of the feeding ground, then stopping with dust-raising sharpness, thrusting his horns this way and that. He now ceased any playing around with younger bulls, for he knew that more serious matters were at hand.

When the rutting season began, he became a violent creature, slashing away at any animal that came his way. And then, one day when Rufous had singled out a cow for himself, he watched with meticulous care for the right moment to assault him, but while he was taking preparatory steps, another young bull stepped forward and boldly challenged the old champion. There was an initial confrontation, the stare, the refusal to back down, the digging in of the hind feet, the colossal charge and the shattering jolt as foreheads crashed.

It was a major fight, a real test of power of the older bull, who met it with distinction, holding his ground and slowly driving the young challenger back. But when he had humbled the younger bull and given the triumphant bellow of the victor, he found that he was not exactly victorious, for while the two had been fighting, the half-lame bull had gone off with the cow and was now breeding her in the lush area between the two pillars.

For the rest of that year Rufous and the young bull were enemies. They did not engage in actual battle, for the younger bull sensed that Rufous was so enraged that victory was impossible. In his canny way he bided his time, and when the great herd assembled that autumn he stayed clear of Rufous.

When the time again came for cows to come into heat, the young bull was at the height of his powers, a handsome creature with heavily matted hair and a long beard. His forequarters were immense and more than compensated for the inadequate left hind leg. Insolently he muscled his way through the younger bulls, always keeping his eye on Rufous.

The confrontation happened with startling suddenness. On the first day of the rutting season he challenged Rufous over the first cow. The two great animals stood glaring at each other for almost a minute and Rufous squared for the initial shock, but when it came he was unprepared for its ferocity. For the first time he backed a little to find a better footing. The second clash was as violent as the first, and again he adjusted his hind feet, but before they found a footing, the younger bull made a feint, followed by a devastating thrust to the other side, and Rufous felt his flank being laid open by a scimitar horn.

For the first time in these fights Rufous was actually hurt, with violent pain coursing through his body. With unprecedented fury he turned upon his assailant and drove at him with such terrible force that he cracked two of the other bull's ribs.

Ordinarily this would have been sufficient to drive a challenger from the field, but the jet-black bull was no ordinary bison. He was an animal trained in adversity and one that would not surrender even in the face of death. Twisting his side so as to accommodate the pain of the broken ribs, he drove directly at Rufous, staggering him with blows to the chest and flank. Here was no stylized dueling; here was a fired-up young bull, trying his best to kill.

Relentlessly he gored and smashed at Rufous, never allowing the older bull a chance to pull himself together. With a mixture of astonishment and panic Rufous sensed that he was not going to defeat this explosive young adversary. Vaguely he acknowledged that a better animal than he had come onto the scene, and with an apprehension of tragedy and lonely years ahead, he began to back away. First one foot moved, grudgingly, then another. He was in retreat.

With a snort of triumph the younger bull charged at him for the last time, knocking him sideways and into confusion. Lowering both his tail and his head, Rufous started running from the battle, disorganized and defeated, while the black bull took possession of the cow he had so clearly won.

The other bison did not react to the fight's outcome as Rufous retreated from the battleground; they displayed neither regret nor satisfaction as he moved disconsolately through their ranks. He had been defeated, and that was that. He was through forever as the commander of the herd and must now make what peace he could with himself.

This proved difficult. For the rest of that summer he stayed apart, taking his position about a quarter of a mile from the edge of the herd.

Throughout the autumn he was a lost soul, and not even the excitement of the massing of the herds inspirited him. Once or twice he caught a glimpse of the handsome new champion, but the two did not travel together this time, and on the return trip even the lead cow ignored him.

Winter was a trying time. When snow covered the prairies and freezing winds with temperatures far below zero strayed in from the west, where the mountains stood, Rufous stayed alone, turning his matted head into the storm and doggedly waiting until the blizzard subsided. Then, alone, he faced the problem of finding enough to eat, so he lowered his massive head into the snow, down two or three feet, and with slow side-to-side rhythmic swings knocked a path in the snow, deeper and deeper, until the frozen grass at the bottom lay revealed. Then he fed, pushing his head into new drifts when the grass in any one spot was gone.

Snow froze in his matted hair. Long icicles formed on his beard. The hair on his cheeks was worn away and his face became raw, but still he stayed by himself, a defeated old bull, fighting the blizzard alone until his bones were weary and his face was heavy with accumulated ice.

He stayed alive. One night wolves tracked him, and once they attempted an attack, but he was too strong for them, much too strong. Methodically and with old skill he slashed them to pieces when they came near. One wolf he caught on his horn, and before it could get away, he dashed it to the ground and stamped it to a pulp, relishing each repeated thrust of his still-powerful feet. After that the wolves left him alone. An outcast he was, by his own volition but food for wolves he would not be for many years.

The snow was extremely heavy that year, and in the mountains it accumulated to a depth of forty feet. When spring came and days of hot sun, the melting was sudden and devastating. Huge bodies of water formed and had to find some way down to the plains, so rivulets became streams and streams became rivers, and the South Platte surged in an awesome flood.

The lead cow, having anticipated this disaster by some intuition, kept the herd at the twin pillars, where the land was high, but since Rufous no longer felt himself a part of the herd and roamed as he wished, he chose the land that lay beside the river, where the ice was thick and the grass would be fresh within the next few weeks. He was therefore not prepared when his refuge was abruptly engulfed in water from the mountains, and he delayed leaving for higher ground. He expected that the water would go away; instead it increased.

Now the main body of the flood inundated new regions, and Rufous was trapped. Ice floes, broken loose by the flooding, began to pile up around him, and he realized that if he stayed in that area he was doomed, so he struck out for what he remembered as higher ground, but here, too, the water had invaded, with large chunks of ice backing up against the cottonwoods.

Abandoning that possible escape route, Rufous decided to try his fortunes on the south side of the river, but this meant that he would have to cross the river itself, something he had often done in the past but could not possibly do now. Before he launched into the water he looked about wildly, as if searching for the lead cow to give him directions. He valiantly plunged into the turbulent river, felt himself carried along by its fury, and struck out forcefully for the opposite bank, now miles distant because of the flooding.

He kept his legs pumping, and had this been a normal river he would have mastered it. Even so, he trusted that he was headed safely for the opposite shore and kept swimming. As he did, he might have dimly reflected that it was the little black bull—the one he had saved and reared—that had driven him from the herd. He knew only that he was an outcast.

Down the middle of the swollen river came a congregation of broken logs, ice chunks, large rolling stones and bodies of dead animals. It was a kind of floating island, overwhelming in its force as it swept along. It overtook him, submerged him, ground him relentlessly in dark waters and passed on.

THE BEAVER

WHEN THE BISON struggled over the land bridge into America, he encountered a huge misshapen creature that was in many ways the opposite of himself. The bison was large in front, slight in the rear, while the native animal was very large in the rear and slight in front. The bison was a land animal; the other lived mostly in water. The beast weighed some three hundred and fifty pounds as it slouched along, and its appearance was fearsome, for its conspicuous front teeth were formidable and as sharp as chisels. Fortunately, it was not carnivorous; it used its teeth only to cut down trees, for this giant animal was a beaver.

It had developed in North America but would spread in desultory fashion throughout much of Europe; its residence in the streams of Colorado would prove especially lucrative, bringing great wealth to those Indians and Frenchmen who mastered the trick of getting its pelt.

The first beavers were too massive to prosper in the competition that developed among the animals of America; they required too much water for their lodges and too many forests for their food. But over the millennia a somewhat smaller collateral strain became dominant, with smaller teeth and softer pelts, and they developed into one of the most lovable and stubborn of animals.

One spring the mother and father beavers in a lodge on a small creek west of the twin pillars made it clear to their two-year-old daughter that she could no longer stay with them. She must fend for herself, find a mate and with him build her own lodge. She was not happy to leave the security in which she had spent her first two years; henceforth she would be without the protection of her hardworking parents and the noisy companionship of the five kits, a year younger than herself, with whom she had played along the banks of the stream and in its deep waters.

Her greatest problem would be to find a young male beaver, for there simply were none in that part of the creek. And so she must leave, or in the end her parents would have to kill her because the space she occupied inside the lodge was needed for future babies.

So with apprehension but with hope, this young female left her family for the last time, turned away from the playful kits and swam down the tunnel leading to the exit. Gingerly, as she had been taught, she surfaced, poked her small brown nose toward the shore and sniffed for signs of enemies. Finding none, she gave a strong flip of her webbed hind feet, curling her little paws beneath her chin, and started downstream. There was no use going upstream, for there the building of a dam was easier and all the good locations would be taken.

One flap of her hind feet was sufficient to send her cruising along the surface for a considerable distance, and as she went she kept moving her head from side to side, looking for three things: saplings in case she needed food, likely spots to build a dam and its accompanying lodge, and any male beaver that might be in the vicinity.

Her first quest was disappointing, for although she spotted quite a few cottonwoods, which beavers could eat if need be, she found no aspen or birch alders, which were her preferred foods. She already knew how to girdle a small tree, strip its bark and fell it so that she could feed on the upper limbs. She also knew how to build a dam and lay the groundwork for a lodge. In fact, she was a skilled housekeeper, and she would be a good mother, too, when the chance presented itself.

She had gone downstream about a mile when there on the shore, preening himself, was a handsome young male. She studied him for a moment without his seeing her, and she judged correctly that he had chosen this spot for his dam. She surveyed the site and knew intuitively that he would have been wiser to build it a little farther upstream, where there were strong banks to which it could be attached. She swam toward him, but she had taken only a few powerful strokes of her hind feet when from a spot she had not noticed, a young female beaver splashed into the water, slapped her tail twice and came directly at the intruder, intending to do battle. It had taken her a long time to find a mate, and she had no intention of allowing anything to disrupt what promised to be a happy family life.

The male on shore watched indifferently as his female approached the stranger, bared her powerful front teeth and prepared to attack. The stranger backed away and returned to the middle of the stream, and the victorious female slapped the water twice with her tail, then swam in triumph back to her unconcerned mate, who continued preening himself and grooming his silky coat.

The wandering beaver saw only one other male that day, a very old fellow who showed no interest in her. She ignored him as he passed, and she kept drifting with no set purpose.

As late afternoon came on and she faced her first night away from home, she became nervous and hungry. She climbed ashore and started gnawing desultorily at a cottonwood, but her attention was not focused on the food, which was fortunate because as she perched there, her scaly tail stretched out behind her, she heard a movement behind a larger tree and looked up in time to spot a bear moving swiftly toward her.

Running in a broken line, as she had been taught, she evaded the first swipe of the slashing paw, but she knew that if she continued running toward the creek, the bear would intercept her. She therefore surprised him by running parallel to the creek for a short distance, and before he could adjust his lunge to this new direction, she had dived to safety.

She went deep into the water, and since she could stay submerged for eight or nine minutes, this gave her time to swim far from where the bear waited—even from the bank a bear could launch a powerful swipe that might lift a beaver right onto the bank. When she surfaced, he was far behind her.

Night fell, the time when her family had customarily played together and gone on short excursions, and she was lonely. She missed the kits and their noisy frolicking, and as night deepened she missed the comfort of diving deep into the water and finding the tunnel that would carry her to the warm security of the lodge.

Where would she sleep? She surveyed both banks and selected a spot that offered some protection, and there she curled up as close to the water as she could. It was a miserable substitute for a proper lodge, and she knew it.

Three more nights she spent in this wretched condition. The season was passing and she was doing nothing about the building of a dam. This bothered her, as if some great purpose for which she had been bred was going unfulfilled.

But the next day two wonderful things happened, the first having no lasting consequences. Early in the morning she ventured into a part of the creek she had not seen before, and as she moved she became aware of a strong and reassuring scent. If it was serious, and not an accident, it would be repeated at the proper intervals, so she swam slowly and in some agitation in the four compass directions, and as she had anticipated, the keen smell was repeated as it should have been. A male beaver, and young at that, had marked out a territory and she was apparently the first female to invade it.

Moving to the middle of the stream, she slapped her tail, and to her joy a fine-looking young beaver appeared on the bank of the creek and looked down into the water. The slapping could have meant that another male had arrived to contest his territory and he was prepared to fight, but when he saw that his visitor was the kind he had hoped to attract, he gave a little bark of pleasure and dived into the stream to welcome her.

With strong sweeps of his webbed feet he darted through the water and came up to her, nudging her nose with his. He was highly pleased with what he found and swam twice around her as if appraising her. Then he dived, inviting her to follow him, and she dived after him, deep into the bottom of the creek. He was showing her where he intended building his lodge, once he found a female to help.

They returned to the surface and he went ashore to fetch some edible bark, which he placed before her. When beavers mated, it was for life, and he was following an established pattern of courtship. The female was eager to indicate her interest, when she noticed that his gaze had shifted from her to something else.

He was looking upstream, where one of the most beautiful young beavers he had ever seen was about to enter his territory. This female had a shimmering coat and glowing eyes, and she swam gracefully, one kick sending her to the corners of his areas, where she checked the markers he had left. Assured that she was in the presence of a serious suitor, she moved languidly to the center of the area and signaled with her tail.

The young male left his first visitor and with lightning strokes sped to this newcomer, who indicated that she was interested in the segment of the creek he had laid out for himself and was willing to move in permanently. In this brief space of time their destiny was determined.

What now to do with the first visitor? When the new female saw her she apprehended immediately what had happened, so she and the male came to where the young beaver waited and started to shove her out of the delineated area. But she had got there first and intended to stay, so she dived at the intruding female and started to assault her. However, the male knew what he wanted and had no desire to settle for second best, so he joined the newcomer and together they forced the unwanted intruder downstream; as she disappeared, chattering in rage, they slapped their tails at her and, making joyous noises, prepared to build their dam.

The outcast drifted aimlessly and wondered whether she would ever find a mate. How could she build a home? How could she have kits of her own? Bitterly she sought the next miserable place to spend a night.

As she explored the bank she became aware of a soft sound behind her and was certain it must be an otter, the most fearful of her enemies. She dived deep and headed for any cranny within the bank that might afford protection, and as she flattened herself against the mud she saw flashing through the waters not far distant the sleek, compacted fur of an otter on the prowl.

She hoped that his first sweep would carry him downstream, but his sharp eye had detected what could have been a beaver hiding against the bank, so he turned in a graceful dipping circle and started back. She was trapped and, in her anxiety, fought for any avenue of escape. As she probed along the bottom of the bank she came upon an opening that led upward. It could well be some dead end from which there was no escape, but whatever it was, it could be no worse than what she now faced, for the otter was returning and she could not swim fast enough to escape him.

She ducked into the tunnel and with one powerful kick sent herself upward. She moved so swiftly that she catapulted through the surface and saw for the first time the secret cave that had formed in the limestone, with a chimney that admitted air and a security that few animals ever found. Soon her eyes became accustomed to the dim light that filtered in from above and she perceived what a marvelous spot this was, safe from otters and bears and prowling wolves. If she built her dam slightly below the cave and constructed her lodge in the body of the creek, attaching it by a tunnel to this secret place, and if she then widened the chimney upward and masked its exit so that no stranger could detect it, she would have a perfect home. To add to her delight she found inside the cave and above the water level a comfortable ledge on which she could sleep that night.

Before dawn she was at work. Moving to the prominent places on the shore and to the ledges in the creek, she stopped at each and grabbed a handful of mud. With her other paw she reached to the opening of her body where two large sacs protruded, and from these she extracted a viscous yellow liquid that would become famous throughout the West as castoreum, valued for having one of the most pleasant odors in the natural world.

Kneading the castoreum into the mud and mixing in a few grasses to make the cake adhere, she placed it carefully so that its odor would penetrate in all directions, and when she had set out nine of these she stopped and tested the results of her labors. She swam upstream and down, and wherever she went she reassured herself that she had established a clear signal that this stretch of water belonged to a beaver who intended holding it.

The limestone cavern became not only a place of refuge but also a satisfactory home. She built three secret escape hatches, one leading a good twenty feet inland from the bank of the creek, so that if a bear or wolf did take her by surprise, she could dive into it and make her way back to her home before the predator knew where she had gone.

The cycle of her life, however, was still incomplete. By herself she would not build a dam or a lodge, for they were needed primarily for the rearing of young. She could survive in the limestone cave, but without a lodge and a mate, she was still an outcast.

This did not prevent her from grooming herself as carefully as ever. Each day, when the sun was low, she perched on the bank overlooking her domain and preened. She did this by using the two peculiar toes on each of her hind legs; the nails on these toes were split so as to form small combs, and these she dragged through her pelt until even the slightest tangle was removed. Then she took oil from her body and carefully applied it to each part of her coat, combing it in deeply until her fur glistened in shimmering loveliness. No one saw or applauded this grooming, but it was impossible for her to go to bed until she had completed it.

And then, in early autumn, when she had given up hope of finding a mate, a beaver seven years old who had lost his family in some catastrophe wandered down the river and turned by chance into her creek. He was by no means a handsome creature; a long gash ran down the left side of his face and he had lost the two toes on his left hind leg that he needed for cleaning himself, so that he looked disreputable.

As he moved up the creek he detected the markers and realized immediately that a mistake had been made. The creek spot looked inviting, but any flood from the river would wash it away. He looked about for the family that occupied it to warn them of the danger they faced, and after a while he saw the head of the owner breaking through the surface. She swam out to him cautiously and looked for his mate, while he looked for hers. There was a period of motionless silence.

They stared at each other for a very long time, and each knew all there was to know. There would be no illusions, no chicanery.

It was he who broke the silence. By the way he looked and moved his tail he indicated that this spot was no place to build a dam.

With a fierce toss of her head she let him know that this was where she would live. And she led him underwater to the entrance of her secret cave and showed him the escape hatches and how she planned to link it to the lodge and the dam. But he was still not satisfied, and when they surfaced, he started to swim to a much safer spot, and she followed, chattering and slamming her tail, then halting in disgust as he left her premises.

In the morning he swam back and indicated hesitantly that she was welcome to accompany him if she would consent to build their dam at a proper site.

Again she protested furiously and snapped at him, driving him away. That afternoon he came back quietly with a length of aspen in his teeth, and diving to the bottom of the creek, he fastened it to the floor with mud, the first structure in their new home.

It was then September, and they set to work with a passion. They labored all night, dragging trees and branches into the stream, weighing them with mud and gradually building the whole construction high enough to check the flow of water. Again and again as they worked he almost betrayed his doubt that the dam they were building would hold, but she worked with such fervor that he withheld his misgivings.

When the two beavers were satisfied that the dam would impound the water necessary for their establishment, she began tying branches and tree lengths into the bottom, weighting them with rocks and mud and other trees, and it was now that she realized that in the building of the dam she had done most of the work. He was great on starting things and showed considerable enthusiasm during the first days, but when it came time for doing the hard, backbreaking work, he was usually absent.

She had to acknowledge that she had accepted a lazy mate, one who could not be cured of indolence, but instead of infuriating her, this merely spurred her to greater efforts. She worked as few beavers, an industrious lot, had ever worked, lugging huge trunks of trees and slapping mud until her paws ached. She did both the planning and the execution, and when the pile from which their lodge would be constructed was nearly finished, and she was eleven pounds lighter than she was when she started, he indicated for the final time that when the floods came, this would all vanish. She made no response, for she knew that just as she had done most of the building this time, she would have to do it again if floods ever came.

When the pile in the middle of the small lake behind the dam was completed, they dived to the bottom and began the gratifying task of cutting entrances into it and providing sleeping levels above the waterline as well as places for kits, and digging connecting runways to the secret chamber. At planning he was a master, for he had built lodges before.

Only a few days remained before the freeze, and they spent this period in a burst of superenergy, stripping bark and storing it for their winter's food. Where eating was concerned, he was willing to work, and in the end they had a better lodge than any other on the creek, and better provisioned, too.

In the early days of winter, when they were frozen in, they mated, and in spring, after she gave birth to four lovely babies, the river produced a flood that washed away the dam and most of the lodge. She rescued the babies and took them to higher ground, where a fox ate one.

As soon as the floods had receded, she began to rebuild the dam, and when it was finished, she taught the kits how to help rebuild the lodge, which took less effort.

They then enjoyed four good years in the tight little domain, but in the fifth, sixth and seventh years there were floods, the last of such magnitude that the whole establishment was erased. He had had enough, and he spent considerable time upstream looking for a better site, but when he found one, she refused to move. He found her marking the corners of her estate with castoreum and teaching her children how to start erecting a higher and better dam.

He halted at the edge of her territory and watched as this stubborn little creature proceeded with her engineering, making the same mistakes, dooming her dam to the same destruction.

He was now fifteen years old, an advanced age for a beaver, and she treated him with respect, not requiring him to haul logs or do much actual construction on the lodge. He snapped at the kits when they placed branches carelessly, indicating that if he were in charge he would not accept such sloppy workmanship. As he aged, his face grew uglier, with the scar predominating, and he moved with difficulty. One day while he was helping girdle some cottonwoods, he failed to detect a wolf approaching and would have been snatched had he not been bumped toward the safety tunnel by his mate.

That year there was no flood.

Then one day in early autumn when the food was safely in and the lodge never more secure, she happened to wander up the tunnel into the secret place that the family had enjoyed so much, and she found him lying there on the limestone ledge, his life gone. She nudged him gently, thinking that he might be asleep, then nuzzled him with affection to waken him for their evening swim through the lake they had built and rebuilt so many times. But he did not respond, and she stayed with him for a long time, not fully comprehending what death signified, unwilling to accept that it meant the end of their long companionship.

In the end the children took the body away, and automatically she went about the job of gathering food. Dimly she sensed that now there could be no more babies, no more kits playing in the limestone chamber and scampering down the runways.

She left the security of the lodge and went to each of the compass points and to the salient ridges in between, and at each she scooped up a handful of mud and mixed it with grass and kneaded in a copious supply of castoreum. When the job was done she swam back to the middle of her lake and smelled the night air.

This was her home, and nothing would drive her from it, not loneliness or attacks by otters or by wolves, or the flooding of the river.

THE EAGLE
AND THE SNAKE

THE DINOSAUR diplodocus had evolved in Colorado but had died out. The horse had evolved here but had left. The beaver had originated here but had emigrated. Was there no inhabitant that had originated here and had stayed? Indeed there was, perhaps the most terrifying creature now living on earth.

From man's point of view, the first animals that occupied the land around the twin pillars had ample justification for their existence. Diplodocus was a magnificent creature that harmed no one; the horse would make man more mobile; the bison would make him warm and well fed, and the beaver would make him rich. Even the omnipresent wolf was needed, for he policed the area and kept the bison herds strong through killing off the old and the weak, while the chattering prairie dog could be appreciated for the humor it provided. But for another inhabitant no acceptable justification had ever been proposed; the reason for his presence on earth was a mystery.

On a hot summer's day a female eagle flying lazily in the sky watched as a herd of bison left the shadows of the twin pillars and headed north for a rendezvous on the far side of the North Platte. The eagle watched with unconcern as the great beasts moved out in single file, for there was nothing of advantage to her in the movement of bison or even in their congregation in large numbers. All they produced was dust.

But as the bison moved north she noticed that at a certain spot even the most aggressive bulls shied to the left, and this was worth inspecting, so she hovered for some minutes to confirm her observation, then flew in lazy circles till the herd passed.

As soon as the last straggler had gone, she dropped like an arrow from above, keeping her eye on the spot, and noted with pleasure that her deduction had been right. Below her in the dust beside a rock was food.

Increasing her speed, she swooped down, almost touching the sand with her wings. At the last moment she extended her talons and grabbed at the object that had attracted her—an enormous rattlesnake some five feet long and very thick in the middle. It had a flat, triangular head and on the end of its tail a set of nine hornlike knobs.

The eagle miscalculated slightly, for only one claw of the right foot caught the rattler, well toward the tail. The eagle tried to carry the snake aloft so as to drop it on rocks and kill it, but the snake, with a violent twisting effort, tore free and, with blood flowing from the wound, immediately coiled itself to repel the next attack.

Seeing that the rattler was in a position to strike, the eagle realized that she must try to take it by surprise, so she landed some distance away, her feet and wings throwing up a cloud of dust and, with wary, high-stepping movements, approached to give battle.

The snake watched her come and was geared to defend himself, but he was not prepared for the kind of attack she made. Uttering a wild cry, she ran directly at the snake and raised her wings, encouraging it to strike at the feathers, then brought the edge of her left wing sharply across the snake's backbone. It was a staggering blow, delivered with all the force the eagle could muster, and it flattened the rattlesnake.

Instantly she leaped upon it, catching it squarely in the middle, so that her claws dug all the way through that part of the snake's body. With a flap of her extended wings she soared into the air and began searching not for rocks but for a quite different terrain. Finding what she wanted, she flew with her eyes into the wind to assure herself that it was not strong enough to blow the snake off target when she dropped him. Satisfied, she released the serpent and watched as it plummeted into the middle of a cactus thicket, whose needle-sharp spines jutted upward.

With a thud the rattlesnake fell onto the cactus, impaling itself in a score of places. As it writhed, the jagged edges of the spines cut deep and held fast. There was no way the snake could tear itself loose, and death became inevitable.

Had the eagle realized that exposure to the sun and loss of blood must soon kill the snake, it could merely have waited, then hauled the dead carcass off to its young. But the bird was driven by some deep inner compulsion and felt obligated to kill its enemy, so it flapped its great wings slowly and hovered above the cactus spines before lowering itself and catching the serpent again.

This time the eagle flew in wide circles, searching for an area of jagged rocks on which to drop the rattler. Locating what she wanted, she rose to a great height and shook the snake free, watching with satisfaction as it crashed onto the rocks. The fall did great damage, and the snake should have been dead, but, like all rattlers, he had a terrible determination to survive, so as soon as he struck the rocks he marshaled his remaining strength and took the coiled position.

The eagle had made a sad miscalculation in dropping the snake onto the rocks, for she had counted on the fall to kill him outright, but this it had not done, so now she was forced to leave the flat, sandy terrain where she had an advantage and go among the rocks, where the advantage was his. However, since the snake was obviously close to death, she judged that she could quickly finish him off.

But when she sought to deliver the decisive blow with the edge of her wing, he somehow thrust himself around her body and enclosed it in a constricting embrace, fighting desperately to bring his lethal head into contact with some vital part.

The eagle was too clever to permit this. She strained and clawed and bit until he had to release his hold. For the moment he was defenseless, and she took this opportunity to pierce him for the third time, and now she carried him very high, kicking him free over the rocks again, and once more he crashed into them.

He should not have survived the fall and he feigned death, lying stretched out and uncoiled. Sorely shattered by this last fall and bleeding from numerous wounds, he made no sound, for his rattles were broken.

The eagle was fooled. She inspected him from the air, then landed on the rocks and walked unsteadily over to carry him aloft for the last time. But as she neared, the snake coiled and struck with what force he had left and plunged his fangs into the eagle's unprotected spot where the thin neck joined the torso. The fangs held there for only a moment, but in that brief instant the muscles in the snake's neck contracted to send a jet of lethal poison deep into the enemy's bloodstream. Easily, so easily, the fangs withdrew and the snake fell back upon the rocks.

The startled eagle made no motion. She merely stared with unbelieving eyes at the snake, which fixed on her a basilisk gaze. She felt a tremor across her chest and then a vast constriction. She took two halting steps, then fell dead.

The rattlesnake lay motionless for a long time, one wing of the eagle across his wounded body. The sun started to go down and he felt the coldness of the night approaching. Finally he bestirred himself, but he was too damaged to move far.

For a long period it seemed that he would die, there on the rock with the eagle, but just before sundown he mustered enough strength to drag himself into a crevice where there would be some protection from the night cold. He stayed there for three days, slowly regaining strength, and at the end of this time he started his painful trip home.

He lived, as did several hundred other rattlers, some much bigger than he, in the rocks at the twin pillars. Their kind had lived there for two million years, a mass of snakes that found the area good hunting for rats and prairie dogs, with safe crevices in the rocks for hibernation in the winter. When men reached the area, the twin pillars would become known as Rattlesnake Buttes, reassuring beacons in the desert when spotted from afar, dangerous death traps when approached too closely.

Rattlesnake Buttes! A thousand westward travelers would remark about them in their diaries: 'Yesterday, from a grate distance we seen the Rattlesnake Butes they was like everybody said tall like castels in Yurope and you could see them all day and wondered who will be bit by the snakes like them folks from Missuri?'

The myriad poisonous snakes that infested the buttes served no purpose that man could discern; they terrorized, they ate harmless prairie dogs, they killed whatever they struck, and after a long life they died. Why had they been made custodians of such deadly poison? It was impossible to say.

The two fangs that folded back against the roof of the mouth when not needed dropped into operating position when the snake wanted to kill. They were not teeth as such, but hollow and very sharp hypodermic needles, so formed that pressure from the rattler's throat would not only deposit the poison but inject it to astounding depths. The poison itself was a combination of highly volatile proteins that reacted with the blood of the victim to produce a quick and painful death.

The snakes at Rattlesnake Buttes were apt to leave intruders alone unless the latter did something to frighten them. Bison roamed the area by the thousands, and always had, and as calves had learned to avoid the rattlers. Indeed, even the sound of a rattle, that dreaded clatter in the dust, was enough to make a line of bison move in another direction. Occasionally, some stupid one would put himself into a position from which there was no escape from the rattler, and then the snake would strike him. If the venom entered the bison anywhere near the head or face, it was invariably fatal, but if the snake struck a leg, there was a fighting chance that the poison would be absorbed before it reached the heart, but the bison would thereafter be lame in that leg, its nerves and muscles half destroyed by the venom.

In the days when horses roamed the area, many a fine steed went lame because it had blundered upon a rattlesnake and taken a shot of venom in its fetlock. But if either a bison or a horse saw a rattler about to strike, and saw it in time, it would take protective action and stamp the snake to death. Sharp hooves were more dangerous to rattlers than eagles or hawks, so that if the bison tried to avoid the snakes, so, too, did the rattlers keep out of the way of bison—and they especially avoided deer, whose ultrasharp hooves could cut a snake in half.

The rattler that had defeated the eagle in mortal combat took a long time to recover. For the next two years he was in poor shape, able to leave the buttes for only short trips and always gratified when winter came so that he could sleep for five or six months, but gradually he began to feel better, and the gaping wounds in his body retreated into scars. He started to move about, and when the weather was good he joined some of the other snakes in short expeditions in search of mice and small birds.

Then his full vigor returned and he resumed a normal life. For him this had always consisted of matching wits with prairie dogs, those chattering little squirrel-like animals that build intricate subterranean towns. There was such a town, rather extensive, not far from the buttes, and for a hundred thousand years rattlesnakes had invaded it.

On a warm day, when the sun relaxed and vivified the muscles that had grown stiff in winter, he set out from the buttes and slithered across the desert toward dog-town. From a distance he could see the little mounds that indicated where the creatures lived, and he noticed with gratification that they were as numerous as ever.

As he approached the town, which contained several thousand prairie dogs, he tried to move as inconspicuously as possible, but from a hillock a sharp-eyed lookout spotted the grass moving and gave a loud chirping sound, which lookouts elsewhere in the town repeated, so that within an instant the whole area was alerted. Where there had been thousands of little prairie dogs sunning themselves and chattering, there were now none and all was silent.

He had encountered this tactic before and was prepared for it. Crawling as close as practicable to a concentrated nest of burrows, he coiled the long length of his body and waited. The one thing he could count on was curiosity; no matter what threatened, the prairie dog sooner or later had to come out of his safe burrow to inspect. A hawk could be perched at the opening, his feet showing, but the little dogs had to come out to satisfy themselves that he was really there.

So the snake waited, and before too many minutes had passed, from one of the burrows a furry little head appeared. By chance its first glance was directly into the eyes of the snake, which startled it so, it gave one wild cry and disappeared down its hole, but before it had ceased trembling from fright, another dog from another hole came out to see if there really was a snake, and this one was not so fortunate as to look directly at the rattler. It turned first in the opposite direction and before it ever saw the snake, the fangs had sunk into its neck.

There were many burrows in this town, and sometimes the rattlesnakes, caught far from the buttes in bad weather or when the sun was danger-ously hot—a snake, like the great reptiles before him, would perish if exposed too long to the direct rays of the sun—would crawl into the burrows, and even make them their home for extended periods, in which case the prairie dogs would simply leave by another exit.

Sand owls, which built their nests and raised their young underground, also liked to preempt the burrows rather than take the trouble to dig their own, and it was not unusual to see within one town the prairie dogs inhabiting one set of burrows, the sand owls another, and the rattlesnake a third, with each group allowing the others to go pretty much their own way.

This rattlesnake had no intention of taking up residence in dog-town. It came only to feed, and when it had caught its prey and swallowed it, there were other areas to visit, down by the river, for example, where mice lived among the roots of the cottonwoods. A rattler would always prefer a mouse above any other food, but they were not easy to catch. There were also birds, especially the young, but catching them required unusual pa-tience, and after his encounter with the eagle this rattler was not much attracted to birds.

As autumn approached, it was essential that each rattler fortify himself with abundant food to keep him nourished in the months of hibernation, and the hunting became more intense. In those days he practically lived in the heart of dog-town, picking off whatever inquisitive little animals he could, but as the days shortened he felt an irresistible urge to seek protection at the buttes. It was no trivial thing to go to sleep for a series of months during which he would be vulnerable to any foe that came upon him; it was essential that he return to deep rocky crevices that had protected him in the past.

So he started the trek back to the buttes, and as he went he saw many other rattlesnakes on their way too. As they convened at familiar places they moved together and sometimes formed intertwined balls of writhing forms, a score of large rattlers twisted together. When men reached this area, as they soon would, they would sometimes in autumn stumble upon such a ball of writhing snakes—'they was as big as a watermillion'—and would be horrified. The memory of the sight would haunt them, and years later they would speak of it: 'I was ridin' a gray mustang, a very steady brute, and all at once he shies and like to throw me on my ass and thank God he didn't because there by them red rocks at Rattlesnake Buttes was this ball of snakes all twisted up I like to died.'

Now as the snakes crawled down the path that they had often used before, the old rattler became aware of an unfamiliar creature blundering toward him from the opposite direction. Following his ancient custom, he coiled himself in the middle of the path and produced a sharp rattle. The stranger, unfamiliar with this warning, ignored it and came stumbling directly at the rattler, which made an even sharper sound. At last the intruder took notice, almost too late.

The snake struck at the thing that stood close to its fangs, but this was to be a unique experience, for deftly the target leaped aside, and from above something descended, striking the rattler a heavy blow behind the head. Knocked out of its coil, the snake endeavored in bewilderment to adjust to this unprecedented assault. It formed a half-coil, preparing to strike anew at its assailant.

And then it looked up, and instead of seeing a buffalo or a sharp-hoofed deer, it saw a new creature, standing erect, bearing a heavy weapon he had not seen before, and the last sensation this rattler had was the sight of the weapon descending toward his head with tremendous force, and the strange cry of triumph from the standing figure, and sharp death.

Man had come to the plains. From the far northwest, from a distant origin, across strange bridges and down green corridors, the two-legged one had journeyed to the buttes, where before only the horse and the camel and the mammoth, the sloth and the beaver and the snake, had lived. His first act was symbolic, the instinctive killing of the snake, and for as long as time endured, enmity between these two would continue.

EPILOGUE:
THE DEATH OF ELLY ZAHM

FOR Levi Zendt and Elly Zahm, the newlywed Pennsylvania Dutch couple, the trail west in 1844 contained an unfolding series of surprises—it seemed almost as if a superior dramatist had prepared the script best calculated to excite the imagination. Now the first hills appeared, and the travelers began to realize that the going would be difficult, yet the way was eased with excellent grass and good water, from which they and the other immigrants could take consolation. Farmers from eastern areas saw the hickory, the oak, the plenitude of walnut and birch, and found themselves in reassuring surroundings, but suddenly at the crest of some hill they would catch a glimpse of landscape reaching to the horizon, infinitely far, with few trees and only scrub grass, and they would catch their breath at the strangeness of the land they were penetrating. The whole trip would be like this, one contrast after another.

At the end of the first week it began to rain, not the way it did back East, but in sullen sheets of water. The rain fell with such intensity that it bounced back up from the earth, and Elly Zendt wrote to her friend Laura Lou Booker:

> June 2, Sunday . . . I am writing this at night huddled inside the Conestoga before a flickering candle. It is raining, but not like any you have seen in Lancaster. It falls in great tubfuls, drowning everything. Sometimes the wagon shakes so that I cannot control my pen, and the wind whistles so piercingly that I cannot think. Levi has put an India-rubber sheet over our wagon, but still the rain drips through. I understand how Noah felt. . . .

Summer was nearly over, and with her growing pregnancy Elly had attained a serenity she had not known before, and her thin face was becoming actually beautiful. She was now a mature woman of seventeen with a
burgeoning loveliness, as if the prairie had called forth a miracle.

One evening, while Levi wandered over the prairie, collecting buffalo
chips so that Elly would not have to work, she stayed in the wagon, writing
to Laura Lou. This letter stands as an epistle of hope and prescience,
epitomizing the contributions made by the brave women who crossed the
plains in pioneer days:

> August 27, Tuesday . . . To be pregnant takes away the sting of
> defeat, for just as we shall be starting a new community where the
> rivers meet, so Levi and I shall be starting a new family. Also, the
> land we are traveling is the kind that makes you proud, for it is
> beautiful in a manner that those of us who lived always in Lancas-
> ter could never have dreamed or appreciated. This afternoon we
> came over a hill and saw before us the two red buttes which have
> been our target since we left Fort John. They stood like signal
> towers, or the ramparts of a castle, and they created such a strong
> sense of home that all of us halted on the hill to appreciate the
> noble place to which God had brought us. Levi and I spent only
> a little while looking at the buttes, because our attention was
> taken by the mountains to the west, and we both thought that if
> we were to live within the shadow of such majestic hills we would
> become like them. It was now growing dark, and the sun disap-
> peared and over the prairie which we have come to love so well
> came a bluish haze and then a purple and finally the first dark
> shades of night itself and we were all travelers on the crest of a hill.
> I feel assured that any family which grows up in such novel
> surroundings will be strong and different and I thank God that I
> am pregnant so that I can watch the growing.

Next morning, Elly was up early to prepare breakfast, and as she moved
briskly toward the small pile of buffalo chips that Levi had gathered for
her to be used as fuel for their fire, she did not heed the warning sound,
and as she stooped to lift a large chip, a giant rattlesnake, bigger around
than her arm, struck with terrifying speed and sank its fangs deep into her
throat. Within three minutes she was dead.

'It's God's mercy,' McKeag said as Levi came rushing up, too late for even one last kiss. 'It's God's mercy,' the red-haired Scotsman repeated, as he gripped Levi by the shoulders. 'I've seen 'em die slow from snakebite, all swole up. Levi, it's better this way.'

Of the millions of words I've written, none have affected readers so emotionally as these short paragraphs describing the death of Elly Zahm. Hundreds have written to ask, 'Why did you have to kill her off like that?' An equal number have approached me personally to report that they wept at her death: 'Why did you make her die so soon?' And I reply, 'That's the way things happened in the settlement of the West.'

                                                                —J.A.M.

THE HYENA

IT WAS THE SILENT TIME before dawn, along the shores of what had been one of the most beautiful lakes in southern Africa. Now for almost a decade little rain had fallen; the earth had baked; the water had lowered and become increasingly brackish.

The hippopotamus, lying with only her nostrils exposed, knew intuitively that she must soon quit this place and move her baby to some other body of water, but where and in what direction, she could not decide.

The herd of zebra that came regularly to the lake edged their way down the bare, shelving sides and drank with reluctance the fetid water. One male, stubbornly moving away from the others, pawed at the hard earth, seeking to find a sweeter spring, but there was none.

Two lionesses, who had been hunting fruitlessly all night, spotted the individual zebra and by arcane signals indicated that this was the one they would tackle when the herd left the lake. For the present they did nothing but wait in the dry yellow grass.

Finally there was a noise. The sun was still some moments from rising above the horizon when a rhinoceros, looking in its grotesque armor much the same as it had for the past three million years, rumbled down to the water and began rooting in the soft mud, searching for roots and drinking noisily.

When the sun was about to creep over the two conical hills that marked the eastern end of the lake, a herd of eland—big, majestic antelope that moved with rare grace—came to drink. When they appeared, a little brown man who had been watching through the night, hidden in deep grass, whispered a prayer of thanks: 'If the eland come, there is still hope. If that rhinoceros stays, we can still eat.'

His attention was deflected by a thunder of hooves. Zebra lookouts had spotted the lionesses and had sounded retreat. Like a swarm of beautifully colored birds, the black-and-white animals scrambled up the dusty bank of the lake and headed for safety.

But the male who had seen fit to wander off, dissociating himself from the herd, now lost its protection, and the lionesses, as planned, cut him off from the others. There was a wild chase, a leap onto the hindquarters of the zebra, a piteous scream, a raking claw across the windpipe. The handsome animal rolled in the dust, the lionesses holding fast.

Seven other lions moved in to share the kill, attended by a score of hyenas who would wait for the bones, which they would crush with their enormous jaws to salvage the marrow, while aloft, a flight of vultures gathered to take their share when the others were gone.

It was in October 1766, when Adriaan Van Doorn was at the advanced age of fifty-four, that he and his half-Hottentot companion Dikkop left home to explore the Zambezi River, a wild river some fifteen hundred miles to the north. 'How long will you be gone?' his wife, Seena, and his young brother, Lodevicus, had asked.

'Three years,' Adriaan said, and with a flick of his whip he started his oxen north.

They took with them sixteen reserve oxen, four horses, a tent, extra guns, more ammunition than they would probably need, sacks of flour and four bags of biltong. They wore the rough homemade clothes of the veld and carried a precious tin box containing Boer farm remedies, medicinal herbs and leaves, their value learned through generations of experience.

They moved slowly at first, seven or eight miles a day, then ten, then fifteen. They let themselves be diverted by almost anything: an unusual tree, a likelihood of animals. Often they camped for weeks at a time at some congenial spot, replenished their biltong and moved on.

As the two went slowly north, they saw wonders that no settler had ever seen before: rivers of magnitude and vast deserts waiting to explode into flowers, and most interesting of all, a continual series of small hills, each off to itself, perfectly rounded at the base as if some architect had placed them in precisely that position. Often the top had been planed away, forming mesas as flat as a table. Occasionally Adriaan and Dikkop would climb such a hill for no purpose at all except to scout the landscape ahead, and they would see only an expanse so vast that the eye could not encompass it, marked with these repititious little hills, some rounded, some with their tops scraped flat.

In the second month of their wandering, after they had rafted their luggage wagon across a stream the Hottentots called Great River, later to be named the Orange, they entered upon those endless plains leading into the heartland, and late one afternoon at a fountain they came upon their first band of human beings, a group of little Bushmen who fled as they approached. Throughout the long night Adriaan and Dikkop stayed close to the wagons, guns loaded, peering into the darkness apprehensively. Just after dawn one of the little men showed himself, and Adriaan made a major decision. With Dikkop covering him, he left his own gun against the wheel of the wagon, stepped forward unarmed and indicated with friendly gestures that he came in peace.

At the invitation of the Bushmen, Adriaan and Dikkop stayed at that fountain for a week, during which time Adriaan learned many good things about the ones his fellow Dutchmen called 'daardie diere' (those animals), and nothing so impressed him as when he was allowed to accompany them on a hunt, for he witnessed remarkable skill and sensitivity in tracking. The Bushmen had collected a large bundle of hides, which Dikkop learned would be taken 'three moons to the north' for trade with people who lived there.

Since the travelers were also headed in that general direction, they joined the Bushmen, and twice during the journey saw clusters of huts in the distance, but the Bushmen shook their heads and kept the caravan moving deeper into the plains until they reached the outlying kraals of an important chief's domain.

The Bushmen ran ahead to break the news of the coming of the white stranger, so that at the first village Adriaan was greeted with intense curiosity and some tittering, rather than the fear that might have been expected. The blacks were pleased that he showed special interest in their huts, impressed by the sturdy workmanship in stone and clay and the walls four to five feet high that surrounded their cattle kraals. As he told Dikkop: 'These are better than the huts you and I live in.'

News of their arrival spread to the chief's kraal and the chief sent an escort of headmen and warriors to bring these strangers before him. The meeting was momentous, for Adriaan was the first white man these blacks had seen. They came to know him well, for he stayed with them two months, and were excited when he demonstrated gunpowder by tossing a small handful on an open fire, where it flamed violently. The chief was terrified at first, but after he mastered the trick, he delighted in using it to frighten his people.

'How many are you?' Adriaan asked one night.

The chief pointed in the four compass directions, then to the stars. There were so many people in this land.

When Adriaan studied the communities he was permitted to see, it became obvious to him that these people were not recent arrivals in the area. Their present settlement, the ruins of past locations, their ironwork traded from the north, their copious use of tobacco—all indicated long occupancy. He was especially charmed by the glorious cloaks the men made from animal skins softened like chamois. He liked their fields of sorghum, pumpkins, gourds and beans. Their pottery was well formed, and their beads, copied from those brought to Zimbabwe three hundred years earlier, were beautiful. He accepted their presence on the highveld as naturally as he did the herds of antelope that browsed near the fountains.

In succeeding months he would never be far from such settlements, scattered over the land as they crossed, but he rarely contacted the people, since he was preoccupied with reaching the Zambezi. Besides, he worried that other chiefs might not be as friendly as the man who danced with joy at the flash of gunpowder.

As they moved north they shot only such food as they required, except one morning when Dikkop became irritated with a hyena that insisted upon trying to grab her share of an antelope he had shot. Three times he tried in vain to drive the beast away, and when she persisted he shot her. This might have occasioned no comment from Adriaan but for the fact that when she died she left behind a baby male hyena with fiery black eyes; she had wanted the meat to feed him, and now he was abandoned, snapping his huge teeth at Dikkop whenever he approached.

'What's out there?' Adriaan called.

"Baby hyena, Baas,' Dikkop replied.

'Bring him here!'

So Dikkop made a feint, leaped back, and planted his foot on the beast's neck, subduing him so that he could be grabbed. Struggling and kicking but making no audible protest, the baby hyena was brought before Adriaan, who said immediately, 'We've got to feed him.' So Dikkop chewed bits of tender meat and put them on his finger for the animal to lick off; by the end of the third day the two men were competing with each other for the right to feed the little beast.

'Swartejie, we'll call him,' Adriaan said, which meant something like Blackie or the Little Black One, but the hyena assumed such a menacing stance that Adrian laughed and said, 'So you think you're a big Swarts already?' and that's what he was called.

He showed the endearing characteristics of a domesticated dog without losing the impressive qualities of an animal in the wild. Because his forequarters were strong and high, his rear small and low, he lurched rather than walked, and since his mouth was enormous, with powerful cheek muscles to operate the great, crunching jaws, he could present a frightening appearance. But his innate good nature and his love of Adriaan, who fed and roughhoused with him, made his face appear always to be smiling. With a short tail, big ears, wide-set eyes, he made himself a cherished pet whose unpredictable behavior supplied a surprise a day.

He was a scavenger, but he certainly lacked a scavenger's heart, for he did not slink and was willing to challenge the largest lion if a good carcass was available. But once when the two men came upon a covey of guinea fowl and wounded one, Swarts was thrown into a frenzy of fear by the bird's flapping wings and flying feathers. As winter approached and the highveld proved cold, whenever Adriaan went to his sleeping quarters— eland skin formed like a bag, with soft ostrich feathers sewn into a blanket—he would find Swarts sleeping on his springbok pillow, eyes closed in blissful repose, his muscles twitching now and then as he dreamed of the hunt.

'Move over, dammit!' Adriaan would say. The sleeping hyena would groan, lying perfectly limp as Adriaan shoved him to one side, but as soon as the master was in the bed, Swarts would snuggle close and often he would snore. 'You! Dammit! Stop snoring!' and Adriaan would shove him aside as if he were an old wife.

They saw animals in such abundance that no man could have counted them, or even estimated their numbers. Once when they were crossing an upland where the grass was sweet, they saw to the east a vast movement, ten miles, twenty miles, fifty miles across, coming slowly toward them, raising a dust cloud so huge that it obliterated the sun.

'What to do?' Dikkop asked.

'I think we'll stand where we are,' Adriaan replied, not at all pleased with his answer but unable to think of any other.

Even Swarts was afraid, whimpering and drawing close to Adriaan's leg.

And then the tremendous herd approached, not running, not moving in fear. It was migration time, and in obedience to some deep impulse the animals were leaving one feeding ground and heading to another.

The herd was composed of only three species: vast numbers of wildebeest, their beards swaying in the breeze; uncounted zebras, decorating the veld with their flashy colors; and a multitude of springbok leaping joyously among the statelier animals. How many beasts could there have been? Certainly five hundred thousand—more probably, eight or nine— an exuberance of nature that was difficult to comprehend.

And now they were descending upon the three travelers. When they were close at hand, Swarts begged Adriaan to take him up, so the two men stood fast as the herd came down upon them. A strange thing happened. As the wildebeest and zebras came within twenty feet of the men, they quietly opened their ranks, forming the shape of an almond, a teardrop of open space in which the men stood unmolested. And as soon as that group of animals passed, they closed the almond, going forward as before, while newcomers looked at the men, slowly moved aside to form their own teardrop and then passed on.

For seven hours Adriaan and Dikkop and Swarts stood on that one spot as the animals moved past. Never were they close enough to have touched one of the zebras or the bounding springbok; always the animals stayed clear and after a while Swarts asked to be put down so that he could watch more closely.

At sunset the western sky was red with dust.

In the next months the landscape changed dramatically. Mountains began to appear on the horizon ahead, and rivers flowed north instead of east, where the ocean presumably lay. It was good land, and soon they found themselves in a remarkable gorge where the walls seemed to come together in the heavens. Dikkop was frightened and wanted to turn back, but Adriaan insisted upon forging ahead, breaking out at last into a wonderland of baobab trees whose existence defied his imagination.

'Look at them!' he cried. 'Upside down! How wonderful!'

For several weeks he and Dikkop and Swarts lived in one huge tree, not up in the branches, which would have been possible, but actually inside the tree in a huge vacancy caused by the wearing away of soft wood. Swarts, responding to some ancient heritage in a time when hyenas had lived in caves, reveled in the dark interior spaces, running from one to another and making strange sounds.

He had become an exceptional pet, perhaps the finest animal Adriaan had ever known, placid as the best ox, brave as the strongest lion, playful as a kitten, and of tremendous strength, like a grown rhinoceros. He enjoyed playing a fearsome game with Adriaan, taking the trekboer's forearm in his powerful jaws and pretending to bite it in half, which he could have done. He would bring his teeth slowly together and impishly watch Adriaan's face to see when pain would show. Tighter and tighter the great teeth would close until it seemed that the skin must break, and then, with Adriaan looking directly into the animal's eyes, Swarts would stop, and laugh admiringly at the man who was not afraid, and he would release the arm and leap upon Adriaan's lap and cover him with kisses.

At times Adriaan would think: These years can never end. There will be enough land for everyone, and the animals will multiply forever. When he and Dikkop left a carcass it was good to hear the lions approaching, to see the sky filled with great birds waiting to descend and clean the feast.

They came at last to the river, not the Zambezi, as Adrian had promised, but the Limpopo, the sluggish stream that marked the natural northern borders of the subcontinent. Portuguese explorers had said the natural border was the Zambezi; anyone who had a map, rude and rough, saw that the Zambezi was the natural boundary, but reality dictated that this boundary be the Limpopo. South of here, the land was of a piece; north of here, it altered radically and could never be digested as a coherent part of a manageable unit.

Perhaps Adriaan realized this in December 1767, when he stood at the Limpopo beside his irreparably broken wagon and his oxen and horses that were dying of disease. 'Dikkop,' he said, 'we can't go any farther.' The Hottentot agreed, for he was tired, and even Swarts seemed relieved when the three started south on foot. It was as if the hyena had a built-in compass that reminded him of where home had stood; he seemed to have known that he was heading away from where he ought to have been, and now that he was homeward bound he manifested his joy like a sailor whose ship has turned into a proper heading.

They formed a curious trio as they came happily down the spine of Africa. Swarts, with his big head and small bottom, took the lead. Then came Dikkop, with a small head and enormous bottom. Finally there was Adriaan, a lean, white-haired trekboer, fifty-six years old and striding along as if he were thirty. Once Swarts insisted upon leaving the trail made by antelope and heading to the west, and when the men followed they found a small cave, which they were about to ignore until Dikkop looked at the roof and discovered the images of three giraffes being stalked by little brown men; they had been painted there millennia ago by the ancestors of the Bushmen they had met. This way and that, men and animals moved, colors unfaded, forms still deftly outlined. For a long time Adriaan studied the paintings, then asked: 'Where have they gone?'

'Who knows, Baas?' Dikkop replied, and Adriaan said: 'Good boy, Swarts, we liked your cave.'

Summer that year was very hot, and even though the trio was moving south, away from concentrated heat, Adriaan noticed that Dikkop was exhausted, so he looked for routes that would keep them away from the hot and dusty center and lead them out toward the eastern edge of the plateau, where they were likely to encounter cooling rains. On one such excursion they came upon that quiet and pleasant lake where the little brown man had hunted his rhinoceros.

It was at its apex now, a broad and lovely body of water to which a thousand animals came each evening in such steady profusion that Swarts was benumbed by the possibilities he saw before him. Lurching here and there, chasing birds and elephants alike, he watched for any weakling, placing himself well back of the lions that were also stalking it, and ran in for bits of meat whenever an opportunity arose. When the bigger predators were gone, he would waddle into the lake to drink and wash himself, and he obviously enjoyed this part of the trip above any other.

Dikkop was faring less well. It was 1768 now and he was sixty-three years old, a tired man who had worked incessantly at a hundred different tasks, always assigned him by someone else. He had lived his life in the shadow of white men, and in their shadow he was content to end his final days. He was not indifferent about his fate; eagerly he wanted to get back to the farm to see how Seena was doing, for he loved her rowdy ways and usually thought of himself as 'her boy.' He would be very unhappy if anything happened to him before he saw her again.

He was to be disappointed. As the summer waned, so did his health, and it became apparent that he would not be able to endure the long return journey: 'My chest, he hurts, he hurts.' Adriaan berated himself for having brought so old a man on so perilous an expedition, but when Dikkop saw this he said reassuringly: 'Impossible to come without me. But you get back safe, I think.'

He died before the chill of winter and was buried beside the lake he had grown to love; it was when Adriaan collected the stones for Dikkop's cairn from the ruins of an ancient village dating back to the 1450s that he began talking seriously to his hyena: 'Swarts, we're piling these stones so your filthy brothers don't dig him up and eat him, you damned cannibal.' Swarts showed his enormous teeth in what could only be a grin, and after that whenever Adriaan consulted with him about which eland path to follow or where to spend the night, Swarts bared his teeth and nuzzled his master's leg.

Adriaan now had every reason to pursue vigorously his way homeward, but for reasons he could not explain he lingered at the quiet lake, not exploring its hinterland but simply resting, as if he realized that this was a place to which men fled for refuge. From his sleeping place he studied the low mountains to the east, the twin peaks that looked like breasts, and the flatlands hungry for the plow. But, most of all, he kept his eyes on the rim of the lake, where animals came to drink and across whose placid surface the flamingos flew.

'Vrijmeer!' he cried one day. 'Swarts, this is the lake where everything that moves has freedom.' That night he could not sleep. Restlessly he stepped across the inert body of his pet to stand in moonlight as undisciplined thoughts assailed him: I wish I were young again . . . to bring a family here . . . to live beside this lake. . . .

It was not easy for Adriaan to admit that he was growing lonely. He had never talked much with Dikkop, nor looked to him for intellectual companionship. He was not afraid of traveling alone, because by now he knew every trick for avoiding dangers; he sensed where the kraals of the black people lay, and he swung away from them; he slept where no lion could reach him, relying upon Swarts to alert him if unusual developments occurred. The hyena was not really a good watchdog, he slept too soundly on a full belly, and with his master's constant hunting he had a good supply of guts and bones to gorge upon, but he had a marked capacity for self-defense, and many animals that might have attacked Adriaan sleeping alone would have had to think twice before risking a hyena's great jaws and flashing teeth.

The loneliness came from the fact that he had seen Africa, had touched it intimately along the mountains and the veld, and had reached the point where there were no more secrets. Even the fact that a majestic waterfall lay only a short distance to the northwest would not have surprised him, for he had found the continent to be greater than he had imagined.

Again the vagrant thought struck, this time with pain, and he said in a loud voice: 'God, Swarts, I wish I were young again. I'd cross the Limpopo. Go on and on, past the Zambezi, all the way to Holland.' He had not the slightest doubt that given a good pair of shoes he could walk to Europe. 'And I'd take you with me, my little hunter, to protect me from the dik-diks.' He laughed at this and Swarts laughed back at the idea of anyone's needing protection from the tiniest of antelope, who leaped in fear at the fall of a leaf.

Perhaps this recurrent loneliness was a premonition, for as they came down off the spacious central plateau to cross the Great River, he saw that Swarts was becoming restless. The hyena was two and a half years old now, a full-grown male, and as they came into territory where other hyenas hunted in packs, Swarts became aware of them in new ways, and sometimes at dusk gave indications that he wanted to run with them. At the same time he knew deep love for his human companion and felt a kind of obligation to protect him, to share with him the glories of the hunt.

So he vacillated, sometimes running toward the open veld, at other times scampering back in his lurching way to be with his master, but one night, when the moon was full and animals were afoot, he suddenly broke away from Adriaan, ran a short distance into the veld, stopped, looked back as if weighing alternatives, and disappeared. Through his sleepless night Adriaan could hear the sounds of hunting; when day broke, there was no Swarts.

For three days Adriaan stayed in that area, hoping that the hyena would return, but he did not. And so, with regret almost to the point of tears, Adriaan set out for the mountains that protected his farm, and now he was truly alone and, for the first time in his life, even afraid. From the latitude of the stars he calculated that he might be as far as three hundred miles north of his destination, with a diminishing store of ammunition and the necessity of covering that expanse of open country when he was not quite sure where he was.

'Swarts,' he shouted one night, 'I need you!' And later, as he lay fitfully sleeping, he heard the sound of animals, many of them, trampling near to where he was hiding, and he began to shiver, for he had not heard this noise so close before. Then slowly he came awake and was aware of something pressing upon him, and it was Swarts, snoring in the old manner.

Now he talked with the animal more than ever, as if the hyena's return had laid bare his need for companionship; Swarts, for his part, kept closer to his master, as if after tasting the freedom of the wild, he realized that a partnership with a human being could have its rewards, too.

Down the long plains they came. 'It must be over this way, Swarts,' Adriaan said, looking at the last line of hills that rose from the veld. 'The farm is probably down there, and when you meet Seena, you two are going to have fun. She's redheaded and she'll throw things at you if you don't look out, but you'll like her and I know she'll like you.' He was not at all sure how Seena would take to sharing her hut with a hyena, but he kept assuring Swarts that it would be all right.

But the hyena's recent experience in the wild had revived animal habits, and one evening after Adriaan shot a gemsbok, a beautiful creature with a white-masked face and imperial horns, a lioness thought it safe to move in and command the kill, whereupon Swarts leaped at her and received a horrible slash of claw across his neck and face.

When Adriaan, screaming at the lioness, reached his companion, Swarts was dying. Nothing that the man might do could save the beast; his prayers were meaningless, his attempts to stanch the blood fruitless. The great jaws moved in spasms and the eyes looked for the last time at the person who had been such a trusted friend.

'Swarts!' Adriaan shouted, but to no avail. The hyena shuddered, gasped for air, got only blood, and died.

'Oh, Swarts!' Adriaan moaned repeatedly through the night, keeping the misshapen body near him. In the morning, he placed it out in the open, where the vultures could attend it, and after an anguished farewell to a constant friend he resumed his journey south.

Now he was truly alone. Almost everything he had had with him at the start of his exploration was gone: Dikkop the trusted Hottentot, ammunition, horses and oxen—lost to the tsetse fly—the wagon, his shoes, most of his clothing. He was coming home bereft of everything, even his hyena, and his memories of the grandeurs he had seen were scarred by the losses he had sustained. Most of all he mourned for Swarts; Dikkop, after all, had lived his life, but the hyena was only beginning his, a creature torn between the open veld and the settled farm that was to have been his home.

As he slogged his way south Adriaan began to feel his age, the weight of time, and idly he calculated the farms he had used up, the endless chain of animals he had bred and passed along, the huts he had lived in and never a house: 'Swarts, I'm fifty-seven years old and never lived in a house with real walls.' Then he braced his shoulders, crying even louder: 'And by God, Swarts, I don't want to live in one!'

He came down off the great central highland of Africa—not defeated, but certainly not victorious. He could still walk many miles a day, but he did so more slowly, the dust of far places in his nostrils. From time to time he shouted into space, addressing only Swarts, for now he was truly Mal Adriaan, the crazy man of the veld, who conversed with dead hyenas, but on he went, a few miles a day, always looking for the trail he had lost.

When he broke through the mountains into unfamiliar terrain, he calculated correctly that he must be a fair distance east of his farm, and he was about to turn westward to find it when he thought: 'If they had any sense, they'd have moved to better land over there.' And like earlier members of his family, he headed east.

But when he reached the new territory that ought to have contained the new farm, he found nothing, so he was faced with the problem of plunging blindly ahead into unknown territory or turning back, and after long consultations with Swarts he decided on the former: 'Stands to reason, Swarts, they'd be wanting better pastures.'

At the farthest edge of where he could imagine his family might have reached, he came upon the shabbiest hut he had yet seen, and in it lived a man and wife who had taken up their six thousand acres, with only the most meager chance of succeeding. They were the first white people Adriaan had seen since setting out on his journey, and he talked with them eagerly: 'You hear of any Van Doorns passing this way?'

'They went.'

'Which direction?'

'East.'

'How long ago?'

'Before I got here.'

'But you're sure they went?'

'We stayed in their old huts. Four months. Trekboer came through, told us they had gone.'

Since Adriaan needed rest, he stayed with the couple for a short time, and one morning the woman asked, 'Who's this Swarts you keep talking to?' and he replied: 'Friend of mine.'

After two weeks, during which the trekboer gave him a supply of ammunition, which he used to bring meat to the hut, Adriaan announced casually that he was about to try to locate his family.

'How long you been gone?' the woman asked.

'Three years.'

'Where'd you say you were?'

'M'popo,' he said, using a name the blacks had taught him.

'Never heard of it.'

For a moment Adriaan felt that he owed it to his hosts to explain, but upon reflection realized that to do so adequately would require another two weeks, so he departed with no further comment.

On and on he went, and one morning as he reached the crest of a substantial line of hills he looked down to see something that disturbed him greatly; it was a valley covering some nine thousand acres and completely boxed in by hills. 'It's a prison, Swarts!' he cried, alarmed that people would willingly submit themselves to such confinement.

What dismayed him especially was that at the center, beside a lively stream that ran from the southwest to the northeast, escaping through a cleft in the hills, stood not the usual Van Doorn huts but solid buildings constructed of clay and stone. Whoever had planned this tight enclave intended to occupy it not for the ordinary ten years but for a lifetime. It represented a change of pattern so drastic that in one swift glance Adriaan realized that his old trekboer days were ended, and he groaned at the error these people were making: Stone houses! Prisons within a prison! To reach this at the end of three years on the most glorious land in Africa was regrettable, to say the least.

But he still was not certain that this was his new farm until an older woman with fading red hair came out of the stone house and walked toward the barn. It was Seena. This stronghold was her home, and now it would be his.

He did not call out to his wife, but he did say to Swarts, 'We've come to the end, old fellow. Things we don't understand . . .' Slowly and without the jubilation he should have felt at reaching the end of so long a journey, he came down the hill, went to the door of the barn and called: 'Seena!' She knew immediately who it was and, leaving the gathering of eggs, ran to him and hugged him as if he were a child. *'Verdomde ou man,'* she cried. 'You're home.'

After the children had screamed their greetings and Lodevicus, now a solid thirty, had come forth with his wife, Rebecca, Adriaan asked the adults, 'How did our farm get to this place?'

'We wanted security,' Lodevicus explained. 'The hills, you know.'

'But why the stone houses?'

'Because this is the last jump that can be made. Because on the other side of the Great Fish River the Xhosa wait.'

'This is our permanent home,' Rebecca said. 'Like Swellendam, a foothold on the frontier.'

'I saw a place up north. It had hills like this, but they were open. There was a lake, and it was open too. Animals from everywhere came to drink.'

The younger Van Doorns were not interested in what their father had seen in the north, but that night when Adriaan and Seena went to bed after the long absence, she whispered: 'What was it like?' and all he could say was 'It's a beautiful country.'

That had to stand for the thundering sunsets, the upside-down trees, the veld bursting in flowers, the great mountains to the east, the mysterious rivers to the north, but as he was about to close his eyes in sleep he suddenly sat upright and cried: 'God, Seena! I wish we were twenty. . . . We could go to a place I saw . . . that lake . . . the antelope darkening the fields.'

'Let's go!' she said, without hesitation or fear.

He laughed and kissed her. 'Go to sleep. They'll find it in time.'

'Who?'

'The ones who come after.'

NERKA
THE SALMON

EAST OF Juneau, Alaska, was Taku Inlet, a splendid body of water that in Scandinavia would be called a fjord; it wound and twisted its way far inland, alternately passing bleak headlands and low hills covered with trees. On all sides mountains with snow-covered peaks rose in the background, some soaring more than seven or eight thousand feet.

A notable feature of Taku was the family of powerful glaciers that pushed their snouts right to the water's edge, where from time to time they calved off huge icebergs that came thundering into the cold waters with echoes reverberating in the hills and mountains. It was a wild, lonely, majestic body of narrow water, and it drained a vast area reaching into Canada almost to the lakes that the Chilkoot miners traversed in 1897 and '98. To travel upstream in the Taku was to probe into the heart of the continent, with the visible glaciers edging down from much more extensive fields inland, where the ice cover had existed for thousands upon thousands of years.

Taku Inlet ran mainly north and south, with the glaciers crawling down to the western shore, but on the eastern bank, directly opposite the snout of a beautiful emerald glacier, a small but lively river with many waterfalls debouched, and nine miles up its course a lake of heavenly grace opened up, not large in comparison with many of Alaska's lakes, but incomparable, with its ring of six, or, from some vantage points, seven mountains that formed a near-circle to protect it.

This remote spot, which not many visitors, or natives, either, ever saw, had been named Lake Pleiades by the Russian explorer Arkady Voronov. As his journal explained:

> On this day we camped opposite the beautiful green glacier which noses into the inlet on the west. A river scintillating in the sunlight attracted my attention, and with two sailors from the *Romanov,*

I explored it for a distance of nine miles. It would be quite unnavigable for even a canoe, because it came tumbling down over rocks, even forming at times small waterfalls eight and ten feet high.

Since it was obvious to us that we were not going to find a better waterway on this course, and since grizzly bears started at us twice, to be deflected by shots over their heads, we had decided to return to our ship with nothing but a fine walk for our labors when one of the sailors, who was breaking the path upstream, shouted back: 'Captain Voronov! Hurry! Something remarkable!'

When we overtook him we saw that his cry was not misleading, for ahead of us, rimmed by six beautiful mountains, lay one of the clearest small lakes I have ever seen. It lay at an elevation, I should guess from the nature of our climb, of about nine hundred feet, not much higher, and it was marred by nothing. Only the bears and whatever fish were in the lake inhabited this magnificent refuge, and we decided on the moment, all three of us, to camp here for the night, for we were loath to depart from such an idyllic place.

I therefore asked each of the men to volunteer for a hurried trip back to the *Romanov* to fetch tents and to bring with him one or two other sailors who might like to share the experience with us, and the man who stepped forward said: 'Captain, with so many bears, I think he should come too,' indicating his partner. 'And he better bring his gun.' I consented, for I realized that I, with my own gun, could protect myself in a settled spot, while they, being on the move, might attract more attention from the bears.

Off they went, and I was left alone in this place of rare beauty. But I did not stay in one place, as planned, because I was lured by the constantly changing attitude of the six mountains which stood guard, and when I had moved some distance to the east, I saw to my surprise that there were not six mountains but seven, and in that moment I determined the name of this lake, Pleiades, because we all know that this little constellation has seven stars, but without a telescope we can see only six. As mythology teaches, the visible six sisters each married gods, but Merope, the hidden seventh, fell in love with a mortal, and thus hides her face in shame.

Lake Pleiades it became, and on three subsequent visits to this eastern area I camped there. It remains the happiest memory of my duty in Alaska, and if, in future generations, some descendant of mine elects to return to these Russian lands, I hope he or she will read these notes and seek out this jewel of a lake.

In September 1900 one hundred million minute eggs of the sockeye salmon were deposited in little streams feeding into that lake. They were delivered by female salmon in lots of four thousand each, and we shall follow the adventures of one such lot, and one salmon within that lot.

The sockeye, one of five distinct types of salmon populating Alaskan waters, had been named by a German naturalist serving Vitus Bering. Using the proper Latin name for salmon plus a native word, he called it *Oncorhynchus nerka,* and the solitary egg of that hundred million whose progress we shall watch will bear that name.

The egg that when fertilized by milt, or sperm, would become Nerka was placed by its mother in a carefully prepared redd, or nest, in the gravelly bottom of a little stream near the lake and left there without further care for six months. It was abandoned not because its parents were negligent but because they were fated to die soon after depositing and fertilizing the eggs that perpetuated their kind.

The site chosen for Nerka's redd had to fulfill several requirements. It had to be close to the lake in which the growing salmon would live for three years. The stream chosen must have a gravel bottom so that the eggs could be securely hidden; it must provide a good supply of other gravel that could be thrown over the redd to hide the incubating eggs; and most curious of all, it had to have a constant supply of fresh water welling up from below at an unwavering temperature of about 47 degrees Fahrenheit and with a supersupply of oxygen.

It so happened that the area surrounding Lake Pleiades had varied radically during the past hundred thousand years, for when the Bering land bridge was open, the ocean level had dropped, taking the lake's level down with it, and as the different levels of the lake fluctuated, so did its shoreline. This meant that various benches had been established at various times, and Nerka's mother had chosen a submerged bench that through the generations had accumulated much gravel of a size that salmon preferred.

But how was the constant supply of upwelling water at a reliable temperature delivered? Just as some ancient river had existed, so another subterranean river, emerging from deep in the roots of the surrounding mountains, surged up through the gravel of that sunken bench, providing the rich supply of oxygen and constant temperature that kept both the lake and its salmon vital.

So for six months, his parents long dead, Nerka in his minute egg nestled beneath the gravel while from below flowed the life-giving water. It was one of the most precise operations of nature—perfect flow of water, perfect temperature, perfect hiding place, perfect beginning for one of the most extraordinary life histories in the animal kingdom. And one final attribute of Lake Pleiades could be considered the most remarkable of all: the rocks that lined the lake and the waters that flowed into it from the submerged rivulets carried minute traces—perhaps one in a billion parts—of one mineral or another, with the result that Lake Pleiades had a kind of lacustrine fingerprint that would differentiate it from any other lake or river in the entire world.

Any salmon born, as Nerka would soon be, in Lake Pleiades would bear with him always the unique imprint of this lake. Was this memory carried in his bloodstream, or in his brain, or in his olfactory system, or perhaps in a group of these attributes in conjunction with the phases of the moon or the turning of the earth? No one knew. One could only guess, but that Nerka and Lake Pleiades on the western shore of Alaska were indissolubly linked, no one could deny.

Still only a minute egg, he nestled in the gravel as subterranean waters welled up through the bench to sustain him, and each week he grew closer to birth. In January 1901, deep under the thick ice that pressed down upon the tributary system, the egg that would become Nerka the salmon, along with the other four thousand fertilized eggs of his group, underwent a dramatic change. His egg, a brilliant orange color, showed through the skin an eye with a bright rim and an intensely black center. Unquestionably it was an eye, and it bespoke the emerging life within the egg. But the natural attrition that decimated these minute creatures was savage. Of the original four thousand, only six hundred survived the freezing gravel, the diseases and the predation by larger fish.

In late February of that year these six hundred eggs of Nerka's group began to undergo a series of miraculous changes, at the conclusion of which they would become full-fledged salmon. The embryo Nerka slowly absorbed the nutrients from the yolk sac, and as the interchange occurred, he grew and developed swimming motions. Now he obtained the first of a series of names, each marking a major step in his growth. He was an *alevin*.

When his yolk was completely absorbed, the creature was still not a proper fish, only a minute translucent wand with enormous black eyes and, fastened to his belly, a huge sac of liquid nutrient on which he must live for the next crucial weeks. He was an ugly, misshapen, squirming thing, and any passing predator could gulp down hundreds like him at a time. But he was a potential fish with a monstrously long head, functioning eyes and a trailing translucent tail. Rapidly in the constantly moving waters of his stream he began to consume plankton, and with the growth that this produced, his protruding sac was gradually resorbed until the creature was transformed into a self-sufficient baby fishling.

At this point Nerka left his natal stream and moved the short distance into the lake, where he was properly called a fry, and in this condition he showed every characteristic, except size, of a normal freshwater fish. He would breathe like one through his gills; he would eat like one; he would learn to swim swiftly to dodge larger predators; and it would seem to any observer that he was well adapted to spend the rest of his life in this lake. In those first years it would have seemed preposterous to think that one day, still to be determined by his rate of growth and maturation, he would be able to convert his entire life processes so radically that he would be completely adapted to salt water.

Ignorant of his strange destiny, Nerka spent the next two years adjusting to life within the lake, which presented two contradictory aspects. On the one hand it was a savage home where salmon fry were destroyed at appalling rates. Larger fish hungered for him. Birds sought him out, especially the merganser ducks that abounded on the lake, but also kingfishers and stiltlike birds with long legs and even longer beaks that could dart through the water with incredible accuracy to snap up a tasty meal of salmon. It seemed as if everything in the lake lived on fry, and half of Nerka's fellow survivors vanished into gullets before the end of the first year.

But the lake was also a nurturing mother that provided young fry with a multitude of dark places in which to hide during daylight hours and a jungle of underwater grasses in which they could lose themselves if light, dancing off their shimmering skin, betrayed their presence to the larger fish. Nerka learned to move only in the darkest nights and to avoid those places where these fish liked to feed, and since in these two years he was not even three inches long, and most things that swam were larger and more powerful than he, it was only by exercising these precautions that he managed to survive.

He was now a fingerling, a most appropriate name, since he was about the size of a woman's little finger, and as his appetite increased, the comforting lake provided him with nutritious insect larvae and various kinds of plankton. As he grew older he fed upon the myriad tiny fishes that flashed about, but his main delight was twisting upward, head out of water, to snare some unsuspecting insect.

Nerka, now three years old, had settled into a routine in freshwater Lake Pleiades that looked as if it would continue throughout his lifetime. But one morning, after a week of agitation, he sprang into unprecedented action, as if a bell had summoned him and all the sockeye of his generation to the performance of some grand, significant task.

And then, for reasons he could not identify, his nerves jangled as if an electric shock had coursed through his body, leaving him agitated and restless. Driven by impulses he did not understand, he found himself repelled by the once-comforting fresh water of his natal lake and for some days he thrashed about. Suddenly one night, Nerka, followed by thousands of his generation, began to swim toward the exit of the lake and plunged into the rushing waters of the Pleiades River. But even as he departed, he had a premonition that he must one day, in years far distant, return to this congenial water in which he had been bred. He was now a smolt, on the verge of becoming a mature salmon. His skin had assumed the silvery sheen of an adult, and although he was still but a few inches long, he looked like a salmon.

With powerful strokes of his growing tail he sped down the Pleiades, and when he was confronted by rapids tumbling over exposed rocks he knew instinctively the safest way to descend, but when waterfalls of more ominous height threatened his progress he hesitated, judged alternatives, then sprang into vigorous activity, leaping almost joyously into the spray, thrashing his way down, and landing with a thump at the bottom, where he rested for a moment before resuming his journey.

Did he, through some complex biological mechanism, record these waterfalls as he descended them, storing knowledge against that fateful day, two years hence, when he would be impelled to climb them in the opposite direction in order to enable some equally determined female sockeye to spawn? His return trip would be one of the most remarkable feats in the animal world.

But now as he approached the lower reaches of the river he faced a major peril, because at a relatively inconsequential waterfall, which he normally could have handled with ease, he was either so tired or so careless that he allowed himself to be thrown against a rock protruding from the downward current; the result was that he landed with an awkward splash at the foot of the falls, where, awaiting just such mishaps, a group of voracious Dolly Vardon trout, each bigger than the salmon smolts, prowled the waters. With swift, darting motions the trout leaped at the stunned smolts, devouring them in startling numbers, and it seemed likely that Nerka, totally disoriented by slamming against the rock, would be an easy prey and disappear before he ever reached the salt water that was luring him.

But he had already proved himself to be a determined fish, and now he instinctively dodged the first attack of the trout, then dropped into protective weeds from which the larger fish could not dislodge him, and in this manner evaded the hungry attacks of the trout.

Of the four thousand salmon born in Nerka's group in Lake Pleiades in 1901, how many now survived? That is, how many swam down the Pleiades River to fulfill their destiny in the ocean? The constant depletion had been so frightful and so constant that 3,968 had perished, leaving only thirty-two alive and ready for the adventure in the ocean. But upon those pitiful few the great salmon industry of Alaska would be built, and it would be Nerka and the other fighting, self-protective fish like him who would keep canneries like the Totem Cannery on Taku Inlet so richly profitable.

At last, one morning, Nerka, having fended off long-legged herons and diving mergansers, approached the most critical moment of his life so far: this freshwater fish was about to plunge into the briny waters of the sea, not inch by inch or slowly over a period of weeks, but with one sweep of his tail and the activation of his fins. True, the change from lake to seawater had been occurring gradually, but even so, the leap to all seawater was momentous.

When he entered the new medium it was an almost lethal shock. For several days he found himself reeling, recoiling from the salt, and in this virtually comatose condition he faced a terrible danger. An immense flock of voracious white gulls and black ravens hovered low in a sullen sky, eager to dive down and catch the floundering smolts in their beaks and carry them aloft for feeding. The devastation wreaked by these screaming scavengers was awesome: thousands of smolts perished in their sharp claws, and those that miraculously survived did so only by pure luck.

Nerka, slow to adjust to the salt water, was especially vulnerable, because from time to time he drifted listlessly on his side, an easy target for the diving birds. But sheer chance saved him, and after one near miss he revived enough to send himself down deep toward the darkness he loved, and there away from the predators, he worked his gills, forcing the unfamiliar seawater through his system.

Most of that summer Nerka and his fellows lingered in Taku Inlet, gorging themselves on the rich plankton blooms and adjusting to the salt water. They began to grow. Their senses quickened. Surprisingly, they were no longer afraid to battle larger fish. They were now full-fledged salmon, and gradually they worked their way toward the mouth of the inlet as they began to hunger for the squid, shrimp and small fish that flourished there. And as they matured they felt an urge to move out into the open ocean to new adventures in its swirling waters.

Of his thirty-one companions who made it to the mouth of Taku Inlet, about half perished before they reached the ocean, but Nerka survived, and he swam forward eagerly, scraping past the protruding rock of the Walrus, leaving Taku Inlet, and heading westward to the Pacific.

A gyre is a massive body of seawater which retains its own peculiar characteristics and circular motion, even though it is an integral part of the great ocean that surrounds it. The name comes from the same root as 'gyrate' and 'gyroscope' and obviously pertains to the circular or spiral motion of the water. How a gyre is able to maintain its identity within the bosom of a tumultuous ocean poses an interesting problem whose unraveling carries one back to the beginnings of the universe. In our day the great Japan Current sweeps its warm waters from Japan across the northern reaches of the Pacific to the coasts of Alaska, Canada and Oregon, modifying those climates and bringing much rain. But this and all other ocean currents have been set in motion by planetary winds created by the differential heating of various latitudinal belts, and this is caused by the earth's spin, which was set in primordial motion when a diffuse nebular cloud coalesced into our solar system. This carries us all the way back to the original Big Bang that started our particular universe on its way.

A gyre, then, is a big whirl which generates at its edges smaller whirls whose motion increases its viscosity, forming a kind of protective barrier around the parent gyre, which can then maintain its integrity eon after eon. One professor of oceanography, name now unknown, striving to help his students grasp this beautiful concept, offered them a jingle:

> Big whirls make little whirls
> That feed on their velocity
> Little whirls make lesser whirls
> And so on to viscosity.

The Pacific houses many of these self-preserving gyres, one of the most important being the Alaskan, which dominates the area just south of the Aleutian Islands. Reaching more than two thousand fluctuating miles from east to west, four hundred variable miles from north to south, it forms a unique body of water whose temperature and abundant food supply make it irresistible to the salmon bred in Alaska and Canada. This gyre circulates in a vast counterclockwise motion, and the sockeye like Nerka who enter it swim with the current in this unvarying counterclockwise direction. Of course, the very fine salmon bred in Japan start from a contrary orientation, so they swim their ordained route clockwise, against the movement of the gyre. In doing so, they repeatedly pass through the larger number of Alaskan salmon, forming for a few hours a huge conglomeration of one of the world's most valuable fish.

For two years, starting in 1904, Nerka, accompanied by the remaining eleven survivors of his group of four thousand sockeye, swam in the Alaskan Gyre, forming part of the rich food chain of the North Pacific. Mammoth whales would swim past, with cavernous mouths capable of sucking in whole schools of salmon. Seals had a predilection for salmon and sped through the gyre decimating the ranks. Birds attacked from the sky, and from the deeper waters came big fish like tuna, pollock and swordfish to feed upon the salmon. Each day consisted of a ten-mile swim with the current in an ocean literally teeming with enemies, and in this perpetual struggle the salmon that survived grew strong. Nerka was now about twenty-five inches long, seven pounds in weight, and although he looked almost immature in comparison with the huge king salmon of the Pacific or the even larger members of the salmon family living in the Atlantic, of his type he was becoming a superb specimen.

The reddish color of his flesh stemmed in part from his love of shrimp, which he devoured in huge quantities, although he fed on the larger forms of plankton, gradually shifting to squid and small fish. He belonged to a midrange of the ocean hierarchies. Too big to be an automatic prey of the seal and the orca whale, he was at the same time too small to be a major predator. But, all in all, he was a tough, self-reliant master of the deep.

During his three and a half irregular circuits of the Alaskan Gyre, Nerka would cover a total of about ten thousand miles, sometimes swimming largely alone, at other periods finding himself in the midst of an enormous concentration. For example, when he reached the halfway point, where sockeye more mature than he began to break away and head back to their home streams, he was drifting along the lower edges of the Aleutian chain when a massive concentration of salmon composed of all five Alaskan types—king, chum, pink, coho and sockeye—began to form, and it grew until it contained about thirty million fish, swimming in the same counterclockwise direction and feeding upon whatever they encountered.

But now a large collection of seals heading for their breeding grounds in the Arctic Ocean came rampaging through the middle of the aggregation, devouring salmon at a rate that would have exterminated a less numerous fish. Two female seals swimming with amazing speed came right at Nerka, who sensed that he was doomed, but with a sudden twist he dove. The two seals had to swerve to avoid colliding, and he escaped, but from his vantage point below the turmoil he witnessed the devastation the seals wreaked. Thousands of mature salmon perished in that ruthless onslaught, but after two days the seals passed beyond the outer fringes and continued on their journey north. But Nerka's group was now down to nine.

Nerka was almost an automatic creature, for he behaved in obedience to impulses programmed into his being half a million years earlier. For example, in these years when he thrived in the Alaskan Gyre he lived as if he had belonged there forever, and in his sport with other fish and his adventures with those larger mammals that were trying to eat him he behaved as if he had never known any other type of life. He could not remember ever having lived in fresh water, and were he suddenly to be thrown back into it, he would not have been able to adjust: he was a creature of the gyre as irrevocably as if he had been born within its confines.

But in his second year in the great Alaskan Gyre a genetically driven change occurred in Nerka, compelling him to seek out his natal stream above Lake Pleiades. And now a complex homing mechanism, still not fully understood by scientists, came into play to guide him over thousands of miles to that one stream along the Alaskan coast. Though employing this inherited memory for the first time in his own life, Nerka did so instinctively and unerringly, and thus began his journey home.

The clues guiding Nerka were subtle: minute shifts in water temperature triggered his response, or it could have been electromagnetic changes. Certainly, as he approached the coast his sense of smell, among the most sensitive in all the world's animals, detected trace chemical markers similar to those in his own Pleiades. This chemical distinction could have been a difference of less than one part in a billion, but there it was. Its influence persisted and grew, guiding Nerka ever more compellingly to his home waters. It is one of the strangest manifestations of nature, this minute message sent through the waters of the world to guide a wandering salmon back to his natal stream.

When Nerka began receiving signals warning him that it was time he started for home, the message was so compelling that even though he was far from Lake Pleiades he began to swim undeviatingly toward it. Sweeping his tail in powerful arcs with a vigor not used before, he shot through the water not at his customary ten miles a day but at a speed four or five times that fast.

In his earlier circuits of the Alaskan Gyre he had always been content to string along with his fellows, male or female, and rarely had he distinguished between the two, but now he took pains to avoid other males, as if he realized that with his new obligations, they had become not only his competitors but also his potential enemies.

From his accidental position in the gyre when these signals arrived he could reasonably have headed for Oregon or Kamchatka or the Yukon, but in obedience to the homing device implanted in him years ago, he followed his signal—that wisp of a shadow of a lost echo—and from one of the most isolated parts of the Pacific he launched himself precisely on a course that would lead him to Taku Inlet and Lake Pleiades, where he would undertake the most important assignment of his life.

On the first of May he was still 1,250 miles from home, but the signals were now so intense that he began swimming at a steady forty-nine miles a day, and as he sped through the gyre he began to feed prodigiously, consuming incredible numbers of fish, three or four times as many as ever before. Indeed, he ate ravenously even when not really hungry, as if he knew that once he left the ocean he would never again eat as long as he lived.

In early September he entered Taku Inlet, and when he immersed himself in its fresh waters, his body began to undergo one of the most extraordinary transformations in the animal kingdom—it was an ugly one, as if he sought a frightening appearance to aid him in the battles he would soon be facing. When he was swimming through the gyre, he had been a handsome fish, quite beautiful when he twisted in the light, but now, in obedience to internal signals, he was transformed into something grotesque. He became extremely prognathous, his lower teeth extending so far beyond those in the upper jaw that they looked like a shark's; his snout turned inward, bending down to form a hook; and most disfiguring of all, his back developed a great hump and changed its color to a flaming red. His once svelte and streamlined body thickened, and he became in general a ferocious creature driven by urges he could not hope to understand.

With determination he swam toward his natal lake, but his course brought him to where the trap of Totem Cannery waited with its very long jiggers, making entry to the Pleiades River impossible. Bewildered by the barrier, which had not been operating when he left the lake, he stopped, reconnoitered the situation like a general, and watched as thousands of his fellows drifted supinely along the jiggers and into the trap. He felt no compassion for them, but he knew that he must not allow this unusual barrier to stop him from fighting through to his river. Every nerve along his spine, every impulse in his minute brain warned him that he must somehow circumvent the trap, and he could do so by leaping across the lethal jigger.

Swimming as close to the right bank as he could, he was encouraged by the cold fresh water that came from the Pleiades River carrying a powerful message from the lake, but when he attempted to swim toward the source of the reassuring water, he was once more frustrated by the jigger. Bewildered, he was about to drift toward the fatal center when a sockeye somewhat larger than he came up from behind, detected a sagging spot in the jigger, and with a mighty sweep of his tail leaped over it, splashing heavily into the free water beyond.

As if shot from a gun, Nerka sped forward, activated his tail and fins and arched himself high in the air, only to strike the top strand of the jigger, which threw him roughly backward. For some moments he tried to fathom what had caused him to fail when the other fish had succeeded, then, with a greater effort he tried again, and again he was repulsed by the jigger.

He lay for some minutes resting in the cool water drifting down from the Pleiades, and when he felt his strength returning he started swimming with great sweeps of his tail, and mustering all his strength, he sped like a bullet at the jigger, arched himself higher than before, and landed with a loud splash on the upstream side.

A workman from the cannery, observing the remarkable leaps of these two salmon, called to his mates: 'We better add two more strands to the jigger. Those two that got across were beauties.'

It was crucial that Nerka survive to complete his mission, for of the four thousand that had been born in his generation, only six remained, and upon them rested the fate of the Pleiades sockeye.

When Nerka the salmon leaped over the jigger in order to return to the Pleiades River, he faced the reverse of the problem that had threatened him three years earlier. Now, as a fish acclimated to life in salt water, he must relearn how to live in fresh, and this sharp alteration required two days of slow swimming in the new medium. But gradually he adjusted, and now the excess fat that he had acquired in his hump during his burst of prodigious eating became an asset, keeping him alive and strong enough to ascend the waterfalls of the river, for once he entered fresh water he would never again feed, his entire digestive system having atrophied to the point of nonfunction.

He had nine miles of upstream swimming to negotiate before he reached the lake, and this was a task immeasurably more difficult than swimming down had been. Not only did he have to leap over major obstacles, but he also had to protect himself from the large number of bears that lined the river, knowing that the fat salmon were coming.

At the first rapids he proved his ability, for he swam directly up the middle, breasting the full power of the stream and propelling himself forward with forceful strokes of his tail. But it was when he reached the first waterfall, about eight feet high, that he demonstrated his unusual skill, for after hoarding his strength at the bottom, he suddenly darted at the falling plume of water, lifted himself in the air, and leaped the full eight feet, vibrating his tail furiously. With an effort not often matched in the animal kingdom, he overcame that considerable obstacle.

The third waterfall was not a vertical drop but a long, sliding affair of rapidly rushing, turbulent water some eighteen feet long and with such a sharp drop that it looked as if no fish could scale it, and certainly not in a single bound.

Here Nerka used another tactic. He made a furious dash right at the heart of the oncoming flow, and within the waterfall itself he swam and leaped and scrambled until he found a precarious lodging halfway up. There he rested for some moments, gathering energy for the greater trial to come.

Trapped in the middle of the fall, he obviously could not build up forward motion, but rising almost vertically, with his tail thrashing madly, he could resume his attack. Once more he swam, not leaped, right up the heart of the fall, and after a prodigious effort he broke free to reach calm water, in which he rested for a long time.

The most perilous part of his homeward journey now loomed, for in his exhausted state he failed to practice the cautions that had kept him alive for six years, and in his drifting he came within range of a group of bears that had gathered at this spot because their kind had learned centuries ago that after the homecoming salmon finished battling the waterfall, they would for some time flop aimlessly about and become easy prey.

One large bear had waded some feet into the river, where it was scooping up exhausted salmon and tossing them back onto the bank, where others fell on them to tear at their flesh. This bear, spotting Nerka as the most promising salmon of the morning's run, leaned forward like an ardent angler, caught Nerka full under the belly with its right paw and with a mighty swipe tossed him far behind it, like an angler landing a prize trout.

As Nerka flew through the air he was aware of two things: the bear's claws had ripped his right flank but not fatally, and the direction in which he was flying contained some areas that looked like water. So as soon as he landed with a hard thump on dry land, with two large bears leaping forward to kill him, he went through a series of wild gyrations, summoning all the power his tail, fins and body muscles could provide. Just as the bears were about to grab him he leaped toward one of the shimmering areas, which turned out to be a sluggish arm of the river, and he was saved.

Now, as he neared the lake, the unique signal composed of mineral traces, the position of the sun, perhaps the gyration of the earth and maybe the operation of some peculiar electrical force, became overwhelming. For more than two thousand miles he had attended to this signal, and now it throbbed throughout his aging body: This is Lake Pleiades. This is home.

He reached the lake on 23 September 1906, and when he entered the jewellike body of water with its projecting mountains, he found his way to that small feeder stream with its particular aggregation of gravel in which he had been born six years earlier, and now for the first time in his life he began to look about him not just for another salmon but for a female, and when other males swam by he recognized them as enemies and drove them off. The culminating experience of his life was about to begin, but only he and two others of his original four thousand had made it back to their home waters. All the rest had perished amid the dangers imposed by the incredible cycle of the salmon.

Mysteriously, out of a dark overhang that produced the deep shadows loved by sockeye, she came, a mature female who had shared the dangers he had known, who had in her own way avoided the jiggers reaching out to trap her and who had ascended the waterfalls with her own skills and tricks. She was his equal in every way except for the fierce prognathous lower jaw that he had developed, and she, too, was ready for the final act.

Moving quietly beside him as if to say 'I shall look to you for protection,' she began waving her tail and fins gently, brushing away silt that had fallen upon the gravel she intended using. In time, employing only these motions, she dug herself a redd, or nest, about six inches deep and twice her length, which was now more than two feet. When the redd was prepared, she tested it again to ensure that the steady stream of life-giving cold water was still welling up from the hidden river, and when she felt its reassuring presence, she was ready.

Now the slow, dreamlike courtship dance began, with Nerka nudging closer and closer, rubbing his fins against hers, swimming a slight distance away, then rushing back. Other males, aware of her presence, hurried up, but whenever one appeared, Nerka drove him off, and the lyrical dance continued.

Then a startling change occurred: both salmon opened their mouths as wide as their jaw sockets would allow, forming large cavernous passageways for the entrance of fresh water. It was if they wished to purify themselves, to wash away old habits in preparation for what was about to happen, and when this ritual was completed they experienced wild and furious surges of courtship emotions, twisting together, their jaws snapping and their tails quivering. When their energetic ballet ended, with their mouths once more agape, the female released some four thousand eggs, and at that precise instant Nerka ejected his milt, or sperm, over the entire area. Fertilization would occur by chance, but the incredible flood of milt made it probable that each egg would receive its sperm and that Nerka and his mate would have done their part in perpetuating their species.

Their destiny having been fulfilled, their mysterious travels were over, and an incredible climax to their lives awaited. Since they had eaten nothing since leaving the ocean, not even a minnow, and were so exhausted by their travel up Taku Inlet, their battle with traps and their swim upstream against waterfalls, they retained not a shred of the vital force. They began to drift aimlessly, and wayward currents eased them along a nepenthean course to the spot where the lake emptied into the river.

When they entered the lively swirls of that stream they were momentarily revived, and fluttered their tails in the customary way, but they were so weak that nothing happened, and the current dragged them passively to where the falls and the rapids began.

As they reached the fatal spot at the head of the long falls, where bears waited, Nerka summoned enough energy to swim clear, but his mate, near death, could not, and one of the biggest animals reached in, caught her in its powerful claws, and threw her ashore, where other bears leaped at her.

In a brief moment she was gone.

Had Nerka been in possession of his faculties, he would never have allowed the long waterfall to grasp him and smash him willy-nilly down its most precipitous drops and onto its most dangerous rocks, but that is what happened, and the last shuddering drop was so destructive that he felt the final shreds of life being knocked out of him. Vainly he tried to regain control of his destiny, but the relentless water kept knocking him abusively from rock to rock, and the last he saw of the earth and its waters of which he had been such a joyous part was a great spume into which he was sucked against his will and the massive rock which lurked behind it. With a sickening smash, he was no more.

He had returned to the Lake Pleiades system on 21 September 1906. He had fathered the next generation of sockeye on the twenty-fifth, and now on the last day of the month he was dead. He had lived five years, six months and had discharged all obligations courageously and as nature had programmed him to do.

For three miles his dead body drifted downstream, until waves washed it to sanctuary in a backwater where ravens, familiar with the habits of the river, waited. He reached their domain about four in the afternoon of an increasingly cold day when food was essential, and by nightfall only his bones were left.

ONK-OR

IN THE REMOTE wastes of northern Canada, where man was rarely seen except when lost and about to perish, a family of great geese, in the late summer of 1822, made their home on a forlorn stretch of Arctic moorland. Mother, father, six fledglings—because of a freak of nature they had come to a moment of terrifying danger.

The two adult birds, splendid heavy creatures weighing close to fourteen pounds and with wings normally capable of carrying them five thousand miles in flight, could not get off the ground. At a time when they had to feed and protect their offspring, they were powerless to fly. This was no accident, nor the result of any unfortunate experience with wolves; like all their breed, they lost their heavy wing feathers every summer and remained earthbound for about six weeks, during which they could only hide from their enemies and walk ineffectively over the moorland, waiting for their feathers to return. It was for this reason that they had laid their eggs in such a remote spot, for during their moulting period they were almost defenseless.

Onk-or, the father in this family, strutted about the bushes seeking seeds, while his mate stayed near the nest to tend the fledglings, whose appetites were insatiable. Occasionally when Onk-or brought food to the younglings, his mate would run long distances as if pleased to escape the drudgery of tending her brood, but on this day when she reached the top of a grassy mound she ran faster, flapped the wings she had not used for six weeks and flew back toward her nest, uttering loud cries as she did so.

Onk-or looked up, saw the flight and knew that within a day or two he would be soaring too; always her feathers grew back faster than his. As she flew past he spoke to her.

Maintaining a medium altitude, she headed north to where an arm of the sea intruded, and there she landed on water, splashing it ahead of her when her feet slammed down to act as brakes. Other geese landed to eat the seeds floating on the waves, and after weeks of loneliness she enjoyed their companionship, but before long she rose on the water, flapped her wings slowly, gathered speed amid great splashing, then soared into the air to head back to her nest. From long habit, she landed short of where her fledglings lay, moved around them casually to deceive any foxes that might be watching, then collected bits of food, which she carried to her children. As soon as she appeared, Onk-or walked away, still unable to fly, to gather more food.

He and his mate were handsome birds, large and sleek. Both they and their children had long jet-black necks, with a broad snowy white bib under the chin and reaching to the ears. When their wings were folded, as they were most of the time, the heavy body was compact and beautifully proportioned, and they walked with dignity, not waddling from side to side like ducks. Their heads were finely proportioned, with bills pointed but not grotesquely long, and their pleasingly shaped bodies were feathered in differing shades of gray. Their subdued coloring was so appropriate to the Arctic moorland that an observer, had there been one, could have come close to their nest without noticing them.

On this day there was an observer, an Arctic fox who had not eaten for some time and was beginning to feel acute pangs of hunger. When from a distance he spotted the rough nest on the ground, with the six fledglings tumbling about and obviously not old enough to fly, he took no precipitate action, for he had learned respect for the sharp beaks and powerful wings of full-grown geese like Onk-or.

Instead he retreated and ran in large circles far from the nest, until he roused another fox to make the hunt with him. Together they returned quietly across the tundra, moving from the security of one tussock to the next, scouting the terrain ahead and developing the strategy they would use to pick off the young geese.

During the brightest part of the day they lay in wait, for long ago they had learned that it was easier to attack at night, when they would be less conspicuous against the Arctic grass. Of course, during the nesting season of the geese there was no real night; the sun stayed in the heavens perpetually, scudding low in the north but never disappearing. Instead of blackness, which would last interminably during the winter, there came only a diffused grayness in the middle hours, a ghostly penumbra, with geese, young and old, half asleep. That was the time to attack.

So as the sun drifted lower in the west on a long, sliding trajectory that would never dip below the horizon, and as the bright glare of summer faded to an exquisite gray matching the feathers of the geese, the two foxes moved slowly forward toward the nest where the six fledglings hid beneath the capacious wings of their mother. Onk-or, the foxes noted, lay some distance away with his head under his left wing.

It was the plan of the foxes that the stronger of the pair would attack Onk-or from such a direction that the big male goose would be lured even farther from the nest, and as the fight progressed, the other fox would dart in, engage the female briefly, and while she was awkwardly trying to defend herself, grab one of the young geese and speed away. In the confusion the first fox might very well be able to grab a second fledgling for himself. If not, they would share the one they did get.

When the foxes had attained a strategic position, the first made a lunge at Onk-or, attacking from the side on which he had tucked his head, on the logical supposition that if the great goose was not instantly alert, the fox might be lucky and grab him by the throat, ending the fight then and there. But as soon as the fox accelerated his pace, knocking aside grasses, Onk-or was aware of what was happening. He did not try evasive action or do anything unusual to protect his neck; instead he pivoted on his left leg, swung his moulted wing in a small circle and with its bony edge knocked his adversary flat.

Onk-or knew that the fox would try to lure him away from the nest, so instead of following up on his first blow, he retreated toward the low pile of sticks and grass that constituted his nest, making sharp clicking sounds to alert his family. His mate, aware that the family was being attacked, drew the fledglings under her wings and studied the ominous grayness.

She did not have long to wait. As the first fox lunged at Onk-or again, the second swept in to attack the nest itself. She had only one flashing moment to ascertain from which direction the attack was coming, but she judged accurately, rose, spread her wings and pivoted to meet the fox. As he leaped at her, she struck him across the face with her powerful beak, stunning him momentarily.

He soon recovered to make a second attack. This time she was prepared, and a harsh swipe of her wing edge sent him sprawling, but this terrified her, for instinct warned her that he might cunningly have seemed to fall so as to distract her. If she struck at him now, he would slyly dart behind her and grab one of the fledglings. So as the fox fell, she wheeled on her right foot, placing herself and her extended rear wings between him and the nest. As for the rear, she had to depend upon Onk-or to protect that from the other fox.

This he was doing. In the half-light he fought the clever fox, fending him off with vicious stabs of his beak, knocking him down with his powerful wing thrusts and filling the Arctic air with short cries of rage and challenge. The fox, who had never been confident that he could subdue a grown male goose, began to lose any hope that he could even hold his own against this infuriated bird. Furthermore, he saw that his partner had accomplished nothing at the nest and was, indeed, receiving an equal thrashing.

Hoping in vain that the two geese would make some fatal mistake, the two foxes battled on for a while but finally recognized the futility of their attack and withdrew, making short, chattering noises to one another as they did.

When daylight came the two parent geese knew how necessary it was that their children proceed with learning the art of flying. So on this day Onk-or did not leave the nest to forage for his family; he stayed by the odd collection of twigs and grasses and nudged his children out onto the moorland, watching them as they clumsily tried their wings.

They were an ungainly lot, stumbling and falling and vainly beating their long wings, but they were gradually attaining the mastery that would enable them to fly south to the waters of Maryland. Two of the young birds actually hoisted themselves in the air, staying aloft for short distances, then landing with maximum awkwardness and joy.

A third, watching the success of her siblings, flapped her wings clumsily, ran across the rocky ground and with great effort got herself into the air, but as soon as she did so, Onk-or felt a rush of terror, for he saw something she did not.

Too late! The gosling, unable to maintain flight, fluttered heavily to the ground, landing precisely where the two foxes had been waiting for such a misadventure. But as they started for the fallen bird, Onk-or, with supreme effort, flapped his wings, which were not yet ready for flight, rose in the air and endeavored to strike down the foxes. His wings were not equal to the task, and he, too, fell, but he was quickly on his feet and charged at the two foxes. Insolently, the first fox grabbed the gosling, killing it with one savage snap of the jaws, and sped away. The second fox ran in circles, tantalizing Onk-or, then disappeared to join his partner in their feast.

What did this family of seven think as they reassembled? Onk-or and his mate, like their fellow geese, were unusual in the animal kingdom in that they mated for life. They were as tightly married as any human couple in a conventional suburban town; each cared desperately about what happened to the other, and Onk-or would have unhesitatingly sacrificed his life to protect that of his mate. Four times they had flown together down from the Arctic to the Eastern Shore, and four times back. Together they had located safe resting spots up and down eastern Canada and in all the seaboard states of America. Aloft, they communicated instinctively, each knowing what the other intended, and on the ground, when nesting in the Arctic or feeding along the Choptank, each always felt responsible for the safety of the other.

In this habit of permanent marriage they were like few other birds, certainly not like the lesser ducks, who mated at will, staying close to each other only so long as their ducklings needed protection. Beavers also married for life—perhaps because they had to live together during their winters in lodges frozen over—but few other animals did. Onk-or was married to his mate, eternally.

His first response, therefore, as the foxes disappeared with one of his daughters, was to assure himself that his mate was safe. Satisfied on this crucial point, his attention shifted to his five remaining children. They must learn to fly—now—and not stumble into traps set by enemies.

His mate, who had remained on the ground during the loss of the fledgling, had not been able to ascertain what was happening with the foxes, for the incident had occurred behind a cluster of tussocks, and for one dreadful moment she had feared that it might be Onk-or the foxes had taken. She was relieved when she saw him stumbling back, for he was half her life, the gallant, fearless bird on whom she must depend.

But she also possessed a most powerful urge to protect her offspring; she would surrender her own life to achieve this, and now the first of them had been stolen. She did not grieve, as she would have done had Onk-or been killed, but she did feel an intense sense of loss and, like her mate, determined that the other five must quickly learn to fly. In the days to come she would be a rigorous teacher.

As for the goslings, each knew that a fox had stolen the missing fledgling. Each knew that tragedy, from which their parents tried to protect them, had struck, and the nascent urges that had caused them to attempt flight were intensified. They had never made the long pilgrimage to the feeding grounds of Maryland, but intuitively they knew that such grounds must be somewhere and they should ready themselves for the migration. They were determined to master their wings; they were determined to protect themselves from foxes.

Of course, these birds were too young to have selected partners, nor had they associated with other geese. But even at this early stage they were aware of the difference between the sexes, so that the three young males were looking for something quite different from what the two remaining females were awaiting, and as other families of geese flew overhead, each fledgling could differentiate the children in that tentative flock. They knew. At seven weeks it was incredible what these young geese knew, and if by some ill chance both their parents were killed, leaving them orphaned in the Arctic, they would know how to fly to Maryland and find the Choptank cove that had been designated as their home. All they needed for maturity was the strengthening of their wings and the selection of a mate from the other fledglings born that year. They were a doughty breed, one of the great birds of the world, and they behaved as such.

In mid-September, as in each year of their lives, Onk-or and his mate felt irresistible urges. They watched the sky and were particularly responsive to the shortening of the day. They noticed with satisfaction that their five offspring were large and powerful birds; with notable wing spans, and sustaining accumulations of fat, they were ready for any flight. They also noticed the browning of the grasses and the ripening of certain seeds, the unmistakable signs that the time of departure was imminent.

At all the nests in the Arctic this restlessness developed and birds bickered with one another. Males would suddenly rise in the sky and fly long distances for no apparent reason, returning later to land in clouds of dust. No meetings were held; there was no visible assembling of families. But one day, for reasons that could not be explained, huge flocks of birds rose into the sky, milled about and then formed into companies headed south.

This southward migration was one of the marvels of nature: hundreds, thousands, millions of these huge geese forming into perfect V-shaped squadrons flying at different altitudes and at different times of day, but all heading out of Canada down one of the four principal flyways leading to varied corners of America. Some flew at twenty-nine thousand feet above the ground, others as low as three thousand, but all sought escape from the freezing moorlands of the Arctic, heading for warmer feeding grounds like those in Maryland. For long spells they would fly in silence, but most often they maintained noisy communication, arguing, protesting, exulting; at night especially they uttered cries that echoed forever in the memories of men who heard them drifting down through the frosty air of autumn: *'Onk-or, onk-or!'*

The wedge in which Onk-or and his family started south this year consisted of eighty-nine birds, but it did not stay together permanently as a cohesive unit. Sometimes other groups would meld with it, until the flying formation contained several hundred birds; at other times sections would break away to fly with some other unit. But in general the wedge held together.

The geese flew at a speed of about forty-five miles an hour, which meant that if they stayed aloft for an entire day, they could cover a thousand miles. But they required rest, and through the centuries during which they had followed the same route south and north their kind had learned of various ponds and lakes and riverbanks that afforded them secure places to rest and forage. There were lakes in upper Quebec and small streams leading into the St. Lawrence. In Maine there were hundreds of options and suitable spots in western Massachusetts and throughout New York, and the older geese like Onk-or knew them all.

On some days, near noon when the autumn sun was high, the geese would descend abruptly and alight on a lake that their ancestors had been utilizing for a thousand years. The trees along the shore would have changed, and new generations of fish would occupy the waters, but the seeds and the succulent grasses would be the same kind. Here the birds would rest for six or seven hours, and then as dusk approached, the leaders would utter signals and the flock would scud across the surface of the lake and wheel into the air. There they would form themselves automatically into a long V, with some old, sage bird like Onk-or in the lead, and through the night they would fly south.

Maine, New Hampshire, Massachusetts, Connecticut, New York, Pennsylvania! The states would lie sleeping below, only a few dim lamps betraying their existence, and overhead the geese would go, crying in the night *'Onk-or, onk-or,'* and occasionally, at the edge of some village or on some farm a door would open and light would flood the area for a while, and parents would hold their children and peer into the dark sky, listening to the passing of the geese. And once in a great while, on such a night when the moon was full, the children would actually see the flying wedge pass silhouetted against the moon, and they would speak of this for the rest of their lives.

No goose, not even a powerful one like Onk-or, could fly at the head of the wedge for long periods. The buffeting of the wind as the point of the V broke through a path in the air turbulence was too punishing. The best a practiced bird could do was about forty minutes, during which time he absorbed considerable thrashing. After his allotted time in the lead position, the exhausted goose would drop to the back of one of the arms of the wedge, where the weaker birds had been assembled, and there, with the air well broken ahead of him, he could coast along in the wake of others, recovering his strength until it came his time again to assume the lead. Male and female alike accepted this responsibility, and when the day's flight ended they were content to rest. On especially favorable lakes with copious food they might stay for a week.

During the first days of October the geese were usually somewhere in New York or Pennsylvania, and happy to be there. The sun was warm and the lakes congenial, but as the northwest winds began to blow, bringing frost at night, the older birds would grow restive. They did not relish a sudden freeze, which would present problems, and they vaguely knew that the waning of the sun required them to be farther south in some region of security.

But they waited until the day came when the air was firmly frosted, and then they rose to form their final V. No matter where the lake had been upon which they were resting, the geese in the eastern flyway vectored in to the Susquehanna River, and when they saw its broad and twisting silhouette, they felt safe. This was their immemorial guide, and they followed it with assurance, breaking at last onto the Chesapeake, the most considerable body of water they would see during their migration. It shimmered in the autumn sun and spoke of home. Its thousand estuaries and coves promised them food and refuge for the long winter, and they were joyful at the sight.

As soon as the Chesapeake was reached, congregations of geese began to break off, satisfied that they had arrived at their appointed locations. Four thousand would land at Havre de Grace, twenty thousand at the Sassafras. The Chester River would have more than a hundred thousand

and the Miles the same. Enormous concentrations would elect Tred Avon, but the most conspicuous aggregation, more than a quarter of a million birds, would wait for the Choptank, and they would fill every field and estuary.

For more than five thousand years Onk-or's lineal antecedents had favored a marsh on the north bank of the Choptank. It was spacious, well grassed with many plants producing seeds, and multiple channels providing safe hiding places. It was convenient to both fields, so that the geese could forage for seeds, and to the river, so that they could land and take off easily. It was an ideal wintering home in every respect but one: it was owned by the Turlocks, the most inveterate hunters of Maryland, each member of the family born with an insatiable hunger for goose.

'I can eat it roasted, or chopped with onions and peppers, or sliced thin with mushrooms,' Lafe Turlock was telling the men at the store. 'You can keep the other months of the year, just give me November with a fat goose comin' onto the stove three times a week.'

Lafe had acquired from his father and his father before him the secrets of hunting geese. 'Canniest birds in the world. They have a sixth sense, a seventh and an eighth. I've seen one smart old gander haunts my place lead his flock right into my blind, spot my gun, stop dead in the air, turn his whole congregation around on a sixpence, without me gettin' a shot.' He kicked the stove and volunteered his summary of the situation: 'A real goose tastes so good because it's so danged hard to shoot.'

'Why's that?' a younger hunter asked.

Lafe turned to look at the questioner, studied him contemptuously as an interloper, then explained: 'I'll tell you what, sonny, I know your farm down the river. Fine farm for huntin' geese. Maybe a hundred thousand fly past in the course of a week, maybe two hundred thousand. But that ain't doin' you no good, because unless you can tease just one of those geese to drop down within gunshot of where you stand, you ain't never gonna kill a goose. They fly over there'—he flailed his long arms—'or over here, or down there, a hundred thousand geese in sight . . .' He startled the young man by leaping from his chair and banging his fist against the wall. 'But never one goddamned goose where you want him. It's frustratin'.'

He sat down, cleared his throat and spoke like a lawyer presenting a difficult case: 'So what you got to do, sonny, is pick yourself a likely spot where they might land, and build yourself a blind—'

'I done that.'

Lafe ignored the interruption. 'And hide it in branches that look live and all round it put wooden decoys whittled into at least eight different positions to look real, and then learn to yell goose cries that would fool the smartest goose ever lived. And if you don't do all these things, sonny, you ain't never gonna taste goose, because they gonna fly past you, night and day.'

The attractive thing about Lafe was his unquenchable enthusiasm. Each October, like now, he was convinced that this year he would outsmart the geese, and he was not afraid to make his predictions public at the store: 'This year, gentlemen, you all eat goose. I'm gonna shoot so many, your fingers'll grow warts pluckin' 'em.'

'That's what you said last year,' an uncharitable waterman grunted.

'But this year I got me a plan.' And with a finger dipped in molasses he started to outline his strategy. 'You know my blind out in the river.'

'I stood there often enough, gettin' nothin',' one of the men said.

'And you know this blind at the pond in the western end of the marsh.'

'I waited there for days and all I got was a wet ass,' the same man said.

'And that's what you'll get in that blind this year, too. Because I'm settin' them two up, just like always, decoys and all. I want that smart old leader to see them and lead his ladies away.'

'To where?' the skeptic asked.

Lafe grinned and deep satisfaction wreathed his face. 'Now for my plan. Over here, at the edge of this cornfield where everythin' looks so innicent, I plant me a third blind with the best decoys me or my pappy ever carved.' And with a dripping finger he allowed the molasses to form his new blind.

'I don't think it'll work,' the cynic said.

'I'm gonna get me so many geese—'

'Like last year. How many you get last year, speak honest.'

'I got me nine geese.' In six months he had shot nine geese, but this year, with his new tactics, he was sure to get scores.

When Onk-or brought his wedge of eighty-nine back to the Choptank marshes, dangerous innovations awaited. Of course, on his first pass over Turlock land he spotted the traditional blind in the river and the ill-concealed one at the pond; generations of his family had been avoiding those inept seductions. He also saw the same old decoys piled on the bank, the boats waiting to take hunters into the river and the dogs waiting near the boats. It was familiar and it was home.

Giving a signal, he dropped in a tight, crisp circle, keeping his left wing almost stationary, then landed with a fine splash on an opening in the center of the marsh. He showed his five children how to dispose themselves, then pushed his way through the marsh grass to see for himself what feed there might be in the fields. His mate came along, and within a few minutes they had satisfied themselves that this was going to be a good winter. On their way back to the marsh they studied the cabin. No changes there, same wash behind the kitchen.

As the geese settled in to enjoy the marshes the young birds heard for the first time the reverberation of gunfire, and Onk-or had to spend much time alerting them to the special dangers that accompanied these rich feeding grounds. He and the other ganders taught the newcomers how to spot the flash of metal or hear the cracking of a twig under a gunner's boot. And no group must ever feed without posting at least three sentinels, whose job it was to keep their necks erect so that their ears and eyes could scout all approaches.

Eternal vigilance was the key to survival, and no birds ever became more skilled in protecting themselves. Smaller birds, like doves, which presented difficult targets for a hunter, could often trust to luck that an undetected human would miss when he fired at them, but the great goose presented such an attractive target either head-on or broadside that a gunner had the advantage, if he was allowed to creep within range. The trick for the geese was to move out of range whenever men approached, and Onk-or drilled his flock assiduously in this tactic, for any goose who frequented the Turlock marshes was threatened by some of the most determined hunters on the Eastern Shore.

By mid-December it was clear that the geese had outsmarted Lafe Turlock once again; none had landed at the blind in the river and only a few stragglers had landed at the pond. By the end of the first week Onk-or had spotted the cornfield trick, and Lafe had been able to shoot only three geese.

'Them damn honkers must of got eyeglasses in Canada,' he told the men at the store.

'You was gonna feed us all this winter,' one of the men reminded him.

'I will, too. What I got to do is make a few changes in my plan.'

He assembled his five sons, plus four other crack shots, and told them, 'We are gonna get ourselves so many geese, you'll have grease on your faces all winter. We do it this way.'

An hour before dawn he rowed his youngest son out to the river blind, before which they strung a dozen decoys haphazardly. He told his boy, 'I want for the geese to see you. Make 'em move on.'

Another son he placed at the pond, with the same careless arrangement and the same instructions. 'Of course, son, if you get a good shot at a goose, take it. But we ain't relyin' on you.'

At the cornfield he posted yet a third son, expecting him to be seen. The six other men he took on a long walk through loblolly, ending at a cove where he said the canny geese would have to land. 'The trick is to think like a goose. They'll leave the cornfield, fly in a half-circle, see the decoys beyond the pine trees, and come down here.'

When they came down, they were going to land in the middle of a fusillade from the four fastest guns, followed immediately by a second round from the three slower guns, during which time the first four would load again to pick off the cripples, by which time the slow guns could reload to do any cleaning up.

'This is guaranteed to get honkers,' Lafe promised, 'if'n that damned big bird don't catch on.'

The geese were slow this morning in going to their feeding stations. There was fractiousness among the younger birds, but the elders did not protest, for mating time was approaching and there were many second-year geese who had not yet selected their partners, so that confusion was inescapable. But toward six-thirty Onk-or and another old gander began making the moves that would get the flock started. Restlessness ceased and eighty-odd birds began moving into positions from which they could take to the air.

Onk-or led the flight, and within moments the flock had formed into two loose V's that wheeled and dipped in unison. They headed for the river south of the marsh, and Onk-or saw that some hunter was still trying vainly to lure geese into the old blind located there. The big birds landed well upstream, fed for a while on grasses and then took off for better forage. They flew to the pond, where there was futile gunfire, and then toward the cornfield, where Onk-or quickly spotted the lone gunner stationed there. He swung away from the corn, flew left and saw some geese feeding in a stream lined by pine trees. Since the geese already down there proved that the area was safe, he would land his flock there.

The geese came in low, wings extended, feet ready for braking, but just as Onk-or prepared to land, he detected movement among the pine trees lining the shore, and with a brilliant twist to the north he swung out of range, uttering cries of warning as he did so. He escaped, and those immediately behind made their turns, too, but many of the trailing geese did not react in time; they flew directly into the waiting guns and furious blasts of fire knocked them down.

Seven geese were killed, including two of Onk-or's offspring. It was a disaster, and he had been responsible. It must not happen again.

At the store, Lafe basked in his victory. 'To catch a honker you got to think like a honker,' he told his listeners, but his glory was short-lived, because for the rest of the season he got no geese from his own marshes, and only two when he led an expedition farther upstream.

'I never seen honkers so cagey,' he snarled. 'I'm goin' to hire me them trolls from Amos Todkill.' So in January 1823 he sailed up to Patamoke to dicker with Todkill, who specialized in combing the marshes for wounded young geese, which he domesticated, using them as living lures to bring wild geese directly into the muzzles of waiting guns.

Todkill said he'd allow Turlock to rent fifteen of his tame geese, three days for a dollar and a half. 'Pretty steep,' Lafe complained.

'But you know they're foolproof. "Never-fails," we call 'em.'

Turlock tied their legs, tossed them into his boat and sailed back to the marsh. 'I want me fifteen or sixteen reliable guns,' he announced at the store. 'I laid out real money for them damned trolls, and I expect some honkers in return.'

He enlisted a veritable battery, whose members he stationed at strategic spots so that the cross-fire from the muzzle-loaders would be impenetrable. He then spread four dozen of his most lifelike wooden decoys, after which he released Todkill's fifteen live ones. 'As pretty a sight as a honker ever seen, and as deadly,' he said approvingly when all was in position.

Then he and the sixteen other hunters waited. Nothing happened. Occasional geese from the marshes flew past, ignoring the trolls, who cackled to lure them down. Once or twice substantial flocks, headed by the old gander, came tantalizingly close, then veered away as if in obedience to a signal, and the three days passed without one good shot at a honker.

Onk-or from the first had spotted the bizarre assembly of wooden decoys and live trolls, and it was not long before he discerned the guns hiding among the rushes. He not only kept his own geese from the lethal area; he also alerted others, so that Lafe and his artillery could not possibly get themselves the geese he had promised.

At the store one of the hunters said, 'Them trolls fooled me, and they fooled Lafe, but they sure as hell didn't fool that old gander.'

'What they did,' Lafe said, 'was waste my dollar-fifty. It was only through the help of prayer that I kept from stranglin' those birds before I gave 'em back to Todkill.'

The men laughed. The idea of Lafe Turlock's hurting a goose, except to shoot it, was preposterous. He loved the big birds, fed them cracked corn when snow covered the ground, rescued cripples at the end of the season and turned them over to Todkill. Once, after a big revival meeting, he said: 'The life of man is divided into two seasons: "Geese is here. Geese ain't here."' So when the men joshed him over his costly failure, they were surprised that he did not fight back.

He remained silent for a good reason: he was ready to shift into phase three of his grand design. Assembling his sons in early March, he told them, 'Turlocks eat geese because we're smarter'n geese. And a danged sight smarter'n them dummies at the store, because I know somethin' that would rile 'em, if'n they had the brains to understand.'

His sons waited. He looked out the door at the March sky and confided, 'I been trampin' through the woods, and I think I found me the spot where they does their courtin'.' He was referring to those few geese who had either been wounded by ineffective gunfire or seduced by the clemency of the Choptank; they would not be flying north with the others but would remain behind, raising their Maryland-born families in marshes to the south. And when they mated, they would be vulnerable, for as Lafe explained to his sons, 'Geese is just like men. When their minds get fixed on ass, caution goes out the window, and come next week we're gonna knock down enough careless geese to feed us through July.'

It was in the deepest nature of a Turlock to be sanguine where hunting and fishing were concerned: the oysters were down there but they could be tonged; the crabs might be hiding but they could be caught. 'How we gonna do it, Pop?'

'Strategy,' Lafe said.

Onk-or, too, was thinking strategy. He must get his flock through the frenzy of this season without loss, and to accomplish this he must keep them away from the mating grounds, for he had learned that when young geese gawked at their contemporaries in the mating dance, they grew inattentive, and their elders were no better, for they, too, stood about cackling and enjoying the proceedings, unmindful of lurking guns.

So for both Lafe and Onk-or the last days of winter became critical, for the man had to find the mating ground and the goose had to keep its family away from it. Nine days went by without a loss to the Turlock guns.

'No fear,' Lafe assured his boys. 'Honkers has got to mate, and when they do, we come into our own.'

He had anticipated, almost better than the young geese, where those who did not fly north conducted their courtships, and there, along a grassy field deep in the woods, he placed himself and his sons, each with three muskets. The young geese, responding to their own inner urgings, were drawn to this spot, and there they began their dances.

Two males would focus upon one female, who would stand aside, shyly preening herself, as if she held a mirror. She would keep her eyes on the ground, pretending to ignore events that would determine how she would live for the remainder of her life.

The males meanwhile would grow more and more active, snapping at each other and hissing, advancing and retreating and putting on a great show of fury. Finally one would actually attack the other, flailing with wings extended six or seven feet, and crashing heavy blows upon the head and shoulders of the other. Now the fight would become real, with each heavy bird attempting to grab the other's head in its powerful beak.

According to some intricate scoring system, it would become apparent to both contestants, to the rest of the flock and especially to the waiting female that one of the fighting birds had triumphed. The other would retreat, and then would come the most moving part of the dance.

The victorious male would approach the waiting female with mincing steps, swaying from side to side, and as he drew near he would extend his neck to the fullest and gently wave it back and forth, close to the chosen one, and she would extend hers, and they would intertwine, rarely touching, and they would stand thus, weaving and twisting their necks in one of the most delicate and graceful maneuvers in nature.

As the dance approached its climax, the young geese of Onk-or's group started instinctively toward the mating ground, and although Onk-or and his mate moved frantically to intercept them, they bumbled their way into the open area.

'Now!' Turlock signaled, and the guns blazed. Before the startled geese could take to the air, the six Turlocks dropped their guns, grabbed others and blazed away, dropped them and reached for their backups. Geese fell in startling numbers, and by the time Onk-or could get his flock into the air, enough lay dead to stock the icehouse.

When they reassembled in the marsh, Onk-or discovered that one of his sons was dead, and he was about to lament when he found to his terror that his wife was missing, too. He had seen geese falter and fall into the grass offshore, and he knew intuitively that the men would now be combing that margin to find the cripples.

Without hesitation he left his flock and sped back to the mating ground. His arrival disconcerted the men, who, as he had expected, were searching for wounded birds. Flying directly over their heads, he landed in the area at which he had seen the geese falling, and there he found his mate, sorely crippled in the left wing. It was impossible for her to fly, and within minutes the dogs and men would find her.

Urging her with heavy pushes of his bill, he shoved her through ill-defined waterways, heading her always toward the safety of the deeper marshes. When she faltered, he pecked at her feathers, never allowing her to stop.

They had progressed about two hundred yards when a mongrel yellow dog with an especially good nose came upon their scent and realized that he had a cripple somewhere in the bushes ahead. Silently he made his way ever closer to the wounded goose, until, with a final leap, he was upon her.

What he did not anticipate was that she was accompanied by a full-grown gander determined to protect her. Suddenly, from the water near the cripple, Onk-or rose up, whipped his heavy beak about and slashed at the dog. The startled animal withdrew in shock, then perceived the situation and lunged at the gander.

A deadly, splashing fight ensued, with the dog having every advantage. But Onk-or marshaled his powers; he was fighting not only to protect himself but also to save his crippled mate, and deep in the tangled marsh he attacked the dog with a confusing flash of wing and thrust of beak. The dog retreated.

'There's a cripple in there!' Turlock shouted to his sons. 'Tiger's got hisse'f a cripple.'

But the dog appeared with nothing except a bleeding cut on the head. 'Hey! Tiger's been hit by a honker. Get in there and find that cripple.'

Three boys and their dogs splashed into the marsh, but by this time Onk-or had guided his damaged mate to safety. They hid among the rushes as the men splashed noisily, while the mongrels, not eager to encounter whatever had struck Tiger, made little attempt to find them.

A week later, when the crippled wing had mended, Onk-or herded his geese together and they started their mandatory flight to the Arctic: Pennsylvania, Connecticut, Maine and then the frozen moorlands of Canada as they had done for generations. On a similar flight, thirty years earlier, as a flock of great geese flew over a small town in central New York, they made a great honking, and citizens came out to follow their mysterious passage. Among them was a boy of eight. He stared at the shadowy forms and listened to their distant conversation. As a consequence of this one experience he would become attached to birds, would study everything about them, and in his adult life would paint them and write about them and take the first steps in providing sanctuaries for them, and all because on one moonlit night John James Audubon heard the geese pass overhead.

THE INVADERS

IN THE SUMMER OF 1968 a family of immigrants—mother, father, four daughters—moved quietly into the oil town of Larkin, Texas, and within three weeks had the owners of better-class homes in a rage. They were such a rowdy lot, especially the mother, that an observer might have thought: The rip-roaring boom days of 1922 are back!

They were night people, always a bad sign, who seemed to do most of their hell-raising after dark, with mother and daughters off on a toot marked by noise, vandalism and other furtive acts. They operated as a gang, with the weak and ineffective father along at times, and what infuriated the townsfolk particularly was that they seemed to take positive joy in their depredations.

Despite their unfavorable reputation—and many sins were charged against them that they did not commit—they really did more good than harm; they were an asset to the community, and they had about them elements of extraordinary beauty, which their enemies refused to admit.

They were armadillos, never known in this area before, a group of invaders who had moved up from Mexico, bringing irritation and joy wherever they appeared. Opponents of the fascinating little creatures, which were no bigger than small dogs, accused them of eating quail eggs (a rotten lie); of raiding chicken coops (false as could be); and of tearing up fine lawns (a just charge and a serious one). Ranchers also said: 'They dig so many holes that my cattle stumble into them and break their legs. There goes four hundred bucks.'

The indictment involving the digging up of lawns and the making of deep holes was justified, for no animal could dig faster than an armadillo, and when this mother and her four daughters turned themselves loose on a neat lawn or a nicely tilled vegetable garden, their destruction could be awesome. The armadillo had a long, probing snout, backed up by two forefeet each, with four three-inch claws, and two hind feet with five shovel-like claws, and the speed with which it could work those excavators was unbelievable.

'Straight down,' Mr. Kramer said, 'they can dig faster than I can with a shovel. The nose feels out the soft spots and those forelegs drive like pistons, but it's the back legs that amaze, because they catch the loose earth and throw it four, five feet backwards.'

Mr. Kramer was one of those odd men, found in all communities, who measured rainfall on a regular basis—phoning the information to the Weather Service—and who recorded the depth of snowfall, the time of the first frost, the strength and direction of the wind during storms, and the fact that in the last blue norther, 'the temperature on a fine March day dropped, in the space of three hours, from 26.9 to 9.7 degrees Celsius.' He was the type who always gave the temperature in Celsius, which he expected his friends to translate into Fahrenheit, if they wished. He was, in short, a sixty-two-year-old former member of an oil crew who had always loved nature and who had poked his bullet-cropped, sandy-haired head into all sorts of corners.

The first armadillos to reach Larkin were identified on a Tuesday, and by Friday, Mr. Kramer had written away for three research studies on the creatures. The more he read, the more he grew to like them, and before long he was defending them against their detractors, especially to those whose lawns had been excavated: 'A little damage here and there, I grant you. But did you hear about what they did for my rose bushes? Laden down with beetles they were. Couldn't produce one good flower, even with toxic sprays. Then one night I look out to check the moon, three-quarters full, and I see these pairs of beady eyes shining in the gloom, and across my lawn come these five armadillos, and I say to myself: "Oh, oh! There goes the lawn!" but that wasn't the case at all. Those armadillos were after those beetles, and when I woke up in the morning to check the rain gauge, what do you suppose? Not one beetle to be found.'

Mr. Kramer defended the little creatures to anyone who would listen, but not many cared: 'You ever see his tongue? Darts out about six inches, long, very sticky. Zoom! There goes another ant, another beetle. He was made to police the garden and knock off the pests.'

Once when a Mrs. Cole was complaining with a bleeding heart about what the armadillos had done to her lawn, he stopped her with a rather revolting question: 'Mrs. Cole, have you ever inspected an armadillo's stomach? Well, I have, many times. Dissected bodies I've found along the highway. And what does the stomach contain? Bugs, beetles, delicate roots, flies, ants, all the crawling things you don't like. And you can tell Mr. Cole that in seventeen autopsies, I've never found even the trace of a bird's egg, and certainly no quail's eggs.' By the time he was through with his report on the belly of an armadillo, Mrs. Cole was more than ever opposed to the destructive little beasts.

But it was when he extolled the beauty of the armadillo that he lost the support of even the most sympathetic Larkin citizens, for they saw the little animal as an awkward, low-slung relic of some past geologic age that had mysteriously survived into the present; one look at the creature convinced them that it should have died out with the dinosaurs, and its survival into the twentieth century somehow offended them. To Mr. Kramer, this heroic persistence was one of the armadillo's great assets, but he was even more impressed by the beauty of its design.

'Armadillo? What does it mean? "The little armored one." And if you look at him dispassionately, what you see is a beautifully designed animal much like one of the armored horses they used to have in the Middle Ages. The back, the body, the legs are all protected by this amazing armor, beautifully fashioned to flow across the body of the beast. And look at the engineering!' When he said this he liked to display one of the three armadillos he had tamed when their parents were killed by hunters and point to the miracle of which he was speaking: 'This is real armor, fore and aft. Punch it. Harder than your fingernail and made of the same substance. Protects the shoulders and the hips. But here in the middle, nine flexible bands of armor, much like an accordion. Always nine, never seven or ten, and without these inserts, the beast couldn't move about as he does. Quite wonderful, really. Nothing like it in the rest of the animal kingdom. Real relic of the dinosaur age.'

But he would never let it end at that, and it was what he said next that did win some converts to the armadillo's defense: 'What awes me is not the armor, nor the nine flexible plates. They're just good engineering. But the beauty of the design goes beyond engineering. It's art, and only a designer who took infinite care could have devised these patterns. Leonardo da Vinci, maybe, or Michelangelo, or even God.' And then he would show how fore and aft the armor was composed of the most beautiful hexagons and pentagons arranged like golden coins upon a field of exquisite gray cloth, while the nine bands were entirely different: 'Look at the curious structures! Elongated capital A's. Go ahead, tell me what they look like.

A field of endless oil derricks, aren't they? Can't you see, he's the good-luck symbol of the whole oil industry. His coming to Larkin was no mistake. He was sent here to serve as our mascot.'

How beautiful, how mysterious the armadillos were when one took the trouble to inspect them seriously, as Mr. Kramer did. They bespoke past ages, the death of great systems, the miracle of creation and survival; they were walking reminders of a time when volcanoes peppered the earth and vast lakes covered continents. They were hallowed creatures, for they had seen the earth before man arrived, and they had survived to remind him of how things once had been. They should have died out with *Tyrannosaurus rex* and diplodocus, but they had stubbornly persisted so that they could bear testimony, and for the value of that testimony, they were precious and worthy of defense. 'They must continue into the future,' Mr. Kramer said, 'so that future generations can see how things once were.'

'What amazes me,' Mr. Kramer told women he tried to persuade, 'is their system of giving birth. Invariably, four pups, and invariably, all four of the same sex. There is no case of a mother armadillo giving birth to boys and girls at the same time. Impossible. And do you know why? Because one fertilized egg is split into four parts, rarely more, rarely less. Therefore, the resulting babies all have to be of the same sex.

'But would you believe this? The mother can hold that fertilized four-part egg in her womb for the normal eight weeks, or, if things don't seem propitious, for as long as twenty-two months, same as the elephant. She gives birth in response to some perceived need, and what that is, no one can say.'

As he brooded over the mystery of birth, wondering how the armadillo community ensured that enough males and females would be provided to keep the race going, he visualized what he called the Great Computer in the Sky, which kept track of how many four-girl births were building up in a given community. And some morning it would click out a message—'Hey, we need a couple of four-boy births in the Larkin area.' So the next females to become pregnant would have four male babies, and the grand balance would be maintained.

Mr. Kramer could find no one who wished to share his speculation on this mystery, but as he pursued it he began to think about human beings, too: What grand computer ensures that we have a balance between male and female babies? And how does it make the adjustments it does? As what happens after a war, when a lot of men have died in battle. Normal births in peacetime would be a thousand and four males to a thousand females, because males are more delicate in the early years and the adjustment has to be made. But after a war, when the Great Computer knows that there's a deficiency in the number of males, the balance swings as high as one thousand and nine to one thousand.

So when he looked at an armadillo on its way to dig in his lawn, he saw not a destructive little tank with incredibly powerful digging devices but a symbol of the grandeur of Creation, the passing of time, the mystery of birth, the great beauty that exists in the world in so many different manifestations. An armadillo is not one whit more beautiful or mysterious than a butterfly or a pine cone, but it's more fun. And what gave him the warmest satisfaction was that all the other sizable animals of the world seemed to be having their living areas reduced. Only the armadillo was stubbornly enlarging his. Sometimes when Mr. Kramer watched this mother and her four daughters heading forth for some new devastation, he chuckled with delight: 'There they go! The Five Horsewomen of the Apocalypse!'

Another Larkin man had a much different name for the little excavators. Ransom Rusk, principal heir and sole proprietor of the Rusk holdings in the Larkin Field, had a fierce desire to obliterate memories of his unfortunate ancestry: the grand fool Earnshaw Rusk; the wife with the wooden nose; his own obscenely obese father; his fat, foolish mother. He wanted to forget them all. He was a tall, lean man, quite handsome, totally unlike his father, and at forty-five he was at the height of his powers. He had married a Wellesley graduate from New England, and it was amusing that her mother, wishing to dissociate herself from her cotton-mill ancestry, had named her daughter Fleurette, trusting that something of French gentility would rub off on her.

Fleurette and Ransom Rusk, fed up with the modest house in whose kitchen Floyd had maintained his oil office till he died, had employed an architect from Boston to build them a mansion, and he had suggested an innovation that would distinguish their place from others in the region: 'It is very fashionable, in the better estates of England, to have a bowling green. It could also be used for croquet, should you prefer,' and Fleurette had applauded the idea.

It was now her pleasure to entertain at what she called 'a pleasant afternoon of bowls,' and she did indeed make it pleasant. Not many of the local millionaires—and there were now some two dozen in the Larkin district, thanks to those reliable wells that never produced much more than a hundred barrels (of oil) a day, rarely less—knew how to play bowls, but they had fun at the variations they devised.

Ransom Rusk, as the man who dominated the Larkin Field, was not spectacularly rich by Texas standards, whose categories were popularly defined: one to twenty million, comfortable; twenty to fifty million, well-to-do; fifty to five hundred million, rich; five hundred to one billion, big rich; one to five billion, Texas rich. By virtue of his other oil holdings in various parts of the state and his prudent investments in Fort Worth ventures, he was now rich, but in the lowest ranks of that middle division. His attitudes toward wealth were extremely contradictory, for obviously he had a driving ambition to acquire and exercise power in its various manifestations, and in pursuit of this he strove to multiply his wealth. But he remained indifferent to its mathematical level, often spending an entire year without knowing his balances or even an approximation of them. On the other hand, he had inherited his father's shrewd judgment regarding oil and had extended it to the field of general financing, and he always sought new opportunities and knew how to apply leverage when he found them.

He was brooding about his Fort Worth adventures one morning when he heard Fleurette scream: 'Oh my God!' Thinking that she had fallen, he rushed into the bedroom to find her standing by the window, pointing wordlessly at the havoc that had been wreaked upon her bowling green.

'Looks like an atomic bomb!' Ransom said. 'It's those damned armadillos,' but Fleurette did not hear his explanation, for she was wailing as if she had lost three children.

'Shut up!' Ransom cried. 'I'll take care of those little bastards.'

He slammed out of the house, inspected the chopped-up bowling lawn, and summoned the gardeners: 'Can this be fixed?'

'We can resod it like new, Mr. Rusk,' they assured him, 'but you'll have to keep them armadillos out.'

'I'll take care of them. I'll shoot them.' In pursuit of this plan, he went to the hardware store to buy a stack of ammo for his .22 rifle, but while there, he happened to stand beside Mr. Kramer at the checkout counter, and the retired oilman, who had worked for Rusk, asked: 'What are the bullets for?' and Ransom said: 'Armadillos.'

'Oh, you mustn't do that! Those are precious creatures. You should be protecting them, not killing them.'

'They tore up my wife's lawn last night.'

'Her bowling green? I've heard it's beautiful.'

'Cost God knows how much, and it's in shreds.'

'A minor difficulty,' Kramer said lightly, since he did not have to pay for the repairs. And before Ransom could get away, the enthusiastic nature lover had drawn him to the drugstore, where they shared a Dr Pepper.

'Did you know, Ransom, that we have highly accurate maps showing the progress north of the armadillo? Maybe the only record of its kind.'

'I wish they'd stayed where they came from.'

'They came from Mexico.'

'One hell of a lot from Mexico—wetbacks, boll weevils—'

'A follower of the great Audubon first recorded them in Texas, down along the Rio Grande, in 1854. They had reached San Antonio by 1880, Austin by 1914, Jefferson in the east by 1945. They were slower reaching our dryer area. They were reported in Dallas in 1953, but they didn't reach us till this year. Remarkable March.'

'Should have kept them in Mexico,' Rusk said, fingering his box of shells.

'They're in Florida too. Three pairs escaped from a zoo in 1922. And people transported them as pets. They liked Florida, so now they move east from Texas and west from Florida. They'll occupy the entire Gulf area before this century is out.'

'They aren't going to occupy my place much longer,' Ransom said, and that was the beginning of the hilarious adventure, because Mr. Kramer persuaded him, almost tearfully, not to shoot the armadillos but to keep them away from the bowling green by building protection around it. 'These are unique creatures,' he said, 'relics of the past, and they do an infinite amount of good.'

The first thing Rusk did was to enclose his wife's resodded bowling green within a stout, tennis-court-type fence, but two nights after it was in place, at considerable expense, the bowling green was chewed up again, and when Mr. Kramer was consulted he showed the Rusks how the world's foremost excavators had simply burrowed under the fence to get at the succulent roots.

'What you have to do is dig a footing around your green, six feet deep, and fill it with concrete. Sink your fence poles in that.'

'Do you know how much that would cost?'

'They tell me you have the money,' Kramer said easily, and so the fence was taken down, backhoes were brought in, and the deep trench was dug, enclosing the green. Then trucks dumped a huge amount of cement into the gaping holes, and the fence was reerected. Eight feet into the air, six feet underground, and the armadillos were boxed off.

But four days after the job was finished, Fleurette Rusk let out another wail, and when Ransom ran to her room, he bellowed: 'Is it those damned armadillos again?' It was, and when he and Mr. Kramer studied the new disaster the situation became clear, as the enthusiastic naturalist explained: 'Look at that hole! Ransom, they dug right under the concrete barrier and up the other side. Probably took them half an hour, no more.'

The scientific manner in which Kramer diagnosed the case, and the obvious pleasure he took in the engineering skills of his armadillos, infuriated Rusk, and once more he threatened to shoot his tormentors, but Kramer prevailed upon him to try one more experiment: 'What we must do, Ransom, is drive a palisade below the concrete footing.'

'And how do we do that?'

'Simple, you get a hydraulic ram and it drives down metal stakes. Twenty feet deep. But they'll have to be close together.'

When this job was completed, Rusk calculated that he had $218,000 invested in that bowling green, but to his grim satisfaction, the sunken palisade did stop the predators he had named Lady Macbeth and Her Four Witches. The spikes of the palisade went too deep for her to risk a hole so far below the surface.

But she was not stopped for long, because one morning Ransom was summoned by a new scream: 'Ransom, look at those scoundrels!' and when he looked, he saw that the mother, frustrated by the palisade, but still hungry for the tender grass roots, had succeeded in climbing her side of the fence, straight up, and then descending straight down, and she was in the process of teaching her daughters to do the same.

For some minutes Rusk stood at the window, watching the odd procession of armadillos climbing up his expensive fence, and when one daughter repeatedly fell back, unable to learn, he broke into laughter.

'I don't see what's so funny,' his wife cried, and he explained: 'Look at the dumb little creature. She can't use her front claws to hold on to the cross wires,' and his wife exploded: 'You seem to be cheering her on,' and it suddenly became clear to Rusk that he was doing just that. He was reacting to his wife's constant nagging: 'Don't wear that big cowboy hat in winter, makes you look like a real hick.' 'Don't wear those boots to a dance, makes you look real Texan.' She had a score of other don'ts, and now Ransom realized that in this fight of Fleurette versus the lady armadillos, he was cheering for the animals.

But as a good sport he did telephone Mr. Kramer and ask: 'Those crazy armadillos can climb the fence. What do we do?' Mr. Kramer noted the significant difference; always before it had been 'those damned armadillos' or worse. When a man started calling them crazy, he was beginning to fall in love with them.

'Tell you what, Ransom. We call in the fence people and have them add a projection around the upper edge, so that when the armadillos reach the top of the fence, they'll run into the screen curving back at them and fall off.'

'Will it hurt them?'

'Six weeks ago you wanted to shoot them. Now you ask if it'll hurt them. Ransom, you're learning.'

'You know, Kramer, everything you advise me to do costs money.'

'You have it to spend.'

So the fence builders were brought in, and yes, they could bring a flange out parallel to the ground that no armadillo could negotiate, and when this was done Rusk would sit on his porch at night with a powerful beam flashlight and watch as the mother tried to climb the fence, with her daughters trailing, and he would break into audible laughter as the determined little creatures clawed their way the top, encountered the barrier, and tumbled back to earth. Again and again they tried, and always they fell back. Ransom Rusk had defeated the armadillos, at a total cost of $238,000.

'What are you guffawing at in the dark?' Fleurette demanded, and he said, 'At the armadillos trying to get into your bowling green.'

'You should have shot them months ago,' she snapped, and he replied, 'They're trying so hard, I was thinking about going down and letting them in.'

'You do,' she said, 'and I'm walking out.'

JIMMY
THE CRAB

THE WORST STORMS to hit the Chesapeake Bay are the hurricanes that generate in the southeast, over the Atlantic Ocean. There they twist and turn, building power and lifting from the waves enormous quantities of water that they carry north in turbulent clouds.

They first hit Cape Charles, at the southern end of the Eastern Shore, then explode ferociously over the waters of the bay, driving crabbers and oystermen to shore. Their winds, often reaching a fierce ninety miles an hour, whip the shallow waters of the Chesapeake into waves so violent that any small boat runs a good risk of being capsized.

In late August of 1886 such a hurricane collected its force just south of Norfolk, but instead of devastating the bay, it leapfrogged far to the north, depositing in the Susquehanna Valley an incredible fall of rain. In less than a day, nineteen inches fell on certain parts of Pennsylvania. Harrisburg felt the lash as its waterfront homes were submerged; Sunbury was inundated; poor Wilkes-Barre watched the dark waters engulf its jetties; and even Towanda, far to the north, was swamped by raging floods from streams that a day earlier had been mere trickles.

From a thousand such rivulets the great flood accumulated, and as it crested on its way south to the Chesapeake, it inundated small towns and endangered large cities. On it came, a devastating onslaught of angry water, twisting and probing into every depression. Past Harrisburg it swept, and Columbia, and over small villages near the border of Pennsylvania. Finally, in northern Maryland it exploded with destructive fury into the body of the Chesapeake, raising the headwaters of that considerable bay four or five feet.

For three days the storm continued, producing strange and arbitrary results. Norfolk was bypassed completely: merely a heavy rain. Crisfield had no problems: a slow rain of no significance. But the great bay itself was nearly destroyed: it came close to being drowned by the floods cascading down from the north. It lay strangling in its own water.

To understand what was happening, one must visualize the bay as carefully structured in three distinct dimensions. From north to south the waters of the bay were meticulously graduated according to their salt content, and any alteration of this salinity was frought with peril. At Havre de Grace, where the Susquehanna River debouched into the bay, there should have been in autumn three parts of salt per thousand; there was none. On the oyster beds near Devon Island there ought to have been fifteen parts per thousand to keep the shellfish healthy; there were two. And at the crabbing beds farther south the crustaceans were accustomed to nineteen parts; they had to contend with less than six. All living things in the bay were imperiled, for the great flood had altered the bases of their existence. The protection provided by salt water was being denied them, and if relief did not come quickly, millions upon millions of bay creatures were going to die.

When the storm broke, there existed on a small subterranean shelf at the western edge of Devon Island a congregation of oysters that had fastened themselves securely to the solid bottom. Here some of the largest and tastiest oysters of the bay had produced their generations, while the minute spat (young oysters) drifted back and forth with the slow currents until they fastened to the bottom to develop the shells in which they would grow during the years of their existence.

Along this shelf, well known to watermen, oysters had thrived during all the generations watermen had tonged the bay; no matter how many bushels of large oysters were lifted from this location, others replaced them. This was a shelf that could be depended upon.

In its original stages the flood from the Susquehanna did not affect these oysters. True, the salinity of all the water dropped, but at the depth at which they lived the loss did not, in these first days, imperil them. But there was another aspect of the flood that did. The Susquehanna, as it swept down from New York, picked up an astonishing burden of fine silt; for example, a house along the riverbank in Harrisburg might be inundated for only seven hours, but when the owners returned they would find in their second-floor bedrooms six inches of silt. How could it possibly have got there? Well, each cubic centimeter of seeping brown water carried its burden of almost invisible dust lifted from the farms of New York and Pennsylvania, and it was this dust, suspended in water, that was left behind.

The silt that fell in the bedroom of a butcher in Harrisburg could, when it dried, be swept away, but the silt that fell on a bed of oysters could not.

Down it came, silently, insidiously and very slowly. In four days more silt fell than in the previous sixty years. The entire Choptank was chocolate-colored from the turbulent mud, but as soon as the waters began to calm themselves, their burden of silt was released and it fell persistently and inescapably onto the oysters.

At first it was no more than a film such as the propellers of the evening ferry might have deposited on any night. Such an amount caused no problem and might even bring with it plankton to feed the oysters. But this thin film was followed by a perceptible thickness, and then by more, until the oysters became agitated within their heavy shells. The spat, of course, were long since strangled. A whole oncoming generation of oysters had been suffocated.

Still the fine silt drifted down, an interminable rain of desolation. The bottom of the Choptank was covered with the gray-brown deposit; whole grains were so minute that the resulting mud seemed more like cement, except that it did not harden—it merely smothered everything on which it fell; pressing down with fingers so delicate, its weight could not be felt until the moment it had occupied every space with a subtle force more terrible than a tower of stone.

The oysters could have withstood a similar intrusion of sand; then the particles would have been so coarse that water could continue to circulate and plankton be obtained. Submersion of even a month was tolerable, for in time the sand would wash away, leaving the shellfish no worse for their experience. But the flood-swept silt was another matter, and on the tenth day after the flood, when the brown waters bore their heaviest burden of mud, even the mature oysters began to die. No lively water was reaching them, no plankton. They were entombed in a dreadful cascade of silt and they could not propel themselves to a new location or to a new level. Secured to their shelf, they had to rely on passing tides that would wash the silt away. But none came.

On the twelfth day the waters of the Chesapeake reached their maximum muddiness; silt from midland Pennsylvania was coming down now, in a final burst of destruction, and when it reached the relatively calm waters of the Choptank, it broke loose from its carrying waters and filtered slowly down to the bed of the river. This was the final blow. The oysters were already submerged under two inches of silt; now three more piled on, and one by one the infinitely rich beds were covered by an impenetrable mud. The oysters perished in their shells.

In time—say, a year and a half—the currents of the Choptank would eat away the mud and once more reveal the shelf upon which untold generations of new oysters would flourish. The shells of the dead oysters would be there, gnarled and craggy and inviting to the young spat that would be looking for a ledge to grab hold of. The spat would find a home; the nourishing plankton would drift by; the oyster beds would exist once more, but for now they were obliterated in the silt of the great storm.

Another resident of the Chesapeake was also severely affected by the hurricane of 1886, but he was better able to cope with the disaster, for he could move and, by taking precautions, adjust to the altered circumstances. He was Jimmy, who bore the time-honored Chesapeake name for the male blue crab, that delicious crustacean upon which so much of the wealth of the bay depended.

While the storm lay off Norfolk, gathering speed and water, Jimmy, resting in the grassy waters at the edge of Turlock Marsh, perceived that a radical change in the atmosphere was about to occur. And it would probably arrive at the worst possible moment for him. How could he know these two facts? He was exceedingly sensitive to changes in atmospheric pressure or any other factors that affected the waters of the bay. If a storm of unusual force was developing, he would be made aware of it by the sharp drop in barometric pressure and would prepare to take those protective measures that had rescued him in the past. Also, he knew intuitively when he must climb painfully out of his old shell, which was made of inert matter that could not grow in size as he grew. He had to discard it and prepare himself for the construction of a new shell better fitted to his increased body size. The time for such a moult was at hand.

When the storm broke, and no great body of water fell on the Choptank, Jimmy felt no signals that a crisis was at hand, so he prepared to shed his old shell, an intricate process that might consume as long as four hours of painful wrestling and contortion. But before he could begin the moult, he became aware of a frightening change in the bay. The water level was rising. The salinity was diminishing. And when these two phenomena continued, and indeed accelerated, he became uncomfortable.

During any moult, which might take place three or four times a year as he increased in size, he preferred some secure place like the Turlock Marsh, but if it was going to be flooded with fresh water, it could prove a death trap rather than a refuge, so he began swimming strongly out toward the deep center of the bay.

A mature crab like Jimmy could swim at a speed of nearly a mile an hour, so he felt safe, but as he cleared Devon Island and was hit by the rush of saltless water, he felt driven to swim with frenetic energy to protect himself. He would not drop dead in the first flush of fresh water, and he could adjust to surprising variations in salinity for brief periods, but to exist in the way for which his body had been constructed, he needed water with a proper salt content.

But moving into the deeper water meant that he would lose the protection of the marsh for his critical moulting. He would have to go through this complex maneuvering out in the bay, where he would be largely defenseless. But he had no other option.

The silt posed no insurmountable problem. It obscured his vision, to be sure, but it did not settle on him or pin him to the bottom, as it did the oysters. He could flip his many legs and swim clear, so that he was not yet in danger at this stage of the flood, but he sensed that he had to swim down toward the ocean to find the salinity necessary for his survival.

These matters assumed little importance in view of the crucial one at hand. Swimming easily to the bottom of the bay, he found a sandy area, a place he would never have considered for a moult in normal times, and there began his gyrations. First he had to break the seal along the edge of his shell, and he did this by contracting and expanding his body, forcing water through his system and building up a considerable hydraulic pressure that slowly forced the shell apart, not conspicuously, but far enough for the difficult part of the moult to proceed.

Now he began the slow and almost agonizing business of withdrawing his boneless legs from their protective covering and manipulating them so that they protruded from the slight opening. With wrenching movements he dislodged the main portion of his body, thrusting it toward the opening, which now widened under pressure from the legs. He had no skeleton, of course, so that he could contort and compress his body into whatever shape was most effective, but he did continue to generate hydraulic pressures through various parts of his body so that the shell was forced apart.

Three hours and twenty minutes after he started this bizarre procedure, he swam free of the old shell and was now adrift in the deep waters of the bay, totally without protection. He had no bony structure in any part of his body, no covering thicker than the sheerest tissue paper, no capacity for self-defense except a much-slowed ability to swim. Any fish that chanced to come his way could gobble him at a gulp; if he had been in shallower water, any bird could have taken him. In these fateful hours all he could do was hide.

And yet, even at his most defenseless moment his new armor was beginning to form. Eighty minutes after the moult he would have a paper-thin covering. After three hours he would have the beginning of a solid shell. And in five hours he would be a hard-shelled crab once more, and would remain that way until his next moult.

But as he waited deep in the bay for his new life, the results of the storm continued to make themselves felt, and now the water was so lacking in salt that he felt he must move south. He swam forcefully and purposefully, keeping to the eastern edge of the bay where the nutritive grasses produced the best plankton, and after a day he sensed the balance of the water to be more nearly normal.

He was not given time to luxuriate in this newfound security of proper water and a solid shell, for urgings of a primordial character were assaulting him, and he forgot his own preoccupations in order to swim among the grasses, looking for sooks that had been bypassed in the earlier mating periods. These overlooked females, on their way south to spend the winter near the entrance of the bay, where fertile sooks traditionally prepared to lay their eggs, sent out frantic signals to whatever males might be in the vicinity, for this was the final period in which they could be fertilized.

Jimmy, probing the marshes, detected such signals and swam with extraordinary energy into the weeds, from which a grateful sook came rushing at him. As soon as she saw that she had succeeded in attracting a male, she became tenderly passive and allowed him to turn her about with his claws and mount her from behind, forming with his many legs a kind of basket in which he would cradle her for the next three days.

This was her time to moult, and Jimmy gave her a protection he had not enjoyed. Covering her completely, he could fend off any fishes that might attack or beat away any birds. Turtles, too, could be avoided, as well as otters, who loved to feed on shell-less crabs. For three days he would defend her, holding her gently as she went through her own difficult gyrations of moulting.

When she succeeded in escaping from her old shell, she allowed Jimmy to cast it aside with his feet. She was now completely defenseless, a creature without a skeleton or any bony structure, and at this moment it became possible for the two crabs, he with a shell and she without, to engage in sex, an act that required six or seven hours.

When it was completed he continued to cradle her gently for two days, until her new shell was formed. Only when he felt it secure beneath him did he release her, and then the two crabs separated, she to swim to the lower end of the bay to develop her fertilized eggs, he to the northerly areas to spend the winter in the deep.

But in 1886 it was not to be as simple as that, for when the Susquehanna broke its banks, flooding the land on either side of the river for a distance of several miles, a terrible problem developed: the floodwaters upset privies, flushed out septic pools and cleaned out manure dumps, throwing into the swiftly moving waters of the river an incredible accumulation of sewage. In each town that the river inundated on its rampage south, it reamed out the sewage ponds until at the end, when it emptied into the Chesapeake, it was nothing but one mighty cloaca carrying with it enough poisons to contaminate the entire bay.

The effect was worsened by the fact that in the big cities the river picked up huge quantities of industrial waste, especially the newly developed oils, which spread the poisons over the entire surface of the bay. Rarely had the Chesapeake been called upon to absorb such a concentration of lethal agents. It failed.

From the mouth of the river to the mouth of the bay the entire body of water became infected with a dozen new poisons. Those oysters that managed to escape the silt did not escape the fatal germs, and that October all who ate the few oysters that were caught ran the risk of death, and many died. The bluefish were contaminated and typhoid spread where they were eaten. The crabs were sorely hit, their delicate flesh acting as veritable blotting paper to absorb the germs. In New York and Baltimore families that ate them died.

The fishing industry in the Chesapeake was prostrated, and two years would pass before fresh waters from the Susquehanna and the Rappahannock and the James would flush out the bay and make it once more habitable for oysters and crabs.

Jimmy, seeking refuge at the bottom of the bay, and his impregnated mate, heading south to breed her young, had conducted their mating in an eddy of water heavily infected by the sewage of this vast cesspool, and they, too, died.

LUCIFER
AND HEY-YOU

T HE GOLDEN AGE of the eastern shore of the Chesapeake Bay came in that four-decade span from 1880 to 1920 when the rest of the nation allowed the marshy counties to sleep undisturbed. True, in these years the world experienced panic and wars, revolutions and contested elections, but these had almost no impact on the somnolent estuaries and secluded coves. Roads now connected the important towns situated at the heads of rivers, but they were narrow and dusty, and it took wagons days to cover what a speedy boat could negotiate in an hour. When roads paved with white oyster shells did arrive, at the end of this happy age, they were usually one-car width only and formed not a reasonable means of transportation but a lively invitation to suicide.

There was, of course, occasional excitement, but it rarely came from the outside world. A black male servant was accused of assaulting a white woman, and a lynching party (composed mainly of Turlocks and Cavenys) broke into the jail with the intention of stringing the accused from an oak tree, but Judge Hathaway Steed proposed to have no such blot on his jurisdiction; armed only with a family pistol, he confronted the mob and ordered it to disperse.

The Eastern Shore baseball league, composed of six natural rivals, including Easton, Crisfield, Chestertown and Patamoke, flourished and became notorious for having produced Home Run Baker, who would hit in one year the unheard-of total of twelve round-trippers. A luxurious ferryboat left Baltimore every Saturday and Sunday at seven-thirty in the morning to transport day-trippers to a slip at Claiborne, where the throngs would leave the ship and crowd into the cars of the Baltimore, Chesapeake and Atlantic Railroad for a two-hour race across the peninsula to Ocean City on the Atlantic. At four-forty-five in the afternoon the railroad cars would refill, the train would chug its way back to Claiborne, passengers would reboard the ferry and arrive back at Baltimore at ten-thirty at night—all for one dollar and fifty cents.

One of the adventures that caused the most excitement occurred in 1887, when a ship commanded by Captain Thomas Lightfoot, a troublemaker if there ever was one, docked at Patamoke with its cargo of ice sawed from the freshwater ponds of Labrador. When the sawdust had been washed away, and the blue-green cakes were stored in icehouses along the riverfront, Captain Lightfoot produced an object that was to cause as much long-lasting trouble as the golden apple that Paris was required to award to the most beautiful goddess.

'I've somethin' extra for you,' Lightfoot announced as he directed one of his black stevedores to fetch the item from below. 'Before it appears I wish to inform you that it is for sale, ten dollars cash.'

A moment later the stevedore appeared on deck leading by a leash one of the most handsome dogs ever seen in Maryland. He was jet-black, sturdy in his front quarters, sleek and powerful in his hind, with a face so intelligent that it seemed he might speak at any moment. His movements were quick, his dark eyes following every development nearby, yet his disposition appeared so equable that he seemed always about to smile.

'He's called a Labrador,' Lightfoot said. 'Finest huntin' dog ever developed.'

'He's what?' Jake Turlock snapped.

'Best huntin' dog known.'

'Can't touch a Chesapeake retriever,' Turlock said, referring to the husky red dog bred especially for bay purposes.

'This dog,' said Lightfoot, 'will take your Chesapeake and teach him his ABC's.'

'That dog ain't worth a damn,' Turlock said. 'Too stocky up front.' But there was something about this new animal that captivated Tim Caveny, whose red Chesapeake had just died without ever fulfilling the promise he had shown as a pup—'Fine in the water and persistent in trackin' downed birds, but not too bright. Downright stupid, if you ask me.' This new black dog displayed a visible intelligence that gave every sign of further development, and Caveny announced, 'I'd like to see him.'

Captain Lightfoot, suspecting that in Caveny he had found his pigeon, turned the Labrador loose, and with an almost psychic understanding that his future lay with this Irishman, the dog ran to Caveny, leaned against his leg and nuzzled his hand.

It was an omen. Tim's heart was lost, and he said, 'I'll take him.'

'Mr. Caveny, you just bought the best Labrador ever bred.' With grandiloquent gestures the captain turned the animal over to his new owner. The dog, sensing that he had found a permanent master, stayed close to Tim, licking his hand and looking up with dark eyes overflowing with affection.

Tim paid the ten dollars, then reached down and patted his new hunting companion. 'Come on, Lucifer,' he said.

'That's a hell of a name for a dog,' Turlock growled.

'He's black, ain't he?'

'If he's black, call him Blackie.'

'He's Old Testament black,' Tim said. And to Captain Lightfoot's surprise, he recited: ' "How art thou fallen from heaven, O Lucifer, son of the morning!" ' Turning his back to the others, he stooped over the dog, ruffled his head and said in a low voice, 'You'll be up in the morning, Lucifer, early, early.'

Lightfoot then startled the crowd by producing three other dogs of this new breed, one male and two females, and these, too, he sold to the hunters of Patamoke, assuring each purchaser: 'They can smell ducks, and they've never been known to lose a cripple.'

'To me they look like horse manure,' Jake Turlock said.

'They what?' Caveny demanded.

'I said,' Turlock repeated, 'that your black dog looks like a horse turd.'

Slowly Tim handed the leash he had been holding to a bystander. Then with a mighty swipe, he knocked Turlock to the wet and salty boards of the wharf. The waterman stumbled in trying to regain his footing, and while he was off balance Caveny saw a chance to deliver an uppercut that almost knocked him into the water. Never one to allow a fallen foe an even chance, Caveny leaped across the planking and kicked the waterman in his left armpit, lifting him well into the air. This was a mistake, because when Turlock landed, his hand fell upon some lumber stacked for loading onto Captain Lightfoot's ship, and after he had quickly tested three or four clubs he found one to his liking, and with it delivered such a blow to the Irishman's head that the new owner of the Labrador staggered back and fell into the Choptank.

In this way the feud between Tim Caveny, owner of a black Labrador, and Jake Turlock, owner of a red Chesapeake, began.

.   .   .

The first test of the two dogs came in the autumn of 1888 at the dove shoot on the farm of old Lyman Steed, who had spent his long life running one of the Refuge plantations and had now retired to a stretch of land near Patamoke.

Nineteen first-class hunters of the area convened at regular intervals during the dove season to shoot this most interesting of the small game birds—gentlemen like Lyman Steed, middle-class shopkeepers and rough watermen like Jake Turlock and Tim Caveny. A dove shoot was one of the most republican forms of sport so far devised. Here a man's worth was determined by two criteria: the way he fired his gun and how he managed his dog.

Each hunter was allowed to bring one dog to the shoot, and the animal had to be well trained, because the birds came charging in at low altitude, swerved and dodged in unbelievable confusion and, on the lucky occasions when they were hit, fell maliciously in unpredictable spots. If there was a swamp nearby, as on the Steed farm, the doves would fall there. If there were brambles, the dying doves seemed to seek them out, and the only practical way for a hunter to retrieve his dove, if he hit one, was to have a dog trained to leap forward when he saw a dove fall from the sky and find it no matter where it dropped. The dog must also lift the fallen bird gently in its teeth, carry it without bruising it against thorns, and drop it at the feet of his master. A dove hunt was more a test of dog than of master.

Jake Turlock had a well-trained beast, a large, surly red-haired Chesapeake, specially bred to work the icy waters of the bay in fall and winter. These dogs were unusual in that they grew a double matting of hair and produced an extra supply of oil to lubricate it. They could swim all day, loved to dive into the water for a fallen goose and were particularly skilled in breaking their way through thin ice. Like most of his breed, Jake's Chesapeake had a vile temper and would allow himself to be worked only by his master. Every other gunner in the field was his enemy and their dogs were beneath his contempt, but he was kept obedient by Jake's stern cry: 'Hey-You, heel!'

His name was Hey-You. Jake had started calling him that when he first arrived at the Turlock shack, a fractious, bounding pup giving no evidence that he could ever be trained. In fact, Jake had thought so little of him that he delayed giving him a proper name. 'Hey-You! Get the dove!' The pup would look quizzical, wait, consider whether he wanted to obey or not, then leap off when Jake kicked him.

So during his useless youth he was plain 'Hey-You, into the water for the goose!' But at the age of three, after many kicks and buffetings, he suddenly developed into a marvelous hunting dog, a raider like his master, a rough-and-tumble uncivilized beast who seemed made for the Chesapeake. 'Hey-You! Go way down and fetch the dove!' So when this redhaired dog swaggered onto the dove field that October day, he was recognized as one of the best ever trained in the Patamoke area.

Lucifer, Tim Caveny's Labrador, was an unknown quantity, for he had never before participated in a dove shoot; furthermore he had been trained in a manner quite different from the way Hey-You had been treated. 'My children were raised with love,' the Irishman said, 'and my dog was trained the same way.' From the moment Lucifer came down off Captain Lightfoot's ice ship, he had known nothing but love.

His glossy coat was kept nourished by a daily supply of fat from the Caveny table, and his nails were trimmed. In return he gave the Caveny family his complete affection. 'I believe that dog would lay down his life for me,' Mrs. Caveny told her neighbors, for when she fed him he always looked up at her with his great black eyes and rubbed against her hand. A peddler came to the door one day unexpectedly and in a frightening manner; Lucifer's hackles rose, and he leaned forward tensely, waiting for a sign. Startled at seeing the man, Mrs. Caveny emitted a short gasp, whereupon Lucifer shot like a thunderbolt for the man's throat.

'Down, Lucifer!' she cried and he stopped almost in midair.

But whether he could discipline himself to retrieve doves was another matter. Jake Turlock predicted widely, 'The stupid Irishman has spoiled his dog, if'n he was any good to begin with.' Other hunters who had trained their beasts more in the Turlock tradition agreed, adding, 'He ain't gonna get much out of that what-you-call-it Labrador.'

But Caveny persisted, talking to Lucifer in sweet Irish phrases, trying to convince the animal that glory awaited him on the dove field. 'Luke, you and me will get more doves than this town ever seen. Luke, when I say "Fetch the dove!" you're to go direct to the spot you think it fell. Then run out in wider and wider circles.' Whether the dog would do this was uncertain, but Tim had tried with all his guile to get the animal in a frame of mind conducive to success. Now, as he led him to Lyman Steed's farm, he prayed that his lessons had been in the right direction, but when he turned the last corner and saw the other eighteen men with their Chesapeakes awaiting him, eager to see what he had accomplished with this strange dog, his heart fluttered and he felt dizzy.

Pulling gently on the rope attached to the dog's collar, he brought him back, kneeled beside him and whispered in his lilting brogue, 'Lucifer, you and me is on trial. They're all watchin' us.' He stroked the dog's glistening neck and said, 'At my heel constantly, little fellow. You don't move till I fire. And when I do, Luke, for the love of a merciful God, find that dove. Soft mouth, Luke, soft mouth and drop him at my toes, like you do with the rag dolls.'

As if he knew what his master was saying, Luke turned and looked at Tim impatiently, as if to say, I know my job—I'm a Labrador.

The field contained about twenty acres and had recently been harvested, so that it provided a large, flat, completely open area, but it was surrounded by a marsh on one side, a large blackberry bramble on another, and a grove of loblollies covering a thicket of underbrush on a third. The doves would sweep in over the loblollies, drop low, hear gunfire and veer back over the brambles. The placement of gunners was an art reserved for Judge Hathaway Steed, who hunted in an expensive Harris tweed jacket imported from London.

The judge had been a hunter all his life, raised Chesapeakes and sold them to his friends. He had acquired much better intuition concerning doves than he had of the law, and now he proposed to place his eighteen subordinates strategically, about sixty yards apart and in a pattern that pretty well covered the perimeter of the field. Toward the end of his assignments he came to Tim Caveny. 'You there, with the what-you-call-it dog.'

'Labrador,' Caveny said, tipping his hat respectfully, as his father had done in the old country when the squire spoke.

'Since we can't be sure a dog like that can hunt . . .'

'He can hunt.'

The judge ignored this. 'Take that corner,' he said, and Tim wanted to complain that doves rarely came to that corner, but since he was on trial he kept his mouth shut, but he was most unhappy when he saw Jake Turlock receive one of the best positions.

Then everyone stopped talking, for down the road edging the field came a carriage driven by a black man. On the seat beside him sat a very old gentleman with a shotgun across his knees. This was Lyman Steed, owner of the field. He was eighty-seven years old and so frail that a stranger would have wondered how he could lift a gun, let alone shoot it. Behind him, eyes and ears alert, rode a large red Chesapeake.

The carriage came to a halt close to where Hathaway Steed was allocating the spots, and the black driver descended, unfolded a canvas chair and lifted the old man down into it. 'Where do we sit today?' Steed asked in a high, quavering voice.

'Take him over by the big tree,' Hathaway said, and the black man carried the chair and its contents to the spot indicated. There he scraped the ground with his foot, making a level platform, and on it he placed the owner of the farm and one of the best shots in this meet. 'We's ready,' the black man cried, and the judge gave his last instructions: 'If you see a dove that the men near you don't, call "Mark!" Keep your dogs under control. And if the dove flies low, absolutely no shooting in the direction of the man left or right.'

The men took their positions. It was half after one in the afternoon. The sun was high and warm; insects droned. The dogs were restless, but each stayed close to his master, and some men wondered whether there would be any doves, because on some days they failed to show.

But not today. From the woods came six doves, flying low in their wonderfully staggered pattern, now in this direction, now swooping in that. Jake Turlock, taken by surprise, fired and hit nothing. 'Mark!' he shouted at the top of his voice. Tim Caveny fired and hit nothing. 'Mark!' he bellowed. In swift, darting patterns the doves dived and swirled and twisted, and three other hunters fired at them, to no avail, but as the birds tried to leave the field old Lyman Steed had his gun waiting. With a splendid shot he hit his target, and his big Chesapeake leaped out before the bird hit the ground and retrieved it before the dove could even flutter. Bearing it proudly in his mouth, but not touching its flesh with his teeth, he trotted back, head high, to his master and laid the bird at the old man's feet.

'That's how it's done,' Tim Caveny whispered to his Labrador.

There was a long wait and the hunters began to wonder if they would see any more doves, but Hathaway Steed, walking the rounds to police the action, assured each man as he passed, 'We're going to see flocks.'

He was right. At about two-thirty they started coming in. 'Mark!' one hunter shouted as they passed him before he could fire. Jake Turlock was waiting and knocked one down, whereupon Hey-You leaped out into the open field, pounced on the fallen bird and brought it proudly back. Jake looked at Tim, but the Irishman kept his eyes on the sky. He did whisper to Lucifer, 'Any dog can retrieve in an open field. Wait till one falls in the brambles.'

On the next flight Tim got no chance to shoot, but Turlock did, and this time he hit a bird that had come over the field, heard the shooting and doubled back. This dove fell into the brambles. 'Fetch the dove!' Jake told his Chesapeake, but the bushes were too thick. That bird was lost.

But now another dove flew into Tim's range, and when he fired, this one also fell into brambles. 'Fetch the dove!' Tim said calmly, his heart aching for a good retrieve.

Lucifer plunged directly for the fallen bird but could not penetrate the thick and thorny briars. Unlike Turlock's Chesapeake, he did not quit, for he heard his master calling softly, 'Circle, Luke! Circle!' and he ran in wide circles until he found a path back to the brambles. But again he was stopped, and again his master cried, 'Circle, Luke!' And this time he found an entrance that allowed him to roam freely, but with so much ranging that he had lost an accurate guide to the fallen bird. Still he heard his master's voice imploring, 'Circle, Luke!' and he knew that this meant he still had a chance.

So in the depth of the bramble patch, but below the reach of the thorns, he ran and scrambled and clawed and finally came upon Caveny's bird. He gave a quiet yup, and when Tim heard this his heart expanded. Lucifer had passed his first big test, but on the way out of the patch the dog smelled another fallen bird, Turlock's, and he brought this one too.

When he laid the two doves at Tim's feet, the Irishman wanted to kneel and kiss his rough black head, but he knew that all the hunters in his area were watching, so in a manly way he patted the dog, then prepared for his moment of triumph.

It was a custom in dove shooting that if a hunter downed a bird that his dog could not retrieve but another man's dog did, the second hunter was obligated to deliver the dove to the man who had downed it. It was a nice tradition, for it allowed the second man to make a show of carrying the dove to its rightful owner while all the other hunters observed his act of sportsmanship. Implied in the gesture was the comment 'My dog can retrieve and yours can't.'

Proudly Tim Caveny walked the hundred-odd yards to where Jake

Turlock was standing. Lucifer started to follow, but Tim cried sharply, 'Stay!' and the dog obeyed. The other hunters took note of this, then watched as Tim gravely delivered the bird, but at this moment another hunter shouted 'Mark!' and a whole covey flew over.

Automatically Jake and Tim fired, and two birds fell. Jake's Hey-You was on the spot, of course, and proudly ran out to recover the dove his master had knocked down. Lucifer was standing far from where his master had shot and was so obedient to the earlier command 'Stay' that he did not move. But when Tim yelled, 'Fetch the dove,' he rushed directly to the fallen bird and carried it not to where Tim was standing but back to his assigned location.

The hunter next to Tim on the down side of the field called, 'You got yourself a dog, Tim.'

When Caveny returned to his location and saw the dove neatly laid beside his pouch, he desperately wanted to smother the dark beast with his affection, but he said merely, 'Good dog, Luke.'

'Mark!' came the call and up went the guns.

The day was a triumph. Luke hunted in marshland as well as he had in the brambles. He proved he had a soft mouth. He circled well in woods, and on the open field he was superb. And with it all he displayed the sweet disposition of the Labradors and the Cavenys.

It was the tradition on these dove shoots for one member at the end of the day to provide refreshments. At a quarter to five, religiously, the hunting ceased. The dogs were put back on leashes, and if the owners had come by wagon, were stowed in back while their masters ate cold duck and drank Baltimore beer. Turlock and Caveny, having come on foot, tied their dogs to trees, and as they did so the former muttered, 'Doves ain't nothin', Caveny. It's what a dog does in ice that counts.'

'Lucifer will handle ice,' Tim said confidently.

'On the bay proper, my Chesapeake is gonna eat 'im up. Out there they got waves.'

'Your Labrador looks like a breed to be proud of,' old Lyman Steed said as the black servant carried him into position to share the duck.

'Has possibilities,' Judge Hathaway Steed said. 'But we won't know till we see him after geese.'

Each man complimented Tim on what he had accomplished with his strange dog, but each also predicted, 'Probably won't be much on the bay. Hair's not thick enough.'

Tim did not argue, but when he got Lucifer home he hugged him and gave him chicken livers, and whispered, 'Lucifer, geese is just doves, grown bigger. You'll love the water, cold or not.' During the whole dove season, during which this fine black dog excelled, Tim repeated his assurances: 'You're gonna do the same with geese.'

The test came in November. As the four men and their dogs holed up in a blind at the Turlock marshes, Jake reminded them, 'Geese ain't so plentiful now. Can't afford any mistakes, man or dog.' He was right. Once the Choptank and its sister rivers had been home for a million geese; now the population had diminished to less than four hundred thousand, and bagging them became more difficult. Jake, a master of the goose call, tried from dawn till ten in the morning to lure the big birds down, but failed. The hunters had a meager lunch, and toward dusk, when it seemed that the day was a failure, nine geese wheeled in, lowered the pitch of their wings, spread their feet and came right at the blind. Guns blazed, and before the smoke had cleared, Jake's Chesapeake had leaped out of the blind with powerful swimming motions and retrieved the goose that his master had appeared to kill. Lucifer went into the water, too, but many seconds after Hey-You, and he was both splashy and noisy in making his retrieve of Tim's goose.

'Sure doesn't like cold water,' Jake said contemptuously.

'Neither did yours, when he started,' Tim said.

'A Chesapeake is born lovin' water, colder the better.'

It became obvious to the hunters, after eight mornings in the blind, that while Tim Caveny's new dog was exceptional with doves on warm days, he left much to be desired as a real hunter in the only form of the sport that mattered—goose on water. He displayed a discernible reluctance to plunge into cold waves, and they began to wonder whether he would go into ice at all.

Talk at the store centered on his deficiencies: 'This here Labrador is too soft. Can't hold a candle to a Chesapeake for hard work when it matters. You ask me, I think Caveny bought hisself a loser.' Some hunters told him this to his face.

Tim listened and said nothing. In his lifetime he had had four major dogs, all of them Chesapeakes, and he understood the breed almost as well as Jake Turlock did, but he had never owned a dog with the charm of

Lucifer, the warmth, the love, and that meant something—'I come home, the room's bigger when that dog's in it.'

'Point is,' the men argued, 'a huntin' dog oughtn't to be in a room in the first place. His job is outside.'

'You don't know Lucifer. Besides, he's sired the best lot of pups in the region. This breed is bound to catch on.'

The Patamoke hunters were a suspicious clan. The most important thing in their lives, more important than wife or church or political party, was the totality of the hunting season: 'You got to have the right gun, the right mates, the right spot, the right eye for the target and, above all, the right dog. And frankly, I doubt the Labrador.' The pups did not sell.

Tim had faith. He talked with Lucifer constantly, encouraging him to leap more quickly into the cold water. He showed what ice was like, and how the dog must break it with his forepaws to make a path for himself to the downed goose. Using every training trick the Choptank had ever heard of, he tried to bring this handsome dog along step by step.

He failed. In January, when real ice formed along the edges of the river, the men went hunting along the banks of the bay itself, and when Jake Turlock knocked down a beautiful goose, it fell on ice about two hundred yards from the blind—'Hey-You, get the bird!'

And the big Chesapeake showed what a marvelous breed he was by leaping into the free water, swimming swiftly to the edge of the ice, then breaking a way for himself right to the goose. Clutching the big bird proudly in his jaws, he plunged back into the icy water, pushed aside the frozen chunks and returned to the blind, entering it with a mighty water-spraying leap.

'That's what I call a dog,' Jake said proudly, and the men agreed.

Lucifer did not perform so well. He retrieved his goose, all right, but hesitantly and almost with protest. He didn't want to leap into the water in the first place; he was not adept at breaking ice; and when he returned to the blind, he ran along the ice for as long as possible before going back to the freezing water.

'He did get the goose,' Jake admitted condescendingly, and for the rest of that long day on the Chesapeake the two dogs performed in this way, with Hey-You doing as well as a water dog could and Lucifer just getting by.

Tim never spoke a harsh word. Lucifer was his dog, a splendid, loving, responsive animal, and if he didn't like cold water, that was a matter between him and his master. And toward dusk the dog found an opportunity to repay Tim's confidence. Jake had shot a big goose, which had fallen into a brambled sort of marsh from which Hey-You could not extract it. The dog tried, swam valiantly in various directions, but achieved nothing.

In the meantime Lucifer remained in the blind, trembling with eagerness, and Tim realized that his Labrador knew where the goose was. After Hey-You had returned with nothing, Tim said softly, 'Luke, there's a bird out there. Show them how to get it.'

Like a flash, the black dog leaped into the water, splashed his way through the semi-ice into the rushy area—and found nothing. 'Luke!' Tim bellowed. 'Circle. Circle.' So the dog ran and splashed and swam in noisy circles and still found nothing, but he would not quit, for his master kept pleading, 'Luke, circle!'

And then he found the goose, grabbed it in his gentle mouth and swam proudly back to the blind. As he was about to place the goose at Tim's feet the Irishman said quietly, 'No!' and the dog was so attentive to his master that he froze, wanting to know what he had done wrong.

'Over there,' Tim said, and Luke took the goose to Jake and placed it at his feet.

The feud between the two watermen continued. The men at the store fired it with unkind comments about Lucifer's deficiencies, but once or twice Caveny caught a hint that their animosity was weakening, for at some unexpected moment a man would see in Tim's dog a quality that made him catch his breath. Outwardly every hunter would growl, 'I want my dog to be rough and able to stand the weather and ready to leap at anyone attackin' me,' but inwardly he would also want the dog to love him. And the way in which Lucifer stayed close to Tim, anxious to detect every nuance in the Irishman's mood, tantalized the men at the store. All they would grant openly was 'Maybe Tim's got somethin' in that black dog.' But Jake Turlock would not admit even that. 'What he's got is a good lapdog, and that's about it. As for me, I'm interested solely in huntin'.'

Aside from this disagreement over dogs, and a fistfight now and then, the two watermen maintained a respectful friendship. They hunted together, fished together and worked the oyster beds in season. But it was the big gun that cemented their partnership, giving it substance and allowing it to blossom.

In these decades when the Eastern Shore thrived, the city of Baltimore also flourished. Some discriminating critics considered it the best city in America, combining the new wealth of the North with the old gentility of the South. The city offered additional rewards: a host of German settlers who gave it intellectual distinction; numerous Italians who gave it warmth. But for most observers, its true excellence derived from the manner in which its hotels and restaurants maintained a tradition of savory cooking: Southern dishes, Northern meats, Italian spices and German beer.

In 1888 the noblest hotel of them all had opened, the Rennert, eight stories high with an additional three stories to provide a dome at one end, a lofty belvedere at the other. It was a grand hostelry that boasted, 'Our cooks are Negro. Our waiters wear white gloves.' From the day of its opening, it became noted for the sumptuousness of its cuisine: 'Eighteen kinds of game. Fourteen ways to serve oysters. And the best wild duck in America.' To dine at the Rennert was to share the finest the Chesapeake could provide.

Jake Turlock and Tim Caveny had never seen the new hotel, but it was to play a major role in their lives. Its black chefs demanded the freshest oysters, and these were delivered daily during the season by Choptank watermen who packed their catch in burlap bags, speeding them across the bay by special boat. When the boat was loaded with oysters, its principal cargo, the captain could usually find space on deck for a few last-minute barrels crammed with ducks: mallards, redheads, canvasbacks, and, the juiciest of all, the black. It was in the providing of these ducks for the Rennert that Jake and Tim began to acquire a little extra money, which they saved for the larger project they had in mind.

One night at the store, after arguing about the comparative merits of their dogs, Jake said, 'I know me a man's got a long gun he might want to dispose of.'

Caveny was excited. 'If you can get the gun, I can get me a couple of skiffs.'

Turlock replied: 'Suppose we get the gun and the skiffs, I know me a captain who'll ferry our ducks to the Rennert. Top dollar.'

Caveny completed the fantasying by adding, 'We put aside enough money, we can get Paxmore to build us our own boat. Then we're in business.'

So the pair sailed upriver to the landing of a farm owned by an old man named Greef Twombly, and there they propositioned him: 'You ain't gonna have much use for your long gun, Greef. We aim to buy it.'

'What you gonna use for money?' the toothless old fellow asked.

'We're gonna give you ten dollars cash, which Tim Caveny has in his pocket right now, and another forty when we start collectin' ducks.'

'Barrel of that gun was made from special forged iron. My grandfather brought it from London, sixty-two years ago.'

'It's been used.'

'More valuable now than when he got it home.'

'We'll give you sixty.'

'Sixty-five and I'll think about it.'

'Sixty-five it is and we get possession now.'

Twombly rocked back and forth, considering aspects of the deal, then led them to one of the proudest guns ever to sweep the ice at midnight. It was a monstrous affair, eleven feet six inches long, about a hundred and ten pounds in weight, with a massive stock that could not possibly fit into a man's shoulder, which was a good thing because if anyone tried to hold this cannon when it fired, the recoil would tear his arm away.

'You ever fire one of these?' the old man asked.

'No, but I've heard,' Turlock said.

'Hearin' ain't enough, son. You charge it with three quarters of a pound of black powder in here, no less, or she won't carry. Then you pour in a pound and a half of Number Six Shot, plus one fistful. You tamp her down with greasy wadding, like this, and you're ready. Trigger's kept real tight so you can't explode her by accident, because if you did, it would rip the side off'n a house.'

The two watermen admired the huge barrel, the sturdy fittings and the massive oak stock; as they inspected their purchase, the old man said, 'You know how to fit her into a skiff?'

'I've seen,' Turlock said.

But Twombly wanted to be sure these new men understood the full complexity of this powerful gun, so he asked them to carry it to the landing, where he had a fourteen-foot skiff with an extremely pointed bow and almost no dead rise, chocks occupying what normally would have been the main seat and a curious burlap contraption built into the stern area.

Deftly the old hunter let himself down into the skiff, kneeling in the stern. He then produced a double-ended paddle like the ones Eskimos used, and also two extremely short single-handed paddles. Adjusting his weight and testing the double paddle, he told Jake, 'You can hand her down.'

When the two watermen struggled with the preposterous weight of the gun, the old man said, 'It ain't for boys.' He accepted the gun into the skiff, dropped its barrel between the chocks, flipped a wooden lock, which secured it, then fitted the heavy butt into a socket made of burlap bagging filled with pine needles.

'What you do,' Twombly said, 'is use your big paddle to ease you into position, but when you come close to the ducks you stow it and take out your two hand paddles, like this.' And with the two paddles that looked like whisk brooms, he silently moved the skiff about.

'When you get her into position, you lie on your belly, keep the hand paddles close by and sight along the barrel of the gun. You don't point the gun; you point the skiff. And when you get seventy, eighty ducks in range, you put a lot of pressure on this trigger and—'

The gun exploded with a power that seemed to tear a hole in the sky. The kickback came close to ripping out the stern of the skiff, but the pine needles absorbed it, while a veritable cloud of black smoke curled upward.

'First time I ever shot that gun in daylight,' the old man said. 'It's a killer.'

'You'll sell?'

'You're Lafe Turlock's grandson, ain't you?'

'I am.'

'I had a high regard for Lafe. Gun's yourn.'

'You'll get your fifty-five,' Jake promised.

'I better,' the old man said ominously.

Caveny produced the two skiffs he had promised, and their mode of operation became standardized: as dusk approached, Jake would inspect his skiff to be sure he had enough pine needles in the burlap to absorb the recoil; he also cleaned the huge gun, prepared his powder and checked his supply of shot. Tim in the meantime was preparing his own skiff and feeding the two dogs.

Hey-You ate like a pig, gulping down whatever Caveny produced, but Lucifer was more finicky—there were certain things, like chicken guts, he would not eat. But the two animals had learned to exist together, each with his own bowl, growling with menace if the other approached. They had never engaged in a real fight; Hey-You would probably have killed Lucifer had one been joined, but they did nip at each other and a kind of respectful discipline was maintained.

Whenever they saw Jake oiling the gun, they became tense, would not sleep and spied on every action of their masters. As soon as it became clear that there was to be duck hunting, they bounded with joy and kept close to the skiff in which Caveny would take them onto the water.

Duck hunting with a big gun was an exacting science best performed in the coldest part of winter with no moon, for then the watermen enjoyed various advantages: they could cover the major part of their journey by sliding their skiffs across the ice; when they reached areas of open water they would find the ducks clustered in great rafts; and the lack of moonlight enabled them to move close without being seen. The tactic required the utmost silence; even the crunch of a shoe on frost would spook the ducks. The dogs especially had to remain silent, perched in Caveny's skiff, peering into the night.

When the two skiffs reached open water, about one o'clock in the morning with the temperature at 12 degrees, Tim kept a close watch on the necks of the two dogs; almost always the first indication that ducks were in the vicinity came when the hackles rose on Hey-You. He was so attuned to the bay that one night Tim conceded graciously, 'Jake, your dog can see ducks at a hundred yards in pitch-black,' and Turlock replied, 'That's why he's a huntin' dog, not a lapdog—like some I know.'

When the ducks were located, vast collections huddling in the cold, Turlock took command. Easing his skiff into the icy water, he adjusted his double-ended paddle, stayed on his knees to keep the center of gravity low, and edged toward the restive fowl. Sometimes it took him an hour to cover a quarter of a mile; he kept the barrel of his gun smeared with lampblack to prevent its reflecting such light as there might be, and in cold darkness he inched forward.

Now he discarded his two-handled paddle and lay flat on his belly, his cheek alongside the stock of the great gun, his hands working the short paddles. It was a time of tension, for the slightest swerve or noise would alert the ducks and they would be off.

Slowly, slowly he began to point the nose of the skiff at the heart of the congregation, and when he had satisfied himself that the muzzle of the gun was pointed in the right direction, he brought his short paddles in and took a series of deep breaths. Then, with his right cheek close to the stock but not touching it, and his right hand at the trigger, he extended his forefinger, grasped the heavy trigger—and waited. Slowly the skiff drifted and steadied, and when everything was in line, he pulled the trigger.

He was never prepared for the magnitude of the explosion that ripped through the night. It was monstrous, like the fire of a cannon, but in the brief flash it produced he would always see ducks being blown out of the water as if a hundred expert gunners had fired at them.

Now Caveny became the focus. Paddling furiously, he sped his skiff through the dark water, the two dogs quivering with desire to leap into the waves to retrieve the ducks. But he wanted to bring them much closer to where the birds lay, and to do so he enforced stern discipline. 'No! No!'— that was all he said, but the two dogs obeyed, standing on their hind feet, their forepaws resting on the dead rise like twin figureheads, one red, one black.

'Fetch!' he shouted, and the dogs leaped into the water and began their task of hauling the ducks to the two skiffs. Hey-You always going to Turlock's and Lucifer to Caveny's.

Since Tim's job was to maintain his shotgun and knock down cripples, he was often too busy to bother with his dog, so the Labrador had perfected a tactic whereby he paddled extra hard with his hind legs, reared out of the water and tossed his ducks into the Caveny skiff.

In this way the two watermen, with one explosion of their big gun, sometimes got themselves as many as sixty canvasbacks, ten or twelve blacks and a score of others. On rare occasions they would be able to fire twice in one night, and then their profit was amazing.

As soon as the two skiffs reached Patamoke, the watermen packed their catch in ventilated barrels, which waited lined up on the wharf. There they purchased from other night gunners enough additional ducks to make full barrels, which they handed over to the captain of the boat running oysters to the Rennert, and at the end of each month they received from the hotel a check for their services.

One wintry February night the two watermen crept out to a spacious lagoon in the ice; there must have been three thousand ducks rafted there beneath a frozen late-rising moon. Caveny became aware of how cold it was when Lucifer left his spot on the gunwale and huddled in the bottom of the skiff. Hey-You turned twice to look at his cowardly companion, then moved to the middle of the bow as if obliged to do the work of two.

Jake, seeing this tremendous target before him—more ducks in one spot than they had ever found before—decided that he would use not a pound and a half of shot, but almost twice as much. 'I'll rip a tunnel through the universe of ducks.' But to propel such a heavy load he required an an extraheavy charge, so into the monstrous gun he poured more than a pound of black powder. He also rammed home a double wadding. 'This is gonna be a shot to remember. Rennert's will owe us enough money to pay for our boat.'

Cautiously he moved his lethal skiff into position, waited, took a deep breath and pulled the trigger.

Whoooom! The gun produced a flash that could have been seen for miles and a bang that reverberated across the bay. The tremendous load of shot slaughtered more than a hundred and ten ducks and seven geese. It also burst out the back of Jake's skiff, knocked him unconscious and threw him a good twenty yards aft into the dark and icy waters.

The next minutes were a nightmare. Caveny, having seen his partner fly through the air during the brief flash of the explosion, started immediately to paddle in the direction of where the body might have fallen, but the two dogs, trained during their entire lives to retrieve fallen birds, found themselves involved with the greatest fall of ducks they had ever encountered, and they refused to bother with a missing man.

'Goddammit!' Caveny yelled. 'Leave them ducks alone and find Jake!'

But the dogs knew better. Back and forth they swam on their joyous mission, gathering ducks at a rate they had never imagined in their twitching dreams.

'Jake! Where in hell are you?'

In the icy darkness he could find no way of locating the drowning man; all he knew was the general direction of Jake's fall, and now, in some desperation—with almost no chance of finding his mate—he began sweeping the area.

Lucifer swam noisily to the skiff, almost reprimanding Tim for having moved it away from the fallen ducks, and threw two ducks into the boat. Then he swam casually a few yards and, grabbing the unconscious Turlock by the arm, hauled him to the skiff before returning to the remaining ducks.

When Tim finally succeeded in dragging Jake aboard, he could think of nothing better to do than to slap the unconscious man's face with his icy glove, and after a few minutes Jake revived. Bleary-eyed, he tried to determine where he was, and when at last he perceived that he was in

Caveny's skiff and not in his own, he bellowed, 'What have you done with the gun?'

'I been savin' you!' Tim yelled back, distraught by the whole affair and by the mangled ducks that kept piling into his skiff.

'To hell with me. Save the gun!'

So now the two watermen began paddling furiously and with no plan, trying to locate the other skiff, and after much fruitless effort Jake had the brains to shout, 'Hey-You! Where are you?'

And from a direction they could not have anticipated, a dog barked, and when they paddled toward the sound they found a sorely damaged skiff almost sinking from the weight of its big gun and the many ducks Hey-You had fetched.

On the doleful yet triumphant return to Patamoke, Tim Caveny could not help pointing out that it had been his Labrador who had saved Turlock's life, but Jake growled through the ice festooning his chin, 'Granted, but it was Hey-You that saved the gun, and that's what's important.'

THE COLONEL AND GENGHIS KHAN

AN INTRODUCTORY NOTE

T HE TALE THAT FOLLOWS of a fighting man who subdued a vast army of Chinese Communists in the mountains and valleys of snowbound Korea but could not conquer a gray squirrel weighing less than a pound is based on the experiences of three men, good friends of mine, who suffered equal humiliation in their fruitless battles against the determined and resourceful breed.

Joe Shane, persuasive fund-raiser for Swarthmore College in Pennsylvania, had his picture window facing a wooded area, and his campaign against squirrels was of the General Bedford Forrest school: 'Git thar fustest with the mostest.' He tried every device then known to keep his bird feeder inviolate but the enemy invariably defeated him. The description in the story that follows of the squirrel Genghis Khan caroming off the windowpane comes from the Shane battle reports, for I sat with him at breakfast one morning when his squirrel came ricocheting smack into his face, with only the glass of the window protecting Shane. It was awesome.

The second warrior I observed in this endless battle was my longtime editor, whose Connecticut house had a picture window overlooking a woods that sheltered his nemesis, a squirrel that frustrated every attempt Albert Erskine made to drive him away. Erskine, being a more bookish type, did not use Joe Shane's blanket bombardment attack but a more cerebral one, which achieved the same results. His defenses were ingenious and sometimes brilliant but they accomplished nothing. As military tacticians, Connecticut squirrels are just as clever as those in Pennsylvania.

The third battle-scarred victim in this incessant warfare was I. On a wooded hilltop in Pennsylvania's Bucks County, one of the choice areas of the United States, I specialized in attracting birds and spent much time and money in bringing to within eight feet of our picture window a host of lovely birds, including three pairs of cardinals and a family of evening grosbeaks, my favorites among all the creatures that fly. Squirrels destroyed my garden of Eden, and I determined to oust them.

I have loved animals and taken great care of them, but I have also been endlessly tormented by them. I cherish the colorful shrub pyracantha with its thorns and brilliant berries, and I have planted at least a hundred of them at various places from time to time, but deer like them even more than I do and prudently eat them down to the roots before big protective thorns have time to develop. I buy the plants, and they're not cheap. I plant them. I fertilize them, and then sit back and watch the deer eat them. I run a rural restaurant, and I have no pyracantha. I tried erecting a high wire fence around them to bring them to the point where they have big thorns, but two days after the fence was built, I saw the deer leap nimbly inside and feed. I was irritated, but I had to admit that even expensive pyracantha are a small price to pay for having a deer in one's garden.

Dogs can be just as offensive. One of our neighbors, who lived nearly a mile away, kept a large weimaraner to whom I was once friendly. Thereafter he migrated all that distance to defecate not on our lawn but, because the macadam had been warmed by the sun, right in the middle of our lane, and nothing I could do would deter him. When I tried to discipline him, the old bond of friendship would vanish and he would snarl at me so that I would have to retreat.

In Texas we had a family of raccoons that gave us great delight by taking residence in our backyard, but they also had an overpowering curiosity regarding the contents of our garbage pail and insisted on emptying it on the lawn and investigating every item. In Maine we would rise early on Friday mornings and keep careful watch so that we could run out and place the garbage where the truck could pick it up at seven. If we were thoughtless enough to put it out the night before, some of the most determined crows in the world would pick it apart before dawn and leave the remnants scattered over a huge area.

Mosquitoes cherish my wife and prove it by coming great distances to feed on her, and moths invade my study whenever I turn on the lights, but more dangerous are the ticks that attach themselves to me when I walk through the woods. In strange hotel rooms cats in heat have often kept me awake much of the night, and flocks of birds have twice flown into jet-engine air intakes of airplanes in which I was traveling, causing near crashes. On the island in the South Pacific where I was stationed swarms of virulent insects caused the death of men who lost their way in the jungle and had to spend the night there unprotected, and at a game preserve in Africa a monstrous crocodile almost swept me into a lagoon by attacking me while I was on land and swinging at me with his powerful tail.

In Alaska several of my acquaintances were mauled by supposedly friendly grizzlies, and when I explored in the jungles of Sumatra I learned that men in nearby villages were actually eaten by tigers. Nature can be extremely antagonistic.

But despite the dangers of associating with animals too closely, the rewards of knowing them and becoming familiar with their habits and, in the end, growing to love them are manifold and one of the pleasures of living on this earth. I have never in my life knowingly stepped on any crawling thing.

I once had a seven-foot black snake that lived under our kitchen. He and I were friends; I fed him things from time to time and always greeted him with joy when he came to see me whenever I returned home.

One afternoon I came back and saw, to my horror, his lifeless body stretched out before me. A visiting professor from Penn State who had come to see me about an art show had caught a glimpse of the snake, concluded that it was maybe a deadly copperhead, a boa constrictor or a fer-de-lance and, grabbing my hoe, hacked my friend to death. Even writing these words brings back the pain.

Like Colonel Cobb, whose story I tell in fictional form, I could not imagine myself shooting one of my ravaging squirrels, no matter how many of my sunflower seeds he had stolen.

I HAD MET Colonel Cobb under distressful circumstances. New York had wired me: 'Shenstone: Submit fullest explanation why Forty-eighth Artillery Unit hightailed in face of Chinese Communist breakthrough.'

It was a sad demoralized outfit to which I reported in those icy mountains south of the Hungnam Reservoir on the Yalu River in northern Korea. It was in the Christmas season of 1950, and our troops, having marched easily and sloppily up to the Chinese border, suddenly found 1.2 million well-trained, tough Chinese Communist soldiers coming at them. To make it brief but accurate, our troops broke and ran, none faster than the 48th Artillery.

During my first moments with the unit, which barely deserved that name, for there was no unity among the bunch of bedraggled individuals running south along snow-packed roads or across frozen rice paddies, I asked: 'What in hell is going on here? Where's the discipline?'

What I heard was a disgraceful story related by a young West Point captain: 'From the start we were poorly organized. Even more poorly led. Composed mostly of big-city kids drafted against their will and commanded, if I may use that word loosely, by a cadre of the most pathetic colonels, majors and captains I've ever worked with. Hell, our outfit not only wilted under the first enemy fire we encountered, but when we ran we left our heavy guns behind. We did not retreat, we evacuated, each man for himself.'

In fleeing, they exposed a major sector of the line without heavy artillery of any kind, which allowed the Chinese soldiers to rush south with only token opposition. I was a mere scribbler, never an artilleryman, but as I talked with what amounted to a rabble even I could see that much could have been saved if the unit had had a resolute commander who had said and meant it when he said it: 'O.K., men. We've run far enough. Here we stand.' A colonel like that, supported by a handful of young West Pointers like the one who told me of the disaster, could have stabilized his portion of the line and perhaps given courage to the entire front.

No matter where I moved among the dispirited troops I heard the story: 'We should've dug in, but nobody gave the order.'

I was spared the embarrassment of having to interrogate the officers responsible for this abject performance, because by the time I reached the front they had been moved to the rear in obedience to stern orders from the Pentagon: 'Report immediately to field headquarters Pusan,' from where they had been flown to MacArthur's headquarters in Tokyo for a real chewing out.

During the first two days I was with the fleeing unit it was commanded by the young West Pointer, who tried his best to establish some kind of order. He failed, but not for lack of determination. He was too young and he lacked what might be called presence, but the man who flew in on the third day to assume command suffered from neither of these deficiencies.

Lt. Col. Bedford Cobb, from a distinguished army family in the little town of Jefferson in northeast Texas, was a hundred and forty pounds' fighting weight, five feet six, with a jutting lower jaw that asserted: Soldier, I mean business! But the thing about him that I and everyone else remembered best was his prematurely snow-white hair, which he wore cropped close, military style, but combed straight forward over his forehead so that he looked like some Roman emperor leading his legions on the frontiers. I had often remarked, before I met him, that some men of athletic build are fortunate when their hair turns white in their twenties, for it lends them not only distinction but also an impression of being sagacious and therefore extra good at whatever they attempt. And when the man had an erect posture and a jutting jaw, the effect ensured attention. Colonel Cobb was such a man, a tough little fighting machine. In a raspy voice he started the moment he arrived to give orders: 'All officers in my tent, immediate.' When he came to me he asked, machine-gun style: 'Who are you—no uniform?' When I replied: 'Shenstone. Press, sir,' he snapped: 'Tell it as it is, you'll have no trouble from me.' Then he added: 'But this is war, young man. Censor to clear everything before it leaves headquarters.'

His use of that last word was ridiculous, for headquarters consisted of one dirty tent only slightly larger than the other tattered shelters we had, and it had to be moved each night as we continued to retreat. But within a day of his arrival he had that forlorn tent cleaned up and organized so that it resembled, in orderliness at least, an office in the Pentagon. And from it he issued a chain of rapid-fire orders: 'No artillery pieces to be abandoned. If you won't stand fast to defend them, call for me. In this outfit, if a gun has to be lost, I and two other officers are lost with it.'

He was especially tough on the cooks: 'You will be at your stoves oh-four-hundred every morning. And I do not care what you have to use, pisspots if that's all you can find, but I want my men to have hot coffee. That's an order.' But his major contribution was to the ordinary soldiers who had fared so poorly when led by officers with no sense of command, no appreciation of the oldest of military maxims: 'Respect down begets respect up.' He was tireless in moving among them, no matter how difficult the terrain over which they were retreating, and his constant aim was to help them stay put, to make the enemy's forward progress as costly as possible. In this tactic he achieved miracles, and I said so in my dispatches, but what I didn't feel required to point out was that for each hundred yards the Communists chased us, their supply lines lengthened and ours shortened until the day came, as the colonel had known it must, when their job of getting food and ammunition and gasoline down from their base in China was just as difficult as ours had been in getting our supplies north from our base in Pusan.

On the day that balance was attained he announced: 'No more retreating. Now we'll have them on the run,' and he was prophetic, for with the insertion into American lines of fighting commanders like him, our lines did begin to stabilize, and when the new year dawned Colonel Cobb had his segment of the front ready to defend itself, even though it would have been insane to try to counterattack. 'That begins next week,' he told his men, and they cheered. It was the first hopeful sound after two months of despair. The panic bailout from Hungnam would be recorded as one of the bleakest events in American military history.

But once the line was stabilized he intensified his demands on his men: 'Hot water is now available. All hands will shave. There will be no more gypsies in this outfit.' He also wanted his men to sit at some table while they ate their meals; any substitute, especially an ammo crate, would do: 'We are no longer camping out.'

In the four enthusiastic reports of the transformation I had witnessed—demoralized fugitives converted into a disciplined fighting unit—I stressed the contribution that could be made by one man of courage, enthusiasm and the capacity to lead. He was, I said in one of my dispatches, 'an 1870 Texas Ranger transported to Korea with two revolvers, guts and drive.' That lucky combination of words was widely quoted in Stateside papers.

Our headquarters were no longer in tents; the moment we stabilized the lines, he had the men put together, from whatever materials they could find or steal, a respectable building in which everything had its place. I was present one morning when he stood rigidly erect, his favorite stance to create the appearance of height, before a desk made of ammo boxes on which his typing clerk had a mass of papers in disarray. Speaking quietly, as if pleading for enlightenment—he never swore—he asked: 'Pritchard, where are your porkers?'

'My what, sir?'

'Your pigs, your swine.'

'I don't understand, sir.'

'You're obviously not operating an army desk. Obviously you're running a pigsty. Where are your pigs?'

Pritchard, flustered by this approach, mumbled something about getting things cleaned up right away, at which Cobb patted him on the back: 'I would like that, son. I would appreciate it very kindly,' and he saluted his scribe.

He took us by surprise—me certainly—with an innovation that made our outfit more professional. Addressing his entire command, he issued an order: 'From this point on you will refer to the Chinese in only one of two ways, *he* or *the enemy*. First thing you've got to do when trying to best an enemy is to respect him. To accept the fact that he's just as clever as you, just as determined to win.' Allowing some moments for this to register, he continued: 'I do not need to remind you that your present enemy kicked your butts right out of the Reservoir and ten miles down the mountains. This was easy for him to do, since it was downhill all the way so you could get up a good head of steam as you ran away from him, leaving nine of our big guns in his hands.' Again he paused, then resumed in his battle voice, hard and crisp: 'Now we stand and fight, and as we face him he is to be called *the enemy*, and a damned tough enemy he has proved to be.'

So his troops, and we reporters, stopped calling them *slopes* and *slant-eyes*, and *gooks* and *yellow-bellies*, for if there was one thing these big meat-fed men from northern China were not, it was *yellow-bellied*. Morale stiffened, attitudes became constructive and the enemy was at last stopped in his tracks. Cobb told me, when the line was stabilized: 'Respect for your enemy is the first step in discipline.' But he added: 'Shenstone, I still need some visual symbol to consolidate the transformation. I've found that the proper arm patch can do wonders in binding a unit into a real fighting force. You got any ideas?' And I could see that he was disappointed when I replied: 'I'm not big on military embroidery.'

One afternoon he invited me to accompany him to the chaplain's hut. When we were there he asked: 'Any good books arrive in your last shipment?' and the padre, who had the additional role of librarian, pointed to an unopened parcel from chaplains' headquarters in Tokyo. Cutting the cord, Colonel Cobb shuffled through the new arrivals and to my surprise stopped at a most unlikely subject. Holding the book before him, he told me: 'Book listing all the saints. I'm not Catholic but I do envy them their parade of saints, one for every day of the year, a special guardian in heaven to sponsor every human activity or duty. Quite consoling.' It was symbolic, I felt, that he would insert the word 'duty' in a spot that I would never have thought of using it. With Cobb, I was discovering, duty was a word that often surfaced. He handed me the book, and I saw that it was handsomely illustrated, the pictures apparently more important than the text. Some of the lady saints were especially appealing, women of great piety who had been horribly tortured in defense of their faith, always with a beatific smile that would make an ordinary man with a toothache ashamed of himself for complaining.

Retrieving the book, Cobb leafed through the appendix: 'Interesting list here. Seafarers? Saint Elmo is their patron. France? Saint Denis. England? Saint George.' He suddenly stopped his aimless riffling and focused sharply on one entry: 'Artillerymen? Santa Barbara.' Quickly he turned to the entry for this saint and found himself confronted by a handsome woman in medieval dress standing beside a torture wheel on which she had apparently been broken by her pagan persecutors, and with her left arm embracing a cannon, whose role in the affair I could not decipher.

I could see that Cobb was deeply moved by this accidental discovery of his patron saint, for he studied Barbara's brief biography—fictional, I suspected—and read aloud the concluding sentence: 'She was revered by medieval artillerymen, who believed that her intervention kept their dangerous cannon from exploding in their faces when fired.'

'Check me out for this one,' he told the surprised padre. 'You Catholics have always known how to identify with people.' He said this admiringly, and when we were back in his headquarters among the big weapons he commanded, he opened the *Book of Saints* to Barbara and studied her portrait.

'Damn!' he said as he slapped the page. 'There's everything in here to inspire a gunner. A woman he can respect. A reminder of the tortures she suffered, worse than any he'll ever know. And that's a real cannon. Santa Barbara is my kind of symbol.'

I could see that the idea captivated him, for at his officers' mess that night he asked his junior staff: 'Men, do you know who the patron saint of gunners is?' When no one responded, he turned to me: 'Tell them, Shenstone,' and I gave a quick rundown on Santa Barbara.

Before anyone could comment, Cobb said reflectively: 'I remember reading that in the good old days military units often identified themselves with religious figures under whose protection they fought. Englishmen went into battle shouting: "Saint George and England!" With Spaniards it was "Spain and Santiago!" And in France it was: "Saint Denis!" To my surprise he was able to cite several other instances of the emotional relationship between military men and their patron saints: 'Like the sailors' Saint Elmo. When they see his fire dancing on the top of their mast they know he's guarding their ship.'

'If I may, sir,' a young officer said. 'I don't understand. What fire on the mast?' and patiently, like a father, he explained: 'An electrical discharge in a storm. Finding the highest point to discharge. It must have been quite reassuring to men long at sea and far from home,' but when he detected that his junior officers were not interested in this arcane tradition he dropped the subject.

But that night, when I checked into his quarters to verify a few facts for my article, he did not wish to focus on my interests: 'Shenstone, what this unit needs to bind it together, to give it a forward purpose . . . Give a group of men a rallying focus, an inspiration, and you can accomplish wonders with them.'

'You've already done that, and I'm saying so in my story.'

'Shenstone! I've only begun! This outfit is going to be tops in the line. Generals are going to fly out here from Washington to inspect what we've accomplished with this team,' and before I could react he thrust at me a piece of thin white paper about three inches by two on which he had drawn in black, blue and red ink a proposed arm patch for his unit. It was a neat job, and showed Santa Barbara with her shield and cannon standing beneath the carefully printed words 'For God and Santa Barbara.'

'What do you think?'

'You're an artist!'

'I mean, does it catch the military spirit we're after?'

I noticed that he had enlisted me in his grand design. It was our plan, not his, and I indulged him: 'It does what's necessary.'

'I'm glad you approve.'

'The artwork, superb. But those words? Don't they sort of fly in the face of recent Supreme Court decisions?' When he gasped I explained: 'Separation of church and state?'

'Good God, Shenstone! That's how men fought in the old days. For God and country! For God and Saint George! And they ought to fight that way now!' He would accept no part of my caution and surprised me by concluding: 'When you fly back to Tokyo with your story, stop in one of those embroidery shops and ask them to whip me up two or three samples of what they can do in various effective colors. Let them choose whatever makes the boldest display. In the design they can drop the wheel if they wish, but the cannon must be prominent.'

'Then what?'

'Rush them back to me. Use the pouch, and I'll take it from there.' Satisfied that I would discharge my commission adequately, he dismissed me, but ran after me: 'Get me cost figures by the hundred and five hundred.'

Tokyo, in those days in the early fifties, had experts who could do anything, and the bartender at the Press Club on Shimbun Alley had no difficulty in finding a shirtmaker named Nakajima, who assured me as soon as he saw Cobb's design: 'My top seamstress, she can do.'

When I asked: 'That word 'seamstress.' Where'd you learn that?'

'I make many shirts British embassy.' While we spoke his best seamstress studied Cobb's flimsy drawing and started immediately to improve it, using her crayons with impressive speed and skill. Before I left the shop she had simplified the design and highlighted it with her own choice of bright colors.

'Come back three hours,' Nakajima said. 'Finish.'

'Colonel Cobb wants firm quotations. Hundred copies. Five hundred.'

'Wilco. But for samples, five dollars now. Give you credit, your order.'

That seemed a modest price for three samples, but things were cheap in Japan in those days, and later that afternoon I put in the pouch for Dog-Seven, code for the colonel's base, three of the finest arm patches I'd seen. The third impressed me, for Nakajima's seamstress, of her own volition as an artist, had modified Cobb's design by dropping the first word *for* and eliminating the torture wheel. The result was a compelling bit of embroidery in gray, gold and blue that any artilleryman would be proud to wear on his left shoulder as a badge of his profession.

By return pouch Colonel Cobb sent me his personal check to cover an order of five hundred copies of the seamstress's third version bearing the four words 'God and Santa Barbara,' but he added a note to me: 'The word "for" must be reinstated. If a man is to fight well, he must fight *for* something, and there could be no higher goal for an artilleryman than the majestic combination of God and his patron saint.' When Nakajima accepted the money I handed him, he promised: 'Word you like will be there. Pick up tomorrow. Five in afternoon,' and when I came for the patches I understood why the British embassy patronized this man. He was truly an artist, or at least his head designer was.

It has always grieved me to reflect that in acting as Cobb's emissary in acquiring and distributing these beautiful patches I was instrumental in bringing on the disaster that overtook his military career.

As soon as they were sewn on the men's jackets in the winter of 1951, they began to accomplish miracles. When the grunts, as we called our enlisted men, saw the colorful patches on the sleeves of their uniforms, they seemed to undergo a transformation. The disorganized unit that Colonel Cobb had whipped into a good fighting force now became a superb one, as if each of the improvements initiated by the colonel had been not only securely locked in but also given special meaning. The men became a cohesive unit, each proud of his companions, each determined that his team give a manly account of itself. They had adopted the word 'manly' from Cobb, who judged behavior on a rigid scale; it was either manly or it wasn't, and he would not tolerate the latter.

On my return from Tokyo I was privileged to watch the alchemy. A slouching oaf from Missouri suddenly became a true artilleryman, inheritor of a great tradition. A petty thief from San Francisco who had been on the verge of being court-martialed became almost overnight a reliable private with a good chance of becoming a corporal. The men marched better, took better care of their personal gear and the unit's big guns. The alteration was so dramatic that I was inspired to draft a report on the affair that was reprinted widely in the States under the heading given it by an enthusiastic wire-service editor: 'The Power of a Patch.'

The title was suggested by a remark made by a foot soldier from Alabama: 'We was a sorry lot, but now we stand for somethin' powerful.' The articles showed a reproduction of the patch, often in color, and that was the source of the trouble. It was precipitated by the arrival of a six-foot-two, hundred-and-forty-pound private with bedraggled whitish hair and the infuriating habit of taking a bouncy step that made his ugly head jut far above the others in the outfit when we marched. He was from Los Angeles and everyone in the outfit knew his name by the end of the first day, for the sergeants kept yelling: 'Debbish! Keep in step!' In a high, whining voice he would reply: 'I *am* in step.'

'Silence! Keep in step.'

'I *am* in step.'

He was correct. When I heard about the problem, I checked him out, and he was certainly in step, but his unbreakable habit of that extra bounce, plus his above-average height, made him stick out like an unruly lock of hair. He was a sad case, this Max Debbish from Los Angeles, but I never doubted that Cobb's patient, firm way with men could whip even this unlikely prospect into line. For example, I was encouraged when Cobb went out to the drill field to watch the sergeant trying to discipline Debbish, and when the colonel saw the preposterous extra lift the man gave his heels whenever he stepped forward he halted drill and summoned both Debbish and the sergeant to him.

'Private Debbish, have you always had that extra bounce in your step?'

'I have, sir.'

'And you can't control it?'

'I can't, sir.'

'So you're always just a bit out of step? Is that right?'

'No, sir. I'm in step. It's just that my head pops up higher.'

To my surprise, Cobb laughed: 'You're right, son. We have a name for that. Extra levitation, and it's not a crime. We're up here to fight the Chinese Communists, not impress visiting Congressmen with our dress parade.' Turning to the sergeant, he said in an almost brotherly fashion: 'Sergeant, this man is telling the truth. He does have that turkey trot and there's nothing you or he can do about it. Excuse him from drill, but see that he gets some constructive assignment to take its place.' With that he saluted crisply both the sergeant and Private Debbish.

Back at headquarters I told Cobb: 'Masterly. You do know how to keep troops moving forward,' but he said: 'What else could I do? We get a bouncer about one in twenty thousand, and no way's been devised to slow them down.'

There it should have ended, with Debbish neatly out of sight and the detachment burnishing its reputation with each weekly report. But that night I received a rocket from my boss in New York while Colonel Cobb was getting an URGENT from his boss in the Pentagon. Mine said ominously:

Private Max Debbish Cobb's detachment son of famed atheist Martha Mears Debbish. She screaming son must not wear patch For God and Santa Barbara in violation First Amendment. Fullest coverage, quotes from soldiers.

When I ran to Cobb's quarters, I found that his orders were even more ominous:

> Private Max Debbish your detachment son of notorious atheist Martha Mears Debbish. She has goaded Senators and Representatives to protest your unit patch as violation of First Amendment. Who authorized patch? Are non-Christians excused from wearing it? Submit fullest report, explanations.

As soon as I saw that red-flag wording 'non-Christians' I realized that it was my job to interrogate as many Jewish soldiers as possible. I think they realized that I was on Cobb's side and not trying to cause him trouble, for five of them gave me great quotes: 'If it was anyone but Colonel Cobb, I wouldn't want to wear a Catholic saint, but he's done wonders with our patch, so it's O.K. by me.' And: 'I ain't big on saints, but if she's fightin' on my side I say fine, because we need all the help we can get.' One fellow from Boston who proved what he said, told me: 'I wear Saint Barbara outside to please the colonel, the Star of David inside to please me,' and he showed me that under the official patch he had scrawled in black ink a six-pointed star.

I was about to pursue some other potentially interesting Jewish quotes when I received surprising information from New York. Since Private Debbish was proved to be not Jewish, the boss suggested I play down that angle and focus on ordinary Protestants. Debbish's famous—or infamous if you wish—mother was a standard Georgia Baptist married to a Maxim Debbish, a Californian reared in some Central European branch of the Russian Orthodox Church.

The upshot of the affair was that Colonel Cobb was ordered by the Supreme Court to remove the offending patches from his men's uniforms; he was rebuked by his superiors for having earned the army a spate of unfavorable publicity; he became the subject of editorials across the nation; and he was quietly retired from army life. Of course, when he left his artillery unit, to be replaced by a strictly ho-hum fellow from New Hampshire, to whom I took an intense dislike, as did his soldiers, the unit promptly relapsed into its old habits, for it had suffered two grievous wounds: the zeal of Colonel Cobb, who had held it together, was missing;

and the comfort of Santa Barbara was gone. So was Private Debbish, back once more in Los Angeles with his crusading mother.

Now, years later and under rather strange circumstances, the colonel and I were about to renew our acquaintanceship. In the Louisiana city of Shreveport, on the Red River, not far from Jefferson, the son of a wealthy businessman had been kidnapped by three hoodlums with no brains, no plan and no possible chance of having their ransom demands fulfilled. In a crude handwritten note smeared with fingerprints, they asked for one million dollars, and should have been arrested within hours, for they were instantly identified. But suddenly they developed catlike cleverness and for two weeks eluded capture, even though their photographs were broadcast, showing three world-class punks who looked exactly like what they were. Their case became a sensation, and when they were captured in a swamp that fed into the Red River I was sent down to write their histories.

When I had my notes in order, I remembered that my old friend Colonel Cobb resided not many miles to the west, and when I telephoned Jefferson I heard the same crisp, manly voice that I had known in that Korean winter: 'Shenstone, it's not as cold as when I last saw you. Come right on over. Julia's always said she wanted to meet you.'

Thus, through the accident of a botched-up kidnapping—the father's total worth was not over two hundred thousand dollars—I was able to meet once again a man I had respected and in whom I had an abiding interest. I had seen him only once since Korea and had tried then to apologize for my role in getting him elbowed out of military service. The occasion had been a public forum on defense at which he was a panelist and I was delighted to find him as self-confident and aggressive as ever. His posture was still so slim and erect that he resembled a white birch, a comparison that was augmented by his gleaming white hair. When it came time for him to speak he did not equivocate. When he finished, no one had to ask: 'Now, what was it he advocated?' His voice was as firm in Washington as it had been in the snow-swept battlefields of Korea: 'I say that if the Communists in Russia make one more threatening move, we use every power in our command to foment revolution along their entire border. Agitate the Baltic states. Help the Ukraine to rebel. They're vulnerable in Armenia, Uzbekistan, Siberia. And keep them pinned down in Afghani-

stan. Our guns do not have to fire shot one. Help them to destroy themselves.'

When a more conciliatory panelist asked: 'But wouldn't that run the
risk of Soviet retaliation in areas over which we have no control?' he
snapped: 'That danger exists right now, has existed for the past forty
years. But one thing's in our favor. Russia grows weaker every year, not
stronger. Do not fear goblins.' He persuaded no one, but that was back
in 1973.

When I reached Jefferson, a sleepy warmhearted little town in that
corner of Texas which preserved the look and customs of the Old South,
I could have been in Georgia or South Carolina, for there was the quiet
air of a village to which local planters would be bringing their wagons of
cotton for baling, and I expected to see Colonel Cobb riding on a white
horse. When I stopped to ask a man lounging outside a drugstore where
I might find Santa Barbara plantation, he said: 'Turn right at the corner,
one mile down that road, the place on the left, painted white, porch with
six columns like in the movies.' When I thanked him he added: 'But if you
want to see the colonel himself, he's over there in the hardware store.'

I parked my car, crossed the street and entered Gravel's Hardware, a
store that seemed to carry one of everything, and there at a counter talking
energetically to a clerk was my old battlefield companion, same weight as
before, same thrust-out lower jaw and same close-cropped military cut to
his white hair.

'Colonel! It's Shenstone. How well you look!'

Turning his head away from the clerk without moving his body, he
cried: 'Damn, Shenstone, it's good to see you,' and with that he indicated
by a gesture of his right hand that I was welcome to be there but that I
must excuse him because he was engaged in important business.

'You say this one is bound to work?' he asked the clerk.

'Guaranteed. Mrs. Wilcox told us that when everything else failed,
Dover Fool Proof did the trick. No more trouble with the enemy raiding
her birdseed.'

'Does she get a lot of birds there on the riverbank?'

'Like the big cage in a zoo.'

As if he were making a decision to attack at dawn, he said crisply: 'I'll
take it, but I have no confidence whatever it'll work.' Slapping two ten-
dollar bills on the counter, he reached for a rather long cardboard box

decorated with a forest scene. Only then did he turn his body to greet me: 'Shenstone, we've not met since Washington, but I do read your things now and then in the magazines. What brings you here?'

'That ugly kidnapping in Shreveport. I'm trying to unravel twisted minds.'

'I'm honored that you found the time to come my way. I remember you as one of the few writers and newsmen who had any sense.' And then, always a military man, he rapped out an order: 'Jump into your car and follow,' and I replied like a second lieutenant: 'Roger, wilco.'

He led me along a tree-lined country road to a high spot overlooking the arm of the waterway connecting with the Red River. It was the site of a rural mansion built sometime prior to the Civil War; its entry gate bore a plaque stating that this was Lammermoor, famous as the seat of the Cobb family, which had emigrated there from South Carolina to play a major role in the fight of Texas on the side of the Confederacy. I had thought my Cobb lived at a plantation called Santa Barbara, and I paid attention when he ignored the big house and continued to a smaller one-story ranch-style house built apparently sometime after World War II. It was easy to identify it as Cobb's residence because its gateway bore the neatly lettered sign: SANTA BARBARA, COLONEL BEDFORD COBB.

Stopping his pickup by the porch, he called loudly: 'Julia! I think we've got the little bugger this time!' His wife, a small, pretty woman in white who looked as if she could have been created by Margaret Mitchell, came to the door, saw the large package he was bringing into the house and said: 'I hope so. This is the fourth surefire system you've tried.' Then she saw me leaving my car and cried: 'This must be Mr. Shenstone, the man who got you fired. I'm amazed he'd have anything to do with you.' When she chuckled, came forward and greeted me warmly, I knew I was going to have a pleasant break in my work.

I still did not have any idea as to what Cobb had purchased at the hardware store, but as I stood by a picture window my attention was attracted by a garden that seemed dedicated to birds. Spacious in dimension, it was edged by shrubs that bore berries on which the birds could feed and contained two Grecian pillars five feet high, topped by large cement basins filled with water for the birds to drink or use for their baths. But what attracted my attention, because it stood so near to the big window, was a solitary telephone pole at least fifteen feet tall. It had a stout wooden crossbar from whose end nearest the house was suspended an intricate bird feeder filled with sunflower seeds and other morsels. Someone had spent effort and money building that feeder.

As I was wondering whether any birds were about, a lovely female cardinal, not a garish red but all gold and brown, flew to the feeder to feast on the sunflower seeds so generously scattered there. I was admiring the muted beauty of the bird and thinking: She's like a nineteenth-century dowager in a story by Edith Wharton, when right at my elbow Julia emitted a piercing scream. Cobb hurried over and asked: 'What's happened, darling?' and without explanation she pointed to an inert object on the lawn near the shrubs. Although I could not ascertain what it was, I did see that it was black, and apparently dead. 'He's done it again, the little bastard,' she cried, leaving us and running out to lift the dead body and carry it reverently to the small table near the house. When she carefully placed it there, as if it were a human corpse, I saw that it was a squirrel, but of a type I did not know; its coat was a silky black and not the rather grubby gray of the squirrels I had grown up with in New Mexico.

When Julia returned to us she was weeping: 'We had two families of these beautiful black squirrels, and that little bastard has killed them all.' As she said this she pointed toward the pole from which the bird feeder hung, and there, on a contraption that had been guaranteed by a dealer in Vermont to prevent squirrels from getting at the expensive seed intended for birds, sat an ugly-looking squirrel gorging on seeds and spitting the husks onto the ground below. His coat was gray and the grin on his face as he picked out only the best seeds was positively evil. He was the murderer, he was the thief, and that was my introduction to Genghis Khan.

'I gave him the name,' Cobb explained, 'because he's a barbarian, some wretched spirit invading our home from the steppes of central Asia.'

Julia broke in tearfully: 'We did our best to protect our black squirrels, lovely little creatures, but he could not abide them. Killed them all to protect what he thought were his rights. And Bedford has done his best to keep the rascal away from our bird feeder. One clever device after another, all failures.' She slumped into a chair by the window and watched disconsolately as Genghis munched away, pausing now and then to sneer at us as if to say: 'Up yours, you clowns!' Then, as the maid prepared the table at which we would be sitting for lunch, Julia wailed: 'The wretched part is, with him monopolizing the feeder, the birds we love so much refuse to come near us.'

'She's right, Shenstone,' Cobb said. 'With great patience, and assisted by those two baths and this feeder right by our window, Julia's attracted an entertaining collection of birds, all types, all colors. They feed so close they seem to be part of this room. You'd see what I mean if that little monster weren't hogging the feeder. With him around, the birds are afraid to visit, and Julia does miss them.'

'So does Bedford,' she said between sniffles, 'but he doesn't like to admit it. Because if he likes the birds so much, why can't he stop that damned squirrel from limiting our enjoyment of our own home?'

As she said this I was not looking at her birds but at Genghis Khan, who was ripping the husks off a large seed that I could not identify, and practically smacking his lips over the morsels inside.

'What is that he seems to favor?' I asked, and Julia wailed: 'My sunflower seeds, damn him. They cost four dollars and ninety-five cents for a smallish bag. The beautiful birds love them. Fly in from miles around, only to be scared away by that greedy monster.' As she spoke a pair of male cardinals ventured in, their red coats gleaming like the uniforms of Hessian soldiers two hundred years ago. Settling close to our window, they had barely started on their share of the seeds when they were driven away by Genghis.

'If I had a gun I'd shoot that pirate!' Julia cried, but the colonel reprimanded her: 'Darling! Never say that. He's our enemy, granted, but an honorable one. We'll defeat him, but we'll do it fair and square. No guns, please!'

As I listened to their plans to defeat the squirrel I concluded that they opposed him for several reasons: he drove away the good birds; he killed the black squirrels; he was a greedy beggar. But most offensive of all, he monopolized the sunflower seeds. They were expensive because they attracted what the blurb on their bag called 'the better type of bird,' by which was meant wrens, cardinals, bluebirds, flickers and grosbeaks. One ravenous gray squirrel could banish them all.

As I stared at the little glutton he stared back, and then he sneered at me, waved his bushy tail in my face and, descending from the foolproof anti-squirrel feeder, ran into the woods, probably looking for more black squirrels to fight.

'That's the last time he stares into our window when we're eating,' Cobb said.

After lunch he and I went into the garden with a ladder. Propping it against the telephone pole and asking me to steady it, he climbed to the top, dismantled the expensive Vermont feeder and threw it disgustedly to the ground. 'It was never worth a damn,' he growled. 'He figured it out in fifteen minutes. Pass me the new one,' and from its careful packaging I extracted a device so intricate that both Cobb and I had to study the instructions intently. When we finally got it assembled, we had a masterpiece so involved and protected by trip-trigger devices that no squirrel was going to be able to climb a nearby tree, leap over to the pole and descend to the feeder. No way could Genghis Khan continue gorging on the sunflower seeds put in this feeder. From now on, those delicacies would be reserved for Julia's cardinals and bluebirds.

It took us two hours to assemble and attach the contraption to the crossbar and plug the electric cord into the outlets in the garden wall, but when we had it finished even I could see that no animal, no matter how clever, could get into that feeder unless it had wings. Normal transit was ooo-oom-possible, as the soldiers in Korea used to say.

There were five barriers a squirrel would have to conquer if he wanted to feed at the Cobb restaurant for robins. It would be easy for him to climb into the nearby trees and leap from some limb onto the pole, but this would place him high above the feeder, and when he started to descend, he would meet eighteen inches of highly polished steel encircling the pole and providing no kind of foothold. Suppose he did manage by some trick to work his way below the slippery steel. Two feet farther down he would encounter another fifteen-inch metal strip, this time carrying a charge of electricity strong enough to knock a squirrel right off the pole. If, by some miracle, he got past this, he would come upon a metal cone, tight about the pole at the top, well flared at the bottom, off which the beast would have to slide. If he used some magic to avoid it, he would have to work his way along the crossbar, which was protected by a large reverse cone which he could enter but not leave. And finally, the long, slim wooden feeder itself was suspended from the crossbar by two wires of a special metal that had great tensile strength but were so thin that nothing could negotiate them but a hummingbird, if it kept its wings beating furiously.

It was midafternoon when we finished installing this fiendishly clever device and turned on the electricity. Each segment of the invention worked, and when I placed my finger on either side of the electrified areas, I received more shock than I expected. 'It's going to be difficult for him to defeat this one,' I said approvingly, and Cobb snorted: 'Impossible.'

As the three of us gathered before the picture window for drinks deftly served by the colonel, he said: 'I expect no wife to serve me except when she's cooked the dinner,' and we had a moment of sheer delight when birds of four different species came to the feeder, including the rare and beautiful evening grosbeak, who, the Cobbs explained, had previously been scared away by the squirrel. Then, as we were congratulating ourselves, through the high branches of one of the trees came Genghis Khan, stopping now and then like an experienced burglar casing the joint. He spotted the new device and must have understood at once that it was intended for him, because he ran swiftly through the branches to reach a spot from which he could study the pole.

From that position he drafted his plan of battle, and he was a wily fellow, for he advanced cautiously to the point at which he usually made his leap into the upper part of the pole, a feat he accomplished easily. 'So far so good, Brother Rat,' Cobb said venomously. 'But now, watch!'

As he made his way down the pole he came upon the eighteen inches of highly polished steel, and before he could catch himself his feet slipped and he tumbled all the way to the ground. 'Aha!' Cobb cried. 'Gotcha!'

The squirrel was shaken but not abashed, for within minutes he was back at the leaping spot, onto the pole, and down to the steel-protected area. Again he fell to the ground, and again Cobb chortled.

Three more times Genghis Khan took that plunge, and I was satisfied that the Cobbs had at last defeated their enemy, but suddenly, as we were enjoying our drinks, Julia uttered another of her patented screams: 'Look at that!' and I turned in time to see the squirrel solve the first of his problems. Coming down the pole cautiously, he reached the slippery steel and instead of trying to negotiate it with his feet, he flattened himself, kept his tail far back as a kind of brake, and slid down, head first, keeping himself against the polished steel and at the last moment digging in his front claws to get a hold on the wooden portion of the pole.

'Damn him!' Julia cried. 'He must have radar.'

'Don't worry,' her husband gloated. 'Watch what hits him now!' and as we studied the squirrel's triumphant descent his forefeet touched the electrified plate and with a screech he found himself flung clear of the pole and on another plunge to the ground.

This was a new sensation for him, and he wandered in a daze to a nearby tree, from where he reconnoitered. Apparently the electricity had shocked him both physically and mentally, for it constituted a new adversary of serious dimensions. But if he was bewildered he was not defeated, for after a longer pause than before, he was once more high in the trees and descending to his jump-off for the pole. I was impressed by how easily he now traversed the polished steel and how gingerly he approached the electrified plate. Prudently he paused for several minutes, trying to fathom the secret of this obstacle, and apparently something that he saw satisfied him, for very slowly he ventured onto the plate, uttered his screech and fell to the ground. Twice more he made the attempt, twice more he screeched, and our party went to bed that night satisfied that as long as we had electricity we had beaten Genghis.

On the next day, a choice Texas morning, we received two reassuring signals. A flock of birds, aware that they could now eat sunflower seeds rather than watch Genghis do so returned to the feeder and chirped merrily as they feasted, and several times during the afternoon we heard Genghis screeching as he hit the electricity. The expensive machine from New Hampshire was doing its work. Indeed, throughout that whole day the squirrel never once got near the feeder, and that night as we dined at the nearby golf club, Cobb was bold enough to inform two couples who had joined us at our table: 'You may not believe it, but at last I've conquered those damned squirrels,' and Julia said: 'Especially that vicious little swine we call Genghis Khan.'

At this a Dallas banker named Gregory who had a country place near Jefferson, burst into laughter: 'Julia, never say you've outtricked a Texas squirrel, especially a gray one. I could tell you a hundred stories about my bird-loving friends who've tried to keep squirrels out of their feeders. Cannot be done.' And another man, an engineer with Texas Instruments, contributed stories of having wrestled with the squirrels at his place: 'I wonder that there's any bird in Texas, the brazen way squirrels eat their food.'

The banker said: 'I'm told there's a man at L. L. Bean's up in Maine who's perfected a gizmo that positively keeps squirrels out of feeders. Man who told me said it wasn't cheap, something like seventy dollars, but he said it does work.'

'Did he install one at his place?' the engineer asked, and the banker said: 'No, but the man at Bean's assured him that it was foolproof,' and the engineer said: 'Maybe with Maine squirrels, but down here the damned things get advanced degrees at Squirrel University, a branch of S.M.U.'

During the next two days I concluded that Cobb would not have to patronize L. L. Bean's because Genghis Khan had figured out no way to circumvent that electric barrier. But as we breakfasted next morning I heard our Cassandra scream her communiqué in the great squirrel war: 'My God! Look at that!' and as Cobb and I stared in disbelief we saw that Genghis, as a result of much trial and error, had learned that if he allowed no part of his body to touch the plate except the nails on his four feet he could sort of ski to safety, throwing sparks but not harming himself. As I watched him doing it several times I got the feeling that he enjoyed it, like riding a sled down a steep, icy hill. I say I watched him several times because after he transited the electric plate he came upon the first metal cone, and then the inverted one, which repelled him, and he had to try again. I felt sure that given enough time he would solve that riddle, but I had the good sense not to predict that to the Cobbs. Let them dream, I told myself. My money's on Genghis.

That night as we dined we forgot the squirrel, for he had accomplished nothing of note in getting closer to the bird feeder, but as we talked he did enter the conversation because I started by saying: 'Julia, I've regretted a hundred times having spread that story about the colonel's battle patch in Korea, FOR GOD AND SANTA BARBARA. It did me no good and him a lot of harm.'

She said: 'For me it was disgusting. People stopping me on the street and either asking why my husband had been sent home in disgrace or assuring me that they too believed in God and that the only people persecuting him were Communists and atheists.'

'But later we laughed,' Cobb said. Then, as darkness fell and both the songbirds and the frustrated squirrel left the feeder, the colonel said: 'I did what I thought was necessary to instill some character in the sorry lot I'd inherited. Gave them self-respect, self-confidence. And it worked.'

Turning to his wife, he explained: 'Shenstone didn't write his story about the patch. He wrote it about the miracle of transformation I'd achieved. It was the Stateside papers that called for a photograph of the patch. Shenstone didn't give it to them.'

I nodded, for that was true. 'However,' I confessed, 'when they radioed for more pictures, I sent them. Never occurred to me that I was putting your neck on the line.'

'Did you ever write a follow-up?' Julia asked. 'Telling the world how Bedford's unit fell apart when the new man took over and outlawed the patch?'

'No. When a sensation dies, the public loses interest.'

We contemplated this for some minutes and then Cobb said quietly but with the force of character and will he had shown in battle: 'I'm a lot like Genghis. I see a job to be done. I barrel ahead, all guns blazing, and I don't really give a hoot or a holler what happens.' He hesitated: 'What I mean is, I don't care what happens to me.' He paused again: 'I've had the curious feeling, all through dinner, that Genghis is out there somewhere regrouping, trying to figure out what's happened and how to overcome it.'

Because we had eased into serious conversation, Julia was encouraged to reveal something she might not normally have liked to discuss: 'I don't think you men appreciate how hard a wife works to achieve a beautiful garden. I slaved to attract birds to our place—planted those shrubs that produce seeds, placed the new trees so that the birds would have a refuge when cats came prowling, and planted that telephone pole—or supervised the men who did plant it so that I could install the bird feeder, right by this window where the birds could entertain us as we dined. And what happens? All my handiwork shot to hell because of that damned squirrel.' His wife's strong language made Cobb wince, but it was nothing compared with his reaction to what she said next: 'I've been so frustrated by that miserable creature that last week I drove down to Marshall and bought myself some of that new poison for vermin—that's what squirrels are.'

Cobb gasped: 'Julia! You can't do that to an animal. Besides, I believe poison has been outlawed in Texas.'

'Not in my garden,' she said, and the force of her antipathy to Genghis echoed in the room. She was not opposed to him merely because he had disrupted her garden and driven away her birds; she hated him for himself. I could see that his mere existence was an affront, and I also saw that her husband did not appreciate the depth of her antagonism.

'To poison an animal in the wild!'

'Don't you want to get rid of the little tormentor?' she asked, and he said: 'I'd like to drive him off our feeder—out of your garden. But kill him? No, that wouldn't be manly.'

'Do you ever consider what might be womanly? She wants a lovely garden and birds and flowers?' I'm not sure that either Cobb or I understood the passion that could motivate such desires.

I shall never forget breakfast the next morning; the three of us were having toast and eggs by the big window. Cobb and I were in chairs right by the window, our faces close to the glass, while Julia sat between us so that she could see what was happening on the telephone pole while Cobb and I could see only a portion. Suddenly she gave an awed shout: 'Watch out, Bedford, here he comes!' and Cobb looked up just in time to see Genghis Khan flying through the air, aimed directly at his face. When the squirrel hit the glass with terrific force, considering his limited weight, he used all four feet to ricochet off, giving him a flight path that landed him right on the feeding platform. In a feat of extraordinary intelligence he had simply bypassed the impediments the New Hampshire genius had placed in his path.

But although he had found a way to land on the feeder he did not on this first flight manage to remain there. Losing his footing, he plunged to the ground, but within minutes he was back up in the trees, on the pole and once more smack in Colonel Cobb's face. Again he landed on the feeder, scattering seeds as he did, and again he fell to the ground. Twice more he smashed into Cobb's face unsuccessfully, but the colonel had been studying the maneuver and had watched Genghis improve his position with each jump.

'This time,' he said with a mixture of admiration and resignation, 'he'll make it,' and I found myself cheering for the squirrel. 'Fifth time lucky,' I said, a statement that irritated Julia, for she said bitterly: 'That damned squirrel runs this place. He kills my black squirrels. He alienates my birds. I hope he breaks his neck.'

He did not. With a mastery of engineering, flight and braking, the determined squirrel solved all his equations. He left the tree with maximum speed, bounded off the pole, ricocheted into Cobb's face, and landed on the feeder with a speed precisely calculated to allow him to hold fast and resume his feast on sunflower seeds, whose husks he contemptuously spat on the ground below, the very ground onto which he had tumbled so many times.

'Bravo!' Cobb said. 'The little bugger did it!'

His wife's response was quite the opposite, for as she watched the invader gorging on the seeds for which she had paid a fair amount of her own money, she felt the most intense hatred for this enemy.

When the colonel was called to the phone, she made her move. Going to the paneled case in which he kept his five guns, one of them captured from the Chinese Communists at Hungnam, she selected a shotgun, loaded it, stalked out into the garden and fired at the feeding station.

Genghis heard the noise but could not have known how close to death he had been.

I had followed her into the garden and had seen that her hands trembled so much that she had no chance of hitting any target. She must have known about her inability, for she tried to hand me the rifle: 'Here, it's loaded. Shoot the little bastard!'

Forcing the rifle into my hands, she commanded me to take aim and kill her enemy, but as I tentatively prepared to do so, Colonel Cobb, alerted by the first shot, dashed up behind me and pushed away my left arm, which was holding the gun. 'Good God, Shenstone! You're not going to shoot the little bugger?'

I was in a difficult position. Relations between the Cobbs regarding the squirrel were already strained, and an accusation from me that she had instigated the shooting might do irreparable harm. 'Yes, I had a mind to. I can see he's a permanent nuisance, and I thought I might aid Julia's birds.'

He drew back and stared at us. There in the morning sunlight, as Genghis remained at the feeder, Cobb said: 'A gentleman never scorns his enemy. That squirrel's conducted an honorable war with us. Protecting his homeland—his turf.' Taking the gun from me, he broke it down, ejected the shells and said quietly as he took his wife by the hand: 'I understand, dear. He is a marauder, and I, too, miss the birds—your birds.' He kissed her, then said to no one in particular: 'One must never denigrate an enemy who conducts his battle in the great tradition.'

When we returned to the house I was aware that I was no longer needed or wanted there, and as I waited at the door to say good-bye to the colonel I heard him on the phone: 'Gregory? Cobb here, Jefferson, Texas. What was the name of that fellow in Maine? L. L. Bean's man, I think you said. The one who had that foolproof device for defeating squirrels?'

ABOUT THE TYPE

This book was set in Times Roman, designed by Stanley Morrison specifically for *The Times* of London. The typeface was introduced in the newspaper in 1932. Times Roman had its greatest success in the United States as a book and commercial typeface, rather than one used in newspapers.